For all the Readers, Good & Evil

IN THE FOREST PRIMEVAL

A SCHOOL FOR GOOD AND EVIL

TWO TOWERS LIKE TWIN HEADS

ONE FOR THE PURE

ONE FOR THE WICKED

TRY TO ESCAPE YOU'LL ALWAYS FAIL

THE ONLY WAY OUT IS

THROUGH A FAIRY TALE

1

THE COVEN

Bad Candy

Some stories are spoiled from the very beginning.

Some stories are rotten to the core.

Like the one that killed her mother, Hester thought, as she hustled through the dark forest. Her mother was minding her own business in her candied house, when two young vandals

ate through her roof. Alone in her crib, Hester had woken from a nap and stared into the faces of two ogreish children, fat cheeks slathered in candy and crumbs. They'd taken one look at the baby they'd just orphaned and fled like cowards, leaving a family and home broken. And they'd been *rewarded* for it, hailed as heroes and legends, while her mother burned in an oven. Ever since that day, whenever Hester sensed an injustice, a story gone wrong, she smelled the sick, sour rot of candy.

Just as she smelled it now.

The story in question was a short one, a statement of simple fact, but Hester's whole body bristled, like a cat amongst snakes. She didn't know how long it had been up there, high over the Endless Woods. But after days of traveling underground from Gnomeland, Lionsmane's message was waiting when she'd resurfaced.

The wedding of King Rhian and Princess Sophie will take place as scheduled, this Saturday, at sundown, at Camelot castle. All citizens of the Woods are invited to attend.

It was penned in gold like King Rhian's other messages, set against the clouds. Rhian was a proven liar and every one of his screeds a trap. But this message had none of the pomp of his others. This was stark and simple . . . yet slithery in a way she couldn't put a finger on. . . .

A shadow appeared at her side.

"This is stupid, Hester. We need to turn back *now*," said

Anadil in a black hood that shadowed her white hair and red eyes. "Sophie's betrayed us. She's marrying Rhian at sundown. *Tonight.* That's what the message says. And the sun's going fast. Either we get back to Camelot and stop this wedding or we all *die.*"

Hester ignored her, spotting the lights of Borna Coric ahead. Once she and her friends entered this new kingdom, they'd need to be careful. Like all citizens of the Woods, those of Borna Coric would be hunting students from the School for Good and Evil.

A second shadow flanked her—

"Ani's right," said Dot, also hooded in black. "Plus, there's no way we'll get inside those caves: it's *impossible.* But if we turn back now, we can sneak onto a Flowerground train from Ravenbow. It can take us back to Camelot in time to stop the wedding—"

"And leave *Merlin?*" Hester said. "That was the assignment Reaper gave us. Rescue the wizard from the Caves of Contempo. Rescue our best weapon. A wedding is not our mission. Sophie is not our mission. *Merlin* is our mission. And if there's one thing our coven abides by, it's doing as we promised."

She powered forward, but Anadil blocked her path.

"Our promise is pointless if Rhian becomes the One True King!" said the pale witch. "He needs two things. Make all hundred kingdoms burn their rings. And marry Sophie as his queen. Do both and he claims the Storian's powers. If the wedding is at sundown, that means all the rings are already gone! Rhian marrying Sophie is the last step. That's what Sophie told us in Gnomeland. Once she's Rhian's queen, Lionsmane will become the new Storian. Rhian can write anything he wants and make it come true! He can erase kingdoms, kill our friends, kill *us* with a penstroke! Our story will be *over*—"

"All the rings can't be gone because Nottingham still has a ring. Dot's *father* has a ring," Hester noted coldly. "And the Sheriff wouldn't burn his ring for King Rhian. Hates him more than we do. Even if the Sheriff were to die, his ring would go to Dot. And we'll go to the ends of the earth to protect Dot *and* that ring. Just like we're going to do for Merlin." Hester shoved past them, pulling her hood tighter.

"Don't you get it? Sophie's *marrying* him!" Anadil said. "Either to save herself or to be Camelot's queen—"

"You really think Sophie would marry *Rhian*?" Hester challenged. "After helping us *escape* him?"

"That's what Rhian wrote!" Dot argued. "That's what his story says!"

"*His* story," said Hester, glaring at the sky. "There's something fishy about that message. And until I figure out what it is, we're sticking to our plan. Besides, if there's one thing I've learned about Sophie, it's that she's a better witch than all of us. I'm sure she has the king right where she wants him."

"Hester, the sun will set within the hour—" Anadil hounded.

"More reason to find Merlin fast. He's our best chance to defeat Rhian. That's why Rhian trapped him in the caves."

"Then why didn't he just *kill* Merlin? For all we know Merlin's already dead or used his Wizard Wish and this is a wild goose chase to get us killed too."

"Wizard Wish?" said Dot. "Is that the wish you make in Aladdin's cave?"

"That's a Genie's Wish, you idiot. No wonder you failed Lesso's class," said Anadil. "Wizards all have one wish. They use their Wizard Wish to choose how and when to die—"

"And no way Merlin would have used his wish while we're still in danger," Hester scorned, approaching the gates of Borna Coric. "Merlin's out there. And he needs our help."

"You're not thinking, Hester. Let's say he is in those caves," Anadil granted. "Caves of Contempo are time traps. Even a few seconds inside and you come out years older. Merlin's been in there for *weeks*."

"Go back without me, then," Hester dared, crossing through the gates—

She stopped short.

So did Anadil and Dot.

The forest floor had disappeared, replaced by the sky instead. No longer were the witches on a dirt path: they were standing on the sunset, a canvas of purple and pink. Lionsmane's message had moved from high above to down by their feet, paving the way ahead. Each gold letter was the size of a house, carved into the horizon beneath their boots, the announcement of King Rhian's wedding become the new path. As the witches inched across it, confused into silence, Hester smelled bad candy again, her eyes cast downwards, searching Rhian's words for the rot at their core. . . .

"Hester?" Dot said, gaping upwards.

Hester blinked.

It wasn't just the sky that had turned upside down.

The whole *kingdom* of Borna Coric was upside down.

She'd known of this topsy-turvy land, where the world swung on its head, but it was quite another thing to see it in real life. Here, the earth was high up in the sky, a ceiling of dirt, and the sky was anchored where the ground should be. Purple beanstalks sprouted downwards from this roof of earth, stretching towards the flat floor of clouds.

Capsized cottages nestled along the beanstalks, the dwellers inside also inverted, together with their furniture and belongings, freed from the laws of gravity. Purple vine ladders and pulleys connected the beanstalks like roads, with a toppled bridge of flowers linking the village to the main square. The witches moved towards this busy arena with levels of overturned shops built between huge upside-down statues. Royal statues, Hester saw now, the stone heads of Borna Coric's king and queen and their children moored to the skyfloor, the statues' feet reaching high over the kingdom. Up close, Hester noticed the king's and queen's sculpted faces looked oddly young. Almost as young as their children.

"Creepy," Anadil murmured. As people bustled above, wrong side up, the two witches stayed hidden in the statues' shadows. "People are going to notice us, Hester. We're the only ones with our heads on straight. Plus, the caves are supposed to be surrounded by a poisonous sea. I don't see *water*, let alone a sea, do you?"

"Must be behind all this," Hester said on tiptoes, glimpsing

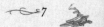

nothing but more shops and statues ahead. "We have to sneak through without anyone recognizing us."

"And then cross a poisonous sea that we can't even find," Anadil added. "Not to mention trespass into cursed caves."

"If you had your rats to scout, you'd be useful instead of a ball and chain," said Hester.

"One is dead. One is missing. The other found Merlin and told Dovey where he is. My rat is the reason we're here. So who's the useful one?" Ani snapped back.

But Hester was already prowling forward, craning up at the floors of upside-down storefronts. Inside Borna's Bread, upturned shoppers filled carts with baguettes and brioches and bottom-up cakes, while inside Toppled Tailors, flurries of purple moths flew mended clothes from reversed racks to waiting customers. Next door, in Sylvie's Salon, men and women sat in upended chairs, perusing newspapers, as floating sylphs cut their hair, none of the patrons' faces the slightest bit swollen, as if their bodies were born to live in the wrong direction.

"Isn't the world upside down enough without it actually being upside down?" Anadil marveled.

"Maybe they see things clearer that way," Hester said.

"Eh, I'd say this group is as blind as the rest," said Anadil.

Hester followed her friend's eyes to a domed theater hanging from the tip of a purple beanstalk like a Christmas bauble—the "Borna Bowl," said the marquee—with the dome inverted and a full audience seated downside up, watching a spellcast of King Rhian's coronation replaying in phantoms of gray light. As the spellcast rehashed the familiar scene, Rhian clutching Sophie, his princess clad in a prim, ruffled dress, the spectators hung on the king's every word, while heads-down vendors hawked Lion memorabilia: mugs, shirts, hats, pins. . . .

"Is this what they do for entertainment? Watch that scum's coronation again and again?" Hester asked, unable to hear Rhian's speech from this far away.

"Probably plays every hour on the hour," said Anadil, tilting her head for better viewing. "Strange, though. I don't remember them spellcasting the coronation."

A brown-skinned family in colorful smocks passed by on the skyroad, heads up like the witches, ogling the Borna Bowl and the rest of the upside-down realm. *Drupathi tourists,* Hester thought, she and Ani forcing smiles, which the family returned before giving Dot weird looks. Dot, who was lurking behind, sucking morosely on vine leaves she'd turned to chocolate with her lit finger.

"People will notice your glow!" Hester hissed, pulling her into the shadows. "And stop sulking!"

"It's just . . . what you said back there . . . ," Dot puled. "If Daddy dies, Nottingham's ring *doesn't* go to me. He changed his will after I freed Robin Hood. Don't think he ever changed it back." She turned more leaves to chocolate, her lit finger trembling. "If Rhian's marrying Sophie, maybe Rhian already got Daddy's ring. Because of *me.* Because Daddy didn't trust me with it. Which means, because of me, Daddy might be . . . might be . . ."

For the first time, Hester's cold facade softened. "That's not how this coven thinks," she said, cupping her hand over Dot's glow and snuffing it out. "Focus on everything we've done to get here. Each of us did our part. Wolves wouldn't have helped us if you hadn't bribed them with chocolate snow. That magic carpet wouldn't have snuck us through tunnels if Ani hadn't threatened it with an unspooling spell. We're still alive, Dot. We're almost to Merlin. Whatever your Dad thought of you when he changed his will, he doesn't think of you that way now. He loves you, Dot. Enough to join forces with Robin Hood—his own Nemesis—to keep you safe. Wherever he is, he'd want you to finish our mission."

Dot mulled this over, gazing at her shoes, before she took a deep breath and tossed her chocolate away. "For the record, I still think Sophie went back to Rhian. Just like the message says. Same story as when she went back to Rafal. Spends too much time around Agatha and Tedros together, gets jealous and desperate and ends up kissing any boy who'll have her, even a lying, murdering pig."

"Could be worse," said Hester. "Could be kissing a Snake."

Dot snorted.

A chill gusted through the square, huddling the witches deeper into their hoods and shivering the spellcast in the dome. Then Hester smelled something on the breeze . . . something that made her muscles tense and her demon twitch. . . .

"The sea," she said, pivoting to her friends. "It's close."

She led them ahead, the three girls gliding along the darkening skyfloor like bats, careful to avoid the glow of over-turned lanterns sparking to life along the beanstalks. Hester navigated the coven past the Borna Bowl, hearing Rhian's voice grow louder, the salty scent of the sea burning stronger and stronger. . . .

"Wait! Look at her dress!" Dot blurted.

"Shhh!" Ani whispered.

"But that's not what Sophie wore at Rhian's coronation," Dot pressed. "You sure it's a replay?"

Hester stopped cold.

So did Anadil.

They cocked their heads in unison, studying the inverted spellcast as Rhian held Sophie in close-up, the king's and princess's figures translucent.

"Citizens of the Woods, I did not expect a day like today to come. This morning, I learned that Japeth of Foxwood, my brother, my liege, has been in league with Tedros and Agatha, plotting against my throne," spoke Rhian. "I thought my brother was the Eagle to my Lion. Instead, he was just another Snake. But the Lion always wins. By the time you view this spellcast, Japeth will be sealed in the dungeons and shall never be seen again. Our Woods is under siege by rebels and even my own blood can't be trusted. I alone can protect us. I alone shall punish our enemies. I alone will keep these Woods safe."

"Dot's right. This isn't from the coronation," said Anadil. "This is . . . *now*."

"Ding Dong, the Snake is gone," Dot chimed. "At least Rhian did one thing right."

But Hester was still studying the king: the chill of his voice, the void in his eyes, the shudder of threads on his jacket like sliding scales. . . . Next to him, Sophie wore a blank smile, like a puppet pulled by strings. The king clasped her tighter.

"But a traitor cannot stop our kingdom from glory," he said. "And though I have lost a liege, soon I will gain a queen. My wedding to my true love will proceed as scheduled, and we shall spellcast it for the Woods to see. I make this promise to you all. With Sophie and I united, *everything* in our world will be possible."

He looked at Sophie, who maintained her perfect smile and spoke directly into the spellcast.

"Long live the Lion!" she proclaimed. "Long live the One True King!"

The scene froze on their image before words magically imposed over it.

THE WEDDING OF
KING RHIAN AND PRINCESS SOPHIE
Live Spellcast will begin in 30 minutes

"See, we were right!" Dot whispered to Anadil. "Sophie *is* marrying Rhian!"

But Hester was fixed on the frozen image of Rhian, honing in on the black holes of his pupils, the serpentine curl of his lips. . . . Slowly Hester's gaze moved to Sophie, trapped in his arms, the light in her eyes extinguished, the witch dead and gone.

Suddenly Hester smelled it again.

That sour, sick rot, overwhelming her.

Bad candy.

"Snake is the Lion . . . Lion is the Snake. . . ." Hester realized softly.

Anadil frowned. "Hester?"

"What is it?" Dot pushed.

The tattooed witch turned to them, face pale.

"The world really *is* upside down."

2

The Girl with No Past

S ophie no longer wanted to kill the boy she was about to marry.

Nor could she make sense of the fleeting thought that she'd wanted to kill him in the first place. From what she could tell, he was gorgeous, eloquent, and cocksure, just like a king should be. And soon, she'd be his queen. *The* queen.

Not that she had the slightest clue how it had happened. The past was fuzzy now, her memories elusive. Any attempt to penetrate them spawned a spearing headache, as if there was an iron spike through her brain, before she'd jolt straight back to the present, the ache gone, as if she'd been born this second, again and again and again. Efforts to recall why she'd ended up like this—a girl with no past—only brought on stronger pain, and it wasn't long before she stopped trying to find her memories altogether.

All she knew was that she'd woken in this prim white dress and tonight she would marry King Rhian, the Lion of Camelot, keeper of Lionsmane, and savior of the Endless Woods. She'd yet to have a private moment with her betrothed: their only time together spent recording a spellcast, which she'd struggled to follow . . . about a brother gone rogue and rebels in the Woods, ending with her pledging allegiance to the Lion, her husband-to-be, just as he'd instructed. . . . But even from this, she knew she loved him, body and soul. Sitting next to him, she'd inhaled his frosty scent and basked in his tan glow, almost too perfect. When the spellcast finished, he stroked her cheek with cold fingers and gave her a snake-eyed smile: "See you at the altar, my sweet." Sophie's heart fluttered like he was her fairy-tale prince.

Any girl would die to be in her shoes, she thought now, powdering her nose in the queen's boudoir and peering in the mirror at her crown of gold braids and the fussy white dress that hijacked nearly every inch of her skin. She had no inkling of where this dress had come from or who had made it, but now that she was about to convene with the Woods-wide press and answer their pre-wedding questions, she wished the dress had a bit more panache . . . straps instead of sleeves or a dash of color around the waist—

On cue, the dress shape-shifted, as if her thoughts were commands, the sleeves whittling to thin strands over her shoulders, while a slash of blue cut across her hips, forming a belt of silk butterflies. Sophie hardly flinched. For something so strange, there was no surprise in the dress's magic, as if she'd had this happen before but couldn't remember when. She glanced into her own eyes in the mirror and saw a flash of sparkle, an emerald gleam, like a light in a tunnel. . . . Then it was gone, as quickly as it came.

"Press is waiting for you, Princess," a voice said.

Sophie turned to the captain of the guard standing at the door to her bedroom, the gold of his jacket specked with dried blood. Kei, he said his name was when he'd woken her from sleep. Handsome as anything, with hawkish eyes and a square jaw, but a glum, tortured expression, as if haunted by a ghost.

They walked towards the ballroom, Kei tight at her side. She noticed him peeking at her, like he was waiting for her to say something. As if they shared a secret. It made Sophie uncomfortable.

A guard cut in front of them, scanty-haired and pock-marked: "Cap, the map inna Map Room's been burnt ta nothin'—one witha rebels' wherebouts!"

Kei flexed his jaw. "Could be one of the maids or cooks. I'll question them."

"But that wazza king's map! Should I tell 'im—"

"Get back to your post," the captain ordered, guiding Sophie past him.

Sophie was mystified by this map business, but whatever it was, it made Kei even more sour than before.

He caught Sophie looking at him.

For the first time, Kei's face changed, replaced by a sharp gaze that seemed to drill into her mind. . . .

"You there?" he whispered.

Sophie stared into his big, dark eyes . . . then snapped from her trance. "Of course I'm here! Where else would I be?" she scolded. "And stop scowling and giving me strange looks. You're the captain of the guard. The king's new liege. Act the part or I'll tell the king to find someone who *will*."

Kei hardened to stone. "Yes, Princess."

"Good," said Sophie. "And clean your jacket while you're at it. Unless there's a coup unfolding in the castle, there's no reason to be flaunting your blood as part of your uniform."

"Rhian's blood," said Kei.

"Excuse me?" said Sophie, stopping.

"It's *Rhian's* blood," Kei repeated, with that drilling gaze again.

"Then kindly return it to him," Sophie quipped, strutting ahead.

She smiled, her white dress puffing up like peacock feathers.

Rhian would be proud of her.

She was settling into the role of his queen already.

"PRINCESS SOPHIE, WHAT'S your reaction to the imprisonment of the king's brother?" asked a blue-haired reporter with a badge labeled *The Pifflepaff Post*. "Are you confident that all traitors have been rooted out from the kingdom?"

"I hardly knew Rhian's brother," Sophie replied, perched on an elevated throne beneath a massive Lion's head. "And I have full confidence in King Rhian to keep Camelot and the Woods safe. Now, if you don't mind, I'm here to answer your questions about tonight's wedding. That is all I wish to speak about. The rest I leave to the king."

As the reporters packed into the Blue Ballroom clamored for the next question—*"Princess Sophie! Princess Sophie!"*— Sophie glanced at two identical women hidden in shadows at the back, barefoot and dressed in lavender robes, who gave her a curt nod of approval. With high foreheads and long noses, they wore the same blithe grin, as if all was going to plan. *The Mistral Sisters*, they'd called themselves when they briefed her before letting reporters in ("Just answer their questions," said the one called Alpa. "Everything will take care of itself," said the other, named Omeida).

A reporter's voice broke through the din—

"And what of the evidence that King Rhian has enlisted the Kingdom Council to reject the Storian's power?" said a man from the *Netherwood Villain Digest*. "Our reporting suggests that in the past week, 99 of the 100 founding kingdoms have destroyed their rings, with these leaders disavowing the Storian and pledging allegiance to King Rhian instead. Does King Rhian believe in the legend of the One True King? Is he seeking to claim the Storian's powers for himself? Is that why kingdoms are burning their rings for him?"

"It's obvious that the Pen has failed our Woods," Sophie replied as reporters furiously transcribed. "The Storian is supposed to tell tales that inspire us and move our world forward. But these days, it fixates only on the students of a school that has become self-indulgent and obsolete. It's why I left my post as Dean. The Pen no longer represents the people. It's time for a Man to rise in its place. *A King*. Someone who can give everyone a chance at glory."

The words slipped effortlessly out of her, as if they had a life of their own.

"The last ring left belongs to the Sheriff of Nottingham, who hasn't been seen since the attack on Tedros' execution," prompted a reporter tagged *Nottingham News*. "Any information as to his whereabouts or the security of his ring?"

"Haven't you heard? The Sheriff is marrying Robin Hood," said Sophie archly.

The press brigade laughed.

"But do you yourself believe in the myth of the One True King?" asked the *Hamelin Piper*. "The legend that the Storian depends on the balance between Man and Pen. A balance protected by our leaders wearing their rings. As long as they wear these rings, Man and Pen share control. Each plays an equal part in writing fate. But if Man forsakes the Pen, if all 100 rulers burn their rings and swear loyalty to a king instead . . . then the balance is gone. The Storian would lose its powers to this new king."

"And it would be about time!" Sophie tossed off. "Men should worship a Man. Not a Pen."

"But what happens when Rhian *is* this One True King?" the *Ooty Observer* pushed. "Lionsmane would become the *new* Storian. King Rhian's own pen. With the Storian's powers, he could use this pen like a sword of fate. He could write anything he wants and have it come true. He could wipe out anyone who challenges him. He could wipe out entire kingdoms—"

"The only thing King Rhian might wipe out is a meddling press," Sophie teased with a wink. "Besides, like you said, he only has 99 rings. Not 100."

The press chuckled once more.

"What can we expect from the wedding?" a toothy woman asked from the *Royal Rot*.

"For Rapunzel's wedding, I heard she floated ten thousand lanterns into the sky, and for Snow White's, the bride rode in on a parade of forest animals." Sophie grinned. "Mine will be *better*." She rose off the throne. "On that note, I'll take my leave—"

"Princess Sophie, any comment on the fact that the rebels sacking kingdoms were not students of the school but paid mercenaries of King Rhian? And that the attacks were King Rhian's ploy to trick leaders into burning their rings?"

The Blue Ballroom went quiet. Slowly the throng of reporters parted, revealing a teenage girl sucking a red lollipop. Her badge was handwritten, dotted with a heart.

The Camelot Courier

"Tell Agatha that Bettina says hello," the girl smiled.

Sophie felt a command fly from her mouth like an arrow: *"Arrest her!"*

Kei and four guards streaked for Bettina, swords out—

The young girl vanished into thin air, leaving only her red lollipop, which fell to the marble and fractured to pieces.

Reporters eyed each other tensely, a chill seeping through the ballroom.

"Apparently local journalists are magicians now," Sophie cooed, untroubled. "We'll see how our little sorceress fares when she and the rest of the *Courier*'s staff are arrested for lies and treason. Now if you'll excuse me, I have a wedding to prepare for."

She sashayed out of the room. The second she stepped into the hall, she was joined by the two Mistral Sisters, hewing to her sides like sentinels, leading her back to the queen's chambers. Little by little, Sophie felt her gait loosen, her head lighten, her sense of direction and purpose disappear. All the words she'd spoken to the press slipped away like smoke out of a chimney. Suddenly, she had no memory of where she was coming from and where she was going, as if time was resetting itself.

She could hear the sisters tittering: *"reporters seen in Putsi"* . . . *"where Bethna is"* . . . *"the girl used a disappearing hex"* . . . *"someone must be helping them"* . . . *"tell Japeth . . ."*

Sophie's brain itched.

Japeth . . . I know that name. . . .

But it vanished into the fog with everything else.

What's happening to me? Sophie searched her mind,

fumbling for an anchor to hold on to. *Who am I? What am I doing here?* A prickle went up her spine. Then a tingling in her nose. She smelled lavender . . . and cucumbers. . . . For a moment, she could see clearly, as if she'd crossed through that emerald light she had glimpsed within her eyes. . . . Again a skullcrushing headache assaulted her, but this time, Sophie fought back, clawing at her memories, trying to hold on—

"That girl, Bettina. What was she saying?" Sophie breathed. "About Rhian plotting the attacks . . ." The pain radiated into her teeth and jaw. Sophie dug in harder. "And Agatha. . . . She told me to say hi to Agatha. . . . Rhian said that name during the spellcast . . . *Agatha*. . . . She isn't a rebel at all! She's my *friend*—"

At once, the sisters raised their hands, twisting them sharply in midair as if to turn a screw—

The pain in Sophie's head exploded, a stabbing blow so deep that she buckled, about to pass out.

The Mistrals caught her, moving her forward.

"You need rest," said Alpa. "Focus on the wedding, my sweet. Once you wed the king, your work will be done."

"You can rest *forever* after that," said Omeida.

The sisters gave each other shrewd looks.

"Just focus on the wedding," Alpa repeated.

The wedding, Sophie thought.

Then I can rest.

Focus on the wedding.

The stabbing pain eased, flooding her with glorious relief.

Yes . . . the wedding would fix everything.

3

Secret School

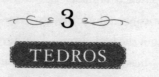

T edros and Agatha stood between two graves.

The light of the fading sun caught the ring on the prince's hand, the silver surface glinting with carved symbols that matched the Storian's.

"That ring belongs to Camelot," said Agatha, stunned. "Your father wouldn't have left it to you if it wasn't yours by right. Which means *you're* the heir, Tedros. Just like he raised you to be."

Tedros blinked at the ring, taking this in, before his eyes sharpened and rose to Agatha's. "Then who's sitting on the throne?"

"Not the heir, that's for sure," said his princess in her rumpled black dress. "We need to get to Camelot and show the people they've been duped by a Snake. And save our best friend from marrying him while we're at it."

"She deserves to marry him," Tedros muttered. "Got herself into this mess going back to Rhian."

"To help us—"

"We don't know that."

"*I* do," Agatha said firmly. "We're going back to Camelot. For your throne. And *my* friend."

Tedros gazed at the grove's two graves, each marked with a glass cross: one his father's, dug up and empty; the other Chaddick's, untouched in the shadows. Tedros' shirt clung to his chest, soaked with his sweat, his breeches smeared with dirt from his father's grave. Pain rattled his body, the exhaustion of the journey and the wounds he'd suffered against his enemies soothed by knowing now that his dad was on his side. He'd followed his heart to Avalon, trusting in his father's last message—*"Unbury Me"*—which brought him here, to King Arthur's tomb, in the Lady of the Lake's secret haven. But there was no body to find. Instead, Tedros had encountered his father's soul, magically preserved by Merlin so that he could appear to Tedros one last time and bequeath his son the ring that would save him. *And* Camelot. For as long as Tedros wore this ring, the Snake couldn't be the One True King. The Snake who had killed his own brother to claim the Storian's power. But it was in vain. With this ring, Tedros' father had ensured that a Snake would never take the Storian's place. That Lions-mane would never replace free will with Japeth's will. That Man would never become Pen. With this ring, Tedros' father had given his son one last chance at his throne.

A king's *true* coronation test.

The prince noticed Agatha peering edgily at the sky, her black clumps shifting.

"Sun will set soon," she worried. "How will we get there in time? We need to mogrify into birds . . . or use Tinkerbell and the school fairies to fly. . . . They're waiting with your mother at the lake—"

"Still won't get there by sunset," Tedros pointed out. "We're half a day's journey, at least, even by flight."

"Maybe the Lady of the Lake knows a way—"

"The Lady who's lost her magic and almost killed me. Twice. We'll be lucky if she lets us out of this cove," said Tedros, his lit finger about to cast a flare for the Lady. "Let's find my mother and use the fairies to fly back to school. Then we can plan our attack."

"I'm not leaving Sophie with the *Snake*!" Agatha blistered, her eyes watering. "I don't care if it's just me, up against every one of his thugs. I'm getting my best friend back."

Tedros clasped her palm. "Look, I know what Sophie means to you. Which is why I'll go to the ends of the earth to keep her safe, even if she and I make better enemies than friends. But there's no way to Camelot in time. There's no way to shrink a hundred miles."

Agatha pulled her hand away. "Does your mother know a

spell? Or Hort or Nicola? They're with her! Maybe they have a talent that's useful—"

"Hort's talent is busting out of his clothes. Nicola's is reminding us how smart she is. And my mother's is an unhelpful mix of cluelessness and evading responsibility. What about *your* talent? You're the one who saved us from that spitfire camel."

"By hearing its wishes, and you can't use that as a means to teleport across half the—" Agatha's eyes sparked. *"Wishes!"*

She bolted past him. "Hurry! Before it's too late!"

He watched Agatha weave between trees, disappearing into the darkness of the grove. Tedros knew better than to ask. Standing between his dad's and his knight's graves, the prince let his fingerglow dim before he sucked in a breath and summoned what strength he had left in his legs to chase her.

HE FOLLOWED THE sounds of Agatha's steps pattering across the forest floor, crackling on fallen branches. But the deeper Tedros drew through the oaks, the more he began to remember his way. Soon, he saw his princess kneeling at the edge of a pond, hidden within the thicket. Just as he'd seen her the *first* time he'd been here.

Back then, it was Hort who'd led Agatha to the pond, when they'd been hiding from Rafal at his mother and Lancelot's safehouse. Tedros had concealed himself behind a tree, listening as the weasel berated Agatha for not following her heart, for sacrificing Tedros instead of fighting for him: a revelation that made Tedros realize just how much Agatha needed him and how much he needed her, right when both of them were doubting it the most. It was here at this pond, only a short distance from two graves, that their love was sealed. The love that would never be broken again, no matter what Evils lay ahead.

Tedros crouched beside her, the mud soft under his boots. Beneath the heavy veil of trees, the pond glistened with embers of sunset. Agatha met her prince's blue gaze in the water's mirror.

"Where are they?" he asked, searching the surface.

The pond stayed still, its inhabitants gone.

Agatha's lips trembled as the sun shimmers faded in the reflection. "But . . ."

Tedros stroked her hair. "Let's get back to the others—"

But then the shimmers changed color, from gold to silver, nuggets of glow pulsing in rhythmic synch. All at once, the glows began to move, rocketing through the pond in crisscrossing patterns like underwater fireworks, rising towards the prince and princess, closer, closer, brighter, brighter, until they splashed through the surface, a thousand tiny fish, spitting tails of water like fountains of light.

"Not gone after all," said Tedros, watching the Wish Fish crowd towards his princess as if they knew her well. "Your secret little school."

"If I put my finger in the water, they'll paint my soul's greatest wish," said Agatha breathlessly. "And my wish is to find a way to rescue Sophie before she marries the Snake. If there's a way, the fish will show it to us!"

Agatha slipped her finger in the water.

Instantly, the Wish Fish dispersed, flickering different colors as they joined fins like pieces in a jigsaw puzzle. At first, Tedros had no clue what he was seeing, with the fish switching hues and rearranging feverishly, as if they were still debating Agatha's wish. But little by little, the fish committed to colors and then to their places, and a painting came into focus across their smooth, silky scales. . . .

A royal garden gleamed beneath a sunset, Camelot's castle silhouetted against the pink and purple sky. Masses of well-dressed spectators gathered, the people and creatures of the Woods watching something attentively, something neither Tedros nor Agatha could make out, since the crowd was obscuring it. But there was something else in the painting, foregrounded and sharply clear, floating over the mob: a pair of watery bubbles, each the size of a crystal ball, two tiny figures enclosed within.

"Those are *us*," Agatha said, peering at the bubbled clones.

"Those are *not* us," Tedros rejected. "You and I are full-grown, we live on the ground, and we breathe *air*."

Agatha turned to him. Her distraction snapped the spell, and the fish splintered, colors draining from their scales.

"Not all that surprised, though. First time I tried Wish Fish after Dad died, it showed me crying in Lancelot's arms. Lancelot, who destroyed my Dad," said Tedros. "Wish Fish are batty."

"Or your soul craved a new father and Lancelot was the

closest you had to one at the time," Agatha disputed. "Wish Fish aren't batty. That painting meant something. And *this* painting is how we get to Sophie."

"By levitating in body-shrinking bubbles?" the prince repelled. "And I would never wish to *cuddle* with Lancelot—"

But Agatha wasn't looking at him anymore. She was looking at the fish, which had rearranged into a stark-white arrow, pointing directly, unmistakably at . . . Tedros.

"Your turn," said Agatha.

Tedros grimaced. "Next thing you know, they'll show me baking cookies with the Snake." He thrust his finger in the water.

Nothing happened.

Instead, the fish clung tighter to their arrow, pointing insistently at Tedros' hand.

"Told you. They're addled, these fish," Tedros carped.

"Wrong finger," his princess said. "*Look*."

The Wish Fish were pointing at another finger of Tedros' hand.

The one with King Arthur's ring.

Tedros' heart beat faster.

Without a word, he dipped the finger in, warm water filling the cold, steel grooves of the ring—

A shockwave of light detonated across the pond.

Prince and princess stared at each other.

"What was *that*?" said Tedros.

But now the fish were gluing into a silver mob, fastening hard around the steel circle, trying to kiss the ring with their bobbing little mouths. With each kiss, the fish flashed with light, as if a secret power had been transferred. Soon they were strobing like stars in the dark, faster and faster, this power magnifying, charging their bodies with mysterious force. Tedros waited for them to disperse, to paint his wish, like they'd done with his princess, but instead, the fish gobbed tighter, a ragged mass, sucking wet and tight to his ring. Then slowly they slid up his palm . . . his wrist . . .

"Wait!" he rasped, yanking at his hand, but Agatha held him in place, the fish surging out of the pond, gripping his elbow, his bicep, his armpit—

"Let go!" he cried, fighting Agatha.

"Trust me," she soothed.

The swarming school was at his shoulder, his throat . . . his chin . . . their interlocked bodies turning clear as glass, revealing small throbbing hearts. Then, all at once, the fish began to swell. Inflating like balloons, they amassed into a clear, gelatinous globe, expanding in every direction, pressing into Tedros' face.

"*Help!*" he yelled, but the warm, slobbery bubble laminated his mouth, his nose, his eyes, suffocating him with a salty smell. He could feel Agatha's arms on him, but he couldn't see her. He couldn't see anything. He closed his eyes, his lashes lacquered in itchy scales, his chest pumping shallow breaths, leaking last bits of air—

Then it stopped. The pressure. The smell. As if his head had separated from his body. The prince opened his eyes to find himself *inside* the fish bubble, floating above the pond.

Agatha was in the bubble with him.

"Like I said," she smiled. "Trust me."

Then his princess began to shrink. And now, so did the prince, his whole body pinching down, inch by inch, to the size of a tea mug. The bubble closed in, too, its watery edges leaving just enough room around them.

Tedros glanced at his pants. "This better not be permanent."

Instantly the bubble split in two, each sealing up whole, separating prince and princess in their own orbs.

"Agatha?" Tedros called, his voice bouncing against liquid walls.

He saw his tiny princess call back, her lips moving but only a squeak coming through.

Rays of light refracted against the bubbles and Tedros watched the pond opening up like a portal, revealing a familiar castle and a pink-purple sky . . . the scene of a Wish Fish painting he'd mocked, now come to life. . . .

"Trust me."

Tedros looked up at Agatha, eyes wide—

He never had time to scream. The two balls plunged into the portal like they'd been shot from a cannon, vanishing into the glare of a faraway sun.

4

THE STORIAN

Altar and Grail

The Pen that tells the tale is just that: the teller, with no place in the story. It should not be a character or a weapon or a prize. It should not be lionized or persecuted or thought of at all. The Pen must be invisible, doing its work in humble silence, with no bias or opinion, like an all-seeing eye committed only to unspooling a story until its end.

Yet here we are: things once held sacred are sacred no longer.

The Pen is under siege.

My spirit is weakened, my powers fading.

I must tell my own story or risk Man erasing it forever.

Man, who despite

thousands of years of trusting in my powers . . . has now come to take them from me.

No ONE KNEW where in the gardens the wedding would take place, for there was no stage or altar or priest and no sign of a bride or groom. But as the sun dipped into the horizon, guards continued to let guests in—men, women, children, dwarves, trolls, elves, ogres, fairies, goblins, nymphs, and more citizens of the Woods—all dressed in their finest as they crammed through the gates of Camelot's castle.

After King Arthur's death, the gardens had fallen to blight, but under a new king, they'd been revived to glory, a sprawling wonderland of color and scent. Packed hip to hip, the people flooded the groves of the Orangerie, the paths of the Sunken Garden, and the lawns of the Rosefield, all of which orbited the long Reflecting Pool crowned with a marble statue of King Rhian hammering Excalibur into the masked Snake's neck. Muddy shoes stained the grass and flattened the willows; restless children tore branches and ate the lilacs; a family of giants broke an orange tree. But still guards continued to let guests in, even as the setting sun halved and quartered and the smell of sweaty bodies clogged the air.

"Is there no end to this?" the Empress of Putsi growled, holding her nose as people jostled against her, nearly knocking her and her goose-feather coat into the Reflecting Pool. "Putsi butchers and millers and maids given the same treatment as their Empress! Ever and Never royalty thrown to the masses and left to fend for ourselves! After all we've done for King Rhian? After we burned our rings in his name? Who ever heard of commoners at a royal wedding!"

"It is the commoners who have *made* him king," said the Maharani of Mahadeva, watching a mountain troll pee in the tulips. "And now that we've burned our rings, our voice has no more weight than theirs."

"We burned our rings to save our kingdoms. To earn the king's protection," the Empress of Putsi argued. "Your castle was attacked like mine. Your sons might be dead if not for you giving up your ring. Your realm is *safe* now."

"Is it? How are we protected if the Kingdom Council no longer has a vote against the king?" the Maharani pressed. "A king who my advisors believe seeks the power of the Storian."

"The 'One True King' is an old wives' tale spread by that Sader family. But even if any of their flimflam *was* true, you of all people should welcome it. The Storian did nothing for Evil kingdoms like yours or for the Nevers of the Woods. If Rhian had the Storian's power, he might do Evil a world of Good." The Empress stood straighter. "King Rhian is a worthy king to *both* sides. He'll listen to us, whether or not we have our rings. King Rhian will always put us above the people—"

Something smacked her face, and she looked up at a chubby boy high on a staircase, pelting people with gooseberries.

"Like he's done today?" the Maharani asked, stonefaced.

The Empress went mum.

As for the berry-pelting boy, he found himself swatted by

his Dean and yanked into place with the rest of her students, who'd traveled with the Dean from Foxwood.

"Behave, Arjun! Or I'll tell King Rhian to throw you in the dungeon with his brother," Dean Brunhilde scolded, swiping her student's ammunition. "And I assure you, you won't last a half second in a cell with RJ. Not an ounce of Good in that boy's body."

"Thought Rhian's brother was called 'Japeth,'" Arjun peeped.

"Even that name sounds Evil," the Dean murmured. "I shortened his birth name to 'RJ.' Came to Arbed House because he, like you, couldn't get along with his mother. I tried to make him Good. Did everything I could. Even his brother thought he could be fixed. But in the end, it seems Rhian learned what I did: some Evil *can't* be fixed."

"Still don't believe we're here. A royal wedding!" piped an older boy with sunken eyes. "A kid like us now the king!"

"And marrying a girl as pretty as Sophie," said a bald boy, his collar littered with dandruff. "Don't forget that, Emilio. That's why *I'd* want to be a king."

"Think I'll get to be a king someday, Dean Brunhilde?" Arjun asked. "Or at least a prince?"

"I don't see why not," Dean Brunhilde said. "Things are different now. Most royal weddings don't allow ordinary citizens. But King Rhian knows to respect every soul, Good or Evil, boy or girl, young or old. All of you have a chance at glory while he's king. Taught him myself, just like I'm teaching you."

"Can we meet King Rhian? Can I get his autograph?" Emilio asked.

"I want to meet him!" another boy prompted.

"Me too! Me too!" clamored the rest of the group.

The Dean blushed. "I'm sure Rhian remembers me fondly. . . . Jorgen! Stop pinching fairies!"

Meanwhile, Arjun pulled a few last gooseberries from his pocket and aimed them over the rail.

"Quit it!" Emilio hissed.

"But if I hit that spellcast bubble roving around, everyone watching in the other kingdoms will see me!" said Arjun. "I'll be famous! Like the king!"

"What bubble are you talking about?" Emilio asked, confused. "The spellcast comes from the shield over the garden. The pink fog up there. That's what beams the scene to everywhere in the Woods."

"Then what's *that*?" Arjun said, pointing down.

Emilio squinted at a watery orb flitting between bodies in the crowd, nearing the edge of the reflecting pool—

But the last light of the sun vanished, and the bubble could be seen no longer, lost in the white mist rising over the lake.

As NIGHT SETTLED, the mist spooled thicker, rolling over the waters in snow-colored waves. Behind the pool, Kei marched the Camelot guard into formation, the armored bodies silhouetted in fog. Standing on a staircase behind were Alpa and

Omeida, the two Mistral Sisters, hooded amongst the crowd, eyes locked on Rhian's statue, each muttering the same incantation under their breaths. On cue, the statue began to glitter a radiant gold, casting rippling light on the king's carved face and the Snake crushed in his arms. The mist over the Reflecting Pool dissipated, revealing the surface had magically frozen, the ice strewn with blue and gold rose petals, the pool now a stage.

Soft music began to play in a strange key, the melody of a wedding march that sounded more like a funeral's.

Then a blur of movement reflected in the ice.

Wedding guests raised their heads.

The sky had bloomed with constellations, Lions repeating endlessly as far as the eye could see, changing pose with every blink of stars. Against these celestial patterns, two more stars appeared: the bride and the king, floating down on the wings of a thousand white butterflies beating across the bride's gown. Her shoes were made of glass, her throat collared with rubies, her face shrouded in a delicate veil. Her groom wore a white fur soaring behind him like a cape, belted with a chain of gold lions. Excalibur's hilt gleamed at his waist. The crown of Camelot fit securely on his head. He made a fine King Rhian, this boy, with his tight copper hair, amber tan, and aqua-green gaze. . . .

But we know better.

"Rhian" was only playing the part of his brother, his wild hair hacked short, his skin painted tan, his eyes dyed by magic. His bride, too, seemed to be playing a role, her smile vacant, her hands clasping him the way she once clasped another boy she'd intended to marry: a young, frost-haired School Master who she thought she loved with all her heart. But now, in her wide green eyes, there was no love. There was nothing but the reflection of her groom, pleased with the emptiness of her gaze.

The young couple floated down towards the statue, "Rhian" gripping Sophie as tightly as the stone Rhian gripped the Snake. They neared the ground, bathed in the statue's light, the Woods' eyes upon them. The king loomed over his bride, placing a hand on her throat, and pulled her mouth to his. The crowd suspended in silence as he kissed her, time standing still. Look closer, the way I can, and one could see the chill in Sophie's cheeks . . . the shudder in her legs . . . the hardness in the groom's lips, repelled by the taste of his bride. . . .

Their feet touched down to the frozen pool.

The mob stayed hushed.

Then King Rhian's statue began to rattle and quake. The edges of the ice pool splintered, shards of ice spraying into the sky, the glassy stage vibrating beneath the bride's and groom's feet. All at once, Rhian's statue lifted out of the ground, taking the Reflecting Pool with it, the thick, frozen lake floating into the air, up, up, up, the bride and groom now high above the gardens, like toy figures on a cake.

Cheers burst out across the land, the crowd unleashing all they'd held back.

The wedding of the king had begun.

Orbiting the grounds, the spellcast shield strobed, record-ing every moment and beaming it to the Woods. Listen well and you might hear the cheers from kingdoms beyond, echoing on the wind . . .

"Rhian" turned from his bride and a flash of gold glowed beneath his cape, pulsing where his heart should be. He reached under the silk and drew out a cocoon of light. Only I know what is hidden within: a black scim disguised as Lionsmane—the king's Pen, my so-called rival—which now rose out of the light, sharp at both ends and gold as the sun, into the night sky over the king's palm.

From its tip came a shimmering dust, the color of pure ore, shapeshifting into the outlines of cuddling puppies, kissing lovebirds, arrows shot through hearts. Children hopped up in the crowd, reaching hands skyward, trying to touch these valentines before they broke apart and golden ash rained down, dusting their hair with sparkles. Sophie, too, clasped her hands to her chest, as if charmed by the sight of happy young souls. (Perhaps the clearest sign yet that this Sophie was as fraudulent as her groom.)

Meanwhile, "Rhian" spoke from the floating stage. "The Storian was the balance of our Woods. The Pen trusted with telling the stories that moved our world forward. That is, until it gave you the last Ever After. Tedros the 'king.' Or as you knew him: Tedros the coward, the fraud, the *snake*. He is no king, regardless of what that Pen says. You learned that the hard way. But this is what happens when we give the Storian free rein. Fate leaves us vulnerable and out of control. Fate leads us to false idols. But the Storian is no longer our future. And neither are the winds of fate. Man's *will* is the future. Man's will can bring glory to all. And tonight, Man becomes Pen. *My* pen. I will write the stories of the future. I will reward those who deserve to be rewarded and punish those who deserve to be punished. The power is with me now. The power is with the *people*."

The crowd roared as Lionsmane rose higher in the sky, throbbing brighter like a north star. Sophie clapped along, not a wick of understanding in her gaze.

The king held her closer. "But as long as the Storian exists, it is a threat. Empower it and it will lead us astray. To more Tedroses, and more like him. So we must not only reject it . . . but destroy it. All but one kingdom in the Endless Woods has renounced faith in the old Pen. All but one of a hundred founding realms has broken their bond with it. Tonight, as a preface to our wedding, the last kingdom breaks its bond too. The 100th realm burns its ring, stripping the Pen's powers and giving the power over Man's fate to me. Tonight, you not only gain a queen." His eyes pierced through the dark. "Tonight, the One True King lives."

Lionsmane spawned flames from its tip: a ball of blue fire that lobbed high in the dark . . . then shot down, blasting past exuberant guests before catching to a halt in front of the Camelot guard. An armored soldier next to Kei stepped forward, the fire lighting up the wrinkles around his greedy eyes and the filthy hair spinning out from his helmet. A discerning Reader would recognize him quickly: this guard who wasn't a guard at all. It was Bertie, the Sheriff of Nottingham's once-steward, now the keeper of his ring. And in Bertie's hands was this very ring, glinting atop a black pillow, the carved steel reflecting the contours of the flames.

I still feel the heat from here.

Little by little, the crowd quieted, sensing the magnitude of the moment, realizing that they too were now pledging loyalty to Man over me. Sophie seemed to stir from her daze, as if deep inside, a kernel of the past had shaken loose in her memory.

"The last piece of the Storian's power," the king declared, fixed on Bertie's ring. "The last tether between Man and Pen."

Bertie stepped forward, his eyes on the king.

"Rhian" nodded.

My spirit cries out in its shell—

The Sheriff's old friend opens his palm. Nottingham's ring falls into the fire.

Crackle! Whish! Pop!

The ring is no more.

All that's left of me is a whisper.

For the first time, the king's face softens, the regal facade falling away, as if he too had dipped into memory. "With my Pen, I vow to write these Woods as they should be. To give all your stories the endings they deserve." His gaze fell on Dean Brunhilde in the crowd. "Including mine."

The Dean locked eyes with "Rhian," a cold tingle worming up her spine. She peered closer at him—

"He sees you!" Arjun blurted, grabbing her. "Rhian remembers!" By the time the Dean turned back, the king had regained his poise, his focus on his bride.

"No more rings left. No more pledges to make," he said,

touching Sophie's cheek. "Except one."

Slowly his eyes lifted.

From Lionsmane's tip birthed two golden rings.

One floated into the king's hand.

One into his bride's.

Lionsmane glowed brighter in the sky, the witness to this moment, both altar and grail.

"With this ring, I thee wed," the king said to Sophie.

He slipped his ring onto her finger.

What power I have left dwindles, my words fainter on the page, as if they cannot sustain another blow.

Sophie stayed lost in his eyes.

"With this ring, I thee wed," she repeated.

No hesitation: she slid her ring onto his finger.

"Then by the power of the Pen, *Man's* Pen," the boy proclaimed, looking up into the sky, "I ask Lionsmane to seal the bonds of this marriage. To crown Sophie my queen. To name me, Rhian of Camelot, the One True King of these Woods!"

Lionsmane burned brighter, brighter, drinking in all the force I have lost. Suddenly, it is alive, becoming *me*, my powers stolen into the hands of this king. Against the night, his pen paints a queen's crown, five ribbons of jewels topped with a ring of fleur de lis—

Instantly, the crown came to life, a dazzling tower of diamonds, as if the king's wish had made it true, before the crown set down upon Sophie's head. Sophie touched its grooves, the blinding glare of jewels casting sparkles on her hands. A strange bubble of light streaked past her, and she swiveled her head to follow it before she remembered what she was *supposed* to focus on: the crowd chanting her name . . . her wedding to the king nearly sealed. . . .

As for this king, his focus was only on the pen, alive with the power of a hundred flames. His eyes quivered with triumph.

The rings had been destroyed.

The queen had her crown.

The prophecy was complete.

Raising his hands, he reached up for Lionsmane, the Pen he'd pillaged and betrayed and murdered for, the Pen that could now bring his deepest wishes to life. He claimed its warm gold in his palm, seizing its powers, seizing immortality, a roar rising into his throat and unleashed to the sky—

The light of the pen snuffed out, its metal turned cold in his hands.

The crown vanished from Sophie's head.

So did the crown on the *king's*.

Their wedding rings disappeared, too.

Across the gardens, the crowd stood stunned.

Sophie startled from her trance, looking to her groom.

"Rhian" was frozen, his teeth clenched.

Here in my school tower, a bolt of heat lights up my steel.

There is one ring left, you see.

A ring which precludes full transfer of my powers. A ring this king does not know of.

And it is closer than he thinks.

Now the last swan in my steel pumps its wings, harder, harder, as if to make up for all the other swans lost, all the other kingdoms who've surrendered their rings.

Over Camelot's castle, silver lightning lashed through the sky, imploding Rhian's statue, and the whole of the frozen stage came plummeting down. People in the mob screamed, diving for cover—

The iced pool shattered to the ground, launching bride and groom in opposite directions. Chunks of ice hailed around them, bashing into spectators.

"Watch out!" Kei yelled, tackling Sophie—

The remnants of Rhian's statue cratered into the dirt behind her, a mountain of rubble.

All went quiet in the gardens, thick with the smell of fire and ice.

Slowly, adults, children, creatures inched out of their hiding places.

Kei lifted his head, Sophie curled up beneath him, her eyes quivering with the blankness of someone who didn't know where or who she was. She spotted the king, flat on his stomach near the statue's ruins, Lionsmane clenched in his fist. Seeing "Rhian" centered her—

But suddenly, from the king's belt, Excalibur rocketed out of its sheath by its own power, flying high over the castle, swordtip gleaming like the point of a pen, before it came axing down into the statue's rubble. It landed blade-first at the top of the heap, its hilt high and standing, like a cross out of a grave.

The hilt magically opened, a scroll rising from inside. As the king and his princess watched, the crowd shellshocked around them, the scroll unfurled in midair, revealing a parchment card, filled with faded words, stamped with Camelot's seal.

Moonlight illuminated the decree.

King Arthur's voice thundered from beyond.

> *"The first test was passed.*
> *Excalibur pulled from the stone.*
> *A new king named.*
> *But <u>two</u> claim the crown.*
> *The sword returns to the stone,*
>   *for only one is the true king.*
> *Who?*
> *The future I have seen has many possibilities . . .*
> *So by my will, none shall be crowned until*
>   *the Tournament is complete.*
> *The Tournament of Kings.*
> *Three trials.*
> *Three answers to find.*
> *A race to the finish.*
> *My last coronation test.*
> *Excalibur will crown the winner*
>   *and take the loser's head.*
> *The first test is coming. Prepare . . ."*

The card crumbled and blew away, like sand in the wind. The hilt of Arthur's sword sealed up, leaving Excalibur in moonlight at the peak of piled stone.

A new altar.

A new grail.

For a moment, there was utter silence, strangers and friends gawking at each other in the gardens. The students of Arbed House looked to their Dean, but she had no words. So too were the leaders of the Woods tongue-tied—the Empress of Putsi, the Queens of Mahadeva and Jaunt Jolie, the Kings of Foxwood and Maidenvale and Bloodbrook and more—scattered across the ice-strewn fields and unsure of what they'd just heard. Even Sophie's vacant sheen had cracked, her eyes narrowing, her soul closer and closer to breaking through. . . .

But now all of them caught sight of a figure rising out of the ruins, climbing the stone heap: the king, crownless and dirt-smeared, Lionsmane cold in his hands, his cheeks a violent red. Slamming a foot onto the highest stone, he seized Excalibur with a single fist, and pulled it hard.

It didn't move.

He shoved Lionsmane into his furs and yanked the sword again, this time with both fists, only to suffer the same result. Sweat soaked his forehead. He raised his eyes to the sky, where King Arthur's voice had spoken. . . .

"*Two* kings?" he shouted mockingly. "What dirty trick is this? I pulled Excalibur from the stone. *I* am the king! Who dares to claim a second?"

A watery orb slammed into the king, then another, bashing him off the stone. The bubbles expanded, two tiny figures growing taller within, rising to full size before they thrust out their hands, peeled their way through watery walls, and left the bubbles behind. Tedros strode atop the stone mountain, muscles clinging to his wet shirt, his princess at his side.

"*Me*," he declared. "And the only trick is how that sword ever came to a Snake in the first place."

Arthur's son raised his hand into the moon's beam, the silver ring stealing its light.

"The last ring lives. Camelot's ring. My father's ring," he thundered, resounding across the castle grounds. "I am the heir. *I am the king*."

The people of the Woods held their breath, their heads whipping between two defiant kings. Sophie, too, stayed still, even though her body told her to run to her groom's side . . . to *her* king. . . . On her knees in shredded roses, she glanced at Kei, who had that same haunted look he'd had in the castle. Slowly, Sophie's eyes went back to Tedros atop the stone. Kei knew this boy . . . and so did *she*. . . .

Tedros glared his rival down. "You heard the king. Excalibur is returned to the stone. The crown no longer belongs to you," he slashed. "Three tests. The sword crowns the winner. No more games. No more lies. . . . Let the *tournament* begin."

Flat on his stomach, "Rhian" peered up at the prince, a hint of fragility in his face. A sliver of fear.

Then it was gone.

He spun to Kei.

"*Kill him*," he ordered.

Kei's gaze hardened. He and the pirates launched for Tedros—the ring on the prince's finger shot a blast of light, reforming the protective bubble, trapping Tedros inside. The prince whirled to Agatha: "Get Sophie!"

But Agatha was already gone from his wing, surging for her best friend and tackling Sophie into her arms. White and black dresses coalesced, like the intermingling of two swans. The girls' eyes locked, dark and light, an eternal connection made. Good and Evil. Boy and Girl. Old and Young. Truth and Lies. Past and Present. Sophie gasped, the color in her cheeks returning, the fire in her eyes pouring forth—

It dampened, like a door slammed shut. Sophie grabbed Agatha by the neck and threw her to the ground.

Lifting her head, Agatha saw the two Mistral Sisters on a staircase behind Sophie, directing their hands, puppeteering her best friend's moves. Sophie grabbed a slab of frozen ice, jagged like a dagger. Grinning, the Mistrals swung their palms. Sophie pounced for Agatha, the ice knife plunging for her best friend's chest—

The ice knife trapped in a wall of water, a hair's width from Agatha's heart.

For a moment, all Agatha could hear were her own shallow breaths, the hammer of her blood. She felt her prince's arms drag her back, the two of them safe in the Wish Fish bubble, Arthur's ring glowing on Tedros' hand like a talisman. Behind the bubble, a portal opened, revealing the gray waters of a lake . . . its vast, snowy shores . . . three shadows in the distance. . . .

But Tedros' gaze was still on Sophie through the bubble, her teeth bared like a rabid animal's, her fist tearing the ice knife into the watery wall again and again, yielding only the tiniest crack.

"Rhian" gently clasped her from behind, staying his princess's hand. Sophie gazed up at him, starry-eyed with love once more, fully under his spell.

Tears rolled down Agatha's cheeks. "What have you done to her! You monster! You creep! What have you done to my friend!"

The boy ignored her, his eyes on Tedros. An eel curled off his wedding robe, so small that no one in the audience noticed as it slithered through the crack Sophie had made in the bubble—

Tedros instantly snatched it into his fist.

But now the eely scim was speaking with the Snake's voice, so only the prince and Agatha could hear. . . .

"Your weak magic can't protect you from what's coming," the scim taunted. Outside the bubble, his master leered at Tedros. "You sniveling coward. You pretty-faced fool. You're no one's leader. No one in the Woods is on your side. And now you think you can win a fight against me?"

"A *fair* fight, yes," Tedros flared, glowering back at his nemesis. "As for the Woods, soon they'll know that their 'king' isn't who he says he is."

"Oh?" said the scim. "Let's see if they believe *anything* you have to say. Tedros the rebel. Tedros the *Snake*."

"I don't need to say a word. They'll know when Excalibur takes your head," the prince seethed, crushing the eel harder. "I'll finish the tests first. I'll win the tournament. The sword will crown *me*."

"Like it did last time? It will never let you be king because you have nothing in you that is a king. *Nothing*."

Tedros vibrated with anger. "I am Arthur's son. I am his *heir*."

"There is only one ending to your tale," said the eel coolly. "You dead and forgotten. That ring in my hands. The Storian's powers mine. You and those you love . . . erased."

"Catch you at the finish," Tedros vowed.

"Rhian" didn't flinch. "I'll kill you long before."

Tedros glared into his black pupils. "I see you, *Japeth*. Like your brother surely did before you murdered him and stole his name. I can believe Rhian was Arthur's son. At least he had a soul. At least he wanted to do Good. But how can a beast like *you* be my brother? How can filth like *you* be my father's child?"

"Isn't it obvious?" the scim replied.

The Snake grinned, his face pressing to the prince's against the slim ball of water, his voice inside a poisoned whisper. . . .

"I'm not."

The words slammed Tedros like a kick to the chest. He killed the scim and smashed it to goo as he choked out a breath—*"Who are you?"*—but Agatha was pulling him back through a portal, lake water flooding his lungs, the prince's question echoing again and again into the dark, dark deep.

5

AGATHA

A Snow of Scrolls

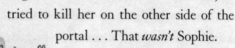

er best friend had tried to kill her before.

Their first year at school.

And again during the third.

Sophie was a witch, after all, and Agatha a princess.

But this time was different, Agatha thought, clawing through water, running out of breath. Because whoever just tried to kill her on the other side of the portal . . . That *wasn't* Sophie.

Agatha tore through the surface, gulping air. She searched the lake for Tedros, her eyes flooding with water before she spotted three shadowy figures on Avalon's shore, shouting out to her—

But Agatha was already back under, prowling through gray depths for her prince. She'd been gripping on to him . . . then suddenly she wasn't, distracted by her fears for Sophie . . .

She squinted in every direction. No sign of him, the lake vast and still. She resurfaced, fueling more air—

"Tedros!" she called across the lake.

"Agatha!" Nicola returned from the shore.

"Where's Tedros!" Agatha gasped at her.

"Don't see him!" said Hort.

"He's not with you?" said Guinevere anxiously.

Agatha dove under. Panic squeezed her throat. Had she left Tedros behind? In worrying about Sophie, had she doomed her prince? She whirled around, limbs flailing—

Flashing gleams winked ahead, like an explosion of pearls.

A swarm of Wish Fish cannoned towards her, Tedros caged within, the school of fish swallowing Agatha too, before they crashed out of the water and spewed the prince and princess to the snow-mounded shore. The two landed in each other's arms, soggy and chilled, as the fish pirouetted in the air and speared back into the lake.

Relieved, Agatha clasped her prince, Tedros still questioning: "Who is he? *Who?*"

"We heard what he said," Hort said, rushing in. "The Snake—"

"Huh? How could *you* hear him?" said Agatha, confused.

"We both heard him," said Nicola, joining her boyfriend.

"That he's not your brother. That he's not Arthur's son."

"But whose son is he, then?" said Hort, ignoring Agatha's perplexed look. "The blood crystal told us Rhian and Japeth were the sons of Evelyn Sader and King Arthur. Rhian's blood can't lie. So what are we missing? Did Japeth say anything else? We couldn't hear it all—"

"Because you kept tilting the mirrorspell to Sophie," Nicola scorched.

"Mirrorspell?" Tedros asked, mystified.

Hort sighed impatiently. "We saw the Lady of the Lake open her portal when the crystal ball shattered. The portal that let you into her secret haven. Before the portal closed, I mirrorspelled inside of it, like Hester taught us. That spell let us follow you, as if we were by your side. We watched everything: from when you went to your father's grave to when you found the Wish Fish to when the sword announced the Tournament of Kings."

"Amazing we watched anything except Sophie's face," Nicola piled on.

"Amazing you can't give me credit for thinking of the spell in the first place," Hort shot back. "I was trying to see what the Snake did to my friend. She's possessed by a curse. I could see the Mistral Sisters controlling her when she attacked Agatha."

"I didn't know the Mistral Sisters *could* use magic," said Agatha, her heart settling down enough for her brain to catch up. She looked up at the weasel, his hair dyed blond, his skin pale, standing beside his girlfriend, her black curls dusted with snow. "They've never used magic before. If they could, wouldn't they have been able to skip the dungeons when Tedros put them there?"

"Can't use magic in Camelot's dungeons," Guinevere reminded, arriving with Tinkerbell on her shoulder, the fairy lighting up at the sight of Tedros. "Though I've known of the sisters for a long time and don't remember them having powers either."

"How could they control Sophie, then?" Agatha pushed.

"How could Arthur gift Tedros his ring so long after his death? How did he know Tedros would need it? How could Excalibur return to the stone after it was pulled?" the prince's mother replied, bending down and touching the carved steel around her son's finger. "From the outside, these things seem impossible. But magic has its own rules. Its own secrets. So if the three sisters are controlling Sophie, then we have to find what that secret is."

"I only saw two sisters," said Hort.

"Me too," Nicola confirmed.

"Third must be up to something," Guinevere suspected. "The Mistral Sisters stick together unless there's good reason."

Tinkerbell nuzzled Tedros lovingly, but he was focused on Agatha. "Sophie would have killed you," he breathed, still haunted. "Nothing would have stopped her."

"Lucky the portal opened," Agatha admitted, glancing at her friends. "Knew we could get back once we saw you."

Guinevere blanched. "You could see us? From Camelot?"

"Why does it matter?" Agatha asked.

Tedros' mother stood up. "The Snake was inches from you.

If you could see this place through the portal, then so could he. You heard him: tournament or no tournament, he wants you dead. We need to leave. *Quickly.*"

"Won't Camelot's ring protect Tedros?" Hort asked. "Like it did back there? Snake would have killed him otherwise."

"You don't think I can take that scum?" Tedros scorned. "That I need a ring's protection?"

"Um, that's not what I was saying, but now that you're asking . . . yes," Hort replied.

"Whatever powers the ring has, the Wish Fish knew how to access it. We *don't*," said Guinevere, moving towards the staircase. "But I wouldn't put our faith in the ring. It's surely bonded by the Storian, like all the other rings—and though we are the Pen's last defenders, it cannot tilt the tale in our favor. That's not how the Storian works. It's why Japeth seeks to replace it with a Pen he can control. Besides, even if the ring *could* protect Tedros, it can't protect Agatha or the rest of us."

"She's right," Tedros said tensely, pulling Agatha towards the stairs, Hort and Nicola scrambling behind them.

As Tedros helped his princess up the steps, his father's ring warm against her palm, Agatha glanced down one last time at the lake, the shores quiet and deserted, the waters dead calm.

Then she saw her.

The bald-headed silhouette beneath the glass of the water, watching as the intruders left her kingdom. The Lady of the Lake met Agatha's gaze for a long moment, her black eyes wide and frozen . . . before she towed back under and disappeared.

Agatha's hand went cold in her prince's.

She'd never seen that emotion in the Lady's face before.

An emotion Agatha knew well.

She was feeling it right now.

Fear.

"Can't they fly faster?" Agatha whispered to Tedros, the two of them shrouded inside a fairy cocoon with Hort, Nicola, and Guinevere.

Tinkerbell retorted with angry squeaks, the light of her wings dimmed like her fellow fairies' to camouflage the cocoon against the night.

"Tink says she let the fairies go feasting while she waited for us," Tedros explained. "Only food in Avalon are those green apples. Must all be drunk on sugar."

The fairy hive stuttered away from Avalon's gates, jostling their concealed passengers like cats in a barrel.

All five members of the team had agreed that they should get far away from Avalon, though each person had competing ideas of where they should go next.

"Living Library," Tedros proposed.

"In Pifflepaff Hills?" said Hort. "Cotton candy land?"

"We can get answers there," Tedros insisted, turning to Agatha. "The scroll that announced the tournament . . . We watched my father write it, remember? When we jumped into the crystal ball and went back in time. Dad was at his desk. He wrote *two* cards. One with my original coronation test. The second must have been the secret one! My second test! Which means—"

"Wait. How did he know he'd *need* a second test?" Nicola interrupted. "How did he know you'd fail the first one?"

"I had the same question," Agatha mulled, eyeing Nicola. "Except . . . that line when he announced the tournament . . ."

"The one that didn't make sense?" Nic caught on. "'*The future I have seen has many possibilities . . .*'"

"Maybe he knew somehow," Agatha guessed. "Maybe he knew all of this would happen."

"Arthur wasn't a seer," Guinevere dismissed.

"Doesn't take a seer to know you have a secret son snaking about," Hort surmised. "Someone who might challenge your other son for your throne."

"But the Snake just said he *isn't* Arthur's son," Nicola reminded.

"Look, all that matters is Dad had that second card ready," Tedros plowed on, trying to make his point. "The one with the tournament. We don't know what the trials are yet, but the Living Library in Pifflepaff Hills has a whole archive about Dad's history—his years at school, his training with Merlin, even his time with Sir Ector and Sir Kay, before he pulled the sword from the stone and became king. Dad kept the archive up to date, so I'd have a place to go if something happened to him. A place where I could still feel close to him . . . The library could give me clues to what the tests might be. So I can be ready for them. It's as good a place as any to start."

"Too risky," his mother countered. "The King of Pifflepaff Hills and his guards will be on Japeth's side. And they keep the ancestry files in the Living Library well protected. Besides, if you have questions about your father, I'm as good a resource as any archive. Arthur confided in me."

"Was that before or after he put a death warrant on your head?" Tedros mumbled.

"Enough, Tedros. I'm trying to keep you alive," said Guinevere sternly. "If you don't want me here, tell me and I'll go."

"Your mother's right," said Agatha, touching her prince. "Library will be a death trap."

"So I'm still a fugitive, then," Tedros blistered, pulling away. "Even after Excalibur went back into the stone. Even with Japeth's crown disappearing. Even with Dad's voice rising from the grave and *telling* people I have a claim to his throne." Pink spots colored his cheeks. "Surely *some* kingdoms will question who the king is now? Surely some leaders will figure out he's the Snake? Surely some will come to my side—"

A blast of light scorched over the Savage Sea like a comet.

Lionsmane's new message lit up the sky.

"Surely not," Hort said.

Agatha, too, had the same sinking feeling as she read the pen's screed.

Tedros thinks he can steal the crown. But the people know better. There is only one king. Your Rhian. The People's King.

Together, we will win the Tournament. For the Lion. For the Woods!

"*'We'?*" said Tedros.

"He's keeping the people on his side," Agatha realized. "Before the tournament starts."

"People don't decide the winner. It's a race. Someone finishes first," her prince dismissed. "That's who Excalibur will crown."

"We don't know the tests, Tedros," said Agatha. "If the people are on his side, they might be able to *help* him with them. Then it's not just you against Japeth. It's you against the entire Woods."

"But that's cheating!" Tedros said. "Excalibur won't crown a cheater!"

"It did once before," his princess pointed out.

Tedros glared up at the Snake's screed. "So I could play these tests honest and fair and act the king . . . and still lose my head."

"Japeth might have the Woods, but you have us. Your family. Your friends. People with real loyalty to you," Agatha encouraged. "We'll find a way to win."

"We just have to keep you safe until you do," Nicola said to Tedros. "Tournament or no tournament, the Snake's coming for your head."

"So many ways to lose a head," Hort quipped.

Tinkerbell bit him.

"Good girl, Tink," said Tedros.

With the prince's safety in mind, the weasel proposed

returning to Gnomeland's underground hideout—

"—where we will have to stay *forever*, because the Snake's scims will track us like last time and surround the stump over Gnomeland until we come out," said Nicola.

"Must you poo on every one of my ideas?" Hort harrumphed. "What's *your* idea?"

"To go back to the School for Good and Evil, where we can join the students and teachers and at least have the semblance of a defense," his girlfriend replied.

"No," Agatha rejected. "First place Japeth's men will look. And this time, there's no Sheriff or enchanted sack to save us."

A sharp rumble thundered behind them—

Between the lattice of fairies, she watched a cavalry of twenty horses, mounted with armed guards, streak across the snow towards Avalon's gates.

The sugar-drunk fairies sprung alert, flying higher and smoother, their wings going dark to conceal their passengers.

"Few more minutes and we'd have been dead," Tedros breathed.

Agatha felt no relief. Japeth's men were already on the hunt. Which meant Tedros didn't just have to win three tests against an insidious Snake. He had to survive long enough to finish them. Her heart seized tighter. If only she could do the tests instead of him . . . if only she could protect him—

She squashed the thought.

Hadn't she learned her lesson about hijacking his battles?

These were *his* tests. Not hers.

Tedros needs a princess, she told herself. A sentinel at his side. Not a nag or a worrywart or a second-guesser. Besides, there were signs it could all end well. They were alive, for one thing. They were still together. And Sophie's wedding to the Snake hadn't been sealed, their rings disappearing before she was his queen. And somewhere out there, the rest of their friends—the witches, Beatrix, Kiko, Willam, Bogden, and others—were hopefully alive too. Tedros still had a chance. Agatha had to let his fate unfold the way it was supposed to. She had to let her prince become a king.

Giving Tedros full command, though, would have to wait. They wouldn't be going to the Living Library like he wanted. Far too dangerous, she insisted. Instead, it was her plan that won out: to fly to Sherwood Forest, the densest part of the Endless Woods, enchanted by magic and impervious to the Snake, his men, or his scims. They could camp there until the first test was revealed, though Agatha hadn't the slightest clue how that would happen. (Would Arthur's voice boom from the sky again? How do you win a race if you don't know when it starts?) All they could do for now was wait, and Robin Hood's lair was the best place to do it. Plus, they'd be able to reunite with Robin, their last possible protector, since Lancelot and the Sheriff were dead, along with Agatha's mother and Professor Sader, Dovey and Lesso too, while Merlin had yet to resurface. Adults didn't fare well in her fairy tale, Agatha thought grimly, glancing at Guinevere, one of the few left, nestled against her son as the fairies flew them over Foxwood. And yet Guinevere didn't quite seem like an adult. To Agatha, she was less sturdy somehow, more precarious, as if all those years with Lance in paradise had left the once-queen unprepared for real life.

"Sorry about pooing on your ideas," Agatha heard Nicola whisper to Hort. "It's just . . . once you saw Sophie in the mirrorspell, you got all lit up. And you never look that way with me."

"Sophie doesn't want me," Hort chortled, then saw his girl-friend's face. "No, I don't mean it like that. I'm abysmal with words. It's why I made a crap History professor at school. How 'bout this: when the Snake has you in a wedding dress and under some terrible spell, I'll get lit up too." He winked at Nic.

"You really are abysmal with words," she laughed.

"With everything, really," said Hort, kissing her.

Agatha couldn't help but smile . . . then noticed Guinevere gazing at her.

"What is it?" Agatha asked.

"I'm just thinking . . . Arthur gave Tedros his ring. Arthur had his second will ready. Arthur *wants* Tedros to win. So why have this tournament at all?" said the old queen. "Why not just tell the people Tedros is the heir?"

"Because the people wouldn't believe him," spoke Tedros quietly. "They know I failed as king the first time. They know Excalibur rejected me for a reason."

"They only know what they've seen," said Agatha.

Her prince looked up at her.

"I know who you are," Agatha expressed. "All of us do. But you're right: the *people* don't. The people never got to know the real Tedros the first time you wore the crown. You were too preoccupied trying to hold on to your place as king to actually stand up and *be* the king. This time is different. There is a Snake on your throne posing as the Lion and you need to save your people from him. Only the true king can make it through that kind of trial. Only the true king can prove he is the real Lion, with everything against him. This is your second chance, Tedros. Excalibur is back in the stone. But the sword can't choose you until you've passed your father's test. *All* of his tests."

Tedros gazed deep and hard into his true love's eyes.

"And even then Excalibur might not choose you," Nicola pointed out. "The Snake could win the race. And, even if he doesn't, Rhian likely pulled Excalibur the first time because he and his brother tricked it. Same trick that made the Lady of the Lake kiss Japeth, thinking he was king. How do we know Japeth can't trick it again? In which case, the sword will never pick you."

"Thanks for that," Tedros grunted, glancing at Hort. "Your dates must be loads of fun."

"It's not like you're marrying Miss Sunshine, either," Hort pipped.

The fairy ball lurched and Tinkerbell flung back a hissy squeak.

"Stay still, she says," Tedros whispered, looking down. "Foxwood hawks. Royal collars. Must be on king's business."

Carefully the fairy hive floated upwards, while Agatha watched a gang of hawks, fitted with red-and-gold neck cuffs, surf low over the Foxwood vales below. They scanned the houses, until their leader gave a winged signal and the hawks dove, ripping through an open window and interrupting a young fairy godmother at work peering into her crystal ball, before the birds swiped the ball from her. The hawks flew to a forest a few miles ahead, where they dumped the ball into a mound of others, birds arriving with various royal collars and dropping more orbs into the pile, as guards in Camelot armor bashed the crystals to pieces with clubs and melted down the shards.

"Only one reason Japeth would be destroying crystal balls," Nicola said to Agatha once they were safely hidden in clouds. "That history you witnessed in Rhian's blood crystal. About Arthur and Evelyn Sader. Clearly Japeth doesn't want you to see anything else."

Tedros bit down. "The way he grinned at me. The way he said it . . . *'I know.'* He got away with making us think he's my brother. Making us think he's my dad's son."

"But he *has* to be Arthur's son. The blood crystal *couldn't* have lied," said Agatha. "I was inside Rhian's blood. His real past. I saw Evelyn Sader put the spansel around Arthur's neck while he slept. She enchanted him to have his child. From what I saw, Arthur *was* Rhian's father. Evelyn Sader *was* Rhian's mother."

"And yet Japeth just told us that Arthur isn't his father," said Nicola. "And Arthur giving Tedros his ring proves it. Camelot's ring can *only* go to the heir."

"Maybe Arthur ignored that rule," Hort offered. "Knowing Evelyn had tricked him, I mean. Maybe he skipped the real heir and gave the ring to the heir he wanted."

"No," said Tedros and Guinevere together, trading looks.

"It's the law of the Woods," the prince added. "Dad would

never flout that, no matter the circumstances."

"So we're back where we started," Agatha muttered. "Rhian's blood says Japeth and Rhian are the sons of Arthur and Evelyn Sader. All other evidence says they aren't. We still have no idea who the Snake is."

"Hmm, could Rhian have one set of parents and Japeth have another?" Hort asked.

"They're *twins*!" Tedros barked, expecting the others to scoff too, but Agatha was thinking about this, and so, it seemed, was Nicola, who was gazing right at the princess, having clearly remembered all the details of *The Tale of Sophie and Agatha*. Twins could have very strange histories, indeed . . . no stranger than the history of Agatha and her best friend . . .

"Maybe the answer has something to do with Sophie," Agatha wondered, thinking of that friend now. "It's her blood that healed the Snake. And it's Sophie he needs as queen. Why *her*? What's special about her blood? Why does Japeth need Sophie to become king?"

"You're the Sophie expert," said Tedros.

Agatha sighed. "Wish we had the witches here. They know magic better than any of us."

"The witches are better off looking for Merlin," said Guinevere. "If Merlin hasn't been killed already. Or used his Wizard Wish."

"Wizard Wish?" Agatha asked.

"A single wish every wizard keeps tucked away where only they can find it," said the old queen. "A wish that can be made for anything, as long as it's said out loud, but usually saved by a wizard to choose the precise moment of his death."

"Merlin's been threatening to use it since I was a kid," Tedros murmured. "Any time I had a tantrum: 'Don't make me use my Wizard Wish, boy!'"

Guinevere looked at her son. "Let's hope the witches find Merlin alive."

"And in time to help me with my first test, whatever it is," said Tedros.

"Maybe it'll be something stacked in your favor," said Hort. "If it was my dad, he'd make the first test something I'd do well. Like picking locks. Or spying on girls." (Nicola frowned.)

"Dad kept a lot of secrets from me," said Tedros, shifting. "Not sure how well we really knew each other."

Agatha waited for Tedros to elaborate, but he put his head between his knees and curled up tighter. Guinevere peered at Agatha expectantly, as if hoping his princess might press the point . . . but Agatha let Tedros be, thinking about how she herself never knew her own father, even if he was there all along.

But there was no more time to think. The fairies were starting to descend.

They'd made it to Sherwood Forest.

AT TEDROS' INSISTENCE, the fairies had landed them near Beauty and the Feast.

"It must be six in the morning. Won't be anyone there. Even

if there was, they're not going to let us in like this," Agatha said, surveying the group's slovenly appearance, as they slid between tight-packed trees.

"They can give us food in a bag for all I care," said Tedros, combing a hand through his thick gold hair. "But I need to eat."

Agatha had learned not to argue with a hungry boy, letting Tedros lead the group towards the dark green cottage hidden in the thicket ahead. She smelled the hot dew of dawn, the sweet scent of leaves brushing her neck . . . then realized it was her prince, slipping his hand around her waist and planting a sly kiss on her cheek.

"I love you," he whispered.

She peeked back and saw his ravenous pace had left the others behind. Raising her eyes to his, Agatha let Tedros pull her to his chest as he kissed her, his warm, minty taste filling her mouth. He pulled her behind a tree.

"I promise you," he whispered, his blue eyes afire. "We will be married. You will be my queen, Agatha. Because you deserve a happy ending. And I will find a way to get us there. Trust me. That's all I ask. I need you to trust me."

Agatha had lost her breath, taken by the heat of his gaze, a passion she'd never seen in him before.

"You must be very hungry," she said, kissing him again.

Tedros guided her out from behind the tree, just in time to join the others.

Agatha was still tasting Tedros, her skin hot, her hair a mess . . . For a second, she'd forgotten why they were here.

She'd forgotten a monster had stolen her best friend and was trying to kill them. All she could think about was the look in her prince's eyes.

The sound of loud banging broke her trance. Tedros and Hort pummeled the door of a green bungalow with a terra-cotta rooftop, the two boys practically drooling. Agatha expected the door to fly open and Masha Mahaprada, the Master of Dining, to appear in a storm of gold feathers and give them each a slap.

Instead, the door popped open.

The prince pushed in, the group crowding behind him. "Let me do the talking—"

Agatha stopped cold. So did the rest of them.

The ballroom of Beauty and the Feast, once glittering with magical chandeliers, peacock-feather tablecloths, singing hummingbirds, and spreads of golden-goose egg fondue, fairy-churned butterbread, and chocolate waterfalls . . . was now completely hollowed out.

"Out of business, loves," said a voice from the corner.

Agatha turned to a matronly fox in a white apron, sweeping the floor, two baby foxes clinging to her.

"Impossible," Guinevere spurned. "How can the most famous restaurant in all the Woods be out of business?"

"No one comin' to Sherwood Forest anymore, love, that's how," the fox replied, going on with her sweeping. "Not since Robin Hood teamed up with the Sheriff. Everyone afraid Sheriff's gonna come and make 'em pay the piper. Why'd you think they loved Robin 'round these parts? Long as Robin and the Sheriff were at odds, no one here paid their taxes, did they? Been goin' on for years. Hoity-toity types takin' shelter in the Forest. There's a reason the last line of Beauty and the Feast's song was *'Always pay in cash'* . . ." The fox chuckled. "Moment Masha heard Sheriff might be in cahoots with Robin, he whisked elsewhere, along with everyone else. Not payin' taxes ain't the only sneak happenin' in Sherwood, if you know what I mean. Had to stay meself 'cause of the pups. Can't be movin' 'em 'til they're older. Suppose I could rustle up somethin' for you lot if you're desperate?" She looked up—

But there wasn't anyone there.

"NEED TO GET to Robin," Agatha insisted, Tedros jogging at her side, the two of them clearing low branches.

"No wonder we haven't seen any people," said her prince.

"The place was a den of vice. Robin's job was to keep the Sheriff away," his mother added, catching up. "Arthur came here too. Mostly right after he was crowned, to escape the pressure. That's how he and Robin became friends. Whole forest was a sinful hideaway, where people could do as they liked. Even the King of Camelot."

"What happens in Sherwood stays in Sherwood," said Hort.

"Until the Sheriff comes. Then no one stays in Sherwood at all," said Nicola.

Agatha bit down. "There's a Snake ruling the Woods and

all people care about is their *taxes*?"

Tedros gripped her wrist, stalling in his tracks.

Agatha followed his stare.

The treehouses were torn down. Robin and his Merry Men's homes, all bashed to filth and strewn to the ground, the paper lanterns that once connected their rogue village ripped apart too, the pieces floating in the morning light like confetti.

Agatha found a handwritten poster tacked to a tree:

WANTED
ROBIN HOOD

DEAD OR ALIVE
BY THE PEOPLE

For ruining their fun!

Agatha pivoted to the others. "Marian's Arrow. *Now.*"

By the time they made it to the clearing, Agatha's heart was in her throat.

Then came the smell.

A putrid scent of rotten eggs and dung that made them hold their noses and gulp for breath.

Marian's Arrow had been pelted with refuse, the familiar painting of a young Robin Hood kissing Maid Marian on its outside wall now vandalized to have Robin Hood kissing the Sheriff instead. The motto of the place—"Leave All Ye

Troubles Behind"—had been scrawled over to read:

YOU ARE OUR TROUBLES

More graffiti littered the door.

SHERIFF LOVER

ROBIN OF NOTTINGHAM

MERRY TRAITORS

Fists clenched, stifling her breath, Agatha pried the door open. A charred, acid smell overwhelmed her, instantly making her eyes water. She heard Hort and Nicola coughing, their footsteps hugging hers as they made their way into Robin Hood's late-night haunt, now burned to ash. Agatha lit her fingerglow, Hort's sapphire glow and Nicola's soft-yellow beaming around hers, illuminating blackened table stumps and toasted fragments of chairs. Shattered beer mugs and plates crunched under their shoes, chunks of a chalkboard hawking daily specials—the Blue Plate Robin, Marian's Mead—

"Wait . . . ," said Nicola.

Agatha followed her glow to a singed countertop, where Maid Marian used to tend bar. Only there was something embedded in the ash . . . something that made a pit in Agatha's stomach . . .

A feather.

A green feather.

Agatha's knees buckled.

"He's dead, isn't he?" said Hort quietly.

Agatha's shaking fingers touched the feather, thinking of the man who'd sacrificed his friends, his home, his *life* to help her. Not Robin, too. Another grown-up cut down by her fairy tale. Another one killed because they'd taken her side. Agatha held the feather closer. Would Readers come to know the real Robin Hood? Would the Storian survive to tell the tru—

Robin's feather shimmered.

Something slipped off it.

A green powder that sprinkled onto the countertop, re-arranging into a pattern in the ash.

The crest seeped into the cinders and vanished.

Agatha gaped at the scorched bar.

Did that happen?

Am I imagining things?

Pitter-patter echoed on the roof. *Plip. Plip. Plip.* A dance of rain, a storm blowing in.

Agatha was still staring at the bar, trying to remember the details of the message Robin left behind—

Then she heard it. Under the rain.

The sharp rustling from the back of the pub.

A closet door vibrating . . . *shaking*.

"Not opening that," Hort said.

Nicola didn't hesitate. She stepped in front of Hort, sucked in a nervous breath, and threw the door open—

"Holy hell," Hort blurted.

Inside the closet were three of Robin Hood's Merry Men, bound with rope and gagged with napkins, their faces and chests painted with red, raging words.

SHERIFF MEN

Instantly, Hort and Nicola were on them, untying their ropes, yanking out their gags, helping them to their feet.

Agatha's neck seared red, anger seizing her like a collar. Merry Men, hog-tied like pigs? Merry Men, once the *heroes* of this place? All because people wanted Robin and the Sheriff to stay enemies so they could hoard more money? Once Tedros was king, she'd find those responsible and punish them—

Tedros.

"Where's Tedros?" she breathed.

Her prince and his mother had never entered the bar.

Panic ripped through her. Through the cracked-open door, Agatha caught a glimpse of movement outside: falling slashes of white . . . like stones . . . or arrows . . .

Plip. Plip. Plip.

It wasn't rain.

She threw aside a crumbling chair, running so hard she lost a clump, and crashed against the front door, sliding outside into the dirt. *"Tedros!"*

He was there.

Exactly where she'd left him.

Standing beneath the trees with his mother.

Surrounded by thousands and thousands of scrolls, blanketing the forest.

Each was identical: a single sheet of parchment, tied with a silver string, stamped with the seal of a Lion.

King Arthur's seal.

Agatha looked up as more scrolls snowed from the sky, whiting out the floor of Sherwood Forest, catching in its trees, the magical storm extending beyond the wood, through the pink-and-gold sky, to kingdoms near and far.

Slowly, she looked back at Tedros, her eyes wide.

Then she saw the opened scroll in his palm, limp at his side, his fingers specked with wax from his father's seal.

Tedros blinked at her, ghost-pale.

"Looks like we found my first test."

6

SOPHIE

Good Little Girl

Excalibur.

That was its name, Sophie thought, gazing at the sword hilt rising out of the mountain of scrolls that swathed the garden.

They'd fallen from the sky at dawn, waking Sophie with their *plip-plop* into the flowers. She heard a boy's voice from the garden, a spew of shouts. By the time she'd run to the window, hair a mess, last night's makeup smudged, the snow had abated, a few last scrolls drifting into the sea of thousands

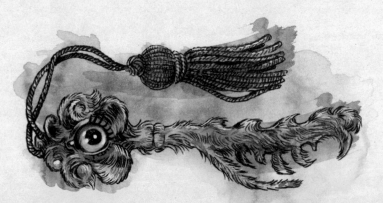

more, reaching far beyond the castle, past the church and stables, to the hills of Camelot.

Sophie's eyes stayed on the sword, glinting in the scroll-covered stone. She could hardly remember anything that happened last night, her brain foggier than ever . . . but she knew a few things for sure.

I'm not married.

Scrolls should not fall from the sky.

The sword's name is Excalibur.

A headache attacked her as if trying to erase these facts, as if determined to clear the slate again, her mind squeezing from both sides like a vise . . .

But Sophie was on to the pain now. There was a crack in it. Things had slipped through.

I'm not married.

Scrolls should not fall from the sky.

The sword's name is Excalibur.

Sophie peered closer at the sword.

Maids shuffled into the garden, marched there by guards. Armed with brooms and buckets, the women in white dresses and bonnets swept the scrolls away, the guards watching them stony-eyed. "King wants every last scrap gone," growled one. "Don't want the princess seein' 'em."

Sophie could feel her gaze hardening, overriding the fog of her mind.

What doesn't he want me to see?

The king had ordered her to stay in her chamber and locked her door. She knew not to disobey him. Until now, her body didn't even know how.

But then the snow happened.

Something had changed.

Her chest thumped faster, hotter.

I'm not married.

Scrolls should not fall from the sky.

The sword's name is Excalibur.

Pain bashed her like a hammer, but Sophie was already moving for the door.

She needed to escape this room.

She needed to find out what the king was hiding.

Her finger glowed pink, aimed at the lock.

She needed to know what was in that *scroll*.

With the guards supervising the maids, Sophie slipped through the hall undetected, ignoring the stabbing in her head getting worse with every step. Her blood slapped so sharply at her temples that she nearly missed the voices, coming from the Blue Tower foyer below. Sophie peeked through the railing.

"I have an appointment with her," said a woman with braided butterscotch hair, thin eyebrows, and stern brown eyes. She wore a cream-colored dress, a crystal tiara, and carried a pearly clamshell purse. "And seeing that I've come here at your demand, on a moment's notice, to help you win your first test, I expect that appointment to be honored—"

"Princess Sophie is ill," said a tan boy, standing at the open door, where outside, that sullen Kei was saddling two horses. Inside, the tan boy glared harder at the woman as he fit a riding coat over his blue-and-gold suit. "Did you bring what I asked for?"

My prince, Sophie recognized, with a swell of love. *My king.*

And yet the king had no crown.

A vague memory snaked through her: crowns vanishing . . . a wedding incomplete . . . a dagger of ice in her fist . . .

She looked down at her hand, no ring on her finger.

What happened last night?

She peered closer at her beloved, taking in the alien green of his eyes, the color not quite real . . . the serpentine lankness of his body . . . the milk-white rim around his ear, as if his tan had missed a spot . . .

That unsettled feeling deepened inside her . . .

Something in the king's eyes flickered. He glanced up to the second floor. Sophie ducked, a new pain shearing her head, pushing her backwards, as if hell-bent on returning her to her room. Suddenly she couldn't remember why she'd left her room to begin with. She couldn't remember why she had this anxious feeling or what she was doing hiding under a rail. But she stayed in place, trusting the moment. Trusting whatever had brought her here.

Slowly she peeked back out.

"The people are in shock, of course," the woman was saying to the king. "Excalibur returning to the stone. Arthur's voice from beyond the grave. A tournament to decide the king when they thought they already had one . . . But the Woods is on your side. For now. Betting has Tedros at 100 to 1 odds."

"Too generous," the king sniped.

"Tedros has his defenders. And many more who are seeing him in a new light," the woman observed. "They wonder if he is the true king that Arthur spoke of. The Lion instead of the Snake you make him out to be. My advice to you: win the first test quickly. Because if Tedros wins the first test . . ." Her eyes drilled into the king's. "Then people will *really* start to wonder."

"Which is why you're here to *help* me," the king said icily. He held out his palm. "Give it to me."

"Princess Sophie looked well enough last night," the woman replied, ignoring the king's outstretched hand. "Unless she too is disturbed by the vanishing of your crown. Unless she questions how Tedros has Camelot's ring instead of its king. Unless she wonders why Arthur's ghost would declare a tournament when his heir already sits on the throne. Perhaps the sum of it left her feeling queasy. Like it has me."

"Sophie's not seeing visitors," said the king.

"Sophie's the one who requested a meeting," the woman answered.

"Impossible," said the king.

"Why's that?" his guest asked. "Is it impossible your queen would reach out to a fellow queen? Is it impossible she wants to control her own life?"

"Give it to me, Jacinda."

"*Queen* Jacinda to you," the woman parried. "I think it perfectly fitting that the Queens of Camelot and Jaunt Jolie be friends. That's a queen's job: *diplomacy*. I myself had meetings this morning with leaders from the Kingdom Council, whose realms were blizzarded by scrolls with Arthur's first test. Naturally, the other leaders still favor you in the tournament over Tedros, given you saved their kingdoms from attacks." She smiled. "Too bad they're not the ones who crown the winner."

"I'm leaving for Putsi," the king intoned. "Did you bring it or not?"

"Will Sophie meet with me or not?" the woman returned. "Just a meeting, King Rhian. That's all."

The boy's eyes cut into her.

Rhian, Sophie thought. *That's his name. Rhian. My king.*

As for the Queen of Jaunt Jolie, Sophie couldn't remember her in the slightest. She certainly didn't recall making an appointment. Nor did she recognize much of what this woman had said to the king: *Arthur? Tedros? Tournament of Kings?* None of it penetrated the pain in her head, worsening by the second. Everything she'd gleaned had slithered back into its cracks.

"So much for diplomacy," the queen sighed, relenting under Rhian's glare. "I will help you with the first test, King Rhian. For the same reason I agreed to burn my ring. Because you saved my children from being hanged by the Snake. But the debt is repaid now. After this, you cannot lord yourself over me anymore. Understood?"

She snapped open her purse roughly, thrusting a hand in. The queen drew out a spotted black-and-white key that seemed to quiver in her palm like a newborn pup. Sophie squinted closer at it through the rail. The key was made of . . . *fur*.

Rhian seized it, pocketing the key into his coat. "We can reschedule your appointment with Sophie. Once Tedros is dead and you're feeling less *queasy* about my place on the throne." He guided the queen towards the door. She pulled from Rhian stiffly, closing her purse—

That's when Sophie noticed it.

The scroll inside the queen's bag.

Sophie homed onto it, a moth to a flame.

Scrolls should not fall from the sky.

Scrolls should not fall from the sky.

Scrolls should not fall from the sky.

The pair were almost through the door—

"Jacinda! Sweetie, darling!"

Queen and king froze. Both looked up at the bedraggled girl in her nightgown.

"My apologies, Jacinda. I was feeling quite poorly this morning, but I'm turned around now," Sophie chimed, forcing words through the pain. "Shall we keep our appointment? The king will be relieved I'm well enough to sit with you. Won't you, pumpkin?"

Sophie smiled down at Rhian, her hair like a wild animal's, her lipstick smeared like a clown's.

The king gave her a stare so cold she thought he'd turned to stone.

SOPHIE BET THAT whatever business lay in Putsi was too important for the king to be waylaid by his princess's sudden appearance. She'd bet well, the king having ridden off with his captain as planned, unable to supervise her meeting with Jaunt Jolie's queen.

What she hadn't accounted for was that he'd leave someone to supervise her in his place.

Now, as she cozied up to Jacinda in a Blue Tower sitting room, laid out with ginger tea and pastries, she endured the watchful eyes of the Mistral Sisters, seated on couches in the corner, notepads and pens in hand.

"Would you prefer to speak . . . privately?" the Queen of Jaunt Jolie asked Sophie, who'd cleaned herself up, her white dress reshaped to its prim, ruffled form. "Perhaps we can meet in your chambers—"

"This is a *scheduled* meeting between dignitaries, is it not?" said Alpa from the corner.

"And all *scheduled* meetings must be recorded," Omeida added. "Besides, there's been mischief in the castle of late. A precious map burned to ash. An intruder at the press gathering. We have to keep our eye on everyone. *Queens* included."

The Queen of Jaunt Jolie turned to them. "When King Rhian pursued the powers of the One True King, I believed he had noble intentions. Now that I know it's the Mistral Sisters advising him, I'm relieved that pursuit came to naught."

"Still holding grudges, are you?" cooed Alpa.

"All because Arthur wouldn't betroth your eldest to his son," said Omeida.

"You took advantage of Arthur when he was grief-stricken and alone. You isolated him and poisoned his mind. You made him believe *he* was the One True King," the queen shot back. "Suddenly, he wouldn't let Tedros and my Betty have their usual playdates. He wouldn't meet with me or any other leaders. Arthur lost respect in the last months of his life because of *you*. Which is why no one trusts you."

"Until now," said Alpa, with a thin smile. "Seems like we found the One True King after all."

"And yet there's one ring still left," the queen replied. "Worn by a son of Arthur who reminds me more of the Arthur *I* knew than the one you currently advise. If there is such a thing as the One True King, perhaps it's *Tedros*."

Alpa's face darkened. "We'll let King Rhian know the next time your children are in danger, he should leave them to their fate."

For the first time, the queen looked shaken.

Sophie hadn't the faintest clue what they were prattling on about. All she knew was she needed that scroll in the queen's bag. Everything else had sloughed away in the pounding thud of her head. Indeed, she'd almost forgotten who the woman seated in front of her was.

The scroll, she reminded herself, clawing the thought back from the brink. *I need that scroll.*

But new thoughts were coming, thoughts not hers, pushing words onto her tongue. Behind the queen, Sophie could see the Mistrals, subtly moving their hands over their notebooks . . .

"What did you want to discuss?" Sophie asked Jacinda,

pouring tea into the queen's cup.

Her brain felt like it was axed in two: one part ramming words and actions through her body; the other trying to hold on to the reason she was here.

The scroll.

She started losing the thought . . .

What scroll?

More words flooded through, the pain in her head evaporating, everything running smooth as milk.

"How is your eldest daughter?" Sophie said, confident and controlled, the way she'd been when she briefed the press. "I wish she and I could have had a chance to be friends at school."

"Betty wasn't taken," Jacinda replied bitterly. "Another from Jaunt Jolie was kidnapped instead. This stultifying Beatrix girl who kept trying to be Betty's friend, hoping it would ingratiate her in royal circles. But it's all worked out in the end. Betty doesn't need that school or the Storian. She's found her own way to tell tales . . ."

"Aren't you glad you burned your ring, then? If Betty doesn't need the school or Storian, the rest of the Woods shouldn't either," quipped Sophie brightly, without a clue what she was saying.

The queen searched Sophie's face. "Something's not right with you," she said quietly. "Tell me what's going on. Even if those two witches are listening. I'll take you to Jaunt Jolie. My Knights of the Eleven are fierce warriors and will keep you safe. And I have the ear of other leaders, Good and Evil. I have the power to protect you, Sophie."

Jacinda looked back at the Mistral Sisters, as if expecting them to revolt or attack, but Alpa and Omeida said nothing, their hands fidgeting over their notebooks.

"Would you like a rum baba?" Sophie offered, on cue, holding out a cream-topped cake. "The new chef here is marvelous."

"Didn't know you were one to eat pastries," the queen said tartly. "And it looks soggy and ill-made." Jacinda locked eyes with Sophie. "I saw you at Tedros' execution. I saw you and your Dean. I know whose side you're really on."

Sophie's mind went stiff, the script aborted.

Behind the queen, the Mistral Sisters mirrored her pause.

"Me and the Dean?" Sophie asked, using her own words now. "Which Dean? What execution? I'm sorry . . . I don't know what you're talking about . . ."

The queen stared into the void of her gaze. "What's happened to you?" she whispered, clasping Sophie's wrist. "Why are you here instead of with Agatha?"

The warmth of touch.

The comfort of skin.

The sound of a name.

Agatha.

It slashed through the fog of Sophie's mind like a lightning bolt to a lake.

Scrolls should not fall from the sky.

Scrolls should not fall from the sky.

Scrolls should not fall from the sky.

She saw the Mistral Sisters' hands moving again, their faces tight, but Sophie was already short-circuiting the script.

"I'm feeling a bit ill," said Sophie, standing up—

As she did, she knocked over the queen's purse, which fell to the floor. "Oopsy," said Sophie, reaching for it, only to punt it farther under the couch.

"Let me—" the queen started.

"I've got it," said Sophie, already on her knees, reaching beneath the couch. "I certainly gave it a good kick . . . oh, here it is . . ." She stood and handed the purse back to the queen. "My advisors will see you out." Sophie smiled at the Mistral Sisters, who looked more at ease now, as if Sophie had steered things back on track.

Jaunt Jolie's queen studied Sophie one last time. "I wish . . ." She shook her head, trying to finish the thought—

Sophie kissed her on the cheek. "Thank you," she whispered.

Then before anyone could say another word, the princess ushered herself back to her chambers, like a good little girl.

Something was inside her head.

Something was controlling this pain.

Sophie had figured it out while sitting with the queen. First, there were those sisters, pretending to take notes. But every time they moved their hands, she lost control, someone else's words coming out of her mouth, someone else's thoughts usurping her mind. And if she tried to reclaim her thoughts, to think for herself, the pain came to hurt her.

Yet the pain attacked even when the Mistrals *weren't* there. She could feel it now, slithering around her mind, waiting to strike.

Which meant the Mistrals might be able to control the pain . . .

But they weren't its source.

The source was her head. *Inside* her head.

She didn't yet know what was causing this pain, exactly. But she knew how to keep it at bay . . .

Don't think.

So rather than thinking about the scroll in her fist, Sophie focused on the sounds of her feet: *plip, plop, plip, plop,* like the patter of rain, pulling her towards her chamber. Her white dress itched at her skin, surely suspecting something, but the dress stopped short of anything more as she slipped into her sun-drenched room and closed the door.

Quickly she tried to lock it, but the latch was broken. Her fault, of course. She'd burned through it to leave this room. Already her head was starting to throb harder, sensing mischief afoot.

She could hear footsteps coming down the hall.

Voices growing closer.

But then something strange happened.

A ribbon of white lace fluttered off her dress, fully alive. For a moment, Sophie thought it might attack her: this dress, which had a mind of its own. Instead, it slid through the broken lock and morphed into a white-stone bolt, jamming the door.

There was no time to think about why the dress was helping her.

The pain was already coming like an alarm.

Sophie flung open her fist, yanking the crumpled scroll out and matting it against a mirror on the wall, the bold, black ink slick in the sunlight—

> *So it begins, the first test arrives*
> *Two kings race to stay alive*
>
> *For a king cannot rule if he is dead*
> *Or lead a kingdom without his head*
>
> *But once upon a time, a man came to my court*
> *Who gave up his head, just for sport*
>
> *He wanted one thing, this headless knave*
> *Tried to claim it and dug his grave*
>
> *What did he want? Only my true heir will know*
> *Now go and find it, where wizard trees grow!*

Sophie couldn't make any sense of it, not with her head about to pop like a balloon. Headless knights . . . wizard trees . . . ? The pain intensified, about to rip open her brain. She shoved the scroll into her pocket. It had to mean something. Something the pain didn't want her to figure out—

Loud knocks attacked the door.

"Sophie!" Alpa said.

Hands jostled the lock, blocked by the ribbon of stone.

"Don't do anything stupid!" Omeida harassed. "The king will know! He'll see you! Wherever he is, he'll come back and punish you!"

Sophie stared at the door, pain blotting out all thoughts but one.

"See" me?

Fists pummeled harder, but the stone held tight.

"Open this door!" Alpa demanded.

How can the king see me if he isn't here? Sophie thought. *Unless . . .*

She peered at the scroll's poem, flattened against the mirror.

Then, slowly, her gaze shifted to her reflection.

She heard guards coming now, the sisters ordering them to bash down the door . . . but Sophie was lost in her own eyes, studying her electric-green irises and big black pupils, the pain cleaving through her head, harder, angrier, as if it knew she was getting close. She couldn't breathe, her mind impaled from every direction, her vision dotting with lights, her body seconds from passing out. But Sophie didn't yield, glaring into the gems of her eyes, mining deeper, deeper, searching the darkness and light for something that wasn't hers . . . until at last she found them.

Hiding like two snakes in a hole.

Guards bludgeoned the door with axes and clubs, the wood splintering.

Sophie had already lit her finger.

Pink glow reflected in her pupils like a torch in a cave.

She could hear their screams, the scaly eels, as they stabbed harder and harder behind her eyes, trying to regain control.

But the truth was in her sights now. Pain had become pleasure.

Sophie raised her finger and slipped it into her ear.

She grinned in the mirror like a devil facing itself.

This is going to hurt.

STONE SHATTERED IN the lock.

The door burst open, guards and Mistrals coming through.

A breeze sifted through the room, rippling across the blood-soaked curtains, the window wide open.

On the windowsill lay two scims crushed to filth.

But it was outside where the real message had been left.

Dripped in crimson across the white snow of scrolls, across the white dresses of maids, lying stunned by a spell.

Five bloody words.

The remnants of a princess.

The warning of a witch.

ALL OF YOU WILL DIE

7

TEDROS

Mahameep

"Your first test to become king . . . ," said Hort, mouth full of cotton candy, "and you don't know what it *means*?"

Tedros ignored him, kicking away scrolls that littered the cotton-candy grove just past the border of Sherwood Forest. He didn't have to answer to the weasel. He didn't have to answer to anyone. He was the heir. He was the king.

Yet he'd failed his first test before it had even begun.

The Green Knight.

Why did it have to be about the Green Knight?

It was the one part of

his dad's history he'd never learned. On purpose. And his dad had known it.

Is that why Dad made it a test? To punish me?

Tedros shook it off, trying to find clues in the poem: *"He wanted one thing, this headless knave . . ." "Tried to claim it and dug his grave . . ." "Now go and find it where wizard trees grow . . ."*

He couldn't focus, his thoughts spiraling—

What did the Green Knight want?

Why didn't I ask Dad!

Does Japeth know?

Suppose he finishes before me? Is he already on to the second test? What if I'm too late—

A hand squeezed his.

Tedros looked up at Agatha, her hair dotted with blue and pink cotton candy.

"I'm sure Japeth doesn't have the answer either," his princess assured, her lips dusted with sugar. "How could he?"

"Well, we can't just loaf around the Woods until I figure it out," said Tedros, watching Hort and Nicola pluck trees and feed each other candy. "This forest is the path into Pifflepaff Hills. Where the Living Library is. We need to go to my dad's archive there. It's the only place where I can find out what the Green Knight wanted."

"Tedros, we decided it's too dangerous—"

"*You* decided. And it's more dangerous for me to lose the first test!" said Tedros. "If Japeth doesn't know the answer, the Living Library is the first place he'll look. We should have gone when I suggested it instead of wasting time back there with Merry Men!"

"They were starving and homeless!" said Agatha. "We got them scraps from Beauty and the Feast and helped fix their houses. It was the Good thing to do."

"Even I know that and I'm Evil," Hort said behind them, mouth stained blue.

"We're going to the Library. My orders," Tedros said firmly, walking ahead.

He glanced up at school fairies tracking him from above, keeping a lookout over sugar-spun trees, while Tinkerbell squeaked at any who snuck down for a bite. Behind him, he could hear Agatha reassuring his mother that she would protect her prince, no matter how dangerous the new plan was.

Having a princess wasn't supposed to be like this, Tedros thought. In all the stories he knew, princes protected their princesses. Princes were in charge and princesses followed. Yes, Agatha was a rebel, which is why he loved her. But sometimes he wished she was less rebel and a little more princess, even if he felt like an ogre for thinking it. Tedros flung aside a pink bough, barreling ahead. One thing was for sure: Agatha couldn't win the first test for him. From here on out, they'd do things *his* way.

A short while later, the prince peeked between a last cluster of sweet-cotton branches.

The Pifflepaff Pavilion was painted pink and blue and nothing in between. There were blue "boy" shops—the Virile Vintner, the Hardy Folk Furriers, the Handsome Barber—and there were pink "girl" shops: Silkmaid's Stockings, the Good Lady's Bookshop, Ingenue's Combs & Brushes. In the morning rush, men in blue stayed apart from girls in pink, including the pink-clad sweepers, who cleaned the pavilion of leftover scrolls. (Tedros' dad had left no kingdom untouched in announcing the first test.) Then there were the trees dotting the streets, like the ones in the forest, blooming with bell-shaped tufts of cotton candy, the trees either blue or pink, from which only the appropriate sex could eat. Pifflepaffers tore off candy as they walked, men inhaling blue, women sucking on pink, as if they lived on nothing but their assigned clouds of color. There was no crossing of lines, no blurring of boundaries. Boys were boys and girls were girls. (Maybe it would rub off on Agatha, Tedros thought grouchily.)

At a coffee stand, a merchant had his blue stall divided into two sides: TEAM RHIAN and TEAM TEDROS, hawking themed drinks for each. Team Rhian's side offered a Lion Latte (turmeric, cashew milk, cloves), a Golden Lions-mane (horchata, chocolate ganache), and the Winner's Elixir (espresso, maca root, and honey) . . . while Team Tedros' side sold a Snake Tongue (matcha powder, hot oat milk, ghee), a Cold Storian (iced coffee, cinnamon), and a Headless Prince (hazelnut, mocha, goat milk). The Rhian aisle was packed with men making orders, picking up drinks, catching up with friends. The Tedros table was deserted. *"Who Will Win the Tournament?"* read two tip jars, one with Rhian's name, over-flowing with copper and silver coins, the other with Tedros' name, toting a few farthings.

Tedros' blood flowed hot.

The Woods thought he had no chance.

Even though Excalibur had returned to the stone. Even though his father spoke from the grave and gave him a claim. These people still thought he would lose.

Why?

Because they'd seen Rhian pull the sword from the stone, while Tedros failed. Because they'd seen Rhian quell attacks on their kingdoms, while Tedros failed. Because Rhian's pen told them what they wanted to hear, while the pen Tedros fought for told them the truth, even if it hurt. All of it was a Snake's tricks, but the people didn't know that. That's why no one was betting on him. To the Woods, Tedros was a loser.

Which is why he had to *win* this first test.

Tedros peered harder through the trees.

The Living Library, a colossal acropolis, stood tall on a hill over the pavilion, its blue pillars and domed roof glowing in afternoon sun. On the stairs, flanking the entrance, were Pifflepaff guards, who despite their comical blue hats, shaped like muffin-tops, came armed with loaded crossbows, Lion badges over their hearts, and small pocket-mirrors, which each guard flashed at anyone who entered or exited the Library.

"Six guards," said Tedros, turning to the others. "And they have Matchers."

"Matchers?" asked Agatha.

"Living Library keeps ancestry files on every soul in the Woods," Tedros explained. "Matchers track those going in and out, in case anyone tries to doctor or steal a file. Those mirrors tell the guards our names and what kingdom we're from."

"So if they'll know who we are, how are we supposed to get inside?" Nicola asked.

Tedros glanced off. "Haven't gotten that far."

"And there's no other way to figure out what the Green Knight wanted?" Nicola pressured, eyeing the scroll peeking out of the prince's pocket. "There isn't something you aren't remembering or something your dad told you—"

"No, there isn't," Agatha defended, "otherwise we wouldn't be here."

"It's his *dad*," Hort snapped at Agatha, then pivoted to Guinevere. "And your *husband*. How can neither of you know a crucial part of King Arthur's history? Even the village idiot knows the story of the Green Knight. Terrorized the Woods because he wanted something from King Arthur. Something secret. We know what happened to the Green Knight but no one ever found out what the secret was. Except Arthur, of course. And now you're telling me you two don't know what it was, either? How can King Arthur's own family not know? Didn't you talk to each other? Or have family dinners or holiday jaunts or the kinds of things Ever families are supposed to have that make them feel so superior to Never ones? If it was my dad, you bet your bottom he woulda told me what the Knight was after, even if it was a secret."

Guinevere grimaced. "I wasn't at the castle when the Green Knight came."

"So much for you being a 'resource' on Arthur," Hort scorned, then glared at Tedros. "And your excuse?"

"He doesn't have to excuse anything—" Agatha started.

"Yes, I do," said Tedros, cutting her off.

He needed to say it out loud.

The reason his dad chose this as the first test.

"The Green Knight came in the weeks after my mother ran off with Lancelot," the prince explained. "I'd stopped talking to Dad. At first, I held him as responsible as I'd held her. For letting her leave. For not keeping her happy. For breaking up our family." He looked at Guinevere, who struggled to hold his gaze. "Eventually I started talking to him again. And only after he came back from defeating the Knight. But we never spoke about his victory. It was a great feat, of course. He tried to bring it up again and again, baiting me to ask the details. Eager to share what happened. And I wanted to know. I wanted him to tell me what the Green Knight came for. But I never did ask. It was my way of punishing him, reminding him that Mother was gone and it was his fault. I wouldn't be the son he could confide in. Not anymore. That's why he made this the first test. Because I failed it when he was alive. Because I chose anger and pride over forgiveness."

Even Hort went quiet.

Tedros suddenly felt the chill of loneliness. Agatha and his friends could only take him so far. In the end, it was him that was on trial. His past. His present. His future.

"We can't change what's already happened. What matters is finding the answer *now*. What matters is winning the first test," Agatha said briskly. Tedros knew that tone: whenever his princess felt helpless or scared, she grasped for control even more than usual. Agatha pushed past her prince and squinted out at the Library. "If the Green Knight was unfinished business between you and your dad, he would have left you the answers. And you've said all along those answers would be here. You're right, Tedros. It doesn't matter if it's dangerous. We need to get past those guards."

"And their Match things," Nicola reminded.

"There's no 'we,'" Tedros corrected Agatha. "I'll go alone."

"I'm coming with you," Agatha insisted.

"It'll be impossible enough getting me past the guards. How can *both* of us get past them?" the prince argued.

"Same way I broke into Camelot's dungeons. Same way Dovey freed us from the execution," said Agatha. "With a distraction."

"And my mother?" Tedros peppered. "Can't just leave her in the middle of the Woods with the weasel and a first year—"

But Guinevere wasn't paying attention.

She and Nicola were watching something else in the forest: a squirrel with a royal collar, carrying a round walnut in its mouth, huffing and puffing past trees, as if it had already come a long way.

The old queen and first year gave each other narrow looks.

"Actually, Nicola and I have other business to attend to," Guinevere said.

"Mm-hmm," said Nic.

The two of them went after the squirrel.

Hort blinked dumbly. "Well, if you're going into the Library and they're going after a rodent, what am I supposed to do—"

He turned to see the Tedros and Agatha staring right at him.

"Oh no," said Hort.

AT THE LIBRARY entrance, there was a lull in the flow of patrons. A guard disguised a yawn, his crossbow limp at his side; a second picked his nose with one of his arrows; a third spied on pretty women with his Matcher—

A blast of blue glow shot it out of his hands, dashing it on the Library steps.

Another blast took out the next guard's Matcher.

The guards looked up.

A blond-poufed boy with no shirt, no pants, and a cotton candy diaper leapt in front of them, wagging his bum—

> *"Singing, hey! Laddie, ho!*
> *Laddie, laddie, ho, ho*
> *Same old shanty,*
> *Sing it front and back,*
> *Ho, ho, laddie, laddie, hey!"*

The boy waited for the guards to attack.

They gaped at him dumbly.

The boy cleared his throat.

This time, he tap-danced too.

"I'm a pirate captain
Hoo ha, hoo ha
My ship is named the PJ Frog
Hoo ha, hoo ha
With a lass named Nic and a friend named Soph,
Ho, ho, laddie, laddie, hey!"

The boy shimmied his hands. *"Olé!"*

Guards still didn't move.

Hort frowned. "Fine."

He burst out of his diaper into a seven-foot-tall, hairy man-wolf.

"Roar," he said, half-heartedly.

The guards charged.

"Never fails," Hort sighed, upending trees as he dragged the men on a chase.

Meanwhile, a boy and girl hurried up the blue library steps, keeping their heads down. Tedros had smeared his shirt with cotton candy, giving it a splotchy blue tint, and hidden his blond locks under a mop of blue spun sugar, so he looked less like a prince and more a homeless elf. Agatha, for her part, had beaded her black gown with pink cotton candy and capped her hair with a towering hive of pink fluff. Together, they motored through the library doors, only to see a large sign.

BOYS ENTRANCE ONLY
By Law of Pifflepaff Hills
"Separate but Equal"

"You've got to be kidding," said Agatha.

But ahead, there was a line of blue-dressed men waiting to get past a librarian—an old goat name-tagged GOLEM—who was checking each entrant with a Matcher, affixing them with their own name tag and letting them through, before he turned his attention to the line of women coming from another entrance.

"I need to use the girls' door," Agatha whispered, heading back outside—

But now the Pifflepaff guards had returned to their posts, Hort's werewolf nowhere in sight. Just as they were about to spot Agatha, Tedros yanked her into the boys' line. He could see the men in line were glaring at her, cracking knuckles and curling fists.

"I know, right?" Tedros chuckled. "Seems like a girl . . . but you'd be surprised."

Agatha frowned at him, but the men glared harder now, prowling towards her.

"Go ahead. Look for yourself," the prince shrugged, offering Agatha up.

His princess gasped, about to clobber him, but the men had stopped in their tracks. They peered at Agatha, weighing Tedros' offer. Then they shook their heads with a collective grunt and went back to their business.

"Told you to trust me," Tedros whispered to his princess.

"Thanks for that," Agatha snapped as they neared the goat, scanning and name-tagging more entrants, "but how we gonna get past *him*?"

Behind the goat's desk, more Pifflepaff guards with Lion

badges were stationed on staircases to the library stacks. Tedros' chest clamped. Guards in here, guards out there. The moment the goat matched their names, he and Agatha were dead.

"It's too risky," he said, grabbing Agatha's wrist, pulling her towards the door. "We need to sneak out—"

"Wait. Not yet," Agatha resisted, studying the old goat as he stamped more names.

"He's going to catch us!" Tedros hissed.

But Agatha's focus stayed on the freckle-faced man in front of them, who was having an argument with the goat. "Trust me," she said to her prince.

Those magic words, Tedros thought.

"I'm called Patrick," the freckled man protested, pointing at the stamp on his chest. "This says . . . 'Poot.'"

"As it should," said Golem, swiveling to the girls' line. "Welcome, Hatshepsut!"

"It's Hanna," said a lady.

But the goat was already back to Tedros and Agatha, next in the boys' line.

Tedros held his breath as he and Agatha approached, the patchy-furred goat eyeing them through thick glasses.

"Good to see strapping boys in a library instead of making mischief," said Golem, his voice hoary and high, honing in on Agatha. "Though at first glance, one might mistake you for a girl, which isn't allowed. Boys must be boys and girls must be girls, through and through. So I really should report you, dear boy. The guards behind me are no doubt itching for my verdict on the matter . . ."

Tedros felt Agatha's palm go clammy.

"But that's to presume we should call you a 'boy' at all," the goat mused. "Because if a boy likes to dress as a girl, one might say he's still a boy, in which case he should use the *boys'* entrance. But if the boy *feels* like a girl, well, he should use the *girls'* door, shouldn't he? Because what you feel often contradicts what 'is' and you can't change what 'is' until you know what you feel. It's rather complicated, isn't it? If only we had a reputable princess to consult. The best princesses can find answers in a way we ordinary goats cannot." He looked at Agatha, as if hoping she could resolve the matter.

"I think the question of which door to use should be left to the one using it," said Agatha, eyeing the Matcher on the desk.

Tedros could see the back of her neck rashing red, anticipating the mirror's scan.

"Must be school aged, you two," the goat rambled, the line of men restless behind them. "My younger brother works as a librarian at the School for Good and Evil. Is that where you went to school?"

"No," said Tedros and Agatha, too forcefully.

The goat gave them a long stare. "No?" He raised his Matcher to reflect them, his whiskers twitching. "Let's see who you are, then . . ."

Tedros' stomach surged into his throat. Why hadn't they run for it? Surely there were other ways to find the answer to his dad's first test . . . to what the Green Knight wanted . . . There was no way of tricking a Matcher! Agatha had put them in a death trap—

"Arise, young Teedum of Coomat!" the goat boomed, stamping him with a tag, before plastering one on Agatha. "And welcome, young Agoff!"

Tedros and his princess gaped at Agatha's name tag.

AGOFF OF WOODLEY BRINK

"May I suggest the exhibit on Floor 5, about Notable Chaplains," the goat prattled. "The one at Camelot happens to be a good friend. Pospisil, his name is. Not that you two would know the slightest thing about Camelot, since Teedum is from Coomat and Agoff from Woodley Brink. Then again, I'm a doddering old bag who's been mixing up my names lately, or at least that's what everyone in Pifflepaff says . . . Imagine if condemned criminals entered my library. I'd hardly notice them."

He gave them a smile.

Tedros saw Agatha grin too, she and the goat locking eyes.

"If only we had a reputable princess to consult on the matter . . ."

Tedros' heart beat faster.

"Dearest Golem," the princess said, keeping her voice low, "might you tell Teedum and I where to find answers about King Arthur's reign?"

"Thought that's what you might be here for," the goat replied keenly. "Floor 3, East Wing. But I'm afraid the Pifflepaff King has closed Arthur's archive for renovation. There's no way inside, unless a trespasser just happened to use the broken door in the south stairwell. But can't imagine anyone would be foolish enough to do that . . ."

"Can't imagine," said Agatha.

Golem winked and waved them away before swiveling to the girls' line: "Next!"

Agatha pulled Tedros towards the stairs ahead.

"How'd you know to trust him?" Tedros whispered.

"Always trust librarians," his princess whispered back.

They heard the goat stamp his book and slap another name—"Hail, Methuselah!"

THE DOOR TO the south stairwell was indeed broken, letting Tedros and his princess steal up to the third floor without the slightest sign of a guard.

As they pushed through the door, Tedros had his first view of the Living Library's halls, he and Agatha stopping short to marvel.

The floor, the walls, the high ceilings were all made of alternating squares of blue and pink mosaic, each tile the size of a biscuit. At first, Tedros thought the mosaic an extension of Pifflepaff's obsession with sex, the alternating pastel colors so relentless that it felt like they'd been stuffed inside a birthday cake. But then Tedros noticed the legions of white mice, wheeling carts loaded with cubes of paper, across the floors, up the walls, along the ceiling, while a large bat supervised from a corner. Each mouse checked the numbers on their cubes, then found a corresponding tile, before popping open the blue or pink square like a safe box and slipping the scroll inside.

Following their lead, Tedros pressed a random pink tile, feeling it pop under his fingers. He pulled out the small cube of paper, labeled "1851," then gently pried open the thin sheet of parchment, crammed with elaborate calligraphy.

Prince Kaveen of Shazabah

Age:	23
Parents:	Sultan Adeen of Shazabah, Mumtaz Adeen of Shazabah
Current Address:	Shazabah Prison
Schooling:	School for Good (Leader)

A long ancestry description followed, marking Kaveen as the great-grandson of Aladdin. Another familiar name caught Tedros' eye: *"Prince Kaveen was briefly married to Princess Uma, now a teacher of Animal Communication at the School for Good—"*

A mouse ran over Tedros' foot with a cart, before it noticed him and Agatha and peered up with pearly, black eyes.

"Moop moop mop mip mip," it meeped.

Tedros and Agatha exchanged baffled looks.

The mouse held up a sign.

WHOSE FILE ARE YOU LOOKING FOR?

Agatha began: "Actually, we're looking for King Arthur's archiv—"

"Japeth of Foxwood. We need his file," Tedros cut in sharply. He glanced at Agatha. "Since we're here, I mean."

The mouse whipped out a notebook, scanning through it.

"Good thinking," Agatha whispered to Tedros, with a smile. The kind of smile princesses gave dashing, quick-thinking princes in the storybooks that Tedros loved growing up. The kind of smile his princess almost never gave him. Maybe this kingdom *was* rubbing off on her, Tedros thought . . . He wasn't sure if he liked it.

"*Japethee*," the mouse piped, pointing at its ledger: "*Matoo cuatro matoo matoo*." Humming a tune, the mouse wheeled its cart up the wall, feet knobbing onto the edges of the tiles, as it scaled columns and slid across rows, until it landed high on a blue tile near the upside-down bat. "*Matoo cuatro matoo matoo*," the mouse double-checked.

Tedros glanced at Agatha hopefully, then back at the mouse, who popped the tile open, pulled out a file, and dropped it, down, down, down, into the prince's waiting palm. "2422," the cube face read. Tedros spread it open, nearly tearing the thin paper—

Sir Kay

Parents: Sir Ector of Foxwood,
             Lady Alessandra of Camelot
Deceased   (Buried in Vault 41, Bank of Putsi)

Sir "Kay," as named by his father, was Arthur's foster

*brother at the home of Sir Ector, where Arthur grew up
before becoming King of Camelot. Kay was later made
King Arthur's first knight, only to leave the Round
Table after a few weeks. According to the Camelot
registry, Kay was Sir Ector's only child, his full name
registered as —*

Tedros crumpled it. "Wrong file," he groaned. "*Japeth*. We wanted Japeth's file. Not my dad's foster brother's."

The mouse skidded down the tiles and yanked the file from him, clearly distressed by Tedros' handling of it before unleashing a barrage of squeaks as it wheeled away: "*Matoo cuatro matoo matoo. Mip moodoo mop!*"

Tedros side-eyed his princess.

"It was worth a try," she sighed, pulling him ahead.

"Mouse?" Tedros called out.

The mouse stopped its cart.

"What about *Rhian* of Foxwood?" Tedros asked.

The mouse grumbled sourly at the prince, slapping open the ledger once more. It continued grouching as it rifled through pages until it came to the one it wanted. The mouse frowned at it intently, then snapped the book shut.

"*Mahameep*," said the mouse.

Tedros shook his head, not following.

The mouse scrawled on the back of a sign and held it up.

MISSING

"*Mahameep*," the mouse repeated, stalking off.

Tedros mumbled: "More dead ends."

"Don't give up yet," said Agatha, peering ahead.

The prince followed her gaze.

Past more mosaic walls and mice scurrying about with carts and scrolls, a flurry of black curtains and yellow rope walled off a wing, the marquee at the entrance hanging askew.

THE HISTORY OF KING ARTHUR
Curated by King Arthur of Camelot
& August A. Sader of Glass Mountain

"August Sader?" Tedros asked, surprised.

Agatha turned to him. "If Professor Sader helped your father . . ."

"He could have helped Dad see the future!" said Tedros, understanding.

"Which means maybe your dad knew we'd come," his princess said, breathless. "You were right, Tedros! He had a plan to help you and it starts here!"

The prince locked eyes with her, both of them swelling with hope—

Then they heard the hammering.

8

AGATHA

Wizard Wish

Behind the curtains and rope, a crew of beavers in blue overalls and yellow hard hats sat on a white floor, alternately passed out or eating ham sandwiches.

Most of the massive East Wing had already been dismantled—busts of Arthur bagged up, tapestries folded away, exhibit walls stripped. All that was left were stenciled plaques: ARTHUR'S ROUND TABLE, THE WEDDING TO GUINEVERE, THE BABY TEDROS . . .

But now Agatha spotted two more beavers ahead, standing on ladders, paint buckets in hand.

"Oh no," she breathed.

Tedros followed her eyes to the

workers, repainting stencils—

RHIAN'S RISE
THE FOUR POINT RESCUE
THE DEATH OF THE SNAKE

Beneath the ladders, busts of Rhian lay wrapped in tissue and bronze Lion heads waited to be hung up, along with painted scenes from the new king's coronation, his claiming of Excalibur, his battle with the Snake.

More hammering detonated and Agatha craned up to see the first team of beavers off their lunch break, walloping at the marquee over Arthur's archive, poised to replace it with a new one.

SON OF ARTHUR: A NEW LION RISES
A Tribute to King Rhian of Camelot

Dust and paint flakes rained down on Agatha's and Tedros' heads. Wary of being spotted, Agatha tried to pull her prince back towards the stairs, but Tedros wouldn't move, his big blue eyes scanning the ruins of his father's archive: portraits strewn, relics dumped in a pile, histories whitewashed over, soon to be replaced with those of his rival.

"You heard the goat. King of Pifflepaff Hills ordered this renovation," said Tedros. "Sucking up to Camelot to earn a king's favor. Same reason he burned his ring. Same reason the others did too. They're all sheep now."

The prince's face reddened. "Dad built his archive here so it'd be safe. Merlin told him to keep it in the Gallery of Good at school, like Merlin's own relics, but Dad thought the school was more vulnerable; that no one would ever desecrate the Living Library . . . let alone in the name of his 'son' . . ." He looked at Agatha. "We're too late. Whatever clues he might have left for us . . . they're gone."

But Agatha was squinting down a dark corridor, away from the beavers.

"What is it?" Tedros asked.

She moved into the hall, ears piqued, eyes narrowing.

With every step, the sound grew louder.

The sound of an unmistakable voice.

A voice she knew as well as her prince's or best friend's.

"The Green Knight came on a Sunday, stalking into the Woods and heading straight for King Arthur's castle—"

The voice glitched, resuming a second later.

"'I'll make you a deal,' said the knight to the king—"

Again the voice glitched.

It was coming from behind a black wall, the surface shiny and smooth, painted with white letters.

ARTHUR AND THE GREEN KNIGHT

With Tedros close behind, Agatha entered the black-painted room, the walls covered in fluorescing green, five-pointed stars, each studded with small silver dots.

Agatha recognized these dots. They'd blanketed her history

textbooks at school instead of words . . . her favorite professor's way of making the past come alive . . .

She counted twenty dot-covered stars on the walls now, with a painted numeral next to each one, ordering them in sequence. "START HERE!" it said near the first.

Meanwhile, two beavers in hard hats were ripping the stars off the wall, their paws activating Professor Sader's narration.

"Arthur launched from his throne and—"

"The sword came down upon—"

"It was a poor decision—"

The beavers dumped more stars in their filthy bucket.

Agatha blushed with fury. She'd already had enough of this sexist kingdom and now these idiots were trashing the clues to Tedros' first test! She charged the beavers, Tedros scrambling too late to stop her—

"You dead-eyed, half-brained fur puppets!" she barked, shoving them. "Go away!"

The two beavers froze, as if no human had ever touched them before. They gave Agatha pursed looks, their noses twitching. One squeezed the Lion badge on his overalls, which flashed gold, before he whispered something into it. Then the beavers went back to stripping stars.

"We need to leave," Tedros warned, pulling Agatha away—

Then they heard a yelp.

The beavers were stuck on the last star, the only one left on the bare black walls. But the harder they pawed at it, the more stubbornly it remained, spewing a few bright sparks, which singed the beavers' fur. Only there was something else happening, Agatha realized: the more they jostled the star, the more its green surface rubbed off, the silver dots shedding, revealing a glowing white star beneath.

Agatha's heart jolted.

That star.

It looks just like . . .

With twin growls, the beavers yanked the star as hard as they could. It exploded with sizzling currents, shocking both rodents to the floor.

Tedros gawked at the comatose beavers, then at the lone white star on the wall. "Is that . . ."

"Only one way to find out," said Agatha, holding her breath.

Down the hall, bootsteps rose, along with the sound of voices.

Human voices.

Quickly, Agatha tugged Tedros to the wall, feeling his chest pound under her grip. If the star was Merlin's, it could hold answers. If it wasn't, then they'd be drooling on the ground with the beavers. Agatha didn't know which outcome to bet on. But she knew one thing for sure: it was worth the chance.

Agatha blinked at her prince. "Ready?"

"Ready," said Tedros.

Both of them thrust hands at the star, slamming their palms against it—

The star went dark.

Instantly the room's walls hopped forward as if they were alive, the black slabs bounding closer, closer, until they pinned to the couple's fronts, backs, sides, sealing them in like a coffin. Agatha felt the cold stone on her nose and bum, her prince's sweaty arm jammed against hers.

"What's happening?" Tedros choked.

The black box upended at lightning speed, knocking them off their feet. It happened so fast Agatha swallowed a scream, the box flipping ninety degrees, leaving her and her prince flat on their spines, the top wall still pinned to their faces.

All of a sudden, the white star reappeared deep in the darkness over their heads, like a light down a tunnel, as if the star was somehow beaming from beyond dimension.

A voice echoed, calm and clear.

"Hello, Tedros. Hello, Agatha. If you're hearing me now, then you've already come a long way. It must be strange to hear your old Professor Sader from beyond the grave, but I assure you it is just as odd for me. Because it is not I who knew you might be hearing this message. As I once told you, I cannot see your future beyond your time at school. In my mind's eye, your fairy tale ends the night Rafal comes for your heads. My sight offers me no further clues as to whether you survive the encounter or what becomes of you.

Instead, it is King Arthur who believes your story will continue long after I'm gone, to a time when Tedros must prove his claim to Camelot's throne. And in pursuit of this proof, you will come here, to this very room, searching for answers to his father's history. Answers the public do not know and which I do not have permission to share with them. Indeed, this particular exhibit in Arthur's archive remains woefully incomplete. As with most fairy tales, the people will only know the beginnings of the tale of Arthur and the Green Knight.

But not you. You will learn more. You must know the full story.

This was Arthur's dying wish to me: that I leave you these answers in a way that only you could find. Since Merlin is as much a part of this story as the king, I turned to the wizard for help in hiding what I have to tell you; it is his magic that allows me to be here with you now.

Before Arthur died, I asked him why he wouldn't tell Tedros the story himself. The king replied that his son should learn the facts from someone he trusted. Facts Tedros didn't care to hear from his father. And yet, I suspect there is another reason the king wanted me to tell this story instead of him. Arthur knew that history should not be conveyed by its participants. Man is too emotional, too bound to his ego. Truth only comes with perspective and time.

With the blessing of both wizard and king, then, it is I who will give you the answers you seek. So lie back, clear your mind, and witness the Tale of Arthur and the Green Knight . . ."

In darkness, a phantom history appeared, like one of Professor Sader's textbooks come to life. As the prince and princess floated, a lush forest appeared around them, occupying every dimension, at once richly detailed and yet porous, like a simulation of reality that hadn't entirely been filled in. Trampling through this forest came a tall, mountainous man with bright green skin, the color of young grass or a garden snake. The Green Knight had big black eyes, a high, smooth forehead, and a thick, dark beard that matched the wavy hair on his head. Veiny muscles bulged from his bare green chest and tight green breeches. A gold-plated axe hung from his belt.

"*By now, you know the beginnings,*" Professor Sader's voice narrated, "*about the mysterious Green Knight who appeared in the Woods and made his way to Camelot, insisting on a private meeting with its king. Arthur was not in the practice of humoring nameless strangers—especially demanding ones with axes—but the Green Knight had arrived only a few days after Guinevere had abandoned the king for his best friend. That the Green Knight would come so soon after the queen's disappearance couldn't be a coincidence . . .*"

The scene evaporated, replaced with King Arthur's throne room. There were no guards or advisors or members of the court. The king had honored the knight's request to meet alone, with Arthur now hunched on his gold throne, his bloodshot eyes creased with wrinkles, his gray-flecked hair unkempt. There were crumbs in his beard, stains on the collar of his robes. Excalibur leaned against the throne, mottled and dull. Agatha was reminded of the way Tedros once looked when she'd tried to end their relationship and pair him off with Sophie. Her prince had disappeared for days, returning with this same childlike stupor, as if both he and his father were truly alive only when they had the security of love. And just like Tedros had welcomed Agatha when he thought he might get her back—bone-tired, but renewed—now his father looked down at his green guest the same way.

"Do you know where she is?" Arthur asked, breathless. "Take me to her at once . . . I'll pay you any price . . ."

The Green Knight seemed bemused. "Most kings would be suspicious of a green stranger. Especially the Lion of Camelot, whose kingdom is founded upon his victory over a Snake. But instead, the mighty Arthur asks me for help, convinced I'm a friend." He peered harder at the king. "You don't remember me, do you?"

"Quite sure I'd remember a green hulk of a man," said Arthur swiftly. "If you are indeed man and not monster."

"More man than most kings, I'd say," the knight replied, his stare unwavering. "As to your question, let's say I *could* find your wife. How would that change anything? Would that make her love you? Would that make her come running back to your side?"

Arthur didn't know what to make of this.

"Poor Lion. It won't be long before you call me a Snake," the Green Knight spoke. "But just remember: the real Snake was in your *bed*."

The king's eyes flickered. "Why have you come here, then?"

"To gain your permission," the Green Knight replied.

"My permission for what?"

"To kill Merlin," said the knight.

The answer was so unexpected that Agatha let out a shocked laugh—a laugh that the king himself echoed, rocking forward on his throne.

Then he saw the knight was serious.

"May I ask *why*?" said the king.

"May I ask why you couldn't keep your wife?" said the knight.

Arthur's mood darkened. "You have three seconds to be out of my sight."

"No, that's not how this goes," the Green Knight said. "If I leave now, I will punish your realms and inflict terror like you have never known until you beg me back, seeking a deal. The same deal I will offer you today. If you wish to spare your people, I suggest you take it."

Arthur looked startled that this creature was now issuing him orders.

"The terms are simple," said the Green Knight. "You may strike me a single blow with your sword. Right here. Right now. And in exchange, I will return tomorrow and give the same blow to Merlin."

"If I give you a blow, you won't be returning anywhere tomorrow," Arthur spat, launching to his feet.

"A true king would do more than boast," the Green Knight taunted.

"You want a blow, do you?" Arthur sneered, drawing Excalibur. "As you wish." From the throne's platform, he pointed the sword down at the knight. "You are lucky there are steps between us. I am offering you mercy, insolent cur. I suggest *you* take it."

"I see," the knight spoke. "You don't think my terms are real. So lost in arrogance you ignore the threat in front of you. So insulated from your people you'd let a Snake run free, because you're too cowardly to strike the blow. Actions have consequences, Your Highness. *Non*-action has consequences as well."

Agatha could see Tedros from the corner of her eye, his

cheeks red, his jaw clenched. This was the same charge people leveled at him. The same trap that gave rise to the new Snake that imperiled him now.

"I'm giving you the right to strike me," the knight reminded. "It is also your right to turn a blind eye, of course. To let me leave and wreak havoc in your name. But don't say I didn't warn you. Just as I'm sure your wife warned she didn't love you and you turned a blind eye to that too."

Arthur lowered his sword. Blood flushed his face. He steamed hot through his nostrils. "You know nothing of my wife."

"I know more than you do, it seems," said the knight. "You're the one who still thinks you can get her back."

Agatha could see the king racked with tension, fighting to resist the bait.

"Get out," Arthur seethed. "Get out *now.*"

"Pity your young wart of a son," said the knight.

"Don't talk about my son—" Arthur lashed.

"Mother gone. Father weak . . ." the Green Knight jabbed. "Brother hidden away."

The king went dead cold.

So did Tedros next to Agatha.

"What did you say?" his father breathed.

The knight grinned back. "Long live the *true* heir. Long live the *king.*"

"You snake," Arthur hissed, already moving. "You *LIAR!*" He slashed down the stairs, robes aflight, like a murderous angel, his sword sweeping up over his head. With a primal roar, he swung it through the shadows, catching a last glint of sun—

It cut clean through the Green Knight's neck.

Agatha and Tedros froze, watching the green head roll across the carpet, waiting for the slain knight's body to fall . . .

But then something strange happened.

Something that made Arthur drop his blade in shock.

The knight's body *didn't* fall.

Instead, it ambled a few steps backwards, picked up the severed head, and tucked it under his arm.

"Same time tomorrow," the knight's head spoke. "Bring Merlin."

Then he strolled out of the throne room, head in hand, leaving Arthur stunned and alone.

The scene faded to darkness.

Slowly Agatha looked at Tedros, who was staring into the void, rock still.

"His head," she croaked. "How do you live with no head?"

But her prince had something else on his mind. "Doesn't make sense," he said, shaken. "Dad gave me the ring because *I'm* the heir." Tedros turned to Agatha. "So why did the Green Knight imply that I'm not?"

"The knight lied," Agatha argued. "You heard your dad—"

But Professor Sader's voice had returned, a new panorama filling in.

"Needless to say, the king had no intention of delivering his wizard to the knight and blocked the entrance to his castle with a thousand guards. Yet, to the Green Knight, he and the king had

made a deal. The king had taken his cut; now it was the knight's turn to strike Merlin. And as long as Arthur refused to honor these terms, then his people would pay the price."

Around Tedros and Agatha spawned a montage of destruction: the Green Knight, head restored, setting fire to castles and carriages; slashing through armies with his axe; launching avalanches to crush villages; terrorizing the streets of kingdoms, Good and Evil. Every arrow that pierced his green chest, every sword that drew blood, he easily swatted away, his skin healing instantly, his force invincible. Mobs gathered in Camelot's square and at the castle gates, jeering the blockade of guards, shouting slurs at Arthur, demanding the king come out and kill this green monster.

Instantly Agatha was reminded of Japeth and his brother, slithering into the Woods and terrorizing the people to turn them against Tedros. They had succeeded just as the Green Knight had.

"Past is Present and Present is Past," the Snake's brother once said. *"The story goes round and round again."*

Coincidence? Agatha wondered. Or did Rhian and Japeth have ties to the Green Knight? Ties that made this first test as significant to Japeth as it was to Tedros? Was the Green Knight the key to solving who Rhian and Japeth *really* were?

But now the scene in the black box was changing: this time, to King Arthur's chambers, as the king stood at his window, watching smoke rise over distant kingdoms, along with the protests at his castle gates.

"Should have let him have me," said a voice.

Arthur turned to find Merlin at the door, the wizard in his purple cape, dented cone hat, and violet slippers, his long, thick beard scragglier than ever.

"Don't be ridiculous," said Arthur, turning back around.

"A deal is a deal," said Merlin.

"Our knights are having no luck against him," Arthur confessed stiffly. "Then again, Lancelot left them in quite a state. Gone without warning: their captain revealed to be a traitor, adulterer, *deserter*. No wonder they can't find the strength to take down this green fool. I'll have to ride into battle against him myself."

"You'll die and he'll have me in any case," Merlin replied.

The king said nothing for a moment.

"Why does he want to kill you?" Arthur asked.

"We have history," the wizard answered.

"What kind of history?"

"Personal history."

Arthur kept his eyes out the window.

"He believes I owe him something," the wizard sighed. "Something he can only take if I'm dead."

"And what is that thing? What is it that he wants?"

"I'm afraid I can't tell you."

Arthur whirled around. "I am inflicting pain on the whole of the Woods, in *your* name, and *you can't tell me*?"

"What I can tell you is to stop your martyrdom and deliver me as agreed," said Merlin. "This is between me and the knight."

"Then go, you doddering prat!" Arthur exploded. "Go

like Gwen did! Go like Lance! You and your *personal* history. Settle your business without me!"

"I would have done that from the beginning, but he made the deal with *you*," Merlin answered. "You must deliver me. Or his terror will not stop."

"Why am I a part of this? This has nothing do with me!" Arthur assailed. "He's acting like I should remember him. Like I should know who he is."

"Do you?" Merlin asked.

"Clearly not!" the king snapped. "So why me? Why do *I* have to deliver you?"

"Isn't it obvious?" said Merlin, quietly. "He would like to see us both suffer."

Arthur stared at him.

"Merlin? Is that you?" said a soft, young voice.

A young boy pulled in, eight or nine years old, with sleepy blue eyes, floppy gold hair, and rumpled pajamas. "Can you make me a toddy, double marshmallow and candy cream, like usua—"

The young prince caught his dad at the window. "Oh. Thought you were alone." The boy started to leave.

"Tedros, wait—" Arthur began.

Young Tedros spun around. "Why are you still here? Go find Mother! You promised! Just like you promised to keep the Woods safe. But you're not doing that either! You're not doing anything!"

He stormed out of the room.

Arthur didn't go after him, pain clouding his eyes, looking

even more the child than his son.

Next to Agatha, the grown Tedros was breathing raggedly, reliving this very moment, watching Merlin step towards his dad.

"You've lost your wife, Arthur. You've lost your best friend," the wizard said gently. "Don't lose him too."

A tear rolled down the king's cheek.

"I'll send word to the Green Knight," said Merlin, touching the king. "Tomorrow at dawn in Ender's Forest. Where no one will see us."

The king gazed off into the distance . . . then turned. "Ender's Forest? No one knows how to find that except you and me—"

But Merlin was already gone.

As the scene vanished, Tedros looked more confused than ever. "We still don't know what the Green Knight wanted from Merlin. The secret he came for. Which means we still don't know the answer to my first test."

"The story isn't over yet," said Agatha, watching colors begin to fill in the darkness once more.

Tedros exhaled. "Was your family this messed up?"

"You have no idea," Agatha said, forcing a smile.

Cramped close in the black box, she held her prince's hand.

"We know the end to the tale," Tedros said. "Merlin survives. Dad does too. The Green Knight dies." He looked at his princess. "So why do I feel like something terrible is about to happen?"

This, Agatha had no comfort for.

Because she had the same feeling too.

A purple forest melted into view around them, the leaves and flowers of every tree, bush, and shrub spanning shades of plum, violet, orchid, amethyst, and lavender.

"*Tedros will know Ender's Forest well, of course, for it's where Merlin used to give him lessons,*" Professor Sader spoke.

"When I could find it," Tedros murmured.

"*If the Celestium was the wizard's place to think, then Ender's Forest was the wizard's place to practice—a forest that appeared only to Merlin whenever and wherever he wished, his space to work-shop new spells and hexes and disguises away from prying eyes . . .*"

Merlin and Arthur heard the knight before they saw him, his resounding steps rattling the tree beneath which wizard and king waited, the dust of dawn rippling through darkness.

"Right on schedule," said the wizard, combing his beard with his fingers.

"Took me ten tries to find this place the first time," said Arthur. "How did he know how to get in?"

Merlin didn't answer, the knight's footsteps growing louder.

Arthur instinctively touched the sword on his belt—

"Whatever happens, you are to stay out of it," Merlin ordered the king, his voice sharp. "Our trust has been strained of late, Arthur. You broke into my quarters. Stole my gnome potion so you could snoop after Guinevere. By betraying me, you only hastened her departure. But the stakes now are even higher. You have delivered me to the Green Knight, per the terms of the agreement. You are to play no further role."

Arthur looked distressed. "Merlin, you can't expect me to

stand here and let him—"

"Remember *why* you are here," Merlin retorted, stone-eyed. "To be a good king. To be a good father. Do not undo what is right with what *feels* right. Promise that you will do as I say. Promise that you will trust me to handle myself."

"But—"

"*Promise* me."

The wizard's tone left no doubt, no room for bargaining.

Arthur could see the shadow of the invincible savage approaching, his boots crushing the lilac beds, his golden axe spattered with blood. The king held back tears, faced with the inevitability of what was to come and no recourse to stop it.

"I promise," he said emptily.

Merlin faced the knight.

"No tricks, Merlin," his green nemesis flared, a hot flush already in his cheeks. "You have too much dignity to cheat me. I expect you to honor the terms." He glanced at Arthur. "You, too. Though I can't say the same about your dignity."

Arthur reached for his sword—

He saw Merlin glaring.

The king drew back.

"Let us finish our business, then," the wizard resumed, stepping towards the knight. "Come, Japeth. Strike your blow."

Agatha gripped Tedros so hard she almost broke his hand. Tedros choked on his spit—

Japeth? Agatha screamed in her head.

JAPETH?

The Green Knight hadn't moved, his sad, dark eyes

on the wizard. "How could you choose him over me, Merlin? How could you put your lot in with *that*?" He stabbed a meaty finger at Arthur. "This coward. This cuckold. When you could have had me. When the *Woods* could have had me."

Arthur looked between them. "What is he talking about, Merlin?"

The wizard's gaze stayed with the knight. "I didn't choose Arthur over you, Japeth. Arthur was destined to be king."

"Don't. Lie. No *lies*," the Green Knight spat, his voice sounding younger, uncontrolled. "You favored him over me from the beginning. Even though I was Ector's real son. Even though Father brought you to be *my* tutor. I was always stronger and better than that . . . *wart*. That's what everyone called him, remember? *Wart*. A blemish on our house. A foster brother no one wanted. And still, you shined your light on him. *Only* him. That's why he could pull the sword out of the stone. Because *you* helped him—"

"Not true, Japeth."

"*I* should have been king," the knight said, his eyes welling. "I should be him!"

Agatha's hand went cold in her prince's.

"Your wart of a son . . ."

The pieces slammed together in Agatha's head: the knight's taunts to the king, that wrong file in the Library, the one the mouse said was Japeth's—

The Green Knight wasn't a stranger at all. The Green Knight was . . .

"Kay?" Arthur gasped, big-eyed.

"Don't call me that, *Wart*," the knight snarled. "I'm not Kay anymore. I'm Japeth, the name my mother gave me, not the puffed-up name Dad thought would be better for a knight. 'Sir Kay,' the bold and strong, fated for glory. Until you stole my destiny. Until the Storian made you legend and me the footnote. Sir Kay, the buffoon brother. But you know that wasn't the truth. So you offered me a place as your first knight to make amends—only to mock me by giving Lance all your attention and love, the same way Merlin chose you over me. Not just Sir Kay, the idiot now. Now Sir Kay, the joke. Sir Kay, the Runt of the Round Table. That's why I left Camelot. That's why I waited to take my revenge until the time was right. Until the Woods could see the failure that was their king. I bet that's why your wife left you? Because she knew the Wart *I* knew? Lancelot, too. He didn't just steal your wife, he abandoned you, your choice to love him as wrong as Merlin's choice to love you. You must wonder why everyone leaves you . . . Guinevere, Lancelot, soon Merlin, no doubt. Even Sir Kay has gone. A relic of your fairy tale. It's Japeth, now. Mother named me right. A name fit for a Snake."

He turned on Merlin. "As for you, old man, I only want what you promised me as a boy. You swore when Arthur pulled the sword that I would go on to a destiny even bigger. That I would have a life I'd be proud of. That I wouldn't resent that wart becoming king." His cheeks burned a darker green. "And if I didn't have a good life, a *great* life, if you were proven to have lied to me, then I could claim your Wizard Wish. The one wish every wizard keeps hidden away where only he can find it. A wish that can grant any desire said out loud, but one you save to choose when to leave this world, like all wizards do. Only it's not *your* wish anymore, Merlin. Because you said if I didn't find my destiny like you promised, then I could take your wish for myself. I could wish for anything I wanted to make up for what you deprived me of. Well, Merlin . . ."

He prowled towards the wizard, gripping his axe.

"I wish for a *death*."

Merlin showed no fear, no remorse. "I said you would live a great life if you allowed yourself to have it, Japeth. But you held on to your bitterness towards Arthur. Envy is a green snake that swallows the heart whole. Look at what it's done to you. It's swelled inside you, this green poison, devouring your soul, consuming your humanity, until it's become *bigger* than you. Jealousy has no bounds. It cannot be quenched, even by death. You will live forever this way. Invincible, immortal . . . but eaten alive by the green snake of your heart. Unless you learn to let it go. Unless you learn to forgive. Not just me and Arthur, but yourself too. Only then can you begin again. Only then can you have the life you were meant to, the life I said you could have if you chose it."

"More lies! More excuses!" the Green Knight cried, his lips trembling. His towering form loomed over the wizard's. He smeared at his eyes, forcing composure. "Kneel, you dog. My turn for a blow."

"As you wish," said Merlin.

He slipped off his hat and bent to the ground, laying his

head against a fallen tree, tilting his long beard to the side and bearing his white, scrawny neck.

Chills raced up Agatha's spine, seeing Merlin so vulnerable, remembering the wizard was as mortal as she—

"Wait," Arthur choked out, rushing forward, sword in hand. "Don't do this, Kay!"

Merlin shot a spell, pinning Arthur against a tree, the king's chest invisibly bound, his fist with Excalibur flailing in vain.

"Take your blow, Japeth," the wizard spoke, his cheek to the log. "Do what you've come to do."

Agatha could see the Green Knight quaking harder as he stared down at Merlin's neck, the axe unsteady in his palms.

"Why, Merlin?" he whimpered. "Why didn't you love me?"

The wizard lifted his eyes. "I love you as much as I love Arthur. As much as I love any of my wards. But love has to be received as much as it is given."

Tears spilled across the Green Knight's face. "Tell me I would have made a better king . . . Tell me you made a mistake . . . That I should have been the Lion. Instead of the Snake."

Merlin gave him a warm, loving smile. "I hope you find peace, Japeth."

The knight let out a sob. "Curse you, Merlin."

He raised the axe.

"No!" Arthur screamed, thrashing against the spell.

The Green Knight swung the blade down, cutting through Merlin.

With a cry, Arthur flung his sword across the forest—

Excalibur impaled hard in the knight's chest.

The green-skin hulk glanced down as blood gushed out of him . . . only to flow back in neatly, the wound closing around Arthur's sword, the knight's immortal skin healing once more.

But Arthur wasn't looking at the Green Knight anymore.

He was gaping past him . . . at the wizard over the log . . .

"Agatha . . . ," Tedros said.

Tedros was pointing at Merlin . . . Merlin, who Agatha couldn't bear to look at because he'd have no head . . .

Only he *did* have a head.

Because the axe hadn't cut through it.

The knight hadn't aimed for Merlin's neck at all.

He'd aimed for Merlin's *beard*, shearing the long, raggedy patch of hair from the wizard's chin.

Arthur froze as the Green Knight calmly retrieved the wizard beard from the dirt, the gash in the knight's chest sealed around the blade.

Slowly, Merlin raised his head, surprised to be alive. He watched the Green Knight hold up the shorn beard, a deep steel in the knight's eye. Only then did Merlin understand his plan.

"Listen to me, Japeth. Let's talk first," he said. For the first time, the wizard looked scared.

The Green Knight noticed. "So it *is* still here. You told me you hid it in your beard when you promised it to me. All these years. You could have moved it somewhere else . . ."

"Don't do it, Japeth," Merlin begged.

"Thank you for giving me your Wizard Wish, Merlin,"

said the knight, his voice steadying. "I know you wanted me to be happy. But I need this wish now. More than you."

"There are other ways—" Merlin insisted.

The Green Knight pressed the wizard beard to his heart. "I wish to give up this bitterness, this envy, this hate. I wish to feel love and forgiveness and peace. I wish to be restored to the man I'm meant to be." He looked right at Merlin. "I wish to be . . . *free.*"

"No!" the wizard cried.

Instantly the green started to fade from the knight's skin. His muscles deflated, his veins shriveled, his sculpted cheeks sagged, until the Green Knight was nothing more than a soft-bellied, pallid, middle-aged man, out of place in an enchanted wood. Sir Kay took a deep breath, his chest rising and falling, his focus lifting to the sky.

"So this is what it's like . . . ," he whispered.

He closed his eyes, the last tints of green draining.

The sword in his chest quivered.

The wound reopened, blood flooding his chest.

Kay opened his eyes as bright as the sun.

"Goodbye, Merlin," he said.

Then he fell down dead.

Merlin ran to his side, scooping him into his arms.

But it was too late.

The wish granted.

The deed done.

Not Merlin's death chosen . . . but the knight's own.

The wizard wept softly, cradling Kay like a child.

His spell trapping Arthur broke, dropping the king face-first into dirt.

Arthur scraped himself to his elbows.

The wizard wouldn't look at him.

"Merlin—" the king appealed.

The wizard thrust out a hand, silencing him. When he spoke at last, it was in a cold, harsh voice. "Kay could have had a second chance at life. I would have convinced him. I would have helped him. He might have finally had a path to become the man he was meant to be. But your sword gave him a way out. *You* gave him a way out instead of letting me fight for him." Merlin paused, his back to the king. "People will say you killed the Green Knight. That you are the hero of this tale . . . But we both know the truth, Arthur. You broke your word to me. A king's word." The wizard's voice crackled with anger. "Too many trusts broken between us. Too much gone wrong."

Slowly Merlin lay Kay down and rose into the light.

"I no longer have a Wizard Wish or the choice of when to end my days. But I can choose to end *this*. I'm leaving you, Arthur," he said, standing over the king. "Our time together is done."

Ender's Forest went silent and still.

Merlin and Arthur gazed upon each other for the last time . . .

The scene evaporated into darkness.

So too did the box around Agatha and Tedros, the prince and princess floating back down in the black room, a dim, cold star on the floor between their feet.

"Merlin's beard," said Tedros, choked with emotion. "That's where Merlin hid his wish. That's what the Green Knight wanted. Merlin's beard is the answer to my first test."

Agatha looked at him, lost in a fog. "We have to get Merlin's *beard?*"

"To show Dad I know the truth," said Tedros. "'*Three tests. Three answers to find.*' He wanted me to learn that slaying the Green Knight wasn't a victory. It was his greatest mistake. A mistake I have to learn from."

Voices amplified in the hall. Footsteps clattered closer.

"Beaver saw 'em. Said the girl was that rebel Agatha," a guard echoed. "Apparently she slayed the beaver's cousin in a camel attack. Traveling with that traitor prince. If we kill 'em, imagine the reward—"

Tedros dragged Agatha into shadows.

"How can we get Merlin's beard?" the prince questioned, still clammy and pale. "Merlin's trapped in the Caves of Contempo—"

"Where the witches are supposed to be," Agatha remembered. "They have to rescue him before Japeth figures out the test, before *he* gets to Merlin . . ."

The guards' voices were nearing the exhibit, their steps closing in.

"We need to get in touch with the witches," Tedros said urgently. "We need to know if they have Merlin!"

"We need to get out of this library first!" Agatha pressed.

Frantically, they searched for a door, a window—

But it was too late.

Five guards turned the corner, Matchers reflecting in Tedros' and Agatha's faces, crossbows aimed at their necks.

"No, don't!" Agatha screamed.

Guards cocked their triggers, arrows poised to fly.

"*Fire!*" the leader yelled—

The wall bashed in behind him, crushing the guards in a heap of rubble.

Agatha and her prince gaped as the dust cleared, sunlight filling the giant hole.

A big, hairy man-wolf peeped through, Nicola and Guinevere on his back.

"What'd we miss?" Hort chimed.

9

The Cave at Two O'Clock

"*Now go and find it where wizard trees grow,*'" Dot panted, an open scroll in her fist. "What does that mean?"

"Merlin was Arthur's wizard during the time of the Green Knight. Maybe the answer has to do with Merlin," Hester surmised, a few last scrolls blizzarding upside down, from her feet past her head. "More reason to rescue the wizard quickly."

"But Merlin's in the Caves of Contempo," Anadil noted, hustling across Borna Coric's night sky. "What does that have to do with *trees*?"

"Ani's right," Dot added. "Doesn't say find the wizard. It says find where wizard *trees* grow—"

"Which Merlin will surely know," Hester snapped, passing beneath the last upturned shops, strung between inverted beanstalks. The shops were closed, the crowds back in their upside-down cottages. "Should have been to the caves by now," said Hester, glowering back at Dot. "If someone didn't force us to stop at All Night Pies."

"Excuse me, I had to eat after that wedding spellcast," said Dot. "My nerves were in pieces."

"Well, at least we know Tedros and Agatha are still alive," said Hester. "Let them worry about the first test. Our mission is to get Merlin out of the caves."

"*If* Merlin's even there," Dot noted. "Dovey was the one who told us to go to the caves. She could have been wrong, first off. Plus, those caves are dangerous. People go in and ten minutes later, they come out 50 years older. It's been *weeks* since Merlin's been gone. And he's old to begin with." She shook out a few scrolls that had flooded up her skirt. "Imagine when it rains here. Everyone's knickers must be drenched."

"Just follow the smell of the sea," Hester grouched, irritated that Dot was making sense for once. She tried to focus on the wet, salty scent, getting stronger and stronger. "That's where the caves will be."

"Need to get there before sunrise or we'll be in plain sight," Anadil murmured. The witches pulled into the shadows as two upside-down ministers in purple suits padded across the beanstalk above them, gripping opened scrolls and whispering anxiously.

Hester tailed beneath, catching phrases: "*Rhian saved us*

from Tedros' rebels . . ." "Can't let Tedros win . . ." "King is en route to Putsi . . ." "Says the first answer is there . . ."

The ministers sensed something, glancing down, but Hester was gone.

Putsi? Why would Japeth go to Putsi? the witch thought, rejoining her friends as they hustled under toppled cottages. *Nothing there but sand and geese . . .*

"Hester!" Anadil hissed, yanking her back—

Distracted, Hester had almost barreled over a cliff. She peered down at the dark skyfloor, dropping off into infinite fog.

"If you die and leave me with Dot, I'll find my way to hell just to kill you again," said Anadil.

"How romantic," said Hester. Slowly, she inched towards the white, swirling mist, her boots scratching the cliff edge, but even close-up, she could see nothing through the fog. Nor could she locate the smell of salt water that led them here.

Anadil's nose twitched, noticing the same thing. "How did we lose an entire sea?" She probed over the cliff, squinting into fog—

Her foot slipped. A hand pulled her back.

"You catch me, I catch you," said Hester.

"Is that a Tedros line?" Anadil replied. "Are you quoting princes at me?"

"Should have dropped you."

They noticed Dot behind them, pensive.

"What is it?" Anadil asked.

"Daddy's ring," Dot rasped. "The man who burned it . . .

It was *Bertie*. I saw his face through his helmet. I keep try-ing to tell myself it wasn't . . . But I know it was him. Daddy would never have let his ring fall into Bertie's hands. He knew Rhian was after it. Daddy would have protected it until his last breath. Which means if Bertie had it . . ." Her eyes welled up.

Hester looked at Anadil. Neither knew what to say. Both of them had lost their parents. They knew what it was like to be alone. Dot, now, was part of their tribe. Each took one of her hands, holding their friend close.

"Maybe Daddy's still alive," Dot croaked, tears falling. "Maybe I've got it wrong?"

Hester smiled as best she could. "Maybe."

"You're my real family, you know," Dot said softly to her friends. "And I know I'm a part of yours too. Even if you act like I'm not. Even if you two pretend you don't need me. A coven is three. It has to be three. Because I'd be so lonely with-out you."

Now Hester had teared up, and so did Anadil, which only Hester could tell, since Ani's face never moved, even when she was crying.

"We love you, Dot," Hester whispered, hugging her tight.

"Even if sometimes we want to push you down a well," said Anadil, joining the hug.

"Now I'll look like a fat raccoon," Dot muttered, wiping at her mascara and glancing upwards. "Oh, good heavens. That's where it's been!"

Anadil and Hester looked up.

The Savage Sea glittered high over their heads, where the

sky should be, the dark waters extending into the wall of mist.

"Caves must be up there too," said Anadil. "In that fog . . ."

"But how are we supposed to *get* up there?" Hester pressed.

"Oh, that's easy," Dot sighed.

Two witches turned to the third.

"WALLS CAN BE useful," said Dot as she climbed the fog. "Without a wall, you might not know where to begin. But a wall is a challenge. Put a wall in front of a witch and she'll find her way past it."

Where Hester and Anadil had seen an impossible gap between skyfloor and sea, an insurmountable fog . . . Dot had seen opportunity.

With a lit finger, she'd turned the wall of fog to chocolate: the misty swirls now made of cocoa meringue, buttressed with sticky fudge to help the witches keep grip. One after the other, the witches climbed, Dot in the lead, the coven hidden by night.

For the time being, at least, Hester mulled. Morning was coming fast. They'd been at it for ages and were barely halfway up the wall. Already they'd climbed so high that Hester's demon was chapped, her nose ring frozen, and she couldn't see the stars in the skyfloor anymore. Luckily, she wasn't scared of heights. (What she was scared of was the wall's sugary stench, which reminded her of babies and boyfriends and Easter bunnies, things Hester thought should be outlawed or dead.)

"Let's say we do make it up there," Anadil puffed. "How

will we get *into* the sea? We need to swim through to get to the caves. But we can't just jump in the water. It's upside down. Won't we just fall out and die?"

Hester looked up at the ocean, high over their heads, an undulating ceiling. "Let's hope Dot has the answer to that too."

"I don't," said Dot, dripping sweat and fudge. "Really, I might go back to turning things to kale after this."

But they had bigger problems now, for the first rays of sun had broken through the skyfloor, lighting up the chocolate wall.

Already Hester could see people in the vales, upside down and tiny as newts, stepping out from inverted houses, peering at a chocolate wall that had appeared overnight.

"Climb faster," Hester growled, shoving Anadil, who shoved Dot, but all three were flagging.

"I wish I were Tedros," Dot wheezed. "He has muscles."

"Rather die," said Hester.

"Same," said Ani.

Sunrays detonated through the iced meringue, refracting rainbow beams up the wall. Not only were the three of them visible now, but they were spotlit like roaches on an ice sculpture. Hester glanced down at upturned guards throttling through the village, armed with swords and headed for the clifftop. Even worse, heat was assaulting the wall, the sun rising full-force in the skyfloor.

"Almost there," Dot breathed, the sea getting closer.

But every inch up seemed to slide them two inches down, the chocolate melting to goo under their hands, the meringue starting to crack. Down below, the Borna guards had leapt onto the wall, their bodies closing the gap with alarming speed.

"How are they so quick?" Dot gasped.

"They live on beanstalks! They spend their lives climbing!" said Hester, head-butting Anadil. "Hurry!"

Each witch struggled up the meringue, pieces chipping off and hitting the witch beneath. By the time they were within arm's length of the sea, the guards were more than halfway up the wall.

Dot reached a hand into the waters overhead. "We need a way to stay upside down and swim," she said, scanning the sea beyond the wall, shrouded in fog. "Caves must be out there somewhere."

"The sea around the caves is supposed to be poisonous," said Ani, eyeing Dot's wet, perfectly healthy hand.

"Caves must not be that close, then," Hester grimaced, before peeking down at the guards. "They're getting closer, though."

"Wait a second," Dot said, focused overhead. "Look."

Hester peered up at the waters, shimmering with sun.

Except the shimmers were *moving*. It wasn't sun. It was . . . *fish*. Big and small, swimming in an overturned sea.

"How are *they* managing it?" Anadil wondered.

Dot punched her hand into the fish-filled waters again, keeping it in longer, gauging something . . . Her eyes narrowed. "Only one way to find out," she said.

With a deep breath, she launched upwards, cannoning into the sea.

"Dot, *no!*" Hester and Ani screamed, both prepared to catch their falling friend, even if it meant death for them all—

Only Dot didn't fall.

"Currents!" she pipped, dangling from the water, her head upside down. "They hold you in place, like the air holds birds in the sky. Jump in!"

Anadil didn't hesitate, flinging herself up and bellyflopping onto Dot. A second later, the pair popped their heads out of the sea like lemurs, but Hester still hadn't moved from her spot down the meringue. Fudge crumbled under her fingers, her body slipping. Below, she heard men's shouts . . . the scrape of their boots against chocolate . . .

"You need to jump. *Now,*" Anadil demanded.

Hester didn't know how to put feelings into words: her fear of letting go . . . her inability to trust . . . the vulnerability of a leap . . .

But a true friend can sense these things without them spoken.

"Trust me," said Anadil.

Hester closed her eyes, launched high, and felt Ani's embrace as they dunked underwater. The sea was warm, its currents viscous, sucking onto her body like the arms of a starfish. Hester opened her eyes to a miles-long drop to the sky below. She panicked, blood surging to her head, her limbs thrashing against the waves, but the warmth held her close and she couldn't tell if it was Ani or the sea. Her head felt light and empty. Salt water slipped down her throat. Cold arms wrapped her tighter.

Hester looked into Anadil's eyes, the currents locking them together, fish brushing their legs.

"Sorry to interrupt," Dot chirped, "but what about *them*?"

Hester glanced at the guards bounding higher. They were within ten yards, teeth bared, Lion badges hooked to their armor, reflecting a witch's darkening glare . . .

"What goes up must come down," Hester vowed.

Three friends lit their fingers.

A helix of glow attacked the wall, red, green, and blue, crisscrossing and searing through chocolate. Fudge spewed into guards' faces, the meringue cracking like glass. But the men kept climbing, the first guard within range of the sea. With a bloody yell, he primed to jump at Anadil. Hester locked eyes with him, redoubling her glow—

The wall combusted under his hands.

Chocolate, cream, and meringue shattered, spraying into the air, as the Borna guards plummeted, screams echoing before they were lost to the sun.

"Let's go," Hester ordered, paddling upside down into fog. "Don't know how long we'll last with blood filling our heads like this."

But Dot stayed in place, eyes pinned downwards, throat bobbing, as if their survival had come at a cost she wasn't ready for.

"Dot?"

She turned to her coven mates, both shadowed in mist.

Anadil's red eyes pierced through.

"They wouldn't have mourned for you," she said.

ANADIL HAD ASKED a pertinent question: If the [...] caves was said to be poisonous, why were the witches still alive.

Prowling through fog, heads hanging out of the water, they hunted for the caves, alert for poison. But all they found was more inverted sea, the fog breaking to reveal open water again and again, until Hester's head was so swollen with blood that she began to hallucinate tiny Easter bunnies. Anadil and Dot, too, were swimming slower and slower, their eyes rolling to the backs of their skulls, as if they were lost in their own visions—

"*Stop*," Hester said, throwing out her arm.

Ani and Dot collided with her.

Ahead, the upturned sea ended in a waterfall, plunging at impossible speed . . .

. . . into a new sea, down below, the sky restored overhead.

"Who knew I'd be so excited for a sea to be where it should be," Anadil said.

"Waterfall must be the end of the kingdom," Dot assessed.

But any comfort the witches had in seeing the Woods right side up beyond the waterfall was offset by the hue of this distant sea, thick and red, the color of rust. And, in the middle of the sea: an island of towering rock. The surface of this rock looked like a clock face, with an opening to a cave at every hour—twelve Caves of Contempo in all.

The cave openings were well-protected. First by a rim of sharp rock spikes around the perimeter of each cave. And second, by a mob of long, spiny-white creatures with black-toothed snouts, floating through the red sea around the island . . .

"*Crogs*," said Dot.

"Special taste for girls," Hester added, remembering the beasts that guarded the old School for Boys.

"Maybe that's what they mean by 'poisoned' sea," Anadil guessed.

A seagull glided over it, letting its feet touch the water—

The bird vanished in an acid char of smoke.

"No, they mean actually poisoned," said Dot.

Head hanging, Hester studied the waterfall ahead, a vertical straight shot, blue sea to red, upside down to right side up, a dividing line between a world in chaos and the hope of setting things right.

Now they just had to find a way to cross it.

"That's a death plunge, first off," Hester said. "Then poisoned water. Girl-eating crogs. Armored rock. Caves that mess with time."

"Can your demon fly us one by one?" said Anadil, voice stuffy from all the time inverted. "Like he did at the Four Point?"

"That was a stone's throw. This is half a mile," Hester dismissed, her demon quivering, afraid to fly. "We need a cocoon or raft to ride in. Something to survive the fall."

"Made from what?" Anadil prompted. "What don't crogs eat?"

"Boys!" Dot piped, her face perilously red. "That's how Sophie evaded them at school. By turning herself into a boy."

"Well, we don't have that option, or is there something

about you that we don't know?" Hester blistered.

"Crogs eat *everything*, though," Dot lamented, watching the spiny creatures wrestle over the last of the seagull. "Well, except each other . . ."

Hester wasn't listening.

She was watching a shadow in the fog behind Anadil, getting bigger . . . bigger . . . Hester's finger glowed, prepared to attack—

Slowly, she lowered it.

It was a boat.

A small dinghy, hanging out of the upturned water, made from white wood.

No, not wood, Hester realized as it floated closer . . .

"Bones," she said, gaping at it.

"*Crog* bones," said Anadil, mystified.

The boat had no passengers. No captain.

Like a ghost ship, it moved silently, deliberately, until it stopped hard in front of the coven. Hester held her breath, shielding her friends—

Two rats poked heads up from the prow, like stealth pirates.

"My babies!" Anadil gasped. "You're alive!" She hugged her pets to her chest, then spotted the scrapes and gashes on their bodies, their fur caked with dried blood. "What's happened?" she asked and listened attentively as they babbled in her ear.

"They found Merlin in the caves," Anadil translated breathlessly. "Then one went to tell Dovey where he was, while the other built this boat, knowing the Dean would send someone to rescue him."

"Wait. How'd a rat build this? These are crog bones," said Dot, bewildered. "How'd a rat kill crogs?"

"Talented rats, remember?" Anadil grinned.

The rats started inflating, bigger, bigger, the size of dogs, the size of tigers, the size of elephants, teeth sharpening to fangs. They loomed over Dot in the water—

"I get it," said Dot.

The rats shrank down, showing off the wounds they'd gotten in the fight. But then they looked at Dot and seemed to remember something, their faces sobering. Together, they whispered to Anadil. The pale witch tensed, her gaze moving to the boat's basin.

Wedged between panels of bone was a bloody Sheriff's badge, the gold crest of Nottingham dented and scratched.

Dot went still.

A rat flipped the badge over.

The back was covered in desiccated fireflies, flickering with light, as if they'd held on to life as long as they could.

Gently, the rat stroked the fireflies' bellies.

Shades of orange filled in across their bodies, forming a projection from the past. This was footage from the dark Woods, footage the fireflies had captured of the Sheriff of Nottingham, soaked in blood, cradled by Sophie as he spoke his last words.

"Tell Dot . . . me and her mother . . . it was love," the Sheriff breathed.

The fireflies went dark.

Slowly Hester and Anadil lifted eyes to the Sheriff's daughter.

"Those were scim wounds," Dot said. She picked up her father's badge. Held it close to her chest. "The Snake killed my dad. Japeth *killed* him."

There was a calm to her. A quiet rage.

"Tedros will win the tournament. Even if I have to die to help him," Dot promised, steel-cold. "Excalibur will take that scum's head."

She turned to her friends. "Get in the boat."

Hester and Anadil obeyed.

With the rats pushing from below, Dot seized on to the prow, teeth clenched, eyes afire, as the bone-boat surged forward, plummeting over the fall.

She was the only one who didn't scream.

HESTER AND ANADIL clasped hands as the boat drifted through crogs, their crocodile snouts sniffing at the witches, drool coating their black teeth. Some snapped their jaws, others blew steam through nostrils, but none attacked, recognizing the threat of the bony vessel in which the girls rode.

Dot was relishing their frustration, Hester noticed, the round-bellied witch posed with a foot atop the fore, Anadil's rats on her shoulders, her dress stained with chocolate, like the least menacing sea captain ever. There were times over the years when Hester wondered if Dot was put in the right school . . . if her sweetness and sympathy and soft heart should have made her an Ever instead. But watching Dot clutch her father's bloody badge, her eyes pinned to the brewing crogs, daring them, *wanting* them to attack, Hester sensed a darkness that her friend had held in reserve.

A fly hovered near Dot's ear. *Pzzt. Pzzt.*

Dot snatched it dead.

Hester and Anadil exchanged glances.

Perhaps the School Master had placed their roommate well after all.

As the boat approached the island, Hester saw that penetrating the caves would be no easy feat. First, there was a crumble of jagged rock, twenty feet high, before the main thrust of stone even began—a smooth, circular tower, rising off the crumble, with the entrance to the dozen caves symmetrically arranged at the hours, each opening barbed with closely packed spikes. To rescue Merlin, they'd have to scale the rock heap, regather at the base of the caves, and hope the one with the wizard was closer to the six o'clock end at the bottom than the twelve o'clock end up top.

"Which cave is he in?" Anadil asked her rats.

The rats squeaked back.

"Two o'clock," Anadil groaned.

Hester wasn't surprised. There was too much on the line for this to be easy.

As the witches started climbing, another fly besieged Dot,

this one peskier and more frenzied than the last.

"Today is *not* the day to mess with me," she seethed, swatting at it.

"Wait!" Hester cried, staying her hand just in time.

It wasn't a fly.

The witches kneeled atop a flattish rock, looking up at Tinkerbell, sour-faced and droopy-winged, clearly having flown a long way to see them and resenting both the journey and murder attempt. Panting hard, the fairy drew a wad of parchment from her green dress and stuffed it at Hester, who quickly opened it—

Merlin's Beard
Bloodbrook Inn

"Agatha's handwriting," said Anadil.

"Merlin's beard?" Dot questioned. "What kind of message is that?"

"Answer to Tedros' first test," Hester decoded. "Merlin's beard must be what the Green Knight wanted. Agatha's telling us that they need it. That they need *us*."

"Why Bloodbrook Inn, then?" Anadil asked.

"Halfway between Camelot and Borna Coric. Must be on their way there," Hester ventured. "Bloodbrook's inn is famously haunted. No one ever checks in. It'll be a safe meeting place. Right, Tink?" She turned to the fairy. "We figured out Japeth is king. Killed Rhian and took his name. Which means the Snake's trying to win the first test too."

Tinkerbell jingled, ratifying her conclusions.

Relief burned through Hester's chest. If Merlin's beard was the answer, then clearly Japeth hadn't figured it out. He was headed to Putsi, after all. Nowhere near the wizard.

"This is why our side will win. Because we work together. Because we finish *missions*," Hester boasted, reminding her friends that they'd doubted her. She turned to Anadil's rats. "And you're sure Merlin's inside the caves? That he's still alive?"

The rats responded. "Heard him snoring under his cape," Anadil translated.

"Caves didn't curse him, then," Hester said, resuming her climb. "He is a wizard, after all." She looked back at Tinkerbell. "Tell Agatha we'll be there by nightfall."

Hester scaled higher, watching the fairy fly off. Dot and Anadil followed, the coven pulling over rocks swiftly, bolstered by Agatha's message and the ease of this climb compared to sky-high chocolate. By the time the witches reached the base of the caves, clouds had moved in, a harsh rain falling.

"Doesn't look like anyone's been here in a while," said Anadil, scanning the island perimeter. "No footprints."

"For good reason," said Dot. "Daddy told me the tale of 'The Ill-Timed Queen.' The Storian's history of a queen who discovered the Caves of Contempo that didn't obey time. One of these caves kept the queen and her king young forever. Meanwhile, their children continued to grow old, and soon older than her and the king. Unsettled, the queen tried another cave to keep pace with them, to age her and the king just enough . . .

only to mistime it and revert her and the king to their *real* ages, well over a hundred years old, upon which they dropped down dead. That's why, to this day, rulers of Borna Coric keep the caves fortified and off-limits—not just to stop trespassers from using them, but to stop *themselves*."

Hester thought back to those royal statues in the square: the king and queen, who looked younger than their own children . . . A fitting fairy tale for a realm upside down . . .

Anadil's rats were already bounding up the cave face, dodging the lethal spikes and landing on the barbs outside the two o'clock hole, squeaking urgently for the witches to follow.

Dot probed one of the spikes around the lowest cave, drawing blood at the touch. "No way can we climb all the way up there without getting skewered like a kebab."

Hester looked into the rain. "Dot's talent got us to the sea. Ani's talent got us to the caves." Her dark-painted lips curled into a grin. "*My* talent gets us inside."

The demon on her neck swelled with blood, teeth gnashing, claws flexing . . . this time, ready to fly.

DOT WAS FIRST. Then Ani. By the time the demon flew Hester up, she felt the toll it had taken on them both. His heaving breaths sucked her lungs; his weakened muscles ached as her own. She didn't know where she began and her demon ended. All she knew was between the torture to get to this island and now her soul pushed to its limits, she'd willingly sacrifice a few years of age to crawl into one of these caves and take a nap.

Dot and Anadil were farther down the tunnel, staring upwards.

Anadil blinked. "From the outside, I didn't expect it to be so . . ."

"Pretty," said Dot.

The cave walls were like an aurora borealis frozen in time, a bloom of a thousand neon glows, coated in a glittery sheen. Even Hester found herself hypnotized by the storm of colors, instinctively reaching a hand for the glitter—

Loud squeaks stopped her.

She looked at Anadil's rats, eyes glowing up ahead. They shook their heads.

Hester lowered her hand.

Quickly, the witches tracked the rats through the bending caves, turning off at new forks every few paces, like an impossible maze. And yet somehow the rats knew their way, even with the colors changing at every turn—atomic orange, alien green, sizzling yellow—as if they were burrowing into the deepest part of a rainbow. Soon, they reached a new fork in the path, and for a moment, the two rats diverged, before they glanced at each other and began gibbering intensely.

"Each is saying Merlin is the other way," Anadil muttered.

The rats persisted arguing, neither giving in.

"Take Dot and go right," said Hester. "I'll go left."

"And leave you on your own?" Anadil asked, wary.

"Have your rat, don't I?" said Hester. She patted her demon. "And him."

Anadil frowned at the shriveled tattoo on Hester's neck, clearly in no shape to protect anyone, but Hester was already splitting off, following her rat.

She kept her head down, the tunnel dimming as she went, the colors muting from fluorescing pastels to steel blues, amber browns, foggy grays. She could only see a few yards ahead now. Then Hester noticed a roach skittering overhead, lit by the glow of the ceiling. Suddenly glitter from the ceiling dusted its body, magically shrinking the roach into a young larva, oozing along . . . before glitter of another color coated it and aged it back to a mature insect . . . Onward the roach plowed, old then young, young then old, intent on its destination. Agatha had been a roach like this once, Hester remembered, trying to help Sophie find love. Little did Agatha know Sophie would be the *real* bug in her story. It was Sophie who'd kissed Rhian . . . Sophie who'd thought the Lion a friend instead of a foe . . . Sophie who'd confused Good with Evil . . . Fitting, wasn't it? That a mix-up had been the seed of all these thorns. For it had been a mix-up that had brought Sophie and Agatha to this world in the first place: two girls dropped into the wrong schools . . .

Meanwhile, Hester made sure not to touch any walls.

A rhythmic snuffle echoed from up ahead. *Ffft . . . Ffft . . . Ffft . . .*

Hester's muscles clamped. "Merlin?" she called out.

Ani's rat was scuttling faster now, into a dark part of the passage where the colors faded away. Hester couldn't see anything: not the rat, not the walls, not even her feet. She lit her finger, casting red glow at a dead end ahead, a solid wall lacquered with glittery sheen.

The snuffling grew louder. *Ffft. Ffft. Ffft.*

"Merlin?" Hester tried again.

The closer she got to the dead-end wall, the more she saw shimmer slipping off before magically replenishing, the glitter cascading to the stone floor of the cave.

Then she saw it.

Pressed against the wall, buried in glitter.

A purple cape, swaddled around a lump, the snuffling emanating from beneath.

Hester welled tears of relief.

"Merlin, it's me," she gasped, rushing towards his cape. She knew better than to touch the glitter on it. Using her finger-glow, she magically swept the velvet away, flinging the glitter against a wall and revealing the wizard's body beneath.

Hester gasped.

She fell backwards in shock, her demon letting out the screams Hester couldn't get out of her own throat.

No no no no no no.

She turned to run . . . to find her friends . . . to find help . . .

"Hester!" a voice cried behind her. "Hester, come quick!"

She turned to see Anadil sprinting towards her—

It was only when the witches saw each other's faces that they both stopped cold.

Because whatever horror each had found in their cave . . . it seemed the other had found something worse.

By the time they made it to Bloodbrook, it was nightfall.

The inn was pitch-dark, save a tiny flicker of light in a window on the top floor.

They were prepared to stun the innkeeper, but the Ingertroll on duty was fast asleep, slumped over her guest book, a single name printed on an otherwise blank page.

Agoff of Woodley Brink

A sign next to the register warned: *Do Not Disturb the Haunts.*

They tiptoed past the troll, witch one, two, and three.

Up the stairs they slunk, in their usual formation.

The door at hall's end was unlocked.

Agatha and Tedros sprung up from the bed, overcome with relief. So did Guinevere, Nicola, and Hort, lit by a single candle on a table. All of them looked exhausted—Hort, especially, itching at his receding fur and picking burrs out of his foot as if he'd wolf-carried the others here.

"Where is he?" Agatha lunged breathlessly, accosting Hester and Anadil. "Where's Merlin?"

"And who's *this*?" said Tedros, pointing at the woman with them. "You shouldn't have brought strangers here. You know the risk—"

"It's m-m-me," the woman said, tears rising.

Agatha and Tedros froze.

Slowly the prince and princess honed in on her the same way Hester had when she'd first laid eyes on this paunchy, middle-aged matron with brown skin, thick curls, and a chocolate-stained dress.

"*Dot?*" Agatha choked. "But . . . but . . . you're . . ."

"Old," Dot wept.

The room went so still they could hear the sounds.

Ffft. Ffft. Ffft.

Coming from under Hester's arm.

Horror trickled over Tedros' face.

"Hester . . . ," he whispered, staring at the bundle in her grip. "Where's Merlin?"

Hester's hands were shaking.

She pressed the bundle down onto the bed.

No one moved, listening to the snuffles beneath the purple velvet.

Ffft.

Ffft.

It was Agatha who had the courage to unfold the cape.

To reveal the wizard as he was now.

The answer to Tedros' first test.

Merlin, the wise.

Merlin, the powerful.

Merlin, the sweet,

sleeping,

entirely beardless,

baby.

10

AGATHA

Think Like Me

On the way to Bloodbrook, Agatha couldn't shake the thought. That they were on the wrong track.

She looked at Tedros next to her, clinging to Hort's furry shoulder, but he was lost in his own haze, no doubt still processing what they'd seen in Sader's history. A Green Knight connected by name to a Snake . . .

As the man-wolf bounded through Bloodbrook's crimson-leafed forest, Agatha knew they should be on the lookout. Japeth surely still had his magic map:

the one that tracked their whereabouts. The Snake's men would hunt them down wherever they went. Plus, they'd lost their fairy spies, who'd gotten so drunk on Pifflepaff's cotton candy that Tedros had to cut them loose after Tinkerbell went to find the witches.

But even knowing all this, Agatha struggled to keep watch. All she could think about was what Nicola and Guinevere had told her back in Pifflepaff.

About the squirrel and the nut.

"And you're sure that's what it said?" she pressed the first year and old queen, both cradled in Hort's paws. "That Japeth is heading to *Putsi*?"

"Ate the squirrelly nut and found the message inside," said Guinevere, looking nauseous from the wolf ride. "Secret note from the Queen of Jaunt Jolie to her daughter, Betty. Told her she'd given Japeth the key to the first test. And that he was on his way to Putsi."

"Stealing the squirrelly nut was a holy mess," sighed Nicola, covered in scratch marks. "With every leader against Tedros, Guinevere and I figured any royal squirrel might be carrying valuable information. But soon as this one saw us, it ran like the wind. Then its royal collar started shooting poisoned darts that almost got me in the head. I'd hardly learned magic at school—only managed to stun the squirrel's back legs. Definitely saw our faces. Hope we don't cross paths with it again."

"Murderous beavers, angry squirrels . . . What's with us and vermin?" Hort growled.

"Why is Japeth going to *Putsi*, though?" Agatha contended, asking herself as much as the others. "If he knows the answer, he should be after Merlin. But Merlin isn't in Putsi."

"Which means Japeth doesn't know the answer," Hort puffed.

"So what did the Queen of Jaunt Jolie mean about giving him a key?" Agatha asked.

Tedros snapped out of his daze. He looked at his princess edgily—

A stuttering jingle sounded and they turned to see Tinkerbell collapse on Tedros' shoulder, sweat-soaked and squeaking dully, like a bell dropped into mud.

"The witches found Merlin," Tedros translated, with a smile. "They'll meet us in Bloodbrook."

Agatha slumped with relief against Hort's fur.

"Can't Tink fairy-dust us there? My paws hurt," Hort griped.

"Tink's dust isn't the same as it used to be," Tedros sighed. "Can only fly one of us at most."

Watching him fold Tinkerbell in his pocket, the fairy peacefully asleep, Agatha tried to feel the same peace . . . to hold on to the relief that Merlin was safe . . .

And yet, that squirrelly nut still bothered her.

"Maybe the Queen of Jaunt Jolie is on our side," Nicola offered, sensing her unease. "Giving Japeth false clues to lead him astray."

"Detective Nic at it again," Hort said, patting her with his big thumb.

Agatha stayed quiet. The Queen of Jaunt Jolie had made it a point not to cross Camelot to protect her children. Why would she risk it now? Agatha had that prickly feeling again. The one she had when the story was all wrong. The Snake wielded magic and intelligence. He was always a step ahead. So how'd he end up in Putsi? How'd he end up the fool?

If Agatha had learned one thing from her fairy tale, it was this.

Go looking for the fool and eventually, the path leads straight back to you.

AGATHA GAZED AT baby Merlin fast asleep, snuffling beneath his coned hat, a half-smile on his face, somewhere in the wonderland of dreams.

The princess turned and assessed her team: two stultified witches and a third grown old; a practically comatose prince; a shaken Reader and a helpless once-queen; and a weasel boy saronged in bedsheets, having burst out of his clothes to get them here. To safety. To victory. To a baby.

With no beard.

"Caves of Contempo aged Merlin in reverse," Hester mumbled, the witch more undone than Agatha had ever seen her. "He can't be more than a few months old."

"Ani and I were on the other side of the cave. The side that ages you forward," said Dot, miserable at the sight of her jowly face, saggy arms, and frumpy curls in a mirror.

"Told you not to touch anything, you idiot," Anadil gritted, her two rats shaking their heads. "I *told* you."

"It was just a measly cockroach," Dot puled. "They make for good chocolate . . . I didn't see the dust on it . . ."

"Considered de-aging Dot on my side of the caves," said Hester, "but we were worried we'd end up with *two* babies."

Tedros buckled against a wall. "This can't be happening . . ." His face reddened like he'd been slapped. "HOW IS THIS HAPPENING! How are we supposed to get Merlin back!"

"How are we supposed to get his *beard*?" Hort clarified.

Agatha inched closer to Merlin and his rosy cheeks, his starry purple cape fanned around him, as if he was floating in a sea. His plush hat had shrunk to a baby's bonnet, drooped over his head. Fists at ears, he shivered in his sleep, lips coated with drool. He was so peaceful, so unaware. But as Agatha drew closer, a low sound echoed. Monstrous forms bulged out of the red walls: horned faces and knife-long claws, stretching against the wallpaper and looming over the baby from every direction.

Agatha froze.

So did the walls.

Tedros rushed to protect his princess—

Hester barred him.

"Haunts," she warned. "Faster you move, faster they move." She turned to Agatha. "Get the baby. *Slowly.*"

Agatha took another step. The haunts resumed their prowl towards Merlin, gnarled bodies swelling against the wallpaper, *krrck, krrck, krrck,* like the crushing of ice.

Now both Tedros *and* Hort surged to help—

The haunts spun sharply in the boys' direction, then swooped for Merlin.

"Stay back!" Agatha gasped at the boys, the creatures stretched so far out of the wall that their papered claws kissed Merlin's face. Agatha lunged to grab him—

"Careful," Nicola breathed. "Fairy tales are filled with demon babies."

Agatha hesitated. Her fellow Reader was right. They didn't know the extent of the wizard's transformation. They didn't know his powers anymore. They didn't even know what side he was on. But the haunts' claws were gathering under him from all sides, lifting the baby off the bed, towards the ceiling, where another set of claws stretched out of the plaster to receive him.

No time for fear.

Agatha seized Merlin's soft, stubby arms.

The ghosts wrested them back.

Agatha latched her fists onto Merlin's body, enduring a silent tussle, human against haunt. The more firmly she pulled, the harder the ghosts resisted, grappling the baby higher, the child caught between worlds. Merlin was well over her head now, her arms at full reach. Standing on tiptoes, Agatha struggled to force the baby down. Hard talons curled around her hands, the bulging wallpaper rough against her skin. Finger by finger, the haunts pried Merlin from Agatha, until only her thumbs clung on—

"*No!*" she cried.

Merlin's big blue eyes flew open.

The infant saw the haunts, his face coloring with fear. Then his eyes darted to Agatha, twinkling with recognition . . .

He farted with a cannon's strength, a blast so swift and loud that the haunts dropped him into Agatha's arms and shot back into the walls.

The wizard child shrieked with delight as a terrible smell filled the room.

Tedros wheezed with horror, while the rest shrank for cover. (Tinkerbell groggily poked out of the prince's pocket, only to sniff the air and pass out once more.)

"Worse than a dungbomb," Hort rasped, under the bed.

The baby clapped his hands and flashed a gummy smile at Agatha. "Mama!" he squeaked.

"We're doomed," Tedros moaned.

The others muttered in agreement.

But Agatha didn't flinch. Not at the smell (she'd grown up in a graveyard). Nor at the infant in her arms. This wasn't a demon child. This was Merlin, who'd chosen her over the haunts. Merlin, who'd just saved himself. She gazed down at the beaming wizard, blowing spit bubbles. At the moment, a baby had more nerve than its rescuers.

"We're not doomed," said Agatha, turning to her prince. "Your father left you three tests. *Tests*, Tedros. This is part of the tournament. Things going wrong. You can bet Japeth won't give up at the first sign of trouble."

The room went quiet.

Tedros glared back at her.

It was a harsh thing to say. Especially since Agatha was just as scared and bereft as he was. But if *she* had to act like the king to force her prince to stand up, then she'd do what she had to. Even if her words hurt.

His hot blue eyes locked into hers, fully aware of what she was doing. Tedros' anger cooled to guilt . . . then to steel. The Lion had stirred.

"Witches," he said. "Go back to school. Tell the teachers everything that's happened and find an aging spell that can reverse the cave's curse. Send word to us once you find it." He saw Dot quivering in the corner and gave her a wink. "Get Dot back to her young and beautiful self while you're at it."

Dot went pink, looking embarrassed but standing up straighter. Agatha knew the gift of Tedros' charm, even in the direst of moments.

"Nicola," the prince went on. "Go with my mother to Jaunt Jolie. Find out what their queen meant about giving Japeth a key. I spent time with Betty, the queen's daughter, when I was young; Queen Jacinda's loyalties to the Snake might be softer then they seem. Agatha and I will stay here. Putsi's the neighboring kingdom to the north, which means Japeth is close. But as long as we have Merlin, we're ahead of him. Once the witches find an aging spell, we'll restore Merlin's years, take the beard ourselves, and be on to the second test."

"Something's bothering me," Dot pitched, gnawing on her fingernails. "The scroll said we'd find the answer to the first test where wizard *trees* grow—"

"Not this nonsense again," Hester scowled. "The answer is Merlin's *beard*. Not some tree."

"Then why did the test mention trees at all?" Anadil contested.

Agatha felt that prickling unease again. That niggling doubt that plagued her on the way here.

"Wizard trees aren't real," Guinevere reassured, siding with Hester. "Just an expression. Comes from a fairy tale. About a tree that once grew at the Four Point."

"People thought the tree had magical powers. That it could answer any question you asked it," said Tedros. "Each of the Four Point leaders wanted the tree for themselves. That's how the Four Point War started. The war that killed Dad. Over a tree. In the end, they found it didn't have any powers at all. Just an ordinary birch. Storian told its tale as a warning."

"Think I read that story," Nicola remembered. "The tale of a king who asked a wizard tree a question and climbed it, looking for the answer, but each branch just grew into another tree and then another, until he climbed so high he was burned by the sun . . ."

"See? Just a red herring to throw us off," Hester chastised Anadil. "But if you'd like to go hunting for wizard trees with Dot, be my guest. I'll go to school alone and find a spell that can *actually* save us."

Agatha trusted Hester's confidence, her doubts lifting.

"Should we use the Flowerground from Bloodbrook to get to school?" Anadil reversed, appeasing her tattooed friend. "Never stations are lax about security. We can pretend to be

Dot's daughters. Should keep us from being recognized." (Dot let out a fresh wail.)

Meanwhile, Guinevere huddled with Nicola: "Jaunt Jolie is a few miles north. We'll be there by sunrise. Getting an audience with the queen is another matter. Knights of the Eleven protect her kingdom and they're fearsome warriors."

"Two women alone might just slip through . . . ," said the first year.

"I'll come with you," Hort insisted.

Nicola hesitated.

"You don't want me to?" the weasel asked.

"Of course I do. It's just a boy will mess up our plan—"

"A *boy*? I'm your boyfriend!" Hort blasted. "I'm not allowed to even look at Sophie, my *soulmate*, but you can slag me off like I'm any old boy off the street!"

"And here I thought I was your soulmate," Nicola replied.

Hort blinked at her, realizing what he'd said.

"Stay here with me, mate," Tedros piped awkwardly, slapping a hand on his shoulder. "A man-wolf may come in handy."

"Get a talent of your own, why don't you," Hort murmured, but Tedros was already hastening the rest through the door.

"Report back when you can," the prince ordered. "Sooner we finish the first test, the closer we are to killing the Snake."

The witches hustled out, along with Nicola and Guinevere, no one offering goodbyes. Nicola slammed the door behind her.

They were alone now: Agatha, the prince, and the weasel.

In a haunted room.

With a cursed child.

"Buggered that up, didn't I?" Hort mumbled, his eyes lingering where Nicola had left.

Tedros ignored him and huddled over Agatha's shoulder, the two of them peering down at Merlin, the infant's giggles replaced by a calm, intense stare.

"How'd he stay alive for so long in that cave?" Tedros wondered.

"Must be hungry," Hort said, cramming next to the prince. "How do we feed a baby?"

The two boys turned to Agatha.

"Don't look at me," Agatha shot back.

The baby made a gurgling noise and his wards glanced down to see Merlin clutching his tiny hat, lapping up milk, magically bubbling up from inside it.

"Wizard baby, indeed," Tedros marveled.

Merlin fussed as he finished, wiggling in Agatha's arms.

"Think you're supposed to burp him," said Hort.

"Be my guest," Agatha said, thrusting Merlin at the weasel.

Tedros intercepted him, taking the baby against his chest and gently thumping his back.

"Hi, M," he whispered.

The baby belched softly, wrapping a tiny hand around Tedros' thumb and the other around Agatha's. Princess and prince couldn't help but smile at each other.

"Thought you two were supposed to get married first," said Hort sourly. "You know. Before having a baby."

Agatha shot him a look.

"Thank the stars I wasn't an Ever," Hort grouched. "Zero sense of humor."

"Mama," the baby said, clamoring for Agatha.

"Think he likes you better," Tedros said, parceling him back to his princess. Agatha reached out, taking him—

The baby disappeared.

Everything disappeared.

Agatha was alone in the Celestium, the sky purple around her.

A bearded man sat beside her on a cloud, returned to full age.

"Merlin?" Agatha said, stunned.

The old wizard didn't look at her. Instead, he gazed straight ahead . . . at a sky full of stars, rearranging into a constellation . . . a pattern Agatha recognized . . . a symbol she'd seen only a short while before . . .

Merlin turned to her.

"*Think like me*," said the wizard.

Then he was gone.

The Celestium too.

Agatha was back at the inn, inside a muggy, dim room, her prince at her side, a baby in her arms.

Except the wizard child was watching her now, with a cryptic smile.

You did that, Agatha thought.

Merlin smiled wider.

"What is it?" Tedros asked, confused by Agatha's silence.

Clearly, neither he nor Hort had been transported. Neither had seen what she had.

Quickly, the princess lit her fingerglow. She drew it in the air with slashes of gold . . . the pattern she'd found inside Marian's Arrow and now again in the Celestium . . . the clue that both Robin Hood and Merlin had wanted her to see . . .

"This," she said, swiveling to the boys. "What is it?"

Hort and Tedros exchanged glances.

"Crest with geese on it . . . ," Hort pondered. "Putsi?"

"Definitely Putsi," said Tedros, before looking at Agatha. "Why?"

Agatha looked down at the baby, staring right at her.

Think like me.

Think like me.

Think like—

Agatha's heart thumped.

Putsi.

Now she remembered.

That file.

The one they'd dismissed.

That's where she'd seen the kingdom's name.

Deceased.

Buried in Vault 41.

Bank of Putsi.

"Sir Kay's file. The one in the Living Library," Agatha breathed. "Japeth isn't going after Merlin. He's going after Merlin's *beard*." She looked up at Tedros. "The Snake knows the answer to the test."

Tedros scoffed. "Impossible. How could he know my father's secret?"

"Because Japeth and *Sir* Japeth are linked somehow. The Snake and the Green Knight. There must be more to the story than we know," said Agatha, swaddling Merlin tight. "Come on. We have to get to Putsi. That's where the beard is—"

"But we have the beard!" Tedros fought. "Once we find an aging spell, I mean—"

"Not *that* beard! The beard the Green Knight cut from Merlin! The beard that had the wish! It must be buried with Kay's body in Putsi!" Agatha said, feeling the wizard baby grip her harder, as if she was on the right track. "That's the ending to this test. The beard. The *original* beard. The beard your nemesis is about to steal!" She shuttled Merlin to the door. "We have it all wrong. We're going to Putsi!"

"But that's where the Snake is!" said Hort.

"For a *reason*!" Agatha said. She trusted the baby in her arms more than two boys' fears. The same way she should have trusted the Snake's movements over her own. "Hurry. If it's the next kingdom east, we can go on foot!"

"Weasel's right," Tedros argued, not following her. "Can't take Merlin near Japeth. He could steal the wizard from us—we'd be handing him our best weapon—"

BOOM! BOOM! BOOM!

Pulsing slams thundered outside, like a cosmic hammer shattering the sky.

Baby Merlin started screaming, hands at his ears.

Clutching him tight, Agatha rushed to the window, the two boys flanking her.

To the east, moonlight shined down on green shoots rising, reaching up, up, up, over the land . . .

A tree, shimmering against the night, each branch blossoming into a new tree, which spawned more trees from its boughs, hundreds of them, *thousands*, higher and higher, wider and wider, the lattice of trunks and branches vanishing into the clouds.

For a split second, Agatha thought she saw bodies tossed between branches, *human* bodies, the size of acorns or leaves—

A cry echoed on the wind.

A cry she knew.

Clouds passed over the moon, sweeping the east into darkness.

Whatever she'd seen faded into the night, like a vision or a dream.

Three pairs of eyes stayed glued out the window, into the void.

Merlin's too, his shrieks gone quiet.

"Uh, guys?" Hort swallowed. "I'm sure it's just me . . . But did that kinda look like . . . you know . . ." He spun to his friends. "A *wizard tree*?"

Agatha held her breath.

One look at Tedros' face and she knew what they were both thinking.

Yes, Hort.

Yes, it did.

SOPHIE

Vault 41

The witch was back.

Sophie strutted through the feather-strewn streets of Putsi, her hair bloodred and cropped into a bob, her white dress skintight and beaded with sharp red spikes.

It was listening to her now, Evelyn Sader's old dress. Helping to disguise her. Melding to her desires. Doing exactly what she wanted it to do. She didn't trust it, of course. But as long it was on her side, she'd use it to her advantage.

Putsi's hoggishly pale citizens shot her looks, yet no one recognized her. They'd all watched the same spellcast. As far as they knew, Sophie was still a blond angel, playing house at Camelot, tending to her king.

How dare he, Sophie raged. How dare he hijack her mind. How dare he control her.

No one controlled her.

No one.

What a coward, she thought. Rhian, at least, had battled her on fair terms.

Japeth *cheated*.

Her ears still throbbed where she'd ripped out those scims.

The reckoning was nigh.

That's why she'd come to Putsi.

To find him.

To stare into his eyes as she cut out his heart.

Until now, she'd been fighting for her friends. To get Tedros and Agatha their Ever After.

Not anymore.

She was fighting for herself now.

Japeth had made this personal.

But how to find him?

All she knew is that he and Kei had set course for this bird-box yesterday. Hoping to track them, Sophie had stolen one of Camelot's horses and made it to Gillikin, where she'd caught a fairy flight from the market.

Wedged on the sea between Kyrgios and Glass Mountain,

Putsi was less a kingdom and more a port of entry, managed by cantankerous goose guards with shiny green hats, who registered new ships at the docks and patrolled the crowded streets, stopping and frisking passersby. ("Foreigners on the rise!" a goose squawked. "Can't trust anyone!") From what Sophie could glean, these "foreigners" were arriving via ships, from lands far, far away: a different side of the Endless Woods, beyond the mapped realms, with names like Harajuku and Mount Batten and Tsitsipas.

"Name. Kingdom. Business," a goose blared at each new body coming off a boat.

"Bao of Vasanta Vale," said a muscled boy with a pet griffin. "Here on royal business for the Sugar Queen."

The goose cuffed Bao in a metal collar. "Sugar Queen has no power here. King Rhian is ruler of these Woods. You're restricted to Putsi's borders until your hearing. Attempts to cross into other kingdoms will activate your collar, causing instant death."

"When's my hearing?" Bao asked.

"A hearing will determine when your hearing is," the goose said. "Next!"

The dusty port was packed with these collared immigrants, seeking clearance into the Woods, along with sour natives, resentful of sharing their city. Word of the tournament had spread here too, with merchants selling cheap Lion crowns for Rhian supporters and Snake crowns for Tedros'. No one was buying the latter. It'd been like this in Gillikin too, Sophie thought. Arthur's will taken seriously. Rhian the presumed winner. They had no idea, of course, that Rhian wasn't Rhian. That the real Snake was their *king*. A traitor to everything Arthur stood for.

Sophie combed the streets, hunting for Japeth. But there were neither signs of his or Kei's horses, nor a royal palace, where he'd have been received—

A trumpet of squawks erupted overhead, as hundreds of geese flew towards the docks from all over the kingdom, awaiting an incoming ship.

No, not a ship, Sophie saw, milling closer.

A *palace*, floating in from offshore, mint-green with gold minarets, scorched in places as if it had been recently attacked. Goose guards kept patrol on the balconies.

The doors flung open and down the dock came Empress Vaisilla, crystal crown askew, swaddled in a goose-feather stole. She paraded past the goose captain, who hustled to keep up, his army of winged guards waddling behind, the Empress throwing shaded looks at anyone with a monitoring collar.

"Good-for-nothings," the Empress murmured as Sophie eavesdropped. "Kingdom Council votes to let them in, because *they* don't have to deal with them. 'Vaisilla's problem! Let them overrun her land like pests!'" Her shoes squashed through goose dung. "Perhaps King Rhian will have sense to ignore the Council and close our borders once and for all—"

She turned sharply and barreled straight into Sophie.

"Idiot," Empress Vaisilla hissed, shoving past her and sidling closer to her captain. "Rhian is riding to the bank. We'll meet him at Albemarle's office. Listen to this: I've heard from

my spies in Camelot that Sophie's gone *missing* from the castle and might be joining the rebels . . . Seems she's up to her old tricks. Send our scouts into the Woods. If we catch her, we'll arrange a trade to Rhian for a seal on our borders—"

Her eyes widened. She stopped cold and whirled to the idiot she'd bumped into . . .

But all she found was feathers and dust.

ALBEMARLE.

Sophie knew that name.

Tedros had a business card with it: *Albemarle, Bank Manager.* He'd found the card with a bank ledger for "Camelot Beautiful" amongst Lady Gremlaine's letters to King Arthur.

Now Sophie just needed to find this bank manager and wait for Japeth to arrive . . .

The Bank of Putsi imposed against the sunset, a circular, jade-green fortress, crowned with flags from around the Woods. Carved into the face of the bank was a gold inscription:

BETWEEN GOOD AND EVIL
LIES
TRUST AND TRADITION

Here, there were no goonish geese or chaotic mobs; the streets were clean and lined with sword-armed men, their chainmail branded with crests from an array of kingdoms, as if the area around the bank was a protected zone, like the Four Point.

As she darted up the steps, Sophie glanced over the rail at a fenced-in plot, where visitors to the bank had secured their horses, magic carpets, and other transports. Still no sign of Rhian's or Kei's horses. Squawks echoed and she turned to see the Empress and her goose caravan nearing the bank. Sophie barreled up the last steps, flashing a flirty smile at a guard with a flip of her new red hair, then scooted through the doors before he could get a better look.

The interior of the bank was a jade temple, rising in a cylindrical hollow to three different levels rimmed by floor-to-ceiling glass, each glass panel stenciled with lettering. The first level up: BRONZE BANKING, packed with patrons in line; the second level: SILVER BANKING, with neon-haired nymphs serving rose water to customers on couches; and the top level, almost higher than Sophie could see, DIAMOND BANKING, obscured by tinted glass. Meanwhile, the bank's atrium, rising all the way to the ceiling, held three statues of gold phoenixes, frozen midair in different poses, like a pretentious art installation.

A bank manager would be somewhere up there, Sophie thought. But there were no staircases on the lobby level. No receptionists or concierge. Down here, the marble was completely bare, except for a quick-moving line of customers waiting for something. Sophie cut to the front, spotting three white circles on the floor. One of these circles started glowing, words materializing inside: **NEXT CUSTOMER**.

The first woman in line, an elegant dowager, stepped into the circle—

Instantly one of the phoenixes came alive, swooping down and seizing her so fast Sophie almost missed it. The statue flew the woman up to the Silver Level and deposited her through the opening in the glass, before the bird refroze in the atrium, the other two phoenixes already plunging for their next customers.

Not an art installation, after all.

Down in the lobby, Sophie inched closer to the circles, noticing the other customers shooting her threatening looks: humans, mogrifs, elves, ogres alike . . .

The next circle glowed.

"Sorry, darling," Sophie chimed, cutting off a troll.

A phoenix dove and swept her into gold-metal wings, glaring hard at her with fire-colored eyes.

"Bank manager, please," Sophie ordered.

The phoenix threw her onto the Bronze floor, where she landed in front of a desk, manned by a smelly, single-browed hag. Sophie noticed her name tag:

Goosha G.
NEW ACCOUNTS

"Poor, Rich, or Filthy Rich?" Goosha inquired, tapping on her desk, a magical tablet Sophie couldn't quite see.

"I'd like to speak with Albemarle," Sophie replied.

"Albemarle handles Diamond accounts only," Goosha snipped.

"Camelot Beautiful," Sophie said. "That's my account."

The hag gave her a prunish look. Tap, tap, tap into her desk . . .

She went still.

Goosha smiled up at Sophie. Fake and tight. The kind Sophie gave to everyone in the world except Agatha. "Thank you for banking with us. I'll fetch Albemarle. Wait right here."

She tapped a few more things, shot Sophie another cramped smile, and headed into a back office.

Sophie immediately leaned over the desk. Red words screamed against a black background—

Impostor Alert
Kill on Sight

In the desk's reflection, Sophie glimpsed armed guards coming from the left. She turned and saw more from the right.

Alarms pealed through the bank: wild and deafening, like a heartbeat out of control. The tinted glass around Diamond Level morphed to iron, locking the floor in.

"THERE!" a cloying voice cried.

Sophie's eyes flew to the Empress in the lobby, pointing up at her, the Empress's goose captain and guards spearing towards Sophie's head, beaks sharp as daggers.

Left, right, down . . . she was cornered from all sides—

Except one.

Sophie was already charging for the glass, kicking up into a flying leap and smashing through the pane, a glitter-rain of shards cascading over her as she fell past storming geese and plummeted through the atrium . . .

. . . straight onto the back of a phoenix.

The metal phoenix screeched and thrashed to life, trying to throw Sophie off its spine. Overhead, the Empress's geese swerved, dive-bombing Sophie and stabbing her with their beaks, drawing blood from her arms and thighs. More and more geese came, Sophie too besieged to light her finger, the birds slashing her head and neck, their hellish squawks melding with the alarms. Panicked crowds scattered from the Bronze and Silver Levels as Sophie's bucking phoenix accidentally batted geese through windows. Sophie couldn't see anymore, her field of view nothing but feathers and blood and falling glass, her breaths shallowing with pain—

Then it stopped.

Geese went limp and dropped out of the air, impaled by small red spikes.

Red spikes from Sophie's *dress*.

One by one they fell dead at the Empress's feet, splattering her with blood.

Empress Vaisilla let out a howl of anguish, patrons fleeing around her.

Gobsmacked, Sophie looked down at her dress, pure white now, all the red spikes gone.

For the second time, the dress had come to her rescue.

Evelyn Sader's dress.

Why?

No time to think about it.

A statue was still trying to kill her.

Make that three statues.

As her phoenix tried to fling her off, its two sisters were upon her, bludgeoning Sophie with iron wings. Together, the three statues grappled her in a headlock, wresting her higher, yet somehow Sophie still clung tight. But now she realized the birds' plans, the three hemming her close and surging towards the ceiling, faster, faster, about to crush her against the stone. Sophie tried to defend herself, but they had a steel hold. *Fight fair*, she seethed. *No one fights fair.* Fear and rage ripped through her blood, lighting up her fingertip—

The statues bashed her into the ceiling at full speed, wings crumpling to shrapnel, before the wreckage plunged, cratering into the lobby and imploding the floor.

The alarms softened . . . then stopped.

A dull silence faded over the bank, as guards and patrons peeked out at the carnage of glass, metal, and dust.

Slowly, the misshapen phoenixes grunted to life, staggering out of the crater, their smooth gold bodies steeling back to form. They smiled at the Empress, expecting to be rewarded for their cleverness, for obliterating the intruder . . .

But the Empress wasn't looking at them.

She was staring at the ceiling, where statues and prisoner had dashed against stone.

Four bodies went up.

Vaisilla had seen it herself.

But only three had come down.

MOGRIFYING OUT OF danger was a cheater's game.

But as Sophie fluttered beneath the doorway of the Diamond Level and down serene hallways sealed from the chaos outside, she didn't feel the slightest twinge of guilt. In her years at school, Good and Evil played by the rules.

But in the Camelot years?

Play by the rules and you die.

Choosing a blue butterfly had been cheeky, but even in the worst danger, Sophie had to find a way to have a *little* fun. It was Evelyn Sader who'd started all this: the twins' wicked mother, who'd duped King Arthur and borne his heirs.

At least that's what she'd seen in Rhian's blood crystal.

Except Japeth had denied it to Tedros at the wedding. She'd heard his voice inside that bubble, the scim tuned to the ones inside her head. Japeth had told the prince that he *wasn't* Tedros' brother . . . that he wasn't Arthur's son at all . . .

Truth, Lies, Present, Past . . . It was all mixed up now.

But sorting it out took short shrift to Sophie's mission.

Finding the Snake.

The Diamond Level was a luxurious fantasy, even by Sophie's standards. As her butterfly wove through, she spotted patrons getting manicures and massages, others partaking in caviar and champagne, even one doing yoga while a bank teller recited the status of their accounts. Unnaturally perfect plants spritzed rosy fragrance into the air, while a choir of green geckos floated in a soap bubble singing dulcet tones. Aside from the guards lining the iron-sealed glass, whispering into Lion badges on their armor, in touch with their colleagues outside, there were no signs that anything in the bank was amiss. Sophie drifted closer to the guards to listen.

"No sign of Sophie up here, Empress," a guard murmured into his badge. "Yes, Empress. As you wish."

He whispered to his fellow guard. "Empty the floor. King Rhian just arrived. He's been briefed on the intruder situation. Wants privacy with the Bank Manager."

Guards began rounding up tellers and patrons—a security situation, they insisted; the floor had to be cleared.

Sophie's wings beat faster. Japeth would be here any minute. She needed to find Albemarle's office and take the Snake by surprise.

Her butterfly zipped through halls, scanning workers' name tags: Rajeev, Vice President . . . Francesca, Vice President . . . Clio, Vice President . . . everyone a Vice President . . . but now Sophie spotted a room set off from everything else, its door heavy and onyx-black.

BANK MANAGER, the plaque read.

Sophie squeezed beneath the door, the space so tight it trapped her. She'd thought she'd finally shed Evelyn's dress when she mogrified, but now she could feel it burning against her thorax as if it was still on, the dress sure to reappear the second she reverted. She jammed harder under the door, about to rip her wings—*ooooof*—

And she was through.

Albemarle, the Bank Manager, was in the heat of conversation with a customer—

Sophie's butterfly leapt in shock.

Albemarle! The woodpecker!

The one from the School for Good and Evil, responsible for tallying ranks!

Sophie had known his name, of course, but she'd never entertained that a middleman at school might be moonlighting at the Woods' most prestigious bank. And yet, here he was, with his white spectacles and red-topped head, perched on a desk, with a massive steel vault looming behind him, as he argued heatedly with a patron.

That was the other surprise.

Seated opposite Albemarle was a skeletal woman with stringy gray hair, a high forehead, and thin, cutting eyes.

Sophie recognized her at once.

Bethna.

The third Mistral Sister, who'd been missing from Camelot.

"You cannot freeze a Diamond account," she contended. "It's our gold—"

"It's *my* bank to manage," said Albemarle. "And it's clear Camelot Beautiful is a fraudulent account. You and your sisters have been stealing Camelot funds and stashing them here for years. And now, *voilà*, the funds flow back to Camelot, just in time for the new king to spend it."

"Irrelevant," Bethna dismissed. "It's Rhian's money now."

"It's *Camelot's* money," Albemarle replied. "And per

Arthur's will, Camelot currently has no king to make use of that money. Not until the Tournament of Kings is won. So until Excalibur names the victor, this account is frozen."

"Let's see what your superior has to say," Bethna challenged. "Someone who I'm sure doesn't spend his free time playing janitor for *students*."

"The bank chose a woodpecker family to manage its accounts for the same reason the school did: we are planners, by nature. Which means my only superior is my father like his father before him and neither is alive for you to appeal to. As for my time at school, I'm lucky that my wings have afforded me a part-time position there when I'm not taking appointments at the bank. And I was even luckier to serve under Clarissa Dovey, who your king saw fit to execute. Like me, Professor Dovey believed money meant little without a compass for spending it." Albemarle stared Bethna down. "And like Clarissa did, I find students more worthwhile than the old and corrupt."

Bethna stood up. "When King Rhian gets here, he will correct your *error*."

"My spy tells me Rhian seeks access to Vault 41," said the woodpecker, feathers puffing. "A vault that belongs to the Four Point kingdoms. Rhian may be planning to enter Vault 41, but I have plans to stop him. It doesn't matter if those in Putsi and elsewhere slave to Rhian's word. I am master of these safes. I decide who enters." Albemarle stood tall against the steel vault. "Because only *my* touch can unlock them."

The door to the office flew open.

"Good to know," said a voice.

Gilded scims ripped across the desk, impaling Albemarle's body.

Sophie's butterfly lunged into the corner, barely eluding Japeth's boot as the Snake swept into the bank manager's office, followed by Kei.

The scims returned to Japeth's blue-and-gold suit as he kneeled down and plucked a feather from the woodpecker's corpse. Sickened, Sophie turned away, before she peeked back to see the Snake approach the steel door behind the desk and slide the feather into the lock.

The door creaked open.

"I hear Sophie's been in this bank," said Japeth.

He glanced at Kei and Bethna, then at Albemarle's dead body.

"Make it look like *she* did this," the Snake ordered.

He entered the vaults, the door closing behind him. Snapping to her wits, Sophie followed, whizzing through the shrinking gap in the steel, her wings shivering at the sudden draft. She glanced back at Kei overturning furniture, Bethna scrawling messages on the walls—"LONG LIVE TEDROS!" "THE WITCH IS BACK"—as Albemarle's blood stained the floor . . .

That's when Sophie caught Kei watching her through the last sliver of closing door, the captain tracking her butterfly with wide eyes, before the darkness sealed him off and locked her inside with the enemy.

AMBUSH IN THE dark.

That's how she would do it, Sophie thought, shadowing the Snake.

She had the beast cornered.

It would be easy.

And yet, her wings were shaking.

She couldn't remember ever being alone with the Snake. Someone had always been there between them: Agatha, Tedros, Hort . . . Rhian. But now, in the dark, she listened to his boots against stone, harsh and clipped, *clack, clack, clack*, the same rhythm he disposed of his enemies. Without pause. Without compunction.

Sophie had to punish him the same way. No hesitation. No mercy. The faster she did it, the sooner it would be over. The Woods spared. The story fixed.

Evil attacks. Good defends.

The first rule of fairy tales.

Not this time.

No one would see this attack as Evil.

It would be an act of Good.

A death well-earned.

But there were obstacles.

She was an insect, first off. A butterfly in a snake pit wouldn't last long. Try reverting to human and he'd hear her instantly, his scims shredding through her the way they had the woodpecker. Plus, it was dark, pitch-dark, to the point Sophie couldn't even see the walls or the floor or ceiling, as if she and her nemesis were floating in a starless sky. Add in the

Snake's scims and magical talents and the fact he'd murdered men bigger than her—Chaddick, Lancelot, the Sheriff, his own *brother*—and Sophie's chances didn't look good, no matter how skillfully she ambushed him. Even if she *did* manage to defeat him, she'd be trapped in this vault with no one to let her out but a bank full of enemies who'd been duped into thinking she just killed their manager.

So for now, Sophie trailed behind Japeth, keeping her distance in the seemingly endless chamber, tracing his frosty scent and the contours of his body.

Then he stopped cold.

Scims curled their heads off his suit like cobras.

"The Witch of Woods Beyond," he cooed. "The Empress claimed she'd had you killed, but I sensed her hesitation. Knew full well that you wouldn't die so easily. Not the Sophie I know. Not my *queen*. In fact, I debated going back to Camelot once you'd escaped. To find you. To punish you. But, in the end, I knew you'd come to me."

His eyes scanned the darkness, like gems in a cave. Sophie's butterfly drifted away from his gaze.

So much for an ambush, Sophie thought.

"Your school magic won't protect you for long, you know." His suit of scims turned black, vanishing him into the dark. "Girls have a stink that can't scrub off. Aric had a good way of describing it. Like a rose gone to rot. I can smell it anywhere. But you . . . I'm afraid you reek of it *worst of all.*"

Sophie's wings grazed a wall: the slightest brush against stone—

Eels shot off Japeth's suit, spearing in her direction. Sophie plunged to the ground, barely dodging them. The scims probed the bricks around her, slimy heads inches above her wings. The Snake's glowing eyes roved down, about to find her . . .

Sophie skidded forward on her tiny thorax. More eels shot off Japeth, following her sound. Sophie dove between scims, the rush of their flight blowing her into a soot-filled corner. She raised her antennae: everywhere she looked, scims hung in the air, inky black ribbons, hunting the darkness for her. Silently, she submerged in soot, blackening her wings, soaking in stale, thick-smelling dust.

Japeth didn't move.

She could hear him sniffing the air.

He waited a moment longer, as if doubting himself.

Why doesn't he light his glow? He'd see me in a second, Sophie thought. *Rhian had a fingerglow . . . which means Japeth should have one too . . .*

Unless Japeth doesn't have one, she realized.

But why would his brother have a student's glow and not him?

Japeth cursed under his breath. "Clever girl. Must have gone before we came and left her stink behind," he snarled, his scims melding back into him. Then he tensed visibly. "The vault . . . if she got there first . . ." He was already pacing ahead. Sophie could see his hand rustling against his suit, pulling something from inside . . . a furry lump . . . moving in the dark . . .

Whatever it was, it was *alive*.

Sophie floated closer to get a better look. Japeth's scim-gloved hands glinted in shadow, caressing the furry form, before he released it into midair.

The creature lit up, electric blue, phosphorescing in the dark, like the Blue Forest at midnight.

Neon glow flooded the chamber, the creature brighter than a torch in a mine, revealing rows of vault doors ahead. Sophie camouflaged herself against the wall, studying the fly-ing rodent made of spotted fur, its body shaped like a . . . *key*.

The same key the Queen of Jaunt Jolie had slipped Japeth before he'd left for Putsi. The key he said he needed to win Arthur's first test.

Vault 41. It belongs to the Four Point kingdoms, Sophie remembered. *And Jaunt Jolie is one of them. So the queen's key will open it . . . The answer to the test must be inside.*

Pieces of memory returned: a scroll fallen from the sky . . . a Green Knight come to Camelot . . . something he wanted from Arthur . . . hidden where "wizard trees grow . . ."

The key peered down the corridor, assessing its surround-ings. The top of the key was the creature's head, with a big fish eye on each side instead of a hole. The shaft was its snout, ridged with teeth, and the tip the opening to its mouth.

It turned back to the Snake, blinking at its new master.

"*Bhanu Bhanu*," it gibbered.

Then it flew down the hall, spotlighting gilded numbers on black doors, left and right, the numbers completely out of order . . . 28 . . . 162 . . . 43 . . . 9 . . . 210 . . . before it turned a corner and vanished.

"Bhanu Bhanu," the key echoed, like a homing signal to track it.

Japeth followed the key's calls, with Sophie flitting behind at a safe distance, dripping soot and trying not to cough.

She wanted to kill him.

She wanted to turn human and rip every scim off his body. And yet . . .

What would Aggie do? Sophie mulled, thinking of her best friend, somewhere in the Woods. A best friend she'd just tried to kill at the wedding to Japeth. Sophie remembered the horror in Agatha's eyes, seeing Sophie under the Snake's control, manipulated into hurting those she loved. But now Sophie was free. She'd come this far. Agatha would be proud. *What would she tell me to do?*

Follow him, she'd say.

Follow the bastard to Vault 41.

Let him find the answer to the first test.

Then steal it from him.

Whatever was in that vault, Sophie had to get it first.

"Bhanu Bhanu," the key blipped.

Butterfly hunted Snake now, her tiny chest beating with the power of two hearts. Right and left she flew, around bends, whisking between vaults—*"Bhanu Bhanu," "Bhanu Bhanu"*— deep into the bowels of the bank, before finally catching up with the key, stopped in front of a door, a vault number gleaming in blue glow.

41

The key stabbed into the lock and yanked the door open, before zipping upwards, gluing to the ceiling, and illuminating the inside of the vault like a skylight.

Japeth swung into the chamber, Sophie's butterfly hot on his heels. Hiding behind the open door, she poked her head over hinges.

Her bug eyes bulged.

Inside the modest room, four copper walls reflected the contents of Vault 41.

There was no gold, no jewels, no treasures.

Instead, there was a tree.

It was a white birch, rooted in the stone floor, with four spindly branches and a broad trunk, slashed with black patches. From each branch hung a small white box, like a Christmas ornament, carved with Camelot's seal.

Japeth grazed his fingers across one of these boxes, looking for an opening . . .

A powdery substance chafed off it, as if the box was made of dust.

"I'd be careful if I was you," said a low, smooth voice. "Human ashes are more delicate than you think."

Japeth pulled his hand away. Sophie gawked at the four boxes, dangling from the tree.

Human ashes?

"And one more thing," said the voice.

Suddenly, Japeth's magical suit curdled, his army of scims crumbling to the floor, like a gameboard upended. The Snake was laid bare, save a strip around his waist.

"No magic in the vaults," the voice finished.

It was the *tree* speaking, Sophie realized, its eyes and mouth formed out of the dark slashes in its bark.

"Beyond the door, you may recover your powers, whatever they may be," said the tree to the Snake.

Quickly Sophie drew back, her wings dangerously close to crossing the plane of the door. One more inch and she would have reverted to human, with nowhere to hide.

The tree continued addressing the Snake. "If you've come this far, you must know this vault safeguards the ashes of Sir Kay. Or more officially, Sir Japeth Kay of Camelot, son of Sir Ector of Camelot and foster brother to King Arthur. It was Kay's will to be cremated and Arthur's will to protect his once-brother's ashes, entrusting them to the Four Point leaders, who maintain this vault. None of them know that Sir Kay was the Green Knight. No one knows the truth of what happened between Arthur and his brother. But *you* do. You have learned what the Green Knight came to Camelot to obtain. *This* is what Arthur wanted his heir to know. The story behind Sir Kay's death. The wish that led to it. Because knowledge is the first step to true power. Except the test is not yet passed. Not until you find the answer you've come here for."

The tree bent its trunk towards the Snake. "Yet which bough holds this answer? Four safeboxes . . . but you only get *one* choice. The true heir of Arthur will feel in his blood where the answer lies. Choose the right box and its contents are yours. Choose the wrong one and . . ."

From the walls, a hundred steel spikes crashed in, slicing

towards the Snake's pale body from every direction, stopping only a hair's width short.

The tree stared hard at Japeth. "Choose wisely."

Without a sound, the spikes retracted into the walls.

Sophie watched as Japeth moved across the four boxes, his cold blue eyes inspecting each one. That they were made of human ashes didn't faze him in the slightest, nor did the chill in the vault, his lean torso hunched forward as he moved between boughs.

What is he looking for? Sophie thought. *What did the Green Knight want?*

It didn't matter.

Whatever it was, she couldn't let Japeth have it.

Assuming he chose the right box, that is.

If he didn't, well . . . problem solved.

At the moment, the latter seemed more likely. The Snake seemed no closer to choosing a box, the four casings of ash identical in every way—

Except then he paused.

The second box.

Something about it stopped him.

The Snake drew closer, his nose to the ashes.

Now Sophie spotted it: the subtle green glow pulsing at its center each time Japeth drew close.

"Oh, that is *unexpected*," said the tree smoothly. "It's not Arthur's soul you're kin to . . . it's the *Green Knight's* . . ."

Japeth's long fingers curled around the box, ashes crumbling off it, the green glow throbbing harder, brighter . . .

The tree searched the Snake's eyes. "Most unexpected. So *who are you*?"

Japeth crushed the box, ashes spewing into the air.

The other three boxes magically combusted too, clouding the vault with dust.

Left hanging on the Snake's branch was a lock of white hair, curled inside a glowing, clear-coated pearl the size of a coin.

The tree seemed to frown. "You've chosen correctly. Merlin's beard is yours," it spoke. "Swallow the pearl to finish the first test. Only then can you learn the second."

Japeth grinned, the hard steel of his gaze returned, any doubts about the outcome of the tournament quelled. He reached up to claim the pearl—

CRACK!

The Snake whirled to see the vault door rip off its hinges and crash into the room. He leapt out of its way, almost crushed by the heavy slab. Startled, he lunged towards the hall—

No one there.

The Snake went back to the tree—

Merlin's beard was gone.

The pearl missing.

The tree wearing a vague smile.

Japeth gaped for a moment, as if he must be seeing wrong.

That's when he caught it.

In the vault's copper walls.

The distorted reflection of a girl's bare skin.

He whirled around.

Sophie was backing out of the vault, Evelyn Sader's white

dress magically re-forming on her body.

Merlin's pearl was in her hand.

Witch and Snake watched each other across the threshold.

Sophie eyed his undressed body.

"The emperor really has no *clothes*," she said.

Scims flew onto the Snake the moment he crossed the door, eels rocketing off his suit for her—

But Sophie was already ahead, running deeper into the vaults, taking any turn she could, hearing the eels whizzing behind her. She knew there had to be an end to this maze as she swerved around corners, losing more and more scims, until the thrum of the pack became a softer buzz, then a lonely squeal, a single eel left, until she was chased only by silence and the choked sounds of her breath. She clutched the pearl with the beard tighter, slippery in her palm. She'd hide here until she could escape and find Agatha. She'd bunker for days, weeks, whatever it took. She had Tedros' salvation in her hand. She'd won the opening test for him. She'd outwitted the enemy. As long as she was the one with Merlin's beard, the prince was ahead in the race. All she had to do was wait. Relief hit her hard—

So hard she didn't see it coming.

The single, sharp blow to the back of her head.

She gasped, more at the irony than the pain.

Ambushed in the dark.

A witch dead instead of a Snake, falling, falling, gone before she ever hit the ground.

12

SOPHIE

Back to the Beginning

When you're sure you've died, it's strange to wake up.

Especially to the sound of two boys who are very clearly in love.

"Look, Willam, she's got it. She's got Merlin's beard!"

"Shouldn't have hit her that hard, Bogden. She's a girl!"

"My sisters beat me up all the time. You're the one who told me to stop her—"

"I meant call her *name*, like a civilized person."

"Snake would have heard us!"

"Do you clods ever shut up?" growled a third voice, deep and gravelly, as Sophie felt rough fingers pry apart her eyelids. "Pupils dilated . . . nostrils flared . . . Just a bit of shock. It's how I wake up after a good night at the Arrow. Or used to, at least."

Sophie's eyes flickered open to a ruddy, handsome face, floppy red-brown curls dangling over his brow.

"R-R-Robin?" she sputtered.

"Nice hair," Robin Hood cracked, glancing at her bright red bob. "So inconspicuous. A wonder no one noticed you."

Sophie sat up to a dark vault, the faces of Willam, Bogden, and Robin lit by the weak glow of Merlin's pearl. She could feel a lump rising off her skull, pain pulsing behind her eyes. More disconcerting, the floor was moving. Sophie looked down at a mass of gold coins shifting beneath them like cold, hard sand.

"Where are we?" Sophie breathed. "H-h-how are you here?"

"Remember when Reaper gave us our missions in Gnome-land?" Willam started. "Bogden and I were supposed to keep our eye on Camelot—"

"Then that shady Mistral Sister leaves the castle, so we tailed her to Putsi," Bogden finished. "Plus, Willam is obsessed with geese."

"I fed a duck at Camelot *once* and now I'm obsessed with geese—"

"You should be happy I care enough to pay attention, Willam. Can't say you do the same for me."

"How was I supposed to know you're a *vegetarian*?"

Definitely in love, Sophie thought.

"Meanwhile, I was on my way here," said Robin. "Couldn't stay in Sherwood. Not after the Sheriff and I joined forces. So I left Marian in a sanctuary on Glass Mountain. Figured she and I could sail across the Savage Sea, start somewhere fresh. Needed money first, so I came to my vault. All those years of raiding the rich to help the poor—skimmed a bit off the top in case Marian and I needed a nest egg."

"A nest egg?" Sophie said, ogling the swamp of coins. "This looks like the entire nest."

Robin ignored her. "Left clues at the Arrow about where I was headed, in case you lot tried to find me. Soon as I get to Putsi, I run into William and Boggins, and before I know it, guards seize us and bring us to the woodpecker's office."

"Turns out Albemarle needed our help. He'd heard the Snake was coming for Vault 41, where the answer to Arthur's first test was," Willam picked up. "Bird said he'd try to stop the Snake from getting it. But if he failed, it'd be up to us."

"So we hide in Robin's vault nearby . . . then eavesdrop on the Snake and tree and find out it's Merlin's beard he's after . . . ," said Bogden. "And we wait to ambush him—"

"Only to see *you* come out with the beard instead of the Snake," said Willam.

"And here we are," said Robin. "A girl, a beard, two idiots, and me."

"It's not like you did anything to help!" Bogden heckled.

"Who do you think was distracting the scims from chasing the lass!" said Robin.

"But how are we supposed to get *out* of here?" Sophie asked, pointing a lit finger at her hair and reverting it long and blond. "The Snake's hunting us! Not to mention the Empress and her geese and the bank guards. The second we leave the vaults, we're dead!"

"Bird said his spy would get us out when the time came," Robin touted. "Same spy that told him the Snake was on the way."

"Bird is *dead*," Sophie scorned, seeing Robin flinch. "And so is his spy, no doubt!"

"Plenty of doubt, I'd say," spoke a voice.

Behind them, a body surfaced, rising out of gold like a wakened dragon. Coins sloughed off tan, young skin, the whites of two eyes piercing the darkness.

"Woodpeckers plan for *everything*, remember?" said the stranger.

Sophie shined the pearl's glow, lighting up a familiar girl with brown hair, a pointed nose, and a toothy smile.

She was sucking on a red lollipop.

"Bettina is the name. Executive Editor of the *Camelot Courier*," the girl said, sitting up in a tall pastel dress. She honed in on Sophie. "Nice to meet you. I don't count the last time when you were being mind-controlled by a twin-killing *Snake*."

Sophie's eyes widened.

It was the girl from the press briefing.

The one who knew Japeth was a fraud.

The one who knew everything.

"My mother is the Queen of Jaunt Jolie," Bettina explained, her voice light and fast. "I figured out quick that Rhian was dead and the Snake had taken his place. My mother didn't believe me until she went to visit 'Rhian' and had a good look at him and realized you were under his control. The Snake demanded her key to the Four Point vault and my mother sent a squirrelly nut to warn me. Nut got stolen by rebels—friends of yours, I'm assuming—but the squirrel found me and relayed my mother's message. I'd been hiding in Putsi to begin with; it's easy to disappear here."

"No kidding. Try finding Willam in a goose flock!" said Bogden. He saw Willam's stare. "You know, long neck . . . big nose . . . the way you waddle when you . . . Never mind."

"I was afraid the Snake might win the first test, so I went to see Albemarle, who'd spotted these two with Robin around the bank," Bettina continued. "So the woodpecker and I forged a plan. He'd enlist Robin to stop the Snake from getting into Vault 41. If his team succeeded, I would help them escape. If they failed, I would stop the Snake myself." She peered at Sophie. "Woodpecker planned for everything but you."

Sophie's head thrummed with questions. "But the Queen of Jaunt Jolie said her eldest's name was Betty—"

Bettina.

Betty.

Betty who'd been passed over by the School Master.

"*Doesn't need that school or the Storian*," the queen had said.

"Betty's found her own way to tell tales."

Sophie bristled. "So the *Courier* knew Rhian and the Snake were in cahoots all along? That they staged the attacks?"

"Why didn't you do something, then?" Willam attacked Bettina. "If you and your staff were on the run, why didn't you help us?"

"There *is* no staff," Bettina said, her voice hardening. "The rest fled after Rhian put out a warrant for us. Almost got caught myself when I snuck into Sophie's wedding briefing; luckily I had a mole at Camelot who gave me a hex to escape."

"So your mother must be on our side too," Sophie followed. "She can give us her Knights of Eleven!"

"My mother is on her *own* side," Bettina corrected. "That's why she surrendered her key to Japeth, even knowing he's the Snake. She'll do anything to protect her family. Regardless of who is king."

Willam started to ask something, but Bettina waved him off. "We're wasting time," she said, pointing at the pearl in Sophie's palm. "Tedros has to swallow that and find out what the second test is—before the Snake catches us. Which means first we need to *find* Tedros."

"First we need to get out of this *vault*," Sophie pointed out.

Bettina frowned, as if there wasn't room for two leaders. "Albemarle put me here to help you escape, remember?"

"But we can't go through the bank!" Sophie reminded. "The whole Woods will slaughter us!"

"We're not going through the bank," Bettina clipped, sucking on her lollipop as she headed for the door. "You're a Reader, aren't you?" She glared back at Sophie. "Should have read that first test more *carefully*."

OUTSIDE VAULT 41, Willam kept a lookout. "Bogs, we clear?"

"Clear!" Bogden called somewhere far away.

"Make goose noises if we're not!" Willam called back.

Inside the vault, Bettina and Sophie stood in front of the old birch tree, which looked dull and ordinary, no longer showing any signs of life.

"Last line of Arthur's clue," said Bettina. *"'Now go and find it where wizard trees grow . . .'"*

"Yeah and I already found '*it*,'" Sophie frowned, holding up the pearl in the vault's blue light. "Why are we back here? We have the answer. We have the beard. Now we need to escape—something a *tree* can't help with—"

"Why do you think this tree is in the Four Point vault?" Bettina responded. "Why do you think Arthur hid his first test here? The War of the Four Point was fought over *this* tree."

"*This* is a wizard tree? The tree that can answer any question asked of it?" Robin asked, assessing it skeptically. "I thought it was just legend."

"Legends exist for a reason," said Bettina. "Enough blood was shed over this tree for the Four Point leaders to lock it here forever. But a good reporter always finds the truth." She stepped towards the tree. "Let me do the talking. Whatever you do, don't ask it any questions—"

"This is ridiculous," Sophie poohed, shoving in front of her. "A tree can't get us out of a bank!" She knocked on its bark mockingly. "Hellllooo, Wizard Tree . . . can you show us a way out?"

"*No!*" Bettina gasped—

The tree stirred awake, with a groggy shiver. "It's been a long time since someone asked me a *question*," he said, opening his eyes at Sophie. "Ah. *You.* Well, well. '*Can you show us a way out?*' Not elegant. Ill-conceived. Poorly phrased. But a question, nonetheless. Ask a Wizard Tree and you shall receive. Your answer awaits . . ."

The tree opened its mouth wide, revealing a hole filled with gooey green moss.

Sophie jumped back.

Outside, a hissy squawk echoed. Like a human pretending to be a goose.

"Bogden's signal!" Willam blurted. "Someone's coming!"

Instantly Robin surged towards the mouth of the tree. "Come on!" he said, climbing into the hole, looking behind—

No one was following him.

"Too dangerous!" Bettina said, pointing at Sophie. "The way she asked the question . . . it's all wrong!"

Bogden stumbled in, red-faced. "Guards! Geese!"

"*Hurry!*" Robin snarled, prowling through sticky moss and disappearing into the tree.

Willam pushed the girls towards the trunk. "Follow Robin!"

Before Sophie could balk, Bogden stuffed her into the tree

like a witch into an oven. Sophie's face slimed with moss as she jammed through the hot, muggy hole and landed in a cramped passage, forcing her onto hands and knees. She might as well have been blindfolded; she couldn't see a damn thing, the contours of wood hard under her palms. The air was heavy with a rotten-fruit smell, as if she was trapped in the belly of a troll. Quickly, she hid Merlin's pearl inside her dress. Little by little, her eyes adjusted, Robin's outline materializing ahead, the green-feathered thief crawling deeper into the tree. Grunts and thuds echoed behind her, the sounds of bodies landing, and Sophie turned to find three pairs of eyes in the dark.

"Follow me," Bettina ordered Sophie. "You've already put us in the worst possible position. From here on out, everyone does as I say."

"Bollocks. Not leaving our fate up to a *journalist*," said Robin. "I'm from Sherwood. Know my way around a tree. Keep close, kids." He bounded forward.

Bettina, meanwhile, hadn't moved.

Willam and Bogden blinked at Sophie, waiting for her to choose a leader.

Sophie followed Robin.

Deeper she probed into the tree, Bettina's grumbles obscured by the plods of Willam and Bogden trying to match Sophie's pace.

Suddenly Robin stopped short, causing a pile-up behind him.

"Path drops off," he said. "Almost went over the edge." He peered back at Sophie. "Use your glow."

The tension in Robin's voice made Sophie's heart thump; fear powered her magic, her fingertip beaming hot pink. She cast it over Robin's shoulder, lighting a deep, deep pit, rimmed with ropes of moss, all the way down. Along this moss grew white flower bulbs, hundreds of them, luscious and large, their petals not yet open.

"There! Look!" Robin said, pointing. "That's the way out!"

Sophie directed her glow to the bottom of the pit, which ended in a pool of light. Through the light, Sophie glimpsed an undulating mirage: the dusty hills of Putsi, beyond the bank.

Robin leaned over the pit and tugged hard at one of the moss-ropes. "These lines will hold. We just need to climb down."

"All the way?" Willam said, bug-eyed.

"Willam's scared of heights," Bogden explained. "And beets."

"Heights is the least of your problems," Bettina growled.

The group looked at her.

"Wizard trees answer the exact question asked of it." Bettina glowered at Sophie. "And this fool asked, '*Can you show us a way out?*' Yes, that is a way out down there. Looks like it, at least. But Sophie's question wasn't specific enough. There could be other ways out. *Bad* ways out that lead to death. There's a reason the tree was locked away. There's a reason the king who sought an answer from a wizard tree *died*. Everything here is a trap."

Sophie tugged anxiously at her dress.

"We've come this far," Robin blustered, gripping a rope and

descending into the pit. "Don't touch anything or do anything stupid!"

Bogden slid onto another rope, plunging backwards—"*Whoaaa!*"—before he steadied himself. Dripping sweat, he peeked up at Willam. "Close your eyes and jump on," Bogden panted. "Anything happens and I'll catch you."

His freckled friend didn't hesitate. Willam closed his eyes and joined Bogden on his rope.

Sophie smiled to herself. Agatha would have surely done the same for her. Who knew that two boys could have the same bond as a princess and a witch, she thought, searching for her own vine and finding a tether of moss that looked especially sturdy. Inch by inch, she dragged herself down, lighting up the pit with her glow, surprised by how the gluey moss molded to her hands and bare feet, magically assisting the climb. She glanced over at Bogden and Willam across the pit, Robin at their wing, all descending quickly, smoothly—

A face plunged into view an inch from hers, along with a whiff of cloying sweetness. Bettina sucked a red lollipop, staring Sophie down from the next rope over.

"A thousand vines to choose from," said Sophie, "and you can't stay away."

"Making sure you don't do anything else stupid," Bettina huffed, dropping fast.

Sophie scrambled to keep up. "How did a Jaunt Jolie princess end up a reporter in Camelot anyway?"

"Don't need to go to that school to make a difference," Bettina needled. "After Arthur died, I knew the Woods should keep a close eye on his realm. If your fairy tale proved anything, it's that you school kids are ill-equipped to be in charge."

"Pity you didn't get *into* our school. You would have made a fine wicked stepmother one day."

"More like Cinderella, mopping up your messes."

"Is there a reason you have to do it so odiously?"

"Snake almost hanged my whole family and then *you* give him the throne."

"Me? It wasn't my fault!"

"You kissed Rhian, didn't you?" Bettina attacked. "You fell into his and Japeth's trap. All because you were jealous of your best friend becoming queen."

"Don't you *dare*," Sophie flamed, tailing her. "You don't know the slightest thing about Agatha and me—"

"I covered Agatha's tenure as princess firsthand," Bettina replied. "She confided quite a bit."

Sophie reddened. "Aggie . . . said I was jealous of her?"

"No, but from your tone, now I know it's true," said Bettina, moving along. "Sometimes a reporter has to tease out a story."

"Oh, I remember," said Sophie, chasing her. "Agatha mentioned a vapid, candy-sucking girl from the *Courier* . . . empty in the head . . ."

Bettina slowed, unsure if Sophie was teasing out her own story. "Fair enough. I figured playing stupid was the best way to get close to Agatha. You know, considering her choice in *friends*."

Sophie reeled as if she'd been slapped. By the time she'd

untied her tongue, Bettina was already a long way down. Nothing to do but admit defeat, Sophie sighed. It was a rare feeling: something only Agatha inspired, given her best friend's ability to find her vulnerable spots and lance right through them . . .

Just thinking of Agatha made Sophie's heart sink. Her best friend. Her soul sister. Once upon a time, they had every day together: aimless walks, shared secrets, unbreakable love. But Sophie had wanted more. Sophie wanted a prince. Suddenly, the life she knew with Agatha was gone. Ever since, they'd tried to find their way back to the way things used to be. Would they die trying? Or worse still, was *this* their ending? Blissful moments together, then violent separations, over and over, reminding them of what they'd had and lost? An endless, futile chase into the maze rather than out of it?

She was so deep in her trance that when the whisper started, Sophie thought it was coming from her own head.

"I know a way out . . . the real way out . . ."

Only the voice was a boy's: young and assured.

Sophie looked up. No one there. She swept her pink glow, lighting the area near her rope, but her route had pulled her around a serrated ridge, far from the others; she couldn't even see Bettina or Robin or the boys anymore. Sophie quickened her pace, skittering downwards—

"I know the way out of your lonely life."

Louder this time.

Right in her ear.

She spun to find a flower, ghostly white, its petals sealed around a blue glow.

"*The way out is a name . . . ,*" it whispered, bending towards her. "*Your true love's name . . . Your forever prince . . .*"

Sophie's heart drummed faster.

"*Open me up . . .*" The flower caressed Sophie's lips. "*I'll show you the way . . . I'll tell you his name . . .*"

Her blood burned with liquid heat. All rational sense was gone. Without thinking, Sophie thrust her hand at the petals—

"Don't!" a voice yelled.

Beneath her, Bettina appeared, a shadow in Sophie's pink glow, curled around the side of the ridge, glaring blackly at her.

"Coming!" Sophie croaked, leaving the flower behind.

Just a trick, she reminded herself.

What could a tree know about her future?

And yet, the tree had given them a way out of the bank. It had answered the question she'd asked. So why wouldn't this answer be real, too? Plus, the way the bloom spoke . . . that boy's voice . . . so confident and clear . . . as if *he* was her true love . . .

Who was it?

What was his name?

The flower would have told her. After all she'd been through, she'd finally know who he was. Her one true prince. Her Ever After. And with it, the power to shortcut to The End instead of wishing and hoping for the Storian to write it. She would have control back. Man at the helm, instead of a Pen.

Which is how we ended up in this mess to begin with, Sophie thought.

Open that flower and she would be no better than two

monstrous twins who thought *they* should be the Pen . . . that they had the right to bend fate to their will . . . Meanwhile, she and Agatha were fighting to protect the Storian and the stories that set the example for their world. To allow these tales to unfold the way a real flower would, in its own time, instead of plundering them for selfish need. Even if it meant enduring pain and suffering. Even if it led her to a thousand false endings. Nature had a way. The Storian had a plan. One that had brought her to a best friend and a world beyond her own where she'd found purpose and meaning and strength. Only in the realm of the Storian could everyone find their place. Their *true* place. This was the future she was fighting for. And that was worth more than the pleasures of a boy or a kiss.

Except now a new flower was talking to her.

"I know a way out of the Evil in your heart . . ."

The green glow within the petals throbbed, like a magical seed.

"A way you can be as Good as Agatha . . . Just open me . . . I'll show you the way . . ."

Sophie hustled past it, wishing she could plug her ears. She let her feet skid down the rope as she rebounded around the side of the ridge, spotting her teammates once more. But now there were new flowers, bending towards her.

"I know a way out of your dress . . . Evelyn Sader's dress . . . I know how to escape its magic . . ."

Sophie clenched her teeth and rushed past.

"I know a way out of the mystery . . . I can tell you who the Snake's parents really are . . ."

"I know a way out of your question . . . why Rhian had a fingerglow and the Snake doesn't . . ."

"I know a way out of Lady Lesso's secrets . . . I know who fathered her child . . . who Aric's real dad is . . . just open me up . . ."

Sophie resisted these new whispers, each pulling on the strings of her heart, promising to unravel a knot. Nearby, Robin seemed to be battling too, his jaw flexed, his muscles tense. For a moment, Sophie could hear his vine's taunts—

"I know a way out of your resentment towards Marian . . . a way to forgive her for what she did . . . Open me, Robin . . ."

Robin paused, teeth gnashed, before he shook his head and kept going, faster than before. He and Bettina were racing towards the bottom from opposite sides, the *Courier* scribe unfazed by her flowers, as if she'd already investigated every last question of her heart. Willam and Bogden, too, were close to the exit, until Willam hesitated in front of a sealed bloom—

"I know a way out of your brother's grave . . . a way to bring Tristan back to life . . ."

Bogden tugged Willam by the leg, forcing him down.

Tristan, Sophie thought. The name kept coming up when Willam was around. And yet the only Tristan she'd known was a boy who'd gone to the School for Good: a redheaded, freckled waif who'd been brutally killed in a tree by Aric—

Sophie swiveled, looking back at the redheaded, freckled waif with Bogden.

Of course!

Willam was Tristan's brother.

It explained everything: Willam's resentment towards Tedros . . . his insistence that the prince bullied his brother . . .

Does he know how Tristan died?

Does he know the Snake was friends with Tristan's killer?

That he's trying to bring that killer back to life?

It's why Japeth wanted the Pen's power, Sophie remembered. It's why he'd killed his own twin.

For Aric.

This was about more than being king to Japeth, more than killing Tedros or erasing his opponents.

This was about Japeth getting his best friend back.

This was about love.

Sophie knew that story well. She'd climbed out of hell to find her Ever After with her best friend, again and again, and yet there was always something in the way.

"Sophie! Hurry!"

She looked down at Robin, Bogden, Willam, and Bettina, converged on the pool of light, poised to jump through and escape back into the Woods. They'd survived the flower traps. Only she was left to finish. Sophie smiled with relief, hurrying down her vine. More blooms ambushed her, their voices louder, more insistent, but she was untouchable now, like a last wolf charging for her pack.

"I know the way out of being a Dean . . . a way to feel more fulfilled . . ."

(Sophie thought: *I'll feel fulfilled when the Snake is dead.*)

"I know a way to check on your father in Gavaldon . . . to see if he's alive or dead . . ."

(*Stefan has a new family now*, Sophie dismissed.)

"*I know a way for you to look even more beautiful . . .*"

("Impossible," Sophie wisped.)

"*I know a way out of your secret cravings for cheese . . .*"

("Now you're just being daft.")

"*I know a way out of your fairy tale . . . so that you and Agatha can be how you once were . . .*"

Sophie hesitated. The very last flower on her vine loomed over her, white petals cupped by thorns, the trapped glow flashing hot pink.

"*Two best friends . . . before Tedros . . . before princes . . . when you only lived for each other . . .*"

Sophie told herself to keep moving, to shut out the voice. Her body didn't listen.

"*I can restore you like you used to be . . . Agatha and Sophie . . . Sophie and Agatha . . .*"

Her heart was outracing her breaths now, something inside her taking over.

"*Back to two girls . . . Back to the beginning . . .*"

"Sophie!" a boy's voice called below.

"*The true way out . . . Open me, Sophie . . .*"

Sophie dripped with sweat, her fingers curling into a fist.

"*Open me for Agatha . . .*"

"Sophie, *no!*" another voice cried.

She ripped open the petals, pricking her finger on a thorn like the tip of a spindle.

Blood dripped onto her white dress.

Inside the bloom, the pink glow withered, white petals

desiccating to dust. Only the thorns remained, thickening, growing longer and longer.

Sophie snapped out of her trance.

Oh no.

She glimpsed movement below and spotted Robin and Bettina rushing up their vines towards her, as if something was about to happen, something terrible she couldn't understand. She spun back to the flower—

The thorns snatched her like fingers, before green moss lassoed on top of her, binding her in. Harder and thicker these binds grew, morphing into wood—into *bark*—from which a new tree began to grow. Sophie couldn't breathe; a few more seconds, and she'd be fossilized into this new tree. Tearing her hand free, she seared through wood with her glow, freeing herself, and instantly plummeted backwards, ricocheting off a branch, then another, then another. Around the pit, new trees erupted from white flowers, an explosion of branches and leaves, ping-ponging Sophie up into darkness. She could hear the shrieks of her friends, careening off new-growing trees, their bodies tiny shadows in the cast of her glow. More trees detonated to life, volleying Sophie up in an endless white canopy, higher, higher, until she saw a ceiling of earth above. Branches suddenly cradled her like a throne and crashed her through dirt, then through stone—

The wizard tree smashed into the lobby of the bank, multiplying out of the marble, bludgeoning the stunned phoenixes aside, and throttling straight for the ceiling. Sophie hung on tight, ducking under branches . . . *BOOM!* The force of the tree shattered the walls, infinite limbs burgeoning freely into the night, scraps of Ever and Never flags that once flew over the bank now caught limply on twigs. Taller and taller the wizard tree grew, new trees flowering off every branch, with Sophie thrust into the night atop the uppermost bough, like a crowning star. She was so far above ground she couldn't see where the tree began, her body lofted against gravity, angling for the moon. Clinging to the top, she let out a piercing cry—

The tree stopped growing.

Clouds swept in, drenching the land in darkness.

Slowly, Sophie peeked down at the wizard tree.

A storm of life, rooted in the ruins of wealth.

She couldn't see Robin or Bettina or the boys.

She couldn't see anyone.

How am I alive?

Am I alive?

Wind slashed through, shaking Sophie's branch, nearly blowing her off it.

Yeah . . . I'm alive.

She wouldn't last long up here. Nor was her dress any protection against the chill, the ghost of Evelyn Sader useless when she needed her most.

Shivering violently, Sophie started to descend, but the gusts were too strong. Her foot slid and she plunged onto the next branch, which snapped under her, leaving her gripping on to a sliver of wood with a single fist. Reaching her toes for the next limb down, she slowly lowered herself, but new gusts assaulted her, tossing her against the branch, her head tipped over it, her feet kicking in midair. From the inside of her dress, she saw the pearl with Merlin's beard slip out—

Sophie yelped, flailing for it, but she toppled harder, about to fall out of the tree.

She had to choose.

Sophie grabbed on to the branch.

The pearl fell.

The tournament's first test.

Tedros' only hope.

Down, down, down, into the darkness—

And then . . .

And *then* . . .

The pearl started floating back up.

Shielded in sparkly green dust.

A small, pale hand caught it, coated in the same green dust.

"Agatha?" Sophie breathed.

Slowly her best friend landed on Sophie's bough, shimmering like a phantom.

Tears sprung to Sophie's eyes. "Are . . . are you . . . real?"

Agatha pressed her hand to Sophie's cheek, warm and soft.

"But how—" Sophie choked.

A grumpy, green-dressed fairy poked out of Agatha's hair, flinging a spritz of fairy dust into the air as if to make it clear whose magic was responsible.

Agatha raised the pearl into the moonlight, inspecting Merlin's beard. She smiled with relief at her friend. "Quite a team, you and I."

Gobsmacked, Sophie glanced around.

No Tedros.

No Hort.

No boys.

Just her and Agatha, high in a tree.

The way they once were, atop an oak in Gavaldon, before a stymph arrived and kidnapped them into the Woods. It was on a branch, just like this, that they had their final moments together before everything changed.

And suddenly Sophie understood.

That flower she'd opened.

Sophie and Agatha.

Agatha and Sophie.

This was it.

The tree had given her what she wanted.

Back to two girls.

Back to the beginning.

The way they used to be.

The true way out.

Two girls stared into each other's eyes, savoring this Ever After, waiting for the Storian to write it . . . waiting for the Pen to make it real . . .

But Man isn't Pen.

Not yet.

Tinkerbell let out a scream of warning.

Both girls reached for the other, as if to hold on to the moment—

But time was up.

Their beginning had come to an end.

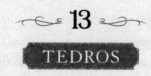
Pride and Princess

"Y ou sure your girlfriend isn't a crackpot?" Hort's man-wolf growled, pacing in the dark forest.

Tedros ignored him as he tried to rock Merlin to sleep.

"Consider the evidence," Hort went on. "First she says

Robin Hood left her a message in magic dust at the Arrow. A message no one else saw. Then she says Merlin appeared to her and told her to come to Putsi. Both sound pretty crackpot to me."

Through the

thicket, Tedros glimpsed the wizard tree in the distance, rising high over the land. Movement flickered in its branches, but they were too far away to see more. Putsi was a well-armed city: the shock of a wizard tree bursting out of the bank would bring the bank's guards and the Empress's flying minions. Tedros' stomach knotted, the baby fussing with his shirt. He shouldn't have let Agatha go off alone.

"You're worrying if she's wrong? I'm worried if she's *right*," the prince returned, so focused on the tree he didn't notice Merlin squiggling out of his arms. "What if the answer was in Putsi all along?"

"Then pray we find it before the Snake," Hort said, rescuing Merlin into his paws before the baby slipped. "Whoever wins the first test gets a head start for the second. And if the Snake gets too far ahead . . ."

Wind axed through the trees, finishing Hort's thought. Tedros watched him cradle Merlin into his dark fur, the baby's eyes starting to close. *How could I be so stupid?* Tedros thought. His dad wouldn't have expected him to track down the wizard in his old age and lop off his beard. Especially after Arthur and Merlin had gone their separate ways. For all his father knew, Merlin would have been long dead. And yet, Tedros had done what he'd always done: made assumptions without thinking.

Agatha was right.

The beard was here in Putsi.

Only he'd come to this realization too late.

Which meant his first test was no longer up to him.

It was up to *her*.

Agatha, who was out there right now, fighting Tedros' battle. All on her own.

And here Tedros was, twiddling his thumbs, just like he had at Camelot when Agatha usurped his quest the first time. Long before there was a King Rhian or King Japeth, there was a masked attacker, daring Tedros to come fight him. But it had been Agatha who answered the call instead of Tedros, the prince willing to stay behind.

The mistake that started it all.

But he'd learned from that, Tedros thought angrily. He was different now. He was ready to be a king. If only his princess would stay out of the way.

Tedros' blood simmered, his father's ring cold on his hand.

That's what this tournament was supposed to be about, wasn't it? Proving himself? Even Agatha had admitted that, back at the inn. So why was he still loitering here like a princess in waiting while she was off hunting the answer to *his* test?

He'd tried to stop her. On the short trip from Bloodbrook, Tedros had assumed they'd battle the Snake together. That they'd track down Merlin's lost beard as a team. But just as they'd gotten to the forest's edge, the wizard tree rising into view, Agatha ordered him and Hort to stay put.

"What? The Snake's out there!" Tedros said, thrown.

"And if he kills you now and takes your ring, we're all dead," said Agatha, dismounting Hort's wolf. "Keep Merlin safe. I'll be back soon."

"Don't be a fool," Tedros scoffed, chasing her. "No way you're going alone—"

Agatha turned. "I won't be alone."

The way she said it.

So sharp and clear that by the time he'd regathered his wits, she was lost in the dark.

"*I won't be alone.*"

I won't be alone?

Then it hit him.

That cry.

The one that echoed as the wizard tree sprung over the land . . . The one that made Agatha's eyes spark before she had taken control of their plans.

I won't be alone.

The shine in her eyes.

That hint of a smile.

Agatha could only mean one person.

That's why she'd driven Hort so hard on the ride here.

That's why she'd left the prince and man-wolf behind.

Agatha was after more than Merlin's beard.

Agatha was after her own grail.

Sophie.

Sophie, who she'd heard out there, crying for help.

Sophie, always the witch between him and his princess.

Tedros' gut twisted tighter.

Where Sophie went, Evil followed.

He fished Tinkerbell out of his pocket and shook her until she woke up. "Follow Agatha and keep her safe. The moment she's in trouble, send a flare. Understood?"

Tinkerbell yawned and jingled back.

"No, I will not kiss you in exchange," Tedros retorted.

Tink argued her case—

"I don't care if Peter kissed you," said the prince. "*Go.* Before I feed you to Hort."

Grumbling, the fairy flitted off to find Tedros' princess.

And this is how he'd gotten here: pent-up and frustrated, saddled with a baby, while his princess went after her best friend. Again.

"Now you know how I felt with Sophie all those years," a voice groused.

The prince looked up at Hort.

"Always second best," the man-wolf sighed.

Tedros sucked in a breath.

Hort was right.

This was *The Tale of Sophie and Agatha.*

It always would be.

Until he had the courage to make it his story too.

Light flashed through the darkness, a flare of gold.

Tedros and Hort spun—

Flames bounded towards them.

For a second, Tedros thought they were under attack.

Then he saw the blaze had a face.

A fairy, wings afire.

"Tink?" he breathed.

Burning up, Tinkerbell choked out a single squeak.

A word that shook Tedros' soul.

"Snake."

The flare swallowed her.

She was gone.

HE WAS TOO poisoned by rage to have a plan.

Throttling towards the wizard tree, his boots skidding across the forest, Tedros thought only of his true love, out there against an enemy who burned fairies alive.

This was the clarity of Evil. Its humiliation of your weaknesses, its savaging of your mercies. Every time Tedros hesitated, the Snake was there to punish him. Japeth was more than a Nemesis. He was his shadow, like the Green Knight to King Arthur, a curse that had been with him all along and yet one he was fully unprepared for.

Hort had tried to come too, but Tedros had repelled him with orders to stay and protect Merlin. (He made no mention of Sophie; if the weasel knew she might be out there, he'd bring the baby into battle.) But without the man-wolf, Tedros had no weapon or shield against someone he still wasn't sure how to kill. Stumbling over a stick, he kicked it into his fist, using his fingerglow to whittle it to a stake.

Soon he heard sounds of war: cries, human and animal; clashes of steel; the groans of a tree under siege. He sprinted out of the Woods, onto open land, the ruins of the bank covered in ghostly white leaves.

As Tedros drew nearer, he saw spatters of blood.

The corpses of geese.

Twelve, he counted.

Then the body of a bank guard, his limbs twisted, as if he'd fallen from a great height.

Closer and closer Tedros came to the tree, the silhouettes in its branches sharpening, two pearls of glow flickering at the top, pure gold and hot pink—

He stopped short.

High in the wizard tree, Agatha and Sophie clung to branches, fending off a storm of scims, the girls' fingerglows strobing in the night. From this far down, Tedros couldn't see their faces or a sign of Japeth himself, but he heard their shouts—"*Sophie, watch out!*" "*Behind you, Aggie!*"—before they disappeared behind white leaves. Eels stabbed in and out of these leaves, Agatha's and Sophie's screams getting louder, prompting the prince to shove the wood stake into his pants and start climbing.

Only now did he see the war in his way.

Geese and guards swarmed branches, angling for the girls but were held off by a team of familiars: Willam . . . Bogden . . . Robin Hood? Plus a female, with brown hair, who looked like . . . *Betty*? They'd been playmates once upon a time. What was she doing *here*?

Questions could wait.

Right now, his friends needed him.

Tedros plunged into the fray, head-butting geese aside, before hurling himself at the first guard in his way. She lunged at him with a yell, slashing his shirt open, roping her legs around his throat and squeezing tight. Above, Bogden was in his own fight, pinned to a branch by two guards punching him as the stout first year thrashed. The guard girl crushed Tedros' neck harder. He tried to suck in air, but it made him lose more. The girl bared her teeth as she strangled him, surely imagining the bounty the dead prince would fetch. Tedros had no move to make. Princes didn't hit girls. Those were the rules. He weakened in her grip, choking on saliva, his mind fogging black—

Tedros gritted his teeth.

Times change.

He jammed one foot into the girl's face, then the other behind her ear and slammed her face against a branch. Dazed, she came at him again, but his boots were around her neck as he launched his body upwards, flipping her headfirst into Bogden's attackers, who crashed backwards, the three guards plummeting out of the tree. Wheezing, Tedros grabbed Bogden like a buoy, the bloodied first year blinking at the prince, before his eyes focused past him: "Willam!"

Tedros spun to the red-haired boy above, jerking against a branch as geese attacked.

"Don't . . . love . . . geese . . . ," Willam gagged, shielding his face.

Instantly Tedros was in full flight, bludgeoning geese with his fists, throwing them off Willam. Now the flock came for the prince, flogging him with wings and beaks, shearing through the last of his shirt, before Bogden leapt next to Tedros, clubbing them aside. Again Tedros tried to be Good;

killing animals was a villain's work. But these geese wouldn't stop until he was dead, their beaks crisscrossing his chest with blood, getting closer and closer to his heart. He struggled to fend them off, blinded by feathers in his face, batting futilely with his wood stake. Through the flurry, he glimpsed more geese pummeling Willam, the boy starting to go limp. Next to him, a bird vised Bogden's neck, about to spike its bill through his skull—

"Help!" Bogden squeaked.

Tedros bared his teeth.

Chivalry was over.

He ripped through the wall of birds, flew up over Bogden's goose, and with a primal snarl, stabbed through it with his stake, separating head from body. He whirled around, prepared to kill more, but the flock gawked at him, then fled into the night.

Willam lay crumpled against a branch, his face a mess of blood, wounds on his arms and legs.

Tedros held Willam's skinny torso and put his head to the boy's chest, tracking the weak pulse of his heart.

Bogden grabbed Tedros. "Is he . . ."

"Leave me," Willam breathed. "Save Agatha."

Tedros gazed at the soft redheaded lad and thought of a boy just like him, once upon a time, clinging to life in a tree. Tedros hadn't been able to save Tristan that day. Aric had made sure of it. But the Pen gives the best men second chances.

"Get him to the forest," Tedros ordered Bogden. "Hort's there. Tell him to ride you and Willam to school. The teachers will heal him."

Bogden stared at Tedros, then at the fleet of guards coming for the prince—

"*Now!*" Tedros lashed.

Bogden flung Willam over his shoulder and hoisted him down the tree.

"*Aggie, look out!*" Sophie echoed above.

Tedros squinted high and watched Agatha fall from the top of the tree, landing hard into branches below and vanishing behind leaves. Immediately a cluster of scims swarmed where her body had fallen, their monstrous shrieks resounding.

"*Aggie, you okay?*" Sophie yelled.

As guards converged on him, Tedros waited for Agatha's reply. Or a glint of her glow. Something to tell him she was alive.

It didn't come.

Fire ripped through his heart, a Lion on the hunt.

Anyone in his way didn't stand a chance, Tedros bashing guards aside or clasping hold of their shirts and knifing legs or hands with his stake to disarm them, before flinging them off the tree. He was lethally high above ground, climbing closer to where Agatha had fallen, when he glimpsed another squall of activity. Robin and Betty at war with a shadow balanced on a limb, gripping a gilded sword with two fists—

Kei.

Bettina whipped at him with a long branch, trying to swipe him off the tree, while Robin grappled Kei from behind, straining for the captain's sword. Betty caught sight of Tedros below. "Help me up!" Tedros whispered.

"No! We need you safe!" Betty hissed back.

"I need *Agatha* safe," Tedros steeled, glaring at her like he did when they fought as children.

Bettina wavered under his stare . . . then surrendered her branch towards him.

Across the tree, Robin had Kei in a chokehold.

"Listen to me—" Kei wheezed, fighting Robin, but Hood stripped Kei of his sword and stalked towards him, gold blade pointed, Kei stumbling as he retreated.

"Agatha . . . It's about Agatha . . . ," Kei pressed.

Tedros vaulted off Betty's bough, landed in front of Robin, and slammed Kei against bark. Before Kei could speak, Tedros' hands were around his throat. "What about Agatha?" Tedros dug his fingers in harder—

But something in Kei's eyes stopped the prince. He'd seen it before. The night Tedros caught him burying Rhian. A look that said whatever side Kei had been fighting for, he was on his own side now.

"Agatha has the answer," Kei panted. "I saw it in her hand. The pearl with the beard. Swallow it before Japeth gets it. That's how you learn the second test."

Tedros was speechless.

"He's a monster," said Kei. "He always has been, since we were in school. He killed Rhian. My best friend. The *real* king. That's why I burned the tracking map. That's why I've been protecting you. I pretended to be loyal to that snake as long as I could. So I could avenge Rhian when I had the chance." He glanced high into the tree. "Stabbed him before he could get the beard from Agatha. Before he could kill them. He escaped or I would have finished him off." He turned to Tedros. "Go. Quickly. Find the pearl. I'll help you figh—"

A gold sword impaled him.

Kei didn't make a sound. His face went the color of clouds. Then he keeled out of the tree, revealing Betty behind him . . .

. . . locked under the Snake's arm.

Japeth's eyes were cold. His torso gleamed with blood through his torn king's suit, now morphing to black scims. One of his hands squeezed Tedros' friend by her neck. The other carried Kei's sword, greased with the captain's blood.

The sword, Tedros realized.

Robin had it just moments ago.

Which meant . . .

Tedros swiveled—

Robin was hanging from the branch, his neck noosed by scims, his face purpling, seconds from death.

"Let's play my favorite game," Japeth said, gripping Betty. "You can only save *one*."

Tedros stiffened.

There was no time to think—

He ran for Robin, ripping the noose. Robin crashed down onto a lower bough, barely catching himself in time. But Tedros was already sprinting for Bettina, reaching out for her—

Japeth held Betty close.

"Rules are rules," he said.

He threw her off the tree.

"*No!*" Tedros yelled.

Bettina fell backwards, arms flailing, with a scream—

Darkness swallowed her.

Tedros froze, midstride.

A friend dead, in the width of a moment.

Like the Sheriff and Lancelot and Dovey and more before her.

Another worthy soul he couldn't save.

Slowly, Tedros looked up at the Snake, separated from him by the length of the branch.

"Now you know how it feels," Japeth spoke. "Those you love *taken* from you."

"Says the brother killer," the prince spat with rage.

"Rhian lied to me. He broke an oath," Japeth replied evenly. "Where you see Evil, I see justice. You think you're the hero of this tale. You think you're the true king. But you are mistaken. Only I know the truth."

"The truth that *you're* the liar? That you're the *fraud*?" Tedros blasted. He could hear Robin below, struggling to regain breath. "You have Rhian's blood, which showed my father as yours. Except you're not my brother. You said it yourself."

"And yet the tournament is between us. Your *father's* tournament," the Snake replied, clear-eyed. "So who am I?"

Tedros had no answer, still at a loss.

"Or maybe that isn't the question," said Japeth, taking him in. "Maybe we should be asking . . . who are *you*?"

The words chilled Tedros' bones.

He'd assumed his father wanted him on the throne.

That's why his dad left him his ring.

Yet that dad had also given the Snake a chance. A monster. A murderer.

Why?

"*Sophie?*" Agatha's voice called weakly.

"*Where are you!*" Sophie cried back.

Tedros' focus flew upwards. *Agatha.* She had the pearl. He needed to get to her. Win the first test and he'd be on to the next.

Get to Agatha, he told himself.

And yet . . .

His eyes lowered to Japeth.

Kill the Snake now and there would be no more tests.

The Snake seemed to read his thoughts, his pupils glimmering in the dark. He fixed on Tedros' ring.

"Maybe you *are* my brother," he said. "Because you're as much a fool as the last one."

Tedros stormed at him across the tree.

Japeth charged, scims curling off his suit—

Robin launched up from below, landing in front of Tedros like a shield.

"Get to Agatha. Get the pearl," he told the prince. "I'll hold him off."

Tedros tried to push past Robin—

"Princess, not pride!" Hood snarled at him.

The words hit Tedros hard.

Robin was right.

If the Snake killed him, Agatha would be next.

Even his nemesis wasn't worth that.

With a leap, he was already on to the next branch, leaving Hood behind. The prince glanced back—scims mobbing Robin as he rushed the Snake—before Tedros bit down and kept moving, telling himself that Robin Hood thrived in trees, that he'd find a way to survive. The Snake couldn't kill another friend . . . not today . . .

Up and up into the wizard tree, the prince climbed, sounds of Robin and Japeth trailing away. He was alone now, no geese, no guards, no more enemies to fight. From this vantage point, he could see the specks of villagers, gathering outside houses, beholding the magic tree that had grown over their kingdom like Jack's beanstalk. Putsi guards would be on the way soon, along with others loyal to "Rhian," but Tedros was nearing the summit, his hands torn, his body suffering, yet propelled by the silent chant of a name: *Agatha. Agatha. Agatha.* Many a prince had scaled a tower to rescue his princess, but it was only fitting that his required a climb to the top of the world. And yet, despite all that was lost, there was a steadiness to him now, a harmony of will and fate, Man and Pen. It was Agatha who had left him behind, thinking she could save him. But in the end, he would save her. At last, he was leading this story. At last, he was the prince. He pulled himself up—

Tedros stopped on a branch, eyes wide.

"Teddy?" a blond girl said softly.

Across the limb, Sophie clutched Agatha in her hands.

Tedros' princess was strewn with leaves, her lungs pumping shallow breaths. Her face and arms were cut up. Her leg was broken badly, twisted at the knee. And yet, even in terrible pain, Agatha managed the happiest smile at the sight of her prince.

"You came," she said.

"Says the girl who ordered me not to," Tedros growled, lurching to her side. He snatched her from Sophie and clasped her to his chest, kissing her all over. "You're hurt. This is what happens when you trust her over me. This is what happens when you fight my battles for me."

"And yet, she has the answer to your test," said Sophie. "An answer *I* found. The two of us do just fine without you."

Tedros clenched his teeth. "Where is it?"

Agatha reached into her dress. "Kei saved us. He rescued us from—"

"I know," Tedros said.

Agatha looked at him. The wounds on his chest. The bruises and marks on his face and throat.

"Where's Robin?" asked Sophie. "Where's Betty and Bogden and Willam?"

"We need to get you to school," Tedros pressed Agatha. "Yuba and the teachers can fix your leg. I'll carry you down—"

"There's no time, Tedros. Leave me with Sophie," Agatha argued. "You have to move on to the second test."

Tedros put his nose to hers. "I'm not leaving you here."

Agatha held up a glowing pearl. "*This* is what matters. Winning the race. Taking the Woods back. For *Good*."

Tedros studied the small frosted orb, Merlin's beard a tight circle inside it.

"Swallow it, Tedros," Agatha ordered. "Learn the next test."

"Whatever it is can wait 'til you're safe," Tedros resisted.

"No, it can't," Sophie snapped. "Swallow now. Fight later."

She's right, Tedros admitted, even if he had no intention of leaving his princess behind. He took a deep breath, focused on the pearl in Agatha's hand. Then he reached his mouth for it—

The branch shook hard from beneath.

In a split second, the pearl slipped from Agatha's fingers, cascading off Tedros' lips.

Startled, the prince, his princess, and Sophie watched Merlin's beard tumble to the next bough and nestle in a canopy of leaves.

The tree continued to rattle beneath them, the pearl quivering precariously, branches bending below.

Someone was coming.

Tedros scanned the darkness with his glow.

"Robin?"

Through leaves, the outlines of a face appeared.

Agatha went rigid under Tedros' arm. Next to him, Sophie stopped breathing.

Japeth loomed closer, slithering towards their branch.

His hands were covered with blood.

Robin's blood, Tedros thought, going cold.

The prince darted a glance at the pearl, couched between leaves.

Japeth caught him looking.

He, too, honed in on the glass orb.

Silence hung between the prince and the Snake.

Both leapt for it.

They smashed into each other, vaulting the pearl upwards. Scims shot off Japeth's suit, about to claim it—

Sophie snatched Merlin's beard in her fist, her body balanced over a branch, before the branch broke and sent her crashing three limbs down. Instantly, eels spiked towards her, Japeth heading her way.

"Tedros! Swallow it!" she yelled, flinging the beard in the prince's direction—

Tedros lunged, losing the pearl in the glare of Sophie's glow. It bounced off his skull, rebounding into the night sky.

Tedros, Japeth, and Sophie dove for it, each from a different direction, each with a chance—

But one was faster than the rest, limbs coated in white leaves, falling through the night like a broken swan.

Agatha.

Her mouth open.

Tedros gasped—

She swallowed the pearl.

Agatha plunged into Tedros' arms, the two plowing hard into tree bark. Sophie and the Snake snagged on branches above them.

For a moment, it was quiet.

All eyes flew to Agatha, crumpled with pain.

Winner of the first test.

Tedros' test.

"Aggie?" Sophie rasped quietly. "What did you do?"

Tedros and Agatha locked eyes, as if the tale had taken a turn both inevitable and unexpected.

Then Agatha choked, her neck convulsing, her cheeks coloring, something brewing inside her. She parted her lips and breathed a silvery dust that lifted into the dark, coalescing into the ghost of a familiar face.

King Arthur glared down at Agatha in the wizard tree.

> *"A twist in the tale . . .*
> *Two vie for my crown.*
> *But you are neither.*
> *Are you friend?*
> *Or are you enemy?*
> *Both can bring down a king.*
> *You have interfered in the quest*
> *And so must die.*
> *That is the second test.*
> *Whoever slays you shall learn the third."*

King Arthur vanished.

Agatha and Tedros whirled to each other—

But now they were floating upwards, Sophie too, as stymph claws hooked under them, rescuing them high into the night, veering west on the command of Ravan, Vex, Mona, and more fourth years astride the bony birds.

Shell-shocked, Tedros looked back at Japeth in the tree, but Japeth hadn't moved. Instead, he posed calmly against white leaves like a shadow, watching the prince recede into the clouds, the Snake gazing up at him with the darkest of smiles . . .

The next test already won before it started.

14

AGATHA

Fatima Finds a Friend

Two kings, ordered to kill her.

That's what the pearl had unleashed.

A victory she thought she'd claimed for her prince.

Instead, a death sentence. For *her*.

But before the pearl had spoken to the boys, it had spoken to Agatha first.

She'd hurled into the night without thinking, streaking past friends and foe hunting an answer and swallowing it herself. The cold glass caught on her tongue,

sliding down her throat with ease. Instantly, it dissolved, spewing harsh, stinging vapors that surged to the roof of her mouth, through her nostrils, and behind the eyes.

Looking inwards, she watched it take shape, this silvery mist, congealing into a ghost . . .

The Snake, in his green mask and suit of scims.

Only then he wasn't the Snake anymore. His muscles swelled, his mask shedding, Agatha faced with the Green Knight instead.

Then he became the Snake again.

Back and forth, the phantoms went, Snake, Knight, Snake, Knight, faster, faster, until they morphed into a third ghost—

Evelyn Sader.

Smiling at Agatha.

As if she, *Evelyn*, was the link between Snake and Knight.

A hidden secret for the winner to find.

But the mist was changing again . . . now the ghost of Arthur, the Lion of Camelot, her true love's father, glowering at Agatha—she, the wrong winner; she, a mistake—the once-king rearing high inside her like a dragon . . .

Then she breathed him out like fire.

WHEN AGATHA WOKE up, she was in her old room at school.

It hadn't changed a bit, Purity 51, as if she'd fallen back in time: jeweled mirrors on pink walls . . . murals flaunting princesses kissing princes . . . a fresco of clouds across the ceiling with cupids shooting love arrows. Over the bed was a white silk canopy shaped like a royal carriage, and at the end of the mattress a glass tray with milk-soaked oats, two hard-boiled eggs, and a chopped banana dusted with sugar. A card propped up against the tray had Sophie's handwriting:

Clearing

Agatha glanced across the room, the middle bed unmade, topped with a bowl of uneaten cucumber salad and a basket of beauty creams and potions. Agatha smelled the cloud of lavender left behind. There was a book open on the bed table: *Black Magic Healing, Level 2*, spread to a page about repairing broken limbs—

She threw aside the sheets, revealing her right leg, shattered badly only a few hours ago.

No longer.

She stood, gently putting weight on it.

Aside from a dull ache within the bone, the leg seemed healed.

Last she remembered, she was nestled into Sophie aboard a stymph, her best friend whispering, "It's okay, Aggie; it's going to be okay," as Agatha lay shell-shocked, unable to speak. In her haze, she must have fainted or fallen asleep. She didn't remember getting to school or making it to this room. She certainly didn't recall her leg being subject to witchcraft.

Agatha mustered a deep breath. She was awake. She could walk. It was time to face what was coming. But she couldn't.

Instead, she ate the food Sophie left her, taking the time to watch the violet sunrise and lick her fingers of every last grain of sugar. After noticing a spare Evergirl uniform in the closet, Agatha ambled to the toilet down the hall, disposing of her torn, filthy gown and stepping into the bath. Scalding water hit her skin, fogging her in with pleasure and silence. She pretended that she could hide away here, closed off from the world, like she once did in a graveyard long ago . . .

But then the dread came, the panic and regret, all the feelings she was trying to keep down.

This whole time they'd been fighting for the Storian.

Fighting for the Pen and the fate of its tales.

Tedros' tale, above all.

The story of a boy trying to prove himself king.

And here she'd gone and hijacked it.

Swallowed it whole, like a whale inhaling the sea.

She wished she could say it was an accident.

But it wasn't.

She saw a way out and took it . . . and lost sight of whose test it was.

And now the price.

For Tedros to become king, she'd have to die.

Not just die. He'd have to kill her.

Chills stung her skin, as if the bathwater had turned cold.

For her true love to defeat Japeth and keep his life—for *all* her friends to keep their lives—she'd have to give hers up.

The same sacrifice her mother made to save her.

Palms sweaty, nausea rising, she armored herself in the

sleek pink uniform, the putrid color offset by the illusion that she was just an ordinary first year again, about to go to class. But there were no other students as she made her way through the halls. No teachers, fairies, wolves. Only a lone nymph, sweeping up candy dust that had shed off the walls of Hansel's Haven, delicate piles of jellybean and gumdrop shavings that Agatha had just tramped through . . .

Once upon a time, she'd been the villain of a fairy tale. The sure pick for the School for Evil, while Sophie was destined for Good. But then came the Great Mistake. Two friends switched into the wrong schools. Only it wasn't a mistake, the Pen said then. Agatha was the princess. Sophie the witch.

But now Agatha was the Evil one.

The witch who ruined a prince's fairy tale.

And the strange thing was: it felt *expected*. As if she never fully believed herself a princess. Not the way Professor Dovey had, who'd insisted she was 100% Good. Not the way everyone else did, either, always trusting her to do the right thing. Deep down, Agatha never felt as Good as people thought her to be. And now, the truth would be clear for everyone to see. The Great Mistake was real—she belonged in Evil after all.

It was only when Agatha was halfway through one of the glass breezeways, still thinking of her old Dean, that she had a thought. That vision in the pearl . . . the riddle Arthur had hidden inside . . . What if she figured it out? The link between the Snake and the Green Knight . . . between two Japeths and Evelyn Sader . . . Then maybe she could expose who the Snake was! Maybe she could fix all this!

Her shoulders slumped, hope fading as quickly as it came.

Who Japeth was didn't matter.

Not when she'd bound her prince to an impossible test.

Kill his princess or hand his throne to a Snake.

That was the trap she'd made for him.

He would protect her, of course.

He would give up Camelot for love.

But the second test wasn't Tedros' alone.

That's why Japeth had smiled so wickedly as the prince flew away.

Because he knew Tedros would never finish the job.

The Snake would, though.

He'd hunt Agatha until it was done, putting him a single test from Excalibur killing Tedros.

Two birds with one swallow.

Agatha had put her and her prince in a death knot.

She was the true Witch of Woods Beyond now.

Even Professor Dovey would have seen that.

Through the glass passage, she gazed out at the School for Good and Evil, connected by Halfway Bridge, the sky over the castles crystal blue—

Agatha's heart jammed.

A new message from Lionsmane glowed to the west.

Tedros uses his princess to
    cheat the first test.
Now he'll pay the price.
His Agatha is the second test.

Help me, my Woods.

Wherever she runs . . .

Bring her to me. Alive.

Agatha's chest clamped so hard she thought her ribs cracked.

She felt someone watching her.

Her focus shifted to the School Master's tower at the center of the bay.

In the spire's window, Bilious Manley stood next to the Storian as the pen hovered over an open book. But the professor's eyes lingered on Agatha. He stared at her long and hard before clouds raided the sun, vanishing him into shadows.

Agatha picked up her pace. She could hear the buzz of conversation as she crossed from the breezeway into the Tunnel of Trees, leading outside.

The Clearing was full, the way it used to be at lunch. Only this time, there was no dividing line between Good and Evil, with friends, faculty, and first years crowded into the intimate picnic field outside the Blue Forest gates. As Agatha exited the tunnel, she spotted the young Everboys and Evergirls in the back: Bodhi, Laithan, Devan, Bert, Beckett, and Priyanka among them. In front of the Evers sat the first-year Nevers: Valentina, Aja, Bossam, Laralisa, and more. Then the crew of fourth years that had rescued them from Putsi—Vex, Ravan, Mona—plus others who had recovered from their quest injuries, including big-boned, flesh-headed Brone, his leg still in a cast. (*Why didn't someone use black magic to heal him too?*

Agatha wondered.) Next was Agatha's own team: shirtless Hort, nursing his feet against ice blocks, his face and arms sunburnt, his chest lily-white, grumbling to himself while swigging cold cider, as if he'd gone from man-wolf to overcooked pirate. Beside him were Bogden and Willam, both bandaged and rubbed with colorful salves. Then Hester, Anadil, and Dot, with Dot still old and baby Merlin clutched to her chest. At the sides of the field, the faculty gathered: Professor Emma Anemone, Professor Sheeba Sheeks, Castor the Dog, and others, both Good and Evil. Only Yuba and Princess Uma were missing. Sophie, too, Agatha realized now. Students and teachers alike took in Agatha as she entered, her once allies, her only family, now silent and grim, like witnesses to a trial.

Overhead, Lionsmane's message shimmered like a golden scar in the sky.

The audience returned their focuses forward: to their leader, seated on a stump between the two tunnels.

Tedros.

He had no shirt on, his body bruised and cut up, his breeches torn and dirt-stained. His gold curls still had leaves in them. Scim scratches blemished his right cheek. While Agatha had slept, eaten, bathed, he'd done none of these things. His cloudy blue eyes zeroed in on her, her prince sitting straighter.

Agatha wanted to say something, but Tedros spoke first.

"Sit down," he ordered.

Agatha obeyed, searching in vain for Sophie, before dropping beside Hort.

"Hello, Fatima," Hort slurred.

Agatha gave him a look.

"Fatima of Neverland whose tale the Storian told because she had so many friends but then did stupid things to lose them, one by one, until she had none." Hort swigged more cider. "Friendless Fatima. That's you."

Agatha tried to tune him out.

"You *knew* Sophie was out there. And *you* didn't tell me," Hort flamed, itching his sunburns. "So instead of protecting her, I end up a wolf chauffeur, ferrying Bilbo Bogden, his boyfriend, and a baby across Mahadeva in a heatwave, this after carrying you and Tedious around the Woods, and now I have sunstroke so bad Castor had to seal me in an ice coffin just to get me to remember my own *name*. But I remember what you did. Oh yes, I do. Taking Sophie for yourself. *Keeping* me from helping her." He glowered at Agatha, who could see Tedros watching her from his stump, just as intensely.

"Witches were saying they were the ones who got the stymphs to rescue us," said Tedros, emotionless.

"No offense, but we didn't trust you out there on your own," Hester explained to Agatha. "Not with the Snake on the loose. Once we got to school, we told the teachers. Figured they should put out a team to protect you."

"Glad you were of some use, considerin' we sent you here to find an aging spell," Hort heckled.

"We did find an aging spell, actually," Anadil said, knife-sharp.

"Not the kind that works," Hort blustered. "Dot's still a fishwife and I can smell Merlin's diaper from here."

"Because it has to be done in steps, you boiled rodent," Hester retorted.

"It's called an Age Defyer," Anadil said, her two rats asleep on her shoulders. "Ages or de-ages you a single year each day, for as long as you take it."

"Same one my mother used to stay young enough to birth me at an old age," said Hester. "Professor Sheeks helped us brew it. A stew of rat tears, turtle scales, and moldy cheese. Piping hot to grow older. Ice cold to turn young."

"Fed some to Merlin and myself this morning," said Dot, snuggling the infant. "Death would have been preferable to the taste."

Agatha inspected Dot closer: indeed, she looked a tad fresher than she had in Bloodbrook, while Merlin was longer, plumper than before, clad in purple velvet robes and fur booties, his eyes radiating intelligence.

"Mama!" he babbled, spotting Agatha and hopping out of Dot's arms to crawl towards her. "Mama llama! Mama llama!"

Limited intelligence, Agatha thought.

She scooped Merlin up, his belly soft against her chest. The wizard baby had new white-blond curls beneath his cone-shaped bonnet, which smelled of sweet milk. Merlin drummed his fingers on Agatha's cheeks. "Mama llama!"

"In a matter of days, Merlin will be able to speak coherent sentences and communicate with us," said Hester. "And in a couple weeks, he'll be our age, equipped with his sorcerer powers."

"*If* he keeps his powers," Professor Sheeks said, concerned.

"We don't know what he's lost."

"AND WE DON'T HAVE WEEKS!" Castor the Dog blared, waving a paw at Lionsmane's message. "WHOLE WOODS IS COMING FOR AGATHA!"

"Castor's right," echoed Professor Anemone, unusually disheveled. "We can't protect Agatha here. Not under that kind of attack."

"Of course we can," said Laithan, the muscled, red-haired Everboy, rising to his feet. "Good always wins. That's our duty as Evers. To hold our ground and fight for our queen."

"Nevers too," said dark-browed Valentina, standing. "We defend Agatha. We defend the school!"

"Like we did against Rafal," said Ravan, bounding up. "We took down him and his army of zombies. We can do it again!"

"No, we can't," Tedros repelled. "Rafal's zombies were *zombies*. Kill Rafal and they died with him. This is the whole Woods, men, women, and creatures from a hundred kingdoms, each fighting for a leader they don't even realize is their *enemy*. A leader far more vicious than Rafal. Robin Hood couldn't defeat the Snake. Kei couldn't either and he was a trained assassin. Japeth murdered Tinkerbell. He slayed my friend Betty like it was nothing. He killed Lancelot, Chaddick, the Sheriff of Nottingham, and so many more. And you think you can win this war for me. The same way Agatha thought she could. Which is why we're here. About to lose."

Agatha reddened, like she'd been slapped.

Everyone's eyes went to her. Even Merlin's, the baby skittish and mute.

Tedros gave her a long stare. Not angry or cold, but weary and defeated, as if when a prince didn't act a prince and a princess didn't act a princess . . . this was the fitting result.

"So what do we do, then?" said blond Bert.

"How do we win?" asked blonder Beckett.

"How else? Make Tedros kill Agatha," a voice said.

The crowd turned to Hort.

"It's the second test, ain't it?" he groused, waving his cup, splashing cider everywhere. "Dear ol' Teddy spears her and he wins. Then all he has to do is finish the third test and the Snake's dead. Trade Agatha's life for ours. That's what a *king* would do."

Agatha gaped at Hort, speechless.

"What you get for hoardin' Sophie to yourself," Hort murmured.

"You have a girlfriend!" Agatha hissed back.

"You have a girlfriend and boyfriend!" Hort scorched. "You kiss everyone!"

"Enough!" Professor Sheeks boomed. "As long as Agatha and Tedros are students at this school, there will be no killing!"

"But Agatha's *not* a student anymore," hairy, three-eyed Bossam pointed out. "And Hort's right. If Agatha dies, we're all safe—"

"You don't think 'King Japeth' will destroy the school the first chance he gets? Along with everyone in it?" Professor Anemone assailed. "As long as Agatha's sitting here, she's a *student*. And our *best* one at that."

"If she's the best, then why did she mess things up?" Bossam pushed.

"Yeah," said Aja angrily, "why do we have to die defending her because of her mistake?"

More Nevers rumbled. Evers too.

"Because it *wasn't* a mistake, you fools," a voice declared from a tunnel, followed by Sophie flouncing into the clearing, hair styled, makeup done, her white dress molded into a glittery winged kimono. "Sorry, I'm late. The hex to fix Aggie's leg picked one of my own bones to break in return." She held up her right hand, wrapped in bandages. "Could have been worse, of course, but beautifying with one hand is about as enticing as a night with Hort." She smiled at the weasel, as if she'd overheard everything he'd said to Agatha in her absence.

Hort went pink.

"Oh right, and this so-called 'mistake,'" Sophie said, fluttering her good hand at the crowd. "Agatha swallowed the answer to stop Japeth from claiming it first. Tedros had plenty of chances to win, but as usual, he didn't get the job done. It was Agatha who *saved* him from losing. It was Agatha who saved us from the Snake being ahead in the race. If anything, it was *she* who acted the king."

Agatha blushed with love. *Sophie.* Her knight in shining armor. Sophie, who'd broken herself to heal her best friend. Sophie, who'd found the Good in her, even when Agatha thought herself Evil. Her friend was never a witch. Just like Agatha wasn't a princess. They were both, always both, the line between princess and witch as thin as the line between stories and real life.

Tedros eyed Sophie stonily. "So I'm to blame, then. My own princess interfering in my test is my fault. My father telling me I have to kill her is my fault."

"Do you think I'd have done it if I'd known what would happen?" Agatha stood up, the baby bobbing against her chest. "I was trying to save us. I wasn't thinking—"

"That much we can agree on," said Tedros.

"Because you're the model of calm, deliberate thought," Sophie chirped, flanking Agatha.

Students and teachers peeked between the prince, his princess, and her best friend, three points of a triangle.

"What should I have done, then?" Agatha challenged Tedros, emboldened by Sophie. "Let Japeth win?"

"You didn't give me a *chance* to win!" Tedros said, jumping to his feet. "I'm the one fighting for the throne. I need you to help me. Not stand in my way!"

"I'm not trying to stand in your way! I want you to have a *head*!" said Agatha.

"So rarely used, though," Sophie chimed.

Merlin clapped with glee.

"This is why the Snake will win," Tedros muttered, sinking to his stump. "Because he doesn't have anyone holding him back. Because he fights for himself!"

"I thought that's what made us Good," Agatha replied. "We fight for each other."

Tedros looked at her.

"And you're wrong. Japeth isn't fighting for himself," Sophie added. "He wants to raise someone from the dead. That's why he wants the Storian's powers. That's why he wants your ring. For love. Just like you."

"Don't compare him to me," Tedros lashed, still riled up. "He wants his mother back. That horrible Sader woman. We already know that."

"No. Not Evelyn," Sophie said, starkly. "That's who Rhian loved. It's why Japeth killed him. The Snake wants someone else back. His best friend. His true love."

Sophie's words hit Agatha like a blow. She turned to Tedros, who'd understood too, his fire dissipating.

"*Aric?*" he said. "That's what he wants? To bring Aric back to life?"

Agatha could feel the whole school tense up, contemplating the return of Lady Lesso's son, a sadist with a black hole for a soul. The only thing worse than a Snake was *two* of them, united by love.

Tedros and Agatha locked eyes, the prince's gaze plaintive, as if the time for blame was over.

"There's nowhere we can go that Japeth won't find you," he said to her. "There's no solution to the test. Not that keeps us both alive."

"But you can stay alive," Agatha answered, damp with sweat, her neck red. Merlin gripped her shirt with small fists. "You can still win the test."

Tedros' expression changed. He leaned forward, looking very much a man. "Listen to me, Agatha. I will *never* hurt you.

Never. I will fight until my last breath to keep you safe."

He spoke with such strength, such clarity, that even with death hanging between them, Agatha felt a rush of love. She didn't want to die. But she needed to hear her prince say it. That they were in this together. That she still meant everything to him. That he loved her, no matter what.

Tedros smiled sadly at her. Even love couldn't save them now. They were cornered, with no way out. He sighed and glanced at Sophie, as if for once in his life, he'd take suggestions from her. But Sophie, too, was at a loss.

The three of them were trapped.

Their story at a dead end.

Until a deep voice broke the silence.

"There *is* a way."

For a second, Agatha thought it'd come from the sky or from the child in her arms.

Then she saw Professor Manley, standing inside the mouth of Evil's tree tunnel, his pale, lumpy flesh and the glare of his eyes reflecting through darkness.

"Come with me," he said, heading back into the tunnel.

Everyone in the Clearing stood up—

"No. You." Manley pointed a sharp, dirty nail at Tedros and Agatha. "*Only* you."

Agatha and her prince exchanged looks. They hurried after him, Merlin at Agatha's breast—

Sophie blocked her path, facing off with Manley. "Where she goes, I go."

Manley was about to retort—

"I still am Dean of the school in which you teach, *Bilious*, given I never resigned the position," Sophie clipped.

Professor Manley's eggish head shivered as if it might explode. "Suit yourself," he snarled, stomping into the tunnel, now three pairs of feet chasing him.

Make that four.

"Ain't leavin' me behind!"

Agatha spun to see Hort bundling after Sophie, half-naked and barefoot. "Not this time, Fatima! Not ever!" the weasel spewed.

Sophie blinked at him. "Who in lord's name is *Fatima*?"

"Don't ask," said Agatha, pulling her best friend ahead.

High in the School Master's tower, the Storian was paused over a nearly blank page. Professor Manley looked down at it, Agatha and her friends circled around him.

There was no painting. No scene.

Only a single line, in bold, black script beneath the empty space.

"There was a way."

Tedros frowned. "That's it? That's all it says?"

"How is *that* supposed to help us?" Sophie asked Manley.

"What good is a 'way' if we don't know what it is?" Hort piled on.

Agatha had the same questions.

Then, suddenly, the Storian began to glow.

A deep, urgent gold.

The ring on Tedros' finger began to glow the same hue.

Tedros' eyes widened. "What's happening—"

The glowing Storian stabbed down to the page, inking a painting in furious sweeps of color. A painting of Agatha and Tedros in this very tower. The couple was standing at the back window, the prince's arm around her waist as Agatha clasped a baby to her chest, the two of them gazing into the sun.

Beneath the painting, the Pen's words remained: "*There was a way.*"

Prince and princess looked at each other, baffled.

Agatha saw Manley peering at her intently, as if she already had the answers.

Then Agatha remembered.

The last time she was in this tower. It happened then too. The Storian painted something that had yet to take place. At the time, she'd questioned why the pen was acting out of turn. The Storian's job was to write the story as it happened. But suddenly the pen was jumping ahead . . . warning them of dangers . . . guiding them to clues . . .

"*Sometimes the story leads you,*" Yuba the Gnome had told her.

Agatha examined the Pen closer.

"The Storian needs our help to keep it alive," she said, studying its steel, a single swan left. Camelot's swan. The last tether of the Pen's power. "That's why it's helping *us.*"

"You're not making sense," Tedros dismissed, pointing at the painting. "How is *this* helping us?"

But Sophie seemed to understand. Sophie, who'd always had her own mysterious connection with the Storian, from the very first time she and her best friend had found it.

Sophie looked at the Pen . . .

Then at Agatha.

In a flash, the two girls were on the move, pushing Tedros towards the back window.

"We have to do it!" Sophie exerted.

"Do what?" the prince asked, mystified.

"Do the *pose*!" said Agatha, matching her stance in the painting, Merlin fussing against her shoulder. "Hold me the way you are in the painting, Tedros! Hurry!"

Tedros slung his arm around Agatha's waist. "I really don't get why—"

"Other side," Sophie badgered.

Tedros growled, letting her position him, but Merlin twitched restlessly, delivering a slap to the prince's eye. "Ow! Why'd you bring the damn baby! Get rid of him!"

"It's Merlin!" Agatha barked.

"Shhh! Both of you!" Sophie snapped. "Now look out the window."

Grumbling, Tedros angled towards the Woods, Agatha trying to subdue Merlin, while Sophie waited carefully out of frame.

Nothing happened.

Hort yawned against the wall. "I've seen a lot of daft things in my life but—"

Manley kicked him. "Stay focused," the teacher directed Agatha and Tedros. "Follow the pen—"

The Storian crackled with blue static, pointing in Manley's direction, as if he risked punishment by interfering any further.

And yet, he'd said all he needed to.

"*When Man Becomes Pen*," Agatha remembered.

That was August Sader's theory.

Man and Pen in balance.

A calm came over Agatha as she nestled against Tedros, the wizard baby settling down, taking her cue. Soon Agatha was as still as the Agatha in the painting. And with Agatha's stillness, Tedros stopped fidgeting, too, and found his own place of quiet, their living selves in union with their ones on the page. Fate and free will in perfect flow, each feeding the other. The silence in the tower thickened, as if the story had taken a breath . . .

Then Agatha heard it.

A galloping sound below.

Tedros' eyes widened.

Together, they looked out into the Woods . . . at the gates of the school flying open . . . a blur of motion rushing through . . .

A masked rider in black atop a horse.

No. Not a horse.

A *camel*.

It skidded to a stop at the edge of the lake, the rider standing atop its hump before tilting masked eyes up towards Agatha and Tedros in the tower window.

"Animals can help you if you help them. First thing I taught you at school!" a bright voice called. "You must have learned your lesson well."

The rider took off the mask.

Princess Uma smiled. "Because this animal's found a way to help you."

The camel grinned, too, craning its head up to Agatha.

A camel Agatha *knew*.

A camel she'd saved from its own trap.

Now come to save her and her prince.

"Mama llama!" Merlin giggled. He pointed at the camel. "Llama! Llama!"

Agatha gaped at the baby.

"*Definitely* keeping him with us," said Tedros.

15

SOPHIE

Trust Is the Way

"What do you suppose they're talking about?" Sophie asked, watching Hort wrap his arms around Tedros in the sky while she wrapped her arms around Agatha on the ground.

"What do boys talk about at all?" Agatha replied, Merlin strapped to her back.

The camel could seat three, anticipating Agatha, Tedros, and Princess Uma as its passengers, only to be confronted with

Sophie and Hort, too, plus a baby. When it became clear that Agatha wouldn't leave Merlin, Sophie wouldn't leave Agatha, and Hort wouldn't leave Sophie, Princess Uma summoned a stymph to ride with the boys, tracking Agatha and Sophie from above, while the girls rode the camel below. ("I can ride with Sophie," Hort volunteered. "And me with Agatha," Tedros seconded. "Uma already assigned teams," Sophie nipped.) As for their destination, they had no clue, because the camel refused to disclose it: "So no one can betray us to the enemy," it told Uma. When the princess pressed the animal to at least reveal the way they were going or the way to save Agatha from the second test, the camel replied: "*Trust* is the way."

"Or at least, that's what I think it said," Uma sighed later. "In Camel tongue, 'trust' and 'death' are the same word, though it's safe to assume it meant the first over the second."

"And you're *sure* we trust it?" Sophie had asked Agatha after Uma and the boys went to find a stymph.

Agatha stroked the camel like a pet. "The Sultan of Shazabah sent it as a gift for Rhian's wedding, before I saved it from the king's hands. It wants to reunite with its family. I heard its wish. But it can't go home to Shazabah. Not without being killed for disobeying orders. Uma said it was hiding in the Woods when it saw Lionsmane's message about me being the second test. The camel knew I needed help, so it sent word for Princess Uma through the forest animals, hoping she'd be able to lead it to me."

Sophie watched Merlin nuzzle his young face in the camel's fur. "Last time we trusted an animal, it was that despicable beaver who tried to murder us with snakes," said Sophie. "I don't trust vermin of any kind. No matter what Uma says."

"Spoken like a true witch," Agatha quipped.

Sophie frowned. "What's that smell?"

The camel had peed on her shoe.

With half the Woods bounty-hunting Agatha, they could only ride at night, leaving sleep for the daytime. As for those left behind, Tedros assigned them new quests. A gang of first years led by Valentina and Laithan would sneak into Camelot to shadow Japeth's movements, while Bogden and Willam were to visit the priest named Pospisil—who Willam once served as an altar boy—to see if he'd be of help against the Snake.

"Librarian at the Living Library hinted he might be a friend to us," said Tedros.

Meanwhile, a squirrelly nut had arrived for Tedros while they'd been in the School Master's tower.

"Message from Jaunt Jolie," Tedros disclosed, addressing the witches. "Queen Jacinda wants to see you."

"Jaunt Jolie?" said Hester. "That's Ever territory."

"Send Beatrix or Reena instead," Anadil agreed.

"Except those two are still missing," matronly Dot pointed out. "Kiko too."

"Not our problem," Hester snapped. "Nor are Ever queens."

"Well, this Ever queen asked for *you*, which is why you three are going," Tedros ordered. "Tell Jacinda that her daughter is dead, at the hands of the Snake. She should know the truth. And find out what happened to Nicola and my mother.

Last we heard, they'd gone to ask for the queen's help. Her Knights of the Eleven are our best chance to help kill Japeth before he finds Agatha. And we have to kill him. Because as long as the second test holds, he won't stop until he kills *her*."

Sophie could see Agatha thinking this over, but Aggie made no argument.

Along the way, Tedros added, the coven should stop at Glass Mountain to find where Robin Hood had hidden Maid Marian. ("How do we tell her Robin's dead?" Dot lamented. "We really are the death parade," Anadil mumbled back.)

The rest of the Evers and Nevers, teachers included, would resume classes as usual, deflecting any suspicions they were harboring Agatha, while keeping the Storian well-protected. Besides, as Professor Sheeks pointed out, the camel had made a wise choice: by withholding its plans for Agatha, the school could play dumb—even the most potent sorcerer couldn't extract information if they had no information to give.

Good, Evil, Boy, Girl, Young, Old . . . the common mission was the same: forward motion, trusting a camel to guide them, even if they hadn't a clue where the camel was going.

Sophie felt this forward motion literally now, their journey begun, the camel bouncing her with every step, Sophie's nose and mouth covered with white silk. Somewhere between the Clearing and the Woods, her white kimono had magically morphed into a chic riding ensemble, complete with headscarf and veil. "You know, I keep trying to get the dress off, but the more I try, the more it refashions into something divine, as if it knows exactly how to charm me. At this point, I can't tell whether it's good magic or bad magic."

"Anything of Evelyn Sader's is bad," said Agatha in a dark hooded cloak behind her, the baby asleep against her back.

"And yet, Evelyn is the link between the Snake and Green Knight," Sophie replied. "Isn't that what you saw in the pearl?"

"It was some kind of riddle hidden inside. A riddle Arthur wanted the winner of the first test to see," said Agatha.

"Must be important, then," Sophie allowed, "even if it makes no sense."

"When we went into Rhian's blood, what did we see for sure?" said Agatha. "We saw Evelyn enchant Arthur to have his child. We saw Evelyn put the spansel around his neck instead of Lady Gremlaine doing it. Which means Arthur *had* a secret son with Evelyn Sader. Or sons. No doubt about it."

"And yet, the Snake isn't Arthur's son at all. Or at least he claimed he isn't," said Sophie. "Then again, he lies about everything, just like his brother did." She shook her head. "But why would he lie about that? Unless the Snake *isn't* the son Evelyn had with Arthur . . . Unless it's the Green Knight who's the Snake's father . . ."

"But Rhian's blood says it's Arthur who's the father!" Agatha argued.

"And yet, the Green Knight has the same *name* as the Snake. Japeth. Plus, the wizard tree said the Snake had a connection to the Green Knight's soul. How can that be unless Japeth shares his blood?" Sophie insisted. "The Green Knight *has* to be the Snake's father."

"And Evelyn Sader his mother? But why did Rhian's blood

lie, then? And how did it fool Excalibur when Rhian pulled the sword from the stone?"

"Maybe it didn't lie," Sophie guessed. "Maybe Rhian had Arthur as his father and Japeth had the Green Knight as his . . . Evelyn Sader the mother to both." Sophie's heart hummed faster. "Twins divided by magic . . ."

"Like us," Agatha spoke softly.

Sophie heard the catch in her friend's voice. They'd never talked about it. What they'd seen in August Sader's history long ago. That they were sisters . . . but sisters in name only . . . Two souls, forever irreconcilable, each a mirror of the other: one Good, one Evil. *What if Rhian and Japeth were the same?* Sophie thought.

"It doesn't make sense," Agatha rejected. "How can twins have *different* fathers?"

Sophie threw up her hands. "But who's their father, then? Arthur or the Green Knight? Is Rhian's blood right or is Japeth's blood right? And if Rhian's blood was wrong, how do we know Evelyn Sader is their mother at all?"

Agatha sighed, both of their brains in knots.

They stopped speaking for a while, Merlin letting out a burble as if he'd been listening all along. Sophie glanced high at Tedros and Hort, silhouetted in their black cloaks, still locked in their own conversation, while Uma steered the stymph to match the camel's pace.

"You really broke your wrist to save my leg?" Agatha asked.

"If the Snake is coming for you, we can't have you hobbling around. Of course the repair spell could have broken my own leg in return or worse, but I figured you and I would take turns healing each other and breaking bones until we found the least inconvenient one."

Agatha snorted. "God, how did we get here?"

"You mean, aboard a smelly camel to nowhere, with your prince ordered to kill you, the Woods stalking you, and a baby wizard on your back?"

The camel spat a gob of fire past Sophie's ear.

"Must everything in our story be twisted and barbarous?" Sophie moaned.

She peeked back at Agatha, expecting the usual wry response. But instead, Aggie looked afraid. More than afraid. She looked lost.

"No, I mean, how did we get *here*?" Agatha said. "So far from a happy ending?"

"We were meant for a bigger life, Agatha," Sophie reminded. "From the beginning. August Sader told the School Master that a Reader would be his true love . . . the Evil soul Rafal had been waiting for. That's why Rafal kidnapped Readers like us to this world. To find his true love. But Sader *lied* to him: because he knew that you and I would kill Rafal. That our love would destroy him. After Rafal died, we thought the story was over. We assumed our happy ending would last forever. Because that's what storybooks taught us. That Good always wins. That Ever After is Ever After. But our fairy tale changed the rules. We punched holes in the old ways of Good and Evil. And now we're in a new tale where it's no longer enough to be Good. The Storian wants more from us. Enough to risk its own destruction. To win, we have to follow our story wherever it leads. Beyond Ever and Never. Beyond Man and Pen. To the End of Ends."

Agatha went quiet behind her, her body no longer rigid, a calm settling into her breath. She touched Sophie's shoulder.

"To the End of Ends," said Agatha.

The words echoed in the dark forest.

Wisps of blue smoke floated down and curdled in front of Sophie, a message in Hort's scraggly glow: "*Tell Agatha to switch with me.*"

Sophie waved away the smoke. "You know, for a boy with a girlfriend, he certainly doesn't act like it."

"Which makes me wonder why Nicola is with him at all," said Agatha, her tone lighter, as if gossiping about someone else's love life was a tonic for doom. "Nicola's as sharp as they come. She's read our fairy tale and knows every detail. She must know Hort can't let go of you."

"And having read our story, she also thinks Hort's too good for me, which is why she continues to date him," said Sophie. "Nic's a Reader like us. She grew up reading tales where witches don't have boyfriends. To her, Hort liking me is unnatural. She truly believes he deserves someone better. Someone like *her*. And that if she stays with him, Hort will eventually see the light. But that implies love is rational. That when backed into a corner, the heart does the sensible thing. But that's where Hort and I are the same. Neither of us has the least control over our heart."

"Hmm. Interesting," Agatha said.

"I don't like the sound of that."

"Our third year, Hort saw a vision in the Wish Fish lake. When we were at Guinevere's safe house. The fish told him that you and him would be married in the end. And we're not yet at The End . . ."

"I know this will surprise you, but I've considered it, Aggie," said Sophie. "Especially after Hort tried to rescue me from Rhian. For the briefest of moments, I saw him as my prince . . . I saw what our story together could be . . . And there are moments, now more than ever, where I think: Take a chance. Date the weasel. Go for the doting, soft boy instead of the sultry hunk who ends up wanting to kill me. At least I'll be loved. At least I'll have kisses without a knife in my back." Sophie paused. "But then I think . . . where's the challenge in *that*?" She grinned back at her friend.

"And you wonder why witches don't have boyfriends," said Agatha.

⁓

NEVER ENTER THE Woods at night.

That had been one of the first rules Sophie had learned at the School for Good and Evil. And with good reason. After sunset, the forest turned into a haunting ground. Red and yellow eyes twinkled like jewels in the underbrush, followed by the gleam of sharp teeth. Dark outlines flitted across trees: snouts, claws, wings. The night came with its own sounds, too, a steady roll of growls and skitters and shrieks. The deeper you prowled into the Woods, the more it prowled back, tickling the crooks of your legs, breathing at your neck. But safe atop the camel, Sophie took in the night with new eyes. Fluorescing green spores on poisonous ivy. Black scorpions, shiny like obsidian. Red and blue snakes twined around a tree. There was beauty in the danger, if you let yourself see it.

The thoughts were fleeting. Sophie knew it was only a matter of time before they ran into someone after Agatha. A few hours into their trek and they'd already caught glimpse of two teenage boys, a lone dwarf, a witch wheeling a cart . . . but all bustled by with hardly a glance, as if using the dark to hide from something themselves.

"That age potion must be working," Agatha said. "Merlin's getting heavier."

Sophie studied the child strapped to her friend, his body bigger, his hair bushier than when they'd left school, the once baby-sized robes seeming to magically grow with him. Merlin eagerly sucked milk from his blue hat, leaking all over Agatha.

"Make Mama wet!" the wizard chimed, rubbing milk into her hair.

"Now I see why you hate children," said Agatha.

"He's in the terrible twos. For the night anyway," Sophie noted. "Hester said to feed him the next dose of potion. That'll grow him to three by tomorrow."

"Already heavy on my back at two."

"Let me hold him, then. At least for a little while."

"He's due for a poo."

"Give him to me, Aggie."

Agatha unhooked Merlin with a sigh and handed him to Sophie, who used her good hand to secure him in her lap—

The Woods vanished.

Sophie was high on a cloud, silver stars winking against a purple sky.

The Celestium.

Someone was sitting next to her.

Tedros.

Tedros, who had no head.

His neck a bloody stump.

"Peekaboo!" a voice said.

She turned and saw Tedros' decapitated head floating in the air behind her.

"Peekaboo!"

Sophie screamed—

But now she was back in the forest, so jolted with shock that she was about to fall off the camel, the baby with her, before Agatha lunged and saved them both.

"Have you lost your mind!" she berated Sophie.

Sophie gaped at Merlin, the child grinning at her. The wizard had done it. Was it a prank? More terrible twos? And yet, the way Merlin was smiling, so calm and assured . . .

"Wait. Did something happen?" Agatha asked suddenly, her expression changing, as if she'd had her own bout with Merlin's tricks. "Sophie, what did you see?"

Your boyfriend in two pieces.

"Nothing," Sophie said out loud. "Just got dizzy."

Hort's glow-smoke drifted in front of her again, a new

message: "*Saw you fall. I'm coming down.*"

Sophie scrawled back in pink glow—"*Come down and I'll give you a slap*"—swatting the message up to him.

Hort stayed where he was.

They rode on. Freed from carrying Merlin, Agatha promptly fell asleep against Sophie's shoulder. The wizard poked at the vial sticking out of Sophie's dress pocket.

"Drinkie," he peeped.

Sophie pulled out the bottle of green goo that Hester had given her and squeezed a few steamy drops onto Merlin's tongue, the child eager for it, despite the potion's hellish smell and the face he made upon swallowing. Sophie tried to shake off what she'd seen in the Celestium, while Merlin sang nonsense and toyed with her veil. Every time she looked at him, he seemed to have grown, his diaper no longer soiled every hour. Instead, he'd tug on Sophie with a spooked look, his new way of indicating he needed to relieve himself. Time slowed to a crawl, the wizard's growth outpacing the night, until at last the black sky started to blue. The camel peered up at Uma, expecting her to scout the path and signal a spot to hide until morning. But the stymph stalled, Uma hesitating . . .

There were campfires ahead, circled by shadows.

"Aggie, *look*," Sophie nudged.

Agatha snored awake. Her eyes widened. "Pirates," she breathed, taking in the fleet of Camelot guards, led by Wesley, his sunburnt face visible through his helmet.

But not just pirates, Sophie realized.

Wolves.

Dozens of them, man-wolves and werewolves alike, mixed with Japeth's army, the wolves' hulking torsos and feral faces flamelit as the teams shared roasted rabbit and squirrel.

Sophie looked to Uma for guidance, but treetops and rising smoke had obscured the stymph. Sophie tugged on the camel's reins, reversing course, but more wolves were coming that way, towing a dead boar. The camel hustled forward, sneaking a narrow path around the camp. Sophie tightened her veil and Agatha grabbed Merlin's blue hat to fashion her own mask, both girls keeping their heads low.

"Bloodbrook ain't no friend to Camelot," Wesley said to the largest man-wolf, as the returning wolves heaped the boar on the fire. "King musta promised yers a pretty penny to help us catch Agatha."

"Storian hasn't written the tale of a Bloodbrook Never in a hundred years. Closest we came was that pathetic Hort, who played the fool in Agatha's tale," said the wolf leader. "No legends or heroes to believe in anymore. Reason we've become a slum instead of the kingdom we once were. If Rhian gets the Pen's powers, he promised to restore Bloodbrook to glory."

"With yer noses helpin' us, king'll win the second test in no time," said Wesley. "Track that wench down like a dog." He smiled at the wolf leader. "No offense."

And yet, with the smoke and meat, none of them caught scent of Agatha, who was slipping right past them, almost out of the thicket. Sophie tried to quiet Merlin, who was squirming for Agatha as the camel skirted the enemy camp, about to break into open Woods. But Merlin thrashed harder in

Sophie's arms, angling for Agatha—

His hat, Sophie realized.

He wanted it back.

Merlin started to swell red.

No, no, no, Sophie prayed.

The wizard went redder, redder, redder.

She covered his mouth—

Merlin exploded.

A loud, piercing wail that startled even the camel.

Agatha and Sophie froze. Merlin, too.

Wolves and guards raised their eyes.

The Woods went still.

Instantly, the camel fled, but wolves surrounded it. The camel spat a blast of fire, torching one, but the rest of the wolves tackled it to the ground, hoisting Sophie and Agatha off, separating them from Merlin, before they cut the camel's reins and stuffed them in its mouth.

As wolves gripped the two veiled girls and a guard gagged Merlin, Wesley approached, sword in hand.

"Heidy-ho, fair lasses. May I ask where yer going inna middle of a night wit a Shazaboo camel?"

Sophie looked at Agatha. Agatha looked at Sophie. Each knew who was the better liar.

"To the island of Markle Markle. Hafsa and I are to dance for the king," Sophie touted, nodding at hat-masked Agatha. The white scarf around Sophie's nose and mouth magically tightened, leaving only her green eyes visible. "We've been sent by the sultan. A diplomatic mission."

"Markle Markle, eh?" said Wesley. "And where izzat? East of Shangri-la and West of Santy Claus' den?"

"Off the shores of Ooty, actually," Sophie replied.

Wesley grinned. "Lies."

"To a guard of Camelot, perhaps," said Sophie. "The island is hidden by fog. Visible only to maidens and pirates, of which you are neither."

Her emerald gaze cut through him.

Wesley stopped grinning.

"Show yer face," he said. "Both of ye."

Neither girl obeyed.

"Then I'll do it meself," he snarled, his sword reaching for Sophie's veil—

"I wouldn't if I were you," said Sophie calmly. "Remove a girl's veil and you'll be cursed to die before the day is done."

Wesley stared at her. Then at Agatha.

"Bad death!" Agatha piped, with a hideous accent.

Wesley turned to his men. "That true?"

No one disputed it.

"Best be on our way then," Sophie said, breaking free—

"Not until you *dance*," said a voice.

The largest man-wolf stepped into the firelight. The pack leader.

"What?" Sophie asked, off guard.

"Whole Woods is searching for a fugitive girl about your age. King Rhian's orders," the man-wolf spoke. "If you are who you say you are, then prove it. One dance and you're free to go."

Sophie hesitated, but Agatha jumped in. "No moosic," she said, sounding like a stuffed-up goat.

"Exactly," Sophie echoed. "No music, no dance."

A steady beat punctured the silence.

Both girls looked up at two wolves, rapping on guard armor with sticks.

Tikka tik tok . . . Tikka tik tok . . .

Another wolf slapped his paw against a stone: *duk duk dop . . . duk duk dop . . .*

A last wolf threw mulch into the fire, with a percussive *pahhh . . . pahhh . . .*

The man-wolf leader bared teeth at Sophie.

"*Dance*," he said.

Sophie glared back at the wolf.

If there was one thing wolves and men had in common, it was that they underestimated the power of a girl.

Sophie could feel Evelyn's dress changing on her skin, as if she had full command over it the same way Japeth controlled his scims. Soon her white riding clothes had become a sparkly fitted halter and matching harem pants, her veil coated in glitterdust.

The wolf stepped back, startled.

Sophie kicked off her shoes, her arms flurrying, her body spinning into motion. Around her enemies she danced, making them dizzy with her whirls and twists, her bandaged hand grazing Wesley and wolf with teasing touches, before her good hand slashed nails across their cheeks, drawing blood. They were too entranced to revolt, watching Sophie twirl with speed and glimmer, like a sylph born out of the fire, yanking guards' hair to jeté over them and clutching wolves' throats to launch into luscious arabesques. The beat quickened, the wolves gaping wet-mouthed. A long time ago, a Beast had punished Sophie by stealing her beauty. Now his kin were slaves to it. Faster and faster, the music went, Sophie heightening her glissades, dropping into splits, capping moves with winks and trills, tossing a guard's meal into the fire for a last spike of flames . . . before she thrust her heel in a high, stabbing kick, which connected hard with Wesley's head, knocking his helmet into the fire and revealing his peeling, mottled face.

"Strange you don't know Markle Markle," Sophie cooed, eyeing him. "Look more *pirate* than Camelot guard to me."

Wolves gave Wesley an odd glance as if they agreed.

"Best of luck finding your fugitive. Come, Hafsah," Sophie said, snatching Merlin from a guard and strutting towards the tied-up camel—

"Stop."

Sophie turned.

The wolf was pointing at Agatha. "She dances *too*."

Sophie cleared her throat. "Hafsah only does *private* dances. For kings who pay their weight in gold."

"*Dance*," Wesley commanded, honed in on Agatha.

A guard stripped Merlin from Sophie.

The music began again.

Tikka tik tok.

Tikka tik tok.

Agatha peeked at the treetops, the stymph long gone, then

at baby Merlin in the guard's arms, as if hoping the wizard would rescue them. But he just chewed on his gag like a pacifier, beaming at his "Mama" and clapping along to the wolves' beat.

The man-wolf tapped his claw in the dirt, his lips curling over jagged teeth.

Sophie gave Agatha an encouraging nod. *Come on, Aggie.* Surely she could muster a competent waltz or volta or *something*. Her friend had received dance lessons at school. And more lessons at Camelot. Besides, dancing was the easiest thing in the world. All it required was comfort of body, grace of movement, and a child's sense of rhythm.

Then she saw the ghostly pallor of her friend's face and remembered that Agatha had none of these things.

Agatha lifted her leg and shook it a few times. At first Sophie thought this was the warm-up for the dance, but no, this *was* the dance, her friend gyrating like a flamingo before dropping into a hideous squat and rocking from side to side, her bony knees cracking. "*Ooh de lally, ooh de lally,*" Aggie mumbled, as if keeping time to a beat that had nothing to do with the one being played. Aggie glanced at Sophie and must have seen her expression because now she was shaking her bottom and waving her arms as if hailing a carriage, before she started running in place as if the carriage had left without her. This went on, the phantom sprint, along with strange hand sweeps like a sad version of tai chi, until she tripped on her cloak and crashed onto her stomach, only to pretend this, too, was the dance, flailing her legs, flashing her dusty petticoat, before lumbering onto her side, caked in dirt, like a mummy washed ashore at the beach.

Her veil fell off.

Agatha and Sophie stared at the shrunken wizard hat on the ground.

Merlin stopped clapping.

The music halted too, the audience stone silent.

Slowly Agatha looked up, face in plain sight.

"Oh, hullo," she said.

Like a storm, they came for her, swords and snouts. Sophie blasted her pink glow, but the wolves were already on her, tying her and Agatha up with pig-smelling rope, while Merlin was stuffed into a burlap sack. Sophie strained for breath, Wesley's knees on her chest, his black nails stabbing her neck, his rancid face in hers—

"King wants yer friend alive. Never said anythin' 'bout *you*."

He strangled her so hard that her heart jolted to a stop, the life squeezed out of her, while Agatha screamed into a gag, forced to watch her best friend die—

Thunder hammered from above.

A roaring wolf-bomb straight for Wesley, shattering his skull with his fists.

A crater imploded beneath, swallowing wolves and guards as the new man-wolf landed, swinging Agatha, Sophie, and Merlin onto his back. He grabbed the boar off the roast, axing it at the remaining wolves, painting them with flames and sending them fleeing into the Woods, before savaging the last few guards with blows to the head. Only when they were all gone did he take a breath, his wolf teeth smeared with blood, his fur lit with embers, before Hort held Sophie up by his paw, gnashing into her face.

"I'll take that *slap* now."

A DAY LATER, they camped on the frigid banks of the Frostplains, under frozen docks that stretched out into the Savage Sea.

When night came, Uma woke her charges, expecting the camel to lead them on the next leg of the journey.

But the camel didn't move, remaining curled up beneath the docks.

"What are we waiting for?" Uma asked, shivering.

"For our ship to come in," the camel told her.

TWO DAYS LATER, the ship still hadn't come in.

While Uma flew the stymph out to sea to forage for more fish, her wards huddled beneath the docks as the sun rose, warmed by a small fire and their own body heat as they cuddled against the camel's belly. None of them could sleep, including Merlin, age five and fully alert, who was skipping around the fire, tossing sticks and seaweed and whatever else he could find into the flames and watching them burn.

"When's this damned ship coming?" Tedros groused, eyeing the sleeping camel. "And where's this blasted beast taking us?"

"As far from Shazabah as it can get," Hort guessed, firesmoking pieces of salmon and handing them to Sophie, who Hort was spooning under his arm. "Probably hiding us in the unmapped realms."

"But how does that help me win the second test without killing Agatha?" said Tedros, harboring his princess to his chest. "Wherever we go, the Snake will hunt us. Running away doesn't stop him or keep Agatha safe. Running away isn't what my father would have wanted me to do. It's just . . . cowardice."

"'*Trust* is the way.' That's what the camel said," Agatha sighed, nestling deeper into her prince's arms.

"Trust also means 'death' in Camel," Tedros cracked.

"It's saved our life before," Agatha reminded. "That's why the Storian pointed us to it."

"Same Storian wrote murdering twins into our fairy tale right when we should have been getting married."

Something about the way Tedros said this, at once angry and loving, made Agatha's face change. "I wish I hadn't swallowed the pearl," she said quietly. "I wish I'd caught it and given it to you. You'd be on to the second test. The *real* second test, whatever it should have been."

Tedros stroked her hair. "Trust is the way, remember?"

Sophie could see Agatha relaxing under her prince's fingers, her eyes closed with pleasure. "Better stop doing that or I'll get used to it," Agatha murmured to him.

"You're very bossy," said Tedros. "Just stop thinking and let go for once."

Agatha settled deeper into his chest. Then she sprung up on her elbows. "And that vision I saw in the pearl means nothing to you? Evelyn Sader as the link between Japeth and the Green Knight?"

Tedros gave up on his massage. "Thought about it on the stymph ride, after you mentioned it. But Evelyn Sader had nothing to do with the Green Knight. Nor does Japeth, as far as we know. Why would my father hide that in the pearl? Doesn't make the slightest sense. Like everything else in this story."

They watched Merlin throw more things into the fire and pip "Shazam!" as if he was the one spawning the flames.

"Our kid is growing up," Tedros mused, pulling Agatha towards him.

Sophie nibbled on salmon, watching them kiss.

"Hope it tastes okay," Hort said, his bicep hugging her. "Tried to cook it just right."

Sophie knew she shouldn't be letting him hold her like this. That it was giving Hort the wrong idea. But it was glacial out here. And Hort was wonderful at spooning, soft in all the right spots. Plus, with Agatha hunkered with Tedros, either she nested with the weasel or slept alone by the camel's buttocks.

But there was something else, of course.

The way he'd saved her.

Not just that Hort had rescued her from death, but also that burn in his glare, that red-hot ardor, as if the boy had molted into a man. She'd always thought him a weenie, a lovestruck sop, but now she'd seen the alpha wolf inside, the one who commanded her love and didn't back down. She'd never admit to being aroused by the thought; she'd plotted the death of any boy or beast who dared to claim her . . . Yet here she was, letting this one touch her, even though his fingers smelled of smoke and fish.

She rolled over to Hort. "What did you and Tedros talk about up there on the stymph? Every time I looked, you two were deep in conversation."

Hort and Tedros exchanged glances.

"Fitness tips," said Hort.

"Rugby," said Tedros.

"Ah," said Sophie.

Liars.

"Maybe this *is* the real second test, though," Agatha wondered, finally freed from Tedros' lips. "The more I think about this tournament, the stranger it is."

"Here she goes again," Tedros said. "Thinking."

"A revelation to you, I imagine," said Sophie. "Aggie, what do you mean?"

"The tournament is a race. Three tests. Whoever stays ahead wins," Agatha reasoned. "If Tedros or Japeth swallowed the pearl, one of them would have had a head start on the next test until the other figured it out. So how did Arthur know neither of them would win? How did he have that second test prepared?"

Tedros sat up. "I don't understand."

"Of course you don't," said Sophie. "But Aggie's right. Arthur's ghost is speaking from the dead. And yet, he was ready for the case that neither you nor Japeth would win."

"My dad is thorough," Tedros defended. "He would have readied for all possibilities."

"Or he knew all along killing Agatha would be the second test," said Sophie. "Because he'd planned for Agatha winning the first."

"You think my dad wants me to kill my future *queen*?" Tedros mocked.

But Agatha was still looking at Sophie. "That line when he announced the tournament. '*The future I have seen has many possibilities . . .*'"

"Somehow he had a view to the future," Sophie said, finishing Agatha's thought.

Tedros scoffed: "My father wasn't a magician. He couldn't have seen the future."

"And yet, he knew we would be at his archive, looking for the first answer. That's why he had Sader leave clues for us there," said Agatha. "Either Arthur made a lot of lucky guesses . . . or your father saw ahead, even when August Sader couldn't."

Tedros' face changed. "But who would have told him? Who would have helped him see the future?"

"You're asking the wrong question," said Hort.

They turned to him.

"The question is whether that person was on your *side*," said Hort.

Sophie and the others fell silent.

Together, they gazed at Merlin, who seemed to have developed command over the fire, summoning magical shapes out of the flames: a tree . . . a cave . . . a sword . . .

"Mama, Mer-Mer is a wizard!" he said, hopping around. "See, look, Mama!"

"I'm looking, Merlin," said Agatha, seemingly both relieved that he had his magic and disconcerted by how fast Merlin was growing. In the last day, he'd become unpredictable: in touch with his powers and still weeks away from knowing his potential.

"So many things we don't know," said Tedros. "Why Dad hid that riddle . . . how the Green Knight and Snake are connected . . . whether my future is fated or within my control . . ." The prince petted the sleeping camel. "Trust better be the way, Sir Camel. Because it's the only way we have left."

"Sir Camel is a 'she,'" said Agatha.

Princess and prince drifted off to sleep.

Hort, too, began to yawn, leaving only Sophie to keep watch as the sun rose, tinting the docks with wintry light. Soon, Uma returned with a scanty stock of fish and fell asleep with the others, while her stymph flew back out to sea. Merlin, meanwhile, was still babbling and pitching things into the fire, conjuring random shapes. But in time, even the wizard child had enough, and after Sophie fed him the next drop of potion, he went down between her and Hort.

Sophie forced herself to stay awake, her eyes pinned on the sea for any incoming ships. Her lids heavied, her focus blurring back to the fire. The flames seemed to heighten, glowing unnatural colors, yielding new shapes, as if Merlin could control them even in sleep, a view into his unconscious. First, a blue butterfly . . . then a black snake . . . then a green, headless man rising from the fire, his neck a bloody stump . . .

But he had a head, Sophie saw now.

He carried it under his arm.

Tedros' head.

"*Peekaboo!*" Tedros said.

Sophie bolted awake to a wash of sun.

The fire was out, the ashes long cooled.

Merlin was sound asleep, snuggled on Hort's chest. Agatha and Tedros, too—

But something was different.

The camel, Sophie realized.

It was gone.

Sophie lifted her eyes.

A ship was at the docks.

Sails, red and gold.

Across the stern, carved letters spelled its name.

Shazabah Sikander

Shadows cast over Sophie and her friends, as if clouds had cloaked the sun.

Only there were no clouds, the sky a vacant white.

Slowly Sophie turned around.

Her blood chilled.

"Aggie?" she croaked.

Agatha stirred, following Sophie's eyes. She jerked upright, snatching Tedros awake. Hort and Uma roused too, with the weasel grabbing Merlin.

At least fifty soldiers glared down at them, wearing red-and-gold armor, wielding curved sabers and spears.

They had the camel, collared and wrapped with chains.

But the camel didn't resist. It wasn't fighting its captors at all.

It was *smiling*.

Grinning at Agatha and Tedros, as if this was the ship it'd been waiting for all along.

It grunted calmly, the same sounds again and again.

Sounds Sophie had heard before, the camel's guiding phrase.

Trust is the way.

Trust is the way.

Trust is the way.

But as guards came towards her and her friends, sabers raised, suddenly Sophie understood.

The camel never meant "trust."

The camel meant something else.

"Trust" and "death" were the same word in Camel.

And they had gotten it wrong.

THE COVEN

The Knights of Eleven

"The queen," the attendant sniffed in his pink-and-yellow uniform, standing tall at the door to Castle Jolie. "I'm to believe the queen sent for *you*."

Hester, Anadil, and middle-aged Dot blinked at him, the three witches in filthy black hoods, held at the necks by a pair of guards.

"Found them sneaking across the border, smelling like skunks," said a guard.

"We weren't sneaking. The queen invited us," Hester snapped. "We've traveled for days to get here. We're her *guests*!"

The attendant snorted. "Throw them out."

"We have an urgent message! About Princess Bettina!" Dot insisted, flapping her arms. "She's been ki—"

"Kin to us. Like family," Hester cut in, glowering at Dot, before puffing up at the attendant: "Is this how you treat friends of the princess? Tell the queen we're here."

"The queen is in a meeting with her knights," the attendant sniffed. "And Nevers aren't permitted inside Castle Jolie. Especially after pirates laid waste to our kingdom, with whom you no doubt sympathize."

"We're Nevers, not thugs," Anadil scorned.

"Would you deny your queen's *guests* because you object to their appearance?" Hester piled on. "No wonder pirates target your realm to punish such arrogance. No wonder the Snake chose your land to occupy, with people like *you* serving it."

The attendant hesitated, with a rankled scowl. Then he rolled his eyes and flung open the door. "Last time someone disturbed the queen, she made him kneel as a dinner table for her children's supper. Let's hope you suffer something far worse." He clacked away, glaring back at the guards. "Don't let them touch anything."

The witches followed the guards inside. "Why didn't we tell the truth?" Dot whispered to Hester. "About Bettina being killed?"

"Who would he think *killed* her? Especially with a creepy adult looming around Ani and me like you've kidnapped us," Hester retorted. "We need to see the queen. That's why Tedros sent us. To get her help fighting the Snake. And for that, we'll tell as many lies as we need to."

"Such a wise leader," said Dot.

Hester looked touched.

Dot smiled back. "But am I lying or telling the truth?"

"Point taken," Hester growled.

Ten minutes later, the witches were still waiting, the two guards keeping watch from across the foyer. Hester's eyes were red, her nose runny, as she sat on a bench beneath a wall of hydrangeas, the pastel, pom-pom-shaped petals blanketing every inch of Castle Jolie.

"Rats can't pick up the scent of Nicola or Guinevere," Anadil fretted, her pets returning to her pocket. "Couldn't pick up Marian's scent in Glass Mountain, either."

"Glass Mountain reeked of fungus and blight. And rats won't pick up the scent of anything here but these damn flowers," Hester muttered, wiping her nose.

"Cleaned up the place nice, at least. Last time we were here, the Snake's pirates pee-peed everywhere," said Dot, plucking a flower and turning it to chocolate. Instantly, the wall began an endless loop of music: "*Tipple Top, Joy and Jaunt, Come and Be Jolie! Tipple Top, Joy and Jaunt, Come and Be Jolie! Tipple Top . . .*" (The guards groaned.) But the music gave the witches cover to talk—

"Let me handle negotiating with the queen," Hester

whispered. "To kill the Snake, we'll need her Knights of the Eleven."

"But what if her message was a trap?" Dot asked. "Nic and Guinevere were supposed to come here and there's no trace of them. What if the queen killed them? What if she's on the Snake's side?"

"Don't be daft," Hester barbed, but now her chest felt tight.

"Think Robin could have left Maid Marian somewhere *else* in Glass Mountain?" Anadil said, still inspecting her rats. "Somewhere we didn't search?"

"Robin told Sophie he hid Marian in a sanctuary," said Hester. "Only place like that is the sacred orchard and she wasn't there."

"Plus, Robin wouldn't have planned on leaving her long," Dot added. "Been four days since the wizard tree battle. She'd have gone searching for him."

"Stink of the blight would have been enough to drive her off," said Hester, sniffing Dot's clothes. "No wonder the guards found us."

"That camel at school smelled worse," said Dot. "Let's hope Agatha's safe."

"Sooner we kill the Snake, sooner we're *all* safe," said Hester.

By now, the music was rattling Hester's skull: "*Tipple Top, Joy and Jaunt, Come and Be Jolie! Tipple Top, Joy and Jaunt, Come and—*"

A black fist went through the flowers. The song sputtered out.

Slowly, the witches raised their eyes to a huge man in gold chainmail tinted with pearlescent colors. A mask of mesh covered his nose and mouth like a veil, his dark eyes slashing through them.

"The queen will see you now," he snarled.

The witches hurried after him.

"You're a Knight of the Eleven," Hester said eagerly. "Fiercest warriors in the Woods—"

"Saddle the horses," the knight barked at a passing page boy. "Queen says the Eleven ride tonight."

The boy looked alarmed. "But I've just seen the Knights. They're in no condition to—"

"*Now!*" the knight roared.

The boy scuttled away. With every step, the knight grew angrier, his jaw grinding, his fists cracking, and only when they turned the corner did Hester see why.

Eight mountainous men stood in their underpants, helping a ninth and tenth disrobe their armor, before they handed this armor to the attendant the witches had encountered outside, now posed at the entrance to a double-doored room.

The black knight sneered at the witches. "Queen is waiting," he said, stabbing a finger at the doors. Then he turned his ire on the attendant. "This is madness, Jorin. An insult to the Knights."

"Turn over your armor, Sephyr," the attendant said. "Queen's orders."

Sephyr growled and stripped off his chainmail. He shoved it at Jorin, who folded it with the two other suits of armor, before opening the doors to the witches. Hester led Anadil and Dot inside, the coven utterly confused, especially since Jorin, who once treated them like fleas, was now bowing his head as they entered, then following them in. Ani and Dot clung to Hester as the witches made their way into a small room, muggy and windowless, the floor creaking underfoot.

Torches illuminated eight knights around a table, wearing the same pearlescent armor and mesh veils the knights outside had been forced to shed.

Three seats at the table were empty.

"The Knights ride with Eleven," the leader spoke at the head of the table, addressing the coven. "And we are eight. Which is why I've brought you here."

The leader's pale hands lifted the armored mask, like a funeral veil. Queen Jacinda gazed intensely at them.

"Welcome, new Knights," she said.

Jorin put a suit of armor in each of the witches' hands.

"New *what?*" Hester said.

"W-w-we don't understand—" Anadil stammered.

The other knights at the table removed their veils.

Dot was so stunned she turned her armor to chocolate.

Nicola.

Guinevere.

Beatrix.

Reena.

Kiko.

Maid Marian.

They faced Hester and the witches, who were now dressed in armor and seated at the table with them, Dot feeling the stares at her adult form.

Together, with the Queen of Jaunt Jolie, they made ten knights.

The eleventh sat at the far end, a stout woman, hair pulled back into a bun.

"Friedegund Brunhilde," she identified herself. "Dean of Arbed House at the Foxwood School for Boys."

Slowly, the story unfolded. Nicola and Guinevere had come to Jaunt Jolie to ask for the queen's help fighting the Snake: help that the queen refused, given her fear of Japeth's retaliation. But then Maid Marian arrived in Jaunt Jolie with news of Bettina's death, which she'd learned of from Robin Hood. When Robin failed to retrieve her from Glass Mountain, Marian had gone searching for him. She found her love in Putsi's forest, scim-stabbed and bleeding. Robin urged Marian to go to Jaunt Jolie . . . to tell Queen Jacinda what became of him and her daughter and ask for shelter . . .

"That was his dying wish," Marian recounted, her voice tremoring. "But what about *my* wish? I can't ever see Robin again. I can't claim the Storian for myself and rewrite the story. No magic can bring him back. Not even a wish in Aladdin's Cave or the darkest sorcerer's spell." She smeared away tears.

"Robin made me promise to hide . . . but there can be no hiding anymore. He's gone. My true love. The Snake took him from me."

"He took my daughter, too," said Queen Jacinda.

"And my dad," said Dot.

"And our Millicent," said Beatrix with Reena.

"And my Lancelot," said Guinevere, white-haired and drawn. "He's made us widows, orphans, and killed our children. He finds the thing you love the most and destroys it, like the darkest curse. But I won't let him take Tedros. Arthur left him his ring for a reason. Tedros can bring us back. To balance. To truth. If only he gets the chance."

"Which is why we're all here," said Queen Jacinda. "To defend your son. To give the true Lion his *pack*."

"Then I am your servant, Your Highness," said Guinevere.

Two queens bowed to each other, bonded by loss.

As for how they'd all made it to this table, Jacinda had the answers to that. After Marian came to her, she'd kept Bettina's murder a secret. Even her husband, the king, was left in the dark. She sent him on a mission in Runyon Mills and packed her younger children off to their grandmother's.

Then she went to work.

"I didn't trust the Knights of Eleven to avenge Bettina's death," said the queen. "For one thing, they still believe in King Rhian and I have no proof of Japeth's ruse. Nor do I even have evidence of my daughter's death; inquiries to both Camelot and Putsi yielded nothing but silence and stonewalling. And then, of course, there was the last time I sent my

Knights to confront the Snake, when his pirates first invaded my kingdom. They were lured by the Snake to a Sleeping Willow and put into a slumber before striking a single blow, while me and my children were noosed up to hang . . . No, I needed to find better knights to fight Japeth this time, equipped with more than weapons or brute strength. Knights who had a stake in this war. Knights who knew the depths of love and loss. Knights who would persist until the end."

Jacinda looked around the table. "Such knights wouldn't be found amongst men."

Thus Nicola and Guinevere were summoned back to the castle, where they joined Maid Marian. At the same time, the queen had been hearing of three warrior princesses who'd been attacking Agatha bounty hunters in the forest, ever since Lionsmane had announced the second test to the Woods. She had these girls brought in, too—Beatrix, Reena, and Kiko—which made seven knights for her table.

The eighth came easier than expected: Dean Brunhilde of Arbed House, who Jaunt Jolie had sent many an Everboy to for rehabilitation. Only this time, it was Dean Brunhilde who had traveled to Jaunt Jolie for help . . . asking if its queen had noticed any similarities between the masked attacker who'd tried to hang her and the new, cold-eyed king . . .

"Which left three knights still to be named," said the queen, turning to the witches. "And I know *The Tale of Sophie and Agatha* well enough to be certain that there are no fiercer protectors of justice than you." She smiled towards Dot. "At any age."

"It's highly temporary," Dot contended.

Jacinda looked at the rest. "So now our work begins, Knights of Eleven."

"But what work, Your Highness?" Beatrix asked. "The whole Woods is after Agatha. If a single person finds her and brings her to Japeth, he'll win the second test. He'll be a step away from being the One True King. From having the Storian's powers and wiping us out before we ever have the chance to fight him."

"Beatrix, Kiko, and I tried to stop the Agatha hunters," Reena agreed. "But every kingdom has people searching for her. Even in my homeland of Shazabah, my father is leading the search for Agatha. He thinks I'm still at school. He has no clue I'm fighting for the 'rebels.' If he did, he'd throw me in prison or have me killed. No one is on Tedros' side anymore. We're outnumbered by thousands."

"And we don't even know where Agatha's gone," said Dot. "The camel swept her, Tedros, and Sophie off to some secret place."

"Which means we don't know how to protect her," said Beatrix.

"If killing Agatha is the second test, imagine what the third test will be," Kiko peeped.

"Nor can we just go riding after the Snake. The Snake killed Robin *and* the Sheriff. The two strongest men I knew," said Marian, with a quick glance at Dot.

"And their strength was surpassed by Lancelot's, who suffered the same fate," Guinevere added. "Marian is right. We're not warriors. We can't succeed in killing a monster where men have failed."

"On the contrary." Jacinda sat taller. "True, we cannot win the second test for Tedros. Surviving the death warrant hung on his princess is his quest alone. But there are other weapons we have to defeat the Snake. Cleverness. Resilience. Insight. Weapons that a woman wields far better than a man. It is why we wear the armor of the Eleven now."

Dot and Anadil peeked at Hester, both unsettled that they'd come here to get the help of knights and were instead asked to *be* those knights . . . But Hester was staring squarely at the queen, intrigued.

"When Betty chose to continue writing for the *Courier*, even after the others fled, I asked her why," the queen said. "Why risk her life when she could be safe? And she told me, with so much conviction, 'Not everyone can see the truth, Mother. It is so easy to be blind to it. But those of us who can see the truth have the responsibility to help others see it too. Even if it's dangerous. Even if it puts us at risk. The truth is worth it.'" The queen's voice wavered. "We know the truth about Japeth. All of us. We just need the Woods to see it. And for that, we must have courage. Like my daughter had. Like your Lancelot and your Robin and your father." She looked at Guinevere, Marian, Dot. "We may not be knights in body. But we are knights in heart. And I'd take that knight against our enemy over any other kind."

This time, there was no argument.

The queen turned to Dean Brunhilde. "You've known the

Snake since he was a boy. What does he want? Why does he seek the Storian's power?"

"He's hateful. Pure Evil. From the beginning," said the Dean, instantly.

"You've made a life out of taking those believed to be Evil and leading them to Good," the queen pointed out. "It was your mission at Arbed House. This one thwarted your efforts, but surely you had a glimpse into his soul along the way. Evil, yes. Hateful, surely. But his hatred might be the chink in his armor, if we can come to understand it."

"He was always a beast," Brunhilde dismissed. "From the moment his mother brought him and Rhian to me. RJ was bitter and cruel in all the ways Rhian was earnest and warm."

"What does RJ stand for?" Nicola asked. "J for Japeth, and R for . . ."

"It's been more than a decade. My files have his records," said Dean Brunhilde.

"We searched for them in your office. Rhian's and Japeth's files," said Nicola. "But we found a squirrelly nut to Merlin that claimed you'd hidden them somewhere."

The Dean bolted straight. "*You?* You were the one who broke in?"

"And now we're on the same side, so it doesn't matter," said Nicola, impatient. "We found other files in your office. A letter from Aric to Japeth. Proof of their friendship. But we couldn't find Japeth's. Where did you hide it?"

Dean Brunhilde crossed her arms. "I'm not confiding in a *thief.*"

"Perhaps you'll confide in us once you, too, lose everyone you love," said Maid Marian.

Dean Brunhilde felt the eyes of Marian and two queens upon her.

"That letter from Aric to Japeth," said Hester delicately, turning to Nicola. "What did it say?"

Nicola opened her mouth, but Dean Brunhilde cut her off. "They were my students," she said briskly. "Aric and RJ were close. Aric was the only one who could keep RJ's rages at bay, even more than Rhian. Perhaps they recognized something in each other. Two poisoned hearts that were each other's antidote. But Rhian was RJ's twin. There was jealousy there. Aric envious of the bond Rhian had with his brother. Rhian resentful of Aric and RJ's friendship. It all boiled over when Aric stabbed Rhian in the head. Somehow Rhian managed to survive. And when the time came, I let the students vote on Aric's fate. RJ begged his brother to forgive Aric . . . if Rhian forgave Aric, so would the others . . . But Rhian voted to expel him instead. Aric was sent back into the Woods. Other than his letters to RJ, I don't know what became of him."

"Ended up at the School for Boys, torturing everyone in sight," Anadil muttered. "Unleashed his fury on all of us. Until Lady Lesso stabbed him. His own mother."

Dean Brunhilde took this in. "So Aric might still be alive today if Rhian had forgiven him."

"At least Rhian did *one* thing right," Kiko sighed.

Hester caught Anadil and Dot staring at her. No one else in the room knew what the coven did. No one else knew what

Sophie had told them at school.

"No, he didn't do it right," Hester said. "Rhian should have forgiven Aric. He should have followed the rules of Good and Evil. Rule #1. The Good forgive. And Rhian wanted to be Good. Taking Aric from Japeth was his fatal mistake."

"What are you saying?" Beatrix asked.

"Japeth killed Rhian. And it all traces back to him losing Aric," said Hester. "That's why Japeth wants to be the One True King. That's why he wants the powers of the Storian. For Aric. He wants to bring his friend back to life."

Dean Brunhilde froze in her seat.

Sweat beaded Hester's forehead, the room sucked of air.

"Love. Friendship. These are the oldest stories of time," said Queen Jacinda finally. "And not just the domain of Good. An Evil School Master believed love gave him the right to claim the Storian, just as the Snake believes love gives him the right to replace it. It's not the pen they ultimately seek to control. It's love itself. But love can't be controlled. Love requires surrender and faith. A trust in the winds of fate that the darkest hearts reject. If Aric and Japeth were meant to be together, they already would be. But fate is a power beyond our grasp. That is why we fight for the Pen. Because Man cannot be trusted to write his own fate. And the Snake shows us why. He believes fate made a mistake in separating him and Aric. That blood must be spilled, over and over, until he claims the power to rewrite that mistake and bring his friend back to him. Even if it spawns nothing but lies and murder and suffering along the way."

She raised her eyes to her knights. "And it is this rejection of fate, this terrible misunderstanding, that is his greatest weakness," said the queen. "We cannot help Tedros win the second test. For him to kill Agatha is unfathomable. He has no way to win. But what if we could make Japeth abandon the test too? What if we could make him surrender the tournament altogether?"

"Now *that* sounds unfathomable," Beatrix scoffed.

Other knights murmured agreement. "Nothing could make Japeth give up the crown," said Dean Brunhilde.

"Nothing except the person that's making him fight for the crown in the first place," Hester countered.

Everyone looked at her.

"Japeth wants his Ever After with Aric," the witch reasoned. "So we have to make him believe that Aric never wanted one with him. That Aric is rejecting his plan. That he doesn't *want* to be brought back. The queen is right. It just might work . . ."

"Um, Aric is *dead*," said Beatrix, "and unless I'm missing something, no one but the Storian has the power to raise people from the grave."

"We don't need to raise him from the grave," said Anadil, catching on to Hester's plan. "We just need to make it *seem* as if he has. Long enough for him to give Japeth a message. A brutal, undeniable message."

"A message which will make him doubt," the queen confirmed. "If his guard is down, then we stand a chance."

Dot frowned. "How can you fake a message from the *dead*?"

"Only one place," Maid Marian realized, looking at Jacinda. "A faraway cave where anything can come true for the right price . . . even a message from the grave . . ."

"Aladdin's Cave," said Guinevere. "The lost Cave of Wishes."

"Lost cave?" Kiko wisped. "How do you find a *lost* cave?"

"You ask the last man who found it, of course," the Queen of Jaunt Jolie replied.

Her eyes fixed on the knight a few seats down.

Eyes wide. Sunk in her chair.

Pale as a ghost.

"My father," Reena gasped.

17

AGATHA

Never Trust a Princess

In the storybooks Agatha read back in Gavaldon, the land of Aladdin was a feast of color and fragrance and earthy delights: loafing camels, dusty spice markets, palaces veiled by storms of sand.

But in real life, that's not what it was like at all.

As the *Shazabah Sikander* had neared its homeland, Agatha, caged in the bowels of the ship, peered out a porthole at a fertile metropolis lording over the desert. Jewel-green palms bowed to each other over paved streets. Sleek red-and-gold buildings speared through the sky, with a controlled traffic of magic carpets transporting citizens around the kingdom. And everywhere she'd looked: camels, squads of them, military-garbed and precise in their march, patrolled the city while also guarding the imperial palace at its center, a pyramid of red-and-gold glass.

It was deep within this palace that Agatha found herself now, imprisoned with her friends, looking out their cell's only window at the royal camel pastures, where the camel that had turned them in was now happily grazing, reunited with its family.

"Still trust that thing?" Tedros growled from Agatha's right, the two crouched in the dark cell.

Agatha couldn't speak. As soon as they'd reached the palace, the guards had stripped Merlin from her. She had no idea where they'd taken the five-year-old wizard. With each passing second, her skin went clammier, her stomach sicker. "Mama!" Merlin had cried. Again, the wizard was prescient. Because she felt like she'd lost her child.

Despairing, she appealed to the camel through the window, but it offered her only the calmest of nods, as if everything was as it should be. As if it hadn't betrayed her. As if *this* was the way to Tedros winning the second test. For a moment, Agatha wondered if she should still have hope . . . if the camel had a larger plan in motion . . .

Then she saw Hort glaring across the cell. "To answer your question, Tedros, yes, she totally still trusts that thing. Same way Sophie trusts guys whose names start with 'R.'"

Sophie let out a long sigh. "You know, Aggie, normally I shield you from boorish boys, but I did warn you about that camel. Animals aren't our friends. Especially ones with *humps*."

"Only a Never would say something so foolish," Princess Uma muttered.

"Oh?" Sophie retorted, nursing her bandaged wrist. "Then why can't you do one of your bird whistles or wolf calls and summon your *friends* to help us?"

"Not in Shazabah," Uma said vaguely, looking away.

"Well, *someone* better help us," Hort said, standing up. "We've been dumped in jail a million miles from home and Rhian and the Sultan were chums, so the Snake's surely on the way to kill Agatha, win the second test, and then kill the rest of us." The weasel paused. "It's that last part I care about."

"Hort's right," Agatha confessed, still thinking about Merlin. "Maybe the camel betrayed us. Maybe I was wrong. But we can't just wait to die."

"What should we do, then? Wish the Snake away? Stick a doll with pins? He's out there and we're in here," Tedros said, clearly frustrated.

"We've gotten out of prison before," said Agatha.

Tedros shook his head. "We shouldn't have tried to run away. I knew it was cowardice. Dad doesn't want me to hide from my own test." He slouched against the wall. "They'll probably give Merlin to the Snake too."

The thought of Japeth claiming Merlin chilled Agatha's blood—

"Sounds like Aladdin's Cave is your only hope now," a voice chuckled.

Agatha and Tedros flashed their gold fingerglows to the back of the cell.

No one there.

"Up here," said the voice.

Agatha cast her glow towards a ceiling pipe—

Hanging by his boots was a young man, with smooth brown skin, thick eyebrows, and a strapping physique, doing stomach crunches upside down.

"Too bad only my father knows where to *find* the Cave of Wishes," he said.

Princess Uma rose slowly. "Kaveen?"

"Thought you'd promised never to return to Shazabah, Uma," said Kaveen, hanging like a bat. "Wasn't that part of our divorce agreement?"

"Your father handled that, just like he handled every other piece of our marriage," said Uma.

"You had a habit of not listening to me," said Kaveen, "and yet you always listened to the Sultan."

"Because if I didn't listen to your father, I would have been thrown in *here*," Uma fired back, "so clearly it's *you* who didn't listen to him in the end."

"Well, we're both here now," said Kaveen, dropping onto the floor. He walked towards Uma. "The cursed Pen pulled us apart. And now it brings us back together."

Agatha watched the distance between them shrink, unsure if they were going to kill or kiss each other—

"Hold on." Tedros stepped in the middle. "You two . . . were *married*?"

Princess Uma, Agatha reminded herself. Because Uma had wed a prince. Prince Kaveen of Shazabah. Aladdin's great-grandson. That's what Kaveen's ancestry scroll had said when she and Tedros had come across it in the Living Library. And yet, Agatha had known of Kaveen before. Years ago, Uma had confided to Agatha about the prince she'd fallen in love with at the School for Good and married soon after. But then the Storian chose Uma for its next fairy tale—the story of a princess whose animal friends rescued her from an Evil warlord when her prince was too late. Uma became famous for her friendship with animals, while Kaveen became a laughingstock for failing to save his true love. Their marriage curdled. But it wasn't their divorce that surprised Agatha now. It was the part about the Sultan being Kaveen's father. Because if the Sultan was his dad . . .

"Why would your own father put you in *jail*?" Agatha asked.

Kaveen's black eyes set upon her. Agatha's neck rashed from the heat of his stare. When Tedros looked at her, there was often a note of uncertainty, as if he was never quite sure of himself. But this prince had no questions about himself, nor was he willing to endure any from her.

"Don't make men like that in Gavaldon, do they?" Sophie whispered in her ear.

Kaveen glowered at Sophie. "Girls like you two are the *reason* I'm here."

"Excuse me?" Sophie bristled.

"I know your fairy tale. Girls who didn't need a prince to find a happy ending. Same story as Uma's. Same rancid ending. The Storian makes fools of the best men. Just look at what it's done to *him*." He pointed his finger at Tedros. "My advice to you, lad: never trust a princess. Not yours, not anyone else's. Not if you want to become the man you're meant to be."

Agatha saw Tedros stiffen slightly, as if this resonated somewhere inside him.

She and her prince certainly had their issues with trust, too. Is this how they would end up? Like Uma and Kaveen? Tedros seemed to be wondering it . . . He caught Agatha looking at him. The prince cleared his throat, addressing Kaveen. "Um, you mentioned a cave that could help us. A cave of wishes?"

"Aladdin's Cave," said Kaveen. He lit a red fingerglow and cast a stream of dust in the dark, which took the shape of vast desert dunes. "The only place where any wish can come true."

The golden sands shifted as if they were alive, opening up the mouth of a cave, the light within a radiant purple.

"The wishes I speak of come from the magic lamp inside the cave. And every soul in the Woods has longed to have this lamp since Aladdin found it. Aladdin, an ordinary slumdog who stumbled upon the cave and the lamp and used his three wishes from the genie within to become the Sultan of Shazabah."

Kaveen's glow conjured this magic lamp . . . a massive half-man, half-tiger unspooling from its tip . . .

"Some accounts suggest that there is no genie or magic

lamp anymore. That Aladdin freed him with his last wish. But the genie knew my great-grandfather's secret—that he'd become Sultan by magic and deceit—and no one with such a secret would ever set its keeper free. But Aladdin was grateful enough to the genie to give him peace. He returned the lamp to the cave, vanishing it deep into the desert . . ."

The genie sucked back into the lamp, extinguishing Kaveen's glow. But then a new ember of light appeared . . . a vision of a Sultan in red-and-gold robes leading an army across the dunes . . .

"After Aladdin's death, his son spent his life searching for the cave, to no avail. Then *his* son took on the quest. My father. Day after day, my dad combed the Shazabah desert . . . until one day he *found* it."

The cave reappeared out of the dunes, towering high in the sand.

"But it would not let my father in. Instead, it gave him a message."

The cave spoke in a tiger's growl: "*I am the genie of the lamp. Master of this cave. Those who seek admission must bring me something in return. Find my true love and deliver her to me. Only then may you enter my Cave of Wishes.*"

Agatha looked up as the cave shape-shifted into the genie they had seen before, half-man, half-tiger . . .

"My father wanted that lamp. So he consulted every sorcerer in Shazabah: *Who* is a genie's true love?" Kaveen went on. "But none had the answer. After all, a genie is neither human nor animal, mortal nor ghost, free nor unfree. Who could possibly be a genie's match? Thwarted, my dad enlisted me and my sister in his hunt, banking on the cleverness and ambition of youth. He baited us with the ultimate prize: whoever found the answer and delivered the lamp to him would be named the *next* Sultan."

Kaveen's glow mirrored his own self along with a second shadow next to him: a girl with a sleek beehive of hair, her tall, shapely form wrapped in red-and-gold furs, and a hawk on her shoulder.

"Who's she?" Sophie whispered to Agatha. "She's *fabulous*."

"My sister and I made a pact. We'd find the answer together and share the throne," said Kaveen. "But we were as stymied by the riddle as our father. Not to mention we were young and soon distracted. I went off to school and then so did she. But after the Storian humiliated me in Uma's tale, I was determined to prove myself. Not just to my father, but to the whole Woods. So without telling my sister, I hunted relentlessly for the genie's true love. But not even the wiliest witch could tell me who it was. Until at last, one night I begged my father to show me the cave. To let me speak to the genie myself. He'd kept the location secret for fear that someone else might find the genie's love and steal the lamp for themselves. But my father honored my plea and took me to the desert in the dead of night, using a map he'd made to mark the cave's spot . . ."

In glowing silhouettes, the Sultan led Kaveen blindfolded across the desert, until the Sultan removed the covering from his eyes. Before Kaveen's eyes, the sand rose up and whittled into the shape of a magic lamp, the tip of the lamp the opening to the cave.

The prince kneeled before this opening, the Sultan watching from a distance.

"I come to you as a humble man, Genie," Kaveen appealed. "The Pen has taken everything from me. My name. My wife. My happiness. Look inside my heart and see my intentions are pure. Let me have the hope of a new life. A *good* life. Like my great-grandfather, who you once opened your cave to. I may have lost my true love. But give me a chance at glory by helping you find yours."

The cave seemed to smile at him, as if he'd said the magic words. Then a golden mist emanated from the cave's opening, seeping into Kaveen's ear. Inside his head, the tiger's growl resounded . . .

"*Find the princess who is every animal's friend,*" said the cave. "*She is my true love.*"

Within Kaveen's mind, the cave's mist spawned an image of a girl with a tiny nose, long hair, and almond-shaped eyes . . .

Agatha jolted in surprise.

"Me?" Princess Uma gasped.

The visions snuffed out, Kaveen's dim fingerglow lighting his face. He didn't look at Uma. "I never told my father what I'd learned. I loved you too much to bind you to a genie and trap you in the lamp. But my dad knew the cave had given me the answer. He'd seen it whisper in my ear. And so he jailed me because I refused to name you to him. All these years, you made your reputation off my humiliation, never looking for me or giving me a thought, while I was in here, protecting you. *Saving* you. Like the Storian told the Woods I'd failed to do."

Slowly Kaveen looked up at Uma, his face hard.

"But here you are now," he said, rising to his feet. "As if the Storian didn't want you protected at all. As if it wants me to name you to my father. As if it wants *me* to be free instead of you. Finally, the Pen is on *my* side."

Kaveen raised his fingerglow, casting a phantom crow in red dust, which flew out of the cell, screeching for the guards.

"Kaveen, no!" Uma cried. Agatha and Tedros shielded her. So did Sophie and Hort—

A fanfare of trumpets exploded outside.

Then somewhere above, the doors to the prison flew open. Agatha thrust her head through the bars.

Bootsteps rattled the stairs, shadows moving across walls.

Guards came off the steps, flooding in front of the cell, five of them, clad in red and gold, scimitars on their belts.

Kaveen addressed them: "Guards, summon my fath—"

Another trumpet blared above, drowning him out: "Presenting the Royal Princess of Shazabah!"

Kaveen drew back in confusion—

A new shadow suddenly appeared over the stairwell. The same silhouette Agatha had glimpsed during Kaveen's tale: a tall, buxom girl with a sculpted mountain of hair and a hawk on her shoulder.

Then she came to life, gliding down the steps and into the light, the Princess of Shazabah, with cinnamon skin, kohl-dusted eyes, and luscious red lips. Two ladies-in-waiting, wrapped in red-and-gold robes, stood at her sides, their heads bowed. The princess took her place in front of the guards and peered into the cell.

"Looks like my father was right about catching you, Agatha," she pronounced. "The King of Camelot is already on a ship to Shazabah to kill you."

"Sister?" said Kaveen, grabbing the bars.

"*Reena?*" said Tedros, grabbing the bars next to him.

"Wait, you *know* these rebels?" Kaveen asked her.

"Dad hasn't a clue, of course," Reena answered. "I told him I was coming down to see you, brother. He said if I could get you to tell me the genie's true love, then *I* could have the throne myself . . . Tempting offer, of course, given you've been secretly searching for the answer, violating our pact. But in truth it's not you I've come to see."

Her brother shook his head. "I—I—I don't understand."

"You see, these aren't rebels, as you say," said Reena. "They're my . . . *friends.*"

The two ladies behind Reena doffed their hoods, revealing Kiko and Beatrix, who sprayed the guards with stun spells, knocking them to the ground.

Agatha was in a daze, watching Beatrix snatch keys off a fallen guard. "How did you—"

"Questions later. If we're going to keep you alive, we don't have much time," Reena said, unlocking the cell. "Follow me. All of you. You too, brother, if you'd like to be out of your cage."

Agatha felt Tedros' arm around her, pushing her out of the cell—

"Stop," said a voice.

Agatha and her friends turned to see Kaveen holding Uma, his fingerglow at her throat.

Beatrix and Kiko aimed their glows at his head. But the prince's eyes were on his sister.

"Reena, it's *her*. The genie's true love. It was Uma all along," said Kaveen breathlessly. "If I give her to Father, I'll be Sultan. I'll have the Woods' respect once more. Take your friends. They're none of my concern. But this one I keep."

Reena narrowed her eyes. "She was your *princess*, Kaveen. Give her to a genie? Bind her to the lamp for eternity?"

"That would be like me killing Agatha to win my test," Tedros berated him. "That would be like me handing my princess to a *Snake*."

Agatha felt a rush of relief. Whatever doubts Kaveen had cast in her prince about her, Tedros had broken the spell.

"But it's what the Storian wants! The *real* happy ending to our story!" Kaveen appealed to his sister. "Me, Sultan. My princess punished. You, free with your friends."

Reena hesitated, considering the offer. "Uma is our friend. Hmm, let's say I do give her to you. There would have to be a steep price. Something me and my friends need . . ." She looked at her brother. "Tell me how Father finds his way to the Cave of Wishes."

Agatha startled. "Reena, we can't leave Uma—"

Kaveen pressed his glow harder to Uma's throat, his eyes on his sister. "I keep her. Promise me."

"You'll have to trust me," said Reena.

"I never trust a princess," said Kaveen. "Not even my own blood."

"Says the one who broke the trust between us," Reena clipped. Beatrix and Kiko fired whips of glow past Kaveen's ears. Kaveen turned his glow on his sister, about to attack—

"Careful. You're quite outnumbered, brother," said Reena.

Kaveen's nostrils flared. "A magical compass on Dad's sash. It has the map to the cave," he snarled. "Now go. Leave Uma with me. Our bargain is complete."

"Thank you," said Reena, walking out. "You were right, you know. To never trust a princess." She glanced back at him. "At least one who doesn't trust you."

Kaveen's eyes widened—

The hawk launched off her shoulder, stabbing Kaveen in the ribs, severing his grip on Uma and sending him writhing to the ground.

"Come on," Reena said, ushering Agatha out of the cell.

Uma gave Sophie a look as she followed. "What was that about animals not being our friends?"

Sophie pursed her lips.

"Once a teacher, always a teacher," said Agatha, dragging her best friend along.

~ 18 ~

Love. Purpose. Food.

Sophie had always found Reena vaporous and dull, a fog of fruity perfume hovering around Beatrix at all times. But just like Beatrix had proved herself to be more than a pretty face, so now had her sidekick. The Storjan might not be able to tell the tale of every soul; but even those it didn't choose could find their way into its light.

The Shazabah princess led them out the prison door, Agatha badgering her: "We have to find Merlin!"

"Leave him to me," Reena answered.

Agatha frowned. "But we need to—"

"What we *need* is to get to Aladdin's Cave," Reena countered. "Do what I say and you and the wizard survive. Try to control things like you always do and we all die. Got it?"

Agatha was speechless.

"I'm loving New Reena," said Sophie.

"Me too," said Tedros.

Agatha shot them both a look.

Reena, meanwhile, was locking the door to the prison, sealing her brother and guards inside, along with her palace hawk, who would keep an eye on both. Beatrix and Kiko had already sprinted ahead. Quickly, Sophie, Agatha, and the rest followed Reena through a dark corridor. "The wishes in the lamp are our best hope to keep Agatha alive and make Tedros king. We just have to make the *right* wishes," the princess explained.

"Just use the wishes to *kill* the Snake!" Tedros argued. "Wish one, wish two, *and* wish three!"

"That isn't the answer," said Agatha thoughtfully, as if it had been on her mind since Tedros had declared his intention to kill the Snake back at school. "I know you want to keep me alive. But killing Japeth means you'll never be king. Not to the people, at least."

"She's right," Sophie agreed. "Use magic to kill your opponent and the Woods will have even more reason to believe Japeth was the Lion and you the Snake."

"There has to be a better answer," said Agatha. "And we have to use the wishes to find it."

"But how else can wishes make me king?" said Tedros. "Second test is to kill *you*. That's not going to happen. Whole Woods knows it. How can a genie change that—"

"Listen up," said Reena, halting in a dark corridor, which led into a palace wing. "Agatha, take Tedros, Hort, and Uma to Pasha Dunes. Mostly sovereign clans there; they won't bother you. Find a pub called the Mirage. The rest of our team will be waiting."

"What team?" asked Agatha, but now they could hear bootsteps in the distance, marching in unison.

Reena spun to Sophie. "You come with me." She shined her fingerglow at two sets of red-and-gold robes, pooled on the floor: Kiko's and Beatrix's. Reena thrust one at Sophie. "Put this on." She grabbed Sophie by the wrist, dragging her into the light—

"Wait!" Agatha whispered, yanking Reena back. "How are the rest of us supposed to get *out* of the palace?"

"Same way you got in," Reena said.

Agatha followed her eyes across the way, where behind glass doors, a family of camels waited in an alley. Two baby ones carried Beatrix and Kiko, who wore pearly chainmail and veils, while a familiar camel smiled right at Agatha, grunting a repeated phrase.

"It's back," Hort grumped.

"Tell me it's not saying what I think it's saying," said Tedros.

"*'Trust is the way,'*" Uma sighed.

The sounds of marching were getting closer now. Sophie could see shadows approaching their hiding place—

"Wait for my signal!" Reena ordered Agatha, before grabbing Sophie.

"No! I can't leave Aggie behind!" Sophie said, but Reena had already pulled her in view of a dozen well-armed guards coming towards them, along with . . .

"Daddy!" Reena chimed.

The Sultan swept towards his daughter, dressed in a formidable gold cape, a matching tunic sashed with feathers, a shiny red turban, and pointy gold shoes. His face had a peculiar carrot-colored tan, along with plucked eyebrows and a curly moustache.

"Where are your guards, my child? With rebels on the loose, I don't want you traveling anywhere alone. Even inside the palace."

"They're keeping an eye on brother before I go down and try again. I'm close to him telling me the genie's true love," Reena assured. "Not that I need guards. I'm safe with Shefali. My lady maid. She's trained in defense."

Sophie glanced around, searching for this Shefali woman, before she saw Reena glaring right at her.

"Shefali. Beautiful name, beautiful girl," the Sultan cooed, appraising Sophie. "My wife had green eyes like yours. We're separated now. Where are you from?"

Sophie delivered a cold stare. "The land of wishful thinking."

"Is that in Ooty?" the Sultan asked. He noticed his guards

hovering behind. "Leave us," he commanded sharply.

The guards dispersed. "So tell me, Shefali," the Sultan asked, shepherding her ahead. "What do you think of my palace?"

Behind him, Sophie could see Reena guiding Agatha, Tedros, and the others out of their hiding spot towards the waiting camels. Reena mouthed at Sophie, pointing at her father's sash: *"Get the compass!"*

Sophie sucked in a breath. It was up to her now. Luckily, she'd had experience in dealing with despicable men.

"What do I think of your palace?" Sophie said, turning to the Sultan. "I find it unnecessarily large and overbearing, as if meant to hide a leader's shortcomings."

The Sultan blinked at her, his face reddening . . . He burst into laughter. "My, my, a joker too! No wonder my daughter enjoys your company!"

"Wasn't joking at all, actually," said Sophie.

The Sultan rambled on. "I shall write to the Queen of Ooty about your charms. Your family should be rewarded! Perhaps we can make arrangements to have you here in the palace, instead of slaving away for the princess. I can show you the world . . . But first, I'll have to pry you from my daughter's grubby little hands. Ha! Reena! Reena!" He turned to search for his daughter, about to spot her helping Agatha onto a camel—

Sophie seized the Sultan's cheeks and swung his face back towards hers. "Have you been poisoned, sir?"

"Poisoned?" said the Sultan, startled.

She pried open his eyelids with her fingers. "Toxins in your iris . . . spots of blood . . . Have you had anything suspicious to eat or drink?"

"Only my usual lamb omelet . . ." He turned ashen. "But it tasted different today. Too salty—"

"Let me look," Sophie said, poking at his eyes and nostrils with one hand, her other palm moving near his sash. "I see . . . cloudy pupils . . . mottled skin . . . foul breath . . ." She backed away from him. "Not poison, I'm afraid. Something far worse."

The Sultan gaped at her, scared.

Sophie leered back. "Old *age*."

"Come, Shefali," Reena said, clasping Sophie's arm intently. "We'll return to the dungeons and give my brother another crack."

"Yes, mistress," said Sophie.

"Wish me luck, Daddy!" Reena piped, towing Sophie from the frowning Sultan.

"Did you get it?" Reena whispered in Sophie's ear.

"Is your father a dog?" Sophie snapped back.

SOPHIE WOULDN'T HAVE suffered fools for anyone but Agatha.

Agatha, who was out in the desert without her, Arthur's death warrant on her head.

They needed to find Aladdin's Cave and use the magic lamp to help Tedros get past the second test *without* killing

Aggie. Sophie had no idea how that was possible, but she'd worry about that once they made it to the Cave of Wishes. She could feel the Sultan's compass rattling in her pocket as she and Reena hustled up a staircase to the top floor. Reena pushed through a door and pink-and-purple light washed over them, the sunset expanding in all directions along with a dizzying rush of fragrance.

On the roof of the palace, a thin brown boy played a sitar as he paced between rows of lavish magic carpets, which were twitching and peeking at each other like toddlers put down for a nap, while sticks of incense burned soothing chamomile from brass holders.

The boy spotted Reena and beamed brightly—

"Where is he?" Reena gasped, scanning around.

Then Sophie heard a familiar giggle. At the other end of the rooftop, Merlin was being tickled by a magic carpet, the young wizard trying to wrestle it down.

Reena slouched with relief. "Thank you, Jeevan," she said to the boy.

"The Sultan was planning on trading him to Hamelin for gold," Jeevan said. "Still a child shortage there after the Pied Piper stole all theirs. Convinced the guards there'd been a mistake; that this very pasty boy was actually my cousin. Luckily they're too dense to ask questions." His smile at Reena hadn't dimmed. "I kept my end of the bargain, then . . . When's our date?"

Reena must have given something away in her expression because now Jeevan noticed Sophie's presence.

"Don't tell me," he said, smile flattening. "Just got them settled for the night."

All the carpets heard this and instantly began clamoring for Reena's attention, waving their tassels at her, jingling with different-pitched bells.

"We'll need Nightwind," Reena said, pointing at a midnight-colored carpet in the corner, dusted with silver patterns. "It's an emergency."

"Sorry, Princess. Can't let you on a carpet without a guard," Jeevan declared, turning stern and official. "Sultan's orders."

"What Daddy doesn't know won't hurt you," Reena replied. "Especially when you and I go on our date tomorrow." She winked at him.

Moments later, Jeevan was helping the girls and Merlin onto Nightwind, the front tassels cuffed around Reena's wrists, the back tassels around Sophie's ankles, securing her and Merlin in place. The carpet began to rise into the hot, heavy evening, giving Sophie a view of Shazabah City and the traffic of magic carpets clogging air lanes between buildings.

"Keep it slow, Reena," said Jeevan. "If you get pulled down for speeding, your dad will take it out of my hide."

"Very slow," Reena promised, pulling her hood over her head.

She smiled back at Sophie. "Ready?"

Nightwind rocketed off the roof so hard that it ripped the maid robes right off Sophie, who lost a scream somewhere in her chest. "Choo-choo!" Merlin whooped.

Her fingers went numb around the five-year-old, Sophie

just starting to catch her breath, before Nightwind plunged into the mid-city jam, weaving and ducking around the other flyers, who were patiently obeying traffic laws. On behalf of their riders, angry carpets jangled their tassels and bells, which wasn't very threatening, like a soothing chorus of protest, before Sophie realized they weren't protesting, but summoning: a fleet of black carpets with bright red tassels that exploded after them, clearly intending to bring Nightwind down.

"Mambas," Reena murmured.

She showed little fear, however, as if she'd thwarted many a Mamba before, her hands seizing the end of the carpet, navigating it between the tightest swerves and tiniest nooks, crashing through windows and upending two sisters playing with their pet peacock, a stately woman reciting poetry to her book club, and a couple kissing over chicken tagine, all the while Reena losing black Mambas one by one. But there was a last Mamba left, gaining on them, its tassel extending with tentacle-like length, about to snare around Merlin's neck . . . Reena launched upwards, doing a full 360-degree loop, which sent Sophie's white dress puffing up like a poisonous fish in terrified response, before Nightwind dropped like a rock, straight into the Mamba, head-driving it, down, down, down and hooking the carpet on a pointy minaret. A few minutes later, they were out of Shazabah City and floating over twilit dunes, with even Nightwind sagging in relief. ("No more choo-choo," Merlin begged, promptly falling asleep.)

"You act like a basic Evergirl . . . you suck up to Beatrix . . . you're like a warrior princess moonlighting as an idiot," Sophie panted, her heart in her throat. "Why? You're clever and fierce. That shouldn't be a secret. You could be anything you want. You could be Sultan—"

"And I choose not to be," said Reena. "If there's one thing I learned from my mother, it's that palace life isn't satisfying. Not to someone who wants to live for *real*. The spotlight of the throne shrivels you up. Turns you into something you're not. Like Dad. He may seem weak-minded and overindulgent, but once he was a fiery warrior himself. That's why I let Beatrix have the limelight. I don't want a fairy tale. Ironic, of course, since I'm risking my life to help your friends win theirs."

"Well, given the way Jeevan looked at you, I'd say you can have your fairy tale anytime you wish," Sophie quipped.

Reena grinned at her, and Sophie suddenly realized that for all the storms of her own love stories, tormenting the Woods with their consequences, there were others, perfectly small and blissful, unfolding with hardly a ripple at all.

Over the desert they flew, skirting a long route around any other flyers in sight, staying as invisible as they could. Night settled in, the moon carved like a scythe. Soon the color of the dunes shifted from a rusted red to a sparkling silver, crowded with small tent villages. Sophie could see teenagers kicking a ball around. Sounds of music emanated from the tents, shadows dancing, drinking, laughing. Farther ahead, Sophie spotted a family of camels on a vacant stretch of sand, feeding from buckets of dried-out grass that someone had laid out for them.

Sophie tensed. "Those camels. They were the ones with Agatha . . . Where is she—"

Reena steered Nightwind down. "I'd say she's right where she's supposed to be."

Over the empty sand, a vision appeared: a tiki hut, strung with a thousand lights and baubles and trinkets of every color, like a chaotic Christmas tree. Outside, crickets gathered, playing a sultry desert beat. A firefly-lit sign beamed out front:

THE MIRAGE
BEST FOOD IN THE DESERT
APPEARING NIGHTLY

Reena landed Nightwind and after jostling Merlin awake, Sophie wobbly dismounted, still dizzy from the ride, her shoes sinking into sand as she hustled the little wizard towards the pub, anxious to find Agatha. She was desperate to have her best friend at her side again and no doubt Aggie was feeling the same. Sophie pushed through the door, scanning the brightly lit pub for her—

Only it seemed Agatha already had friends at her side.

And not just friends . . . *knights*. A whole bunch of them, at least ten, dressed like Beatrix and Kiko had been, in shimmering armor.

For a moment, Sophie wondered if she was seeing straight,

given the carpet ride. But then she realized: *she* knew these knights too. And now they were cheering for her as Reena stood on the bar and held up the compass, pointing at Sophie as the main reason they'd procured it.

Sophie spotted Agatha rushing towards her and Merlin—

"Thank goodness you're both safe!" Agatha said, grabbing Sophie into a hug.

"*Mama!*" Merlin yipped, his arms around Agatha's leg.

But now Dot was hugging Sophie too, looking a tad younger in her adult body, and so were Nicola and Hester and Anadil and Beatrix and Kiko, all her girlfriends in one place, wearing matching suits of armor. Over their shoulders, she spotted Hort alone in the corner, expecting him to pile in, but he was sipping a fizzy drink, lost in his thoughts. Near him, Reena inspected the Sultan's compass, while Tedros was locked in conversation with Guinevere, Maid Marian, Princess Uma, and a stout matron who Sophie didn't recognize, all but Uma in the same pearly chainmail as the other girls.

"Drinkie!" Merlin badgered Agatha, grasping for the aging potion in her pocket and squeezing it on his tongue.

"Am I dreaming, or are our friends all here?" Sophie asked Agatha. "Dressed as *knights*?"

"Hello, Sophie," said a familiar voice.

Sophie turned to find the Queen of Jaunt Jolie, dressed in knight's armor too.

"Jacinda?" Sophie sputtered. "I—I—I don't understand—"

"My *new* Knights of Eleven," said the queen. "Born out of the courage of girls like you and Agatha, who confronted Evil when I was too scared to. Girls like my daughter, who had the bravery to join your fight. If I had her courage before today, maybe she'd still be alive."

"Betty," Sophie said softly, thinking of the girl who had battled so valiantly for her and her friends. "She didn't have to fight for us. But she did. Until the very end. Didn't like me much, of course. But that's probably a testament to her character."

The queen hugged Sophie tight. "I suspect you and Betty were more alike than she would have wanted. Perhaps the two of you would have joined our Knights of Eleven, except for the fact you occupy a place more important." She nodded at Agatha. "You're *this* girl's knight."

"And what am I? Court jester?" Tedros teased, pulling Agatha to his chest. He looked relaxed for once, almost happy, Sophie thought, as if being around his friends made him feel protected, even if this was his quest alone. So much of the prince's life had been spent on his own: no mother, no father, not even Merlin. Tedros had come to school searching for love. Love that could save him. The same kind of love that Sophie had come to this world to find. No wonder they'd both been so insufferable. No wonder they'd never gotten along. They were like two seals trapped underwater, fighting for the same breath of air.

He caught Sophie watching him. "Well, I can't get too jealous," the prince said. "You and Agatha have to stick together while I'm inside the cave."

Sophie raised her brows. This was news to Agatha too.

"You're going inside . . . alone?" said Agatha.

"Me too," Merlin insisted, already looking older than a minute ago. "Merlin go with Tee Tee."

"No, Merlin. No one's going with Tee Tee. It's my test," Tedros reminded. "But I do have a job for you. You'll be six years old soon. Think you can handle it?"

"A *big* job?" Merlin said, hopefully.

Tedros rubbed his head, then looked at the girls. "The cave is close. Reena checked the compass. She said it's less than a mile from here."

"But how will you get *inside* the cave?" Sophie asked. "You heard Kaveen's story. Genie won't let anyone in unless—"

"Leave that to Tedros," said Uma, arriving with Guinevere, who both exchanged looks with the prince.

"The knights have a plan to beat the Snake," Tedros explained to Agatha. "Have my doubts about it, but I'll do anything if it doesn't involve killing you."

"What's the plan?" said Agatha.

"Like Uma said . . . leave that to me," Tedros replied.

Sophie could see Agatha stiffen.

"Though each of us will have a part to play," added Maid Marian cryptically, joining the group, accompanied by the stout matron Sophie had spotted earlier, the last of the knights. This woman reached out a hand to Sophie.

"Dean Brunhilde," she introduced herself. "Rhian and Japeth were my students at the Foxwood School for Boys."

"Aric's too, then," Agatha realized, new to the Dean too.

"I'm afraid so," Dean Brunhilde sighed.

Sophie shuddered even hearing the beast's name. "Well, what are we waiting for? We're all together now. Can't loaf around drinking cider and ordering food. Let's find the genie—"

"Not yet," said Tedros.

Sophie and Agatha looked at each other.

"But what if the Snake comes?" Agatha pressed Tedros.

Sophie piled on: "Didn't you hear what Reena said before? Sultan already told the Snake we're here! Japeth's on a ship to Shazabah! And when the Sultan finds out we've escaped, he'll see his compass is missing. He'll know we've gone to the caves—"

"Japeth will track us there!" Agatha finished.

Tedros grinned. "Exactly."

The two girls stared at him, confused—

"Did someone say 'food'?" a voice trilled.

From the kitchen, a big-bellied woman flounced out in a sequined headscarf and tunic, her face spotted with flour, her arms piled with sumptuous spreads: red lentil soup, cucumber salad, hummus with mushrooms, spinach and feta pies, crispy yellow rice, stuffed grape leaves, garlic shrimp, milky pistachio delights, and towers of cookies and cakes.

"Mother!" Reena said, hugging her. "I told you not to go overboard. Last thing we need before a battle is bloated bellies."

"For once I wish you were more like your father. Eating is exactly what knights should do before battle," her mother ribbed, before barking at a scrawny man, struggling to get more platters through the kitchen doors. "Yousuf! Hurry and bring the kebabs before they all get dry! Then what will we do? Use them as stones?"

Sophie, meanwhile, had forgotten all about arguing with Tedros and was stuffing her face with cucumber salad, savoring the tarty lemon dressing, unable to remember the last time she ate a well-seasoned meal. In the corner, the prince was talking to Merlin, the young wizard surprisingly quiet and attentive, perhaps because of the chocolate cake Tedros seemed to be withholding from him. Nearby, Dot was complaining to Hester over spinach pies: "Maid Marian is the only link I have to Daddy, but she avoids me every time I try to talk to her. Been that way since we met!" (Hester responded: "Ani and I avoid you, but you always corner us. Try that.") Even Agatha was lost in a mound of honeycake, before she caught Sophie's eye. The two girls smiled and moved for each other, before Nicola cut in, pulling Agatha aside. Sophie stopped short—

"So Reena tells me you met my husband," Reena's mother said, appearing next to Sophie. "And from the face you just made, I see nothing about him has changed."

"Wait, you were the *queen*?" Sophie said, understanding. She looked around the smoky, cramped pub. "And now you're . . ."

"Happier than I've ever been," said Reena's mother, unoffended. "I've taught my daughter to ask herself the same question I did. What matters? Look in your heart every day and ask: What *really* matters in life? Doesn't matter who you are. It's the same answers for everyone. Love. Purpose. Food. That's it. That's all we need."

Reena's mother was studying Yousuf, dropping kebabs as he tried to serve them to the witches. Yousuf caught her watching and the two exchanged adoring smiles. Suddenly Sophie understood. At the palace, Reena's mother could have everything she ever wanted. But only in leaving it could she find the things she needed.

Sophie repeated these to herself.

Love. Purpose. Food.

"I don't know if I have any of those," she confessed. She thought of Agatha and Tedros, committed to the cause of Good. She thought of Reena, sacrificing the spotlight to find quiet love with a boy. She even thought of Hort, who wore love and purpose on his sleeve. Tears sprung to Sophie's eyes before she could stop them. "Well, I have food, I suppose," she said weakly. "If you consider what I eat food."

"I probably don't," Reena's mother teased. "Listen to me, sweet girl. So many of us make the mistake of denying ourselves what we want. Out of fear that we don't deserve it. And it's a good thing too. Try to have everything you want and you'll end up like my husband! But the things that matter, those cannot be compensated for or bargained away. They are our birthright in this world. We must find them and hold on to them, even if it takes us deep into the desert, far, far from where we thought we should be . . ." She hugged Sophie so close that Sophie could smell the spices flecked on her skin. "Give yourself permission to be happy. That is the magic spell. Then everything will be possible."

"I'm not sure how to do that," Sophie whispered, but she

was alone again, Reena's mother back to the kitchen.

Sophie wiped her eyes, her hands unsteady.

"You okay?" a gravelly voice asked behind her.

Sophie turned to see Hort holding two plates of rose-colored cookies, the weasel looking especially shifty.

"I asked them if they had anything without sugar or milk or all the other things you don't eat and they said no, but these were pretty, so . . . ," Hort mumbled.

"Shouldn't you be sharing those with your girlfriend?" Sophie asked.

"We broke up," Hort said.

Sophie's eyes widened. She looked over at Nicola, talking animatedly with Agatha. "Does your girlfriend know that?"

"*Ex*-girlfriend. And yes. It was her idea." Hort took a deep breath. "She thinks I'm immature and lost in my own fantasies and a sad, soft boy."

"All true, I suppose . . . ," Sophie considered.

"Thanks," said Hort, wounded. He walked away.

Sophie wanted to finish her sentence: "*That's why I like you.*" But she neither called him back nor moved from her spot, her cucumbers soggy on her plate.

"Nic looks less upset about their breakup than you do," Agatha said, accosting her, clutching another hunk of golden-brown honeycake, "presuming, of course, that's what you two were talking about. She's fine about it, actually. I think she finally realized that Hort from the storybooks is different from the Hort in real li—"

"Can I have some of that?" Sophie asked.

She was pointing at the cake.

Agatha gaped at her like she had two heads. "Um, take it all."

Sophie didn't think, the cake already pried out of her best friend's hands and stuffed into her mouth. She closed her eyes, the fluffy weight of flour collapsing on her tongue into a cool melt of honey, a burst of cinnamon at the center. With each chew, the alchemy repeated, as she let the sensations dance on her tongue, then down her throat, surrendering herself to the riot of flavors, as if for once in her life she wasn't in a rush to make pleasure *mean* something. She'd always thought of cake as fleeting, pointless, but here in the span of one taste, she'd understood why it mattered. Because *life* was fleeting and pointless unless you let yourself enjoy it, *savor* it, down to its lightest, most insignificant moments. She could feel tears falling, as if she'd opened up the forbidden gate . . . as if she'd lost and found something at the same time . . .

"I'll have what she's having," Dot said to Yousuf nearby, pointing at Sophie.

Sophie looked at Agatha. They both cracked up.

Then Agatha stopped laughing.

"What is it?" Sophie asked—

Crickets, she realized.

The music had stopped.

Both girls turned to the Queen of Jaunt Jolie, who'd noticed it too, she and Maid Marian standing very still at the center of the room. Everyone seemed to tune in, the pub going silent.

Then Sophie heard it.

Rattling and thundering, like a faraway quake.

Agatha was already dragging her outside, into the thick desert air, the others close behind—

Together, the two girls looked up into the night and glimpsed the swell of flames sweeping down the dunes like a storm. A thousand Shazabah camels, riders wielding torches and blades, side by side with soldiers astride gold-saddled horses.

Camelot horses.

Tedros stepped between the girls, his eyes locked on the king in blue and gold, charging at the fore of both armies.

"Time to go," said the prince.

19

TEDROS

Secret Weapon

"You are a very strange compass," Tedros murmured, who was used to a brass arrow that oriented you towards a goal. But instead, the Sultan's compass featured a tiny phantom of a belly dancer, shimmying her hips to the left.

"Go *that* way," the belly dancer advised.

Tedros jogged west in the dark, the glowing numbers near the belly dancer's waist counting down the distance to the

caves: *1,000 feet . . . 900 feet . . .* The prince glanced back at the rest of his team, hustling to keep up. Over their heads, he could see the flames of Japeth's army high on the dunes, miles away, but gaining ground. The Sultan had told Japeth everything, no doubt, thinking he was Rhian. Given him soldiers too.

Ten minutes, Tedros guessed.

That's how much time they had.

At the most.

"You sure you know what you're doing?" Agatha asked, rushing to his side.

"The implication being that I don't?" said Tedros. "Uma and Kaveen didn't trust each other. Look how they turned out."

Agatha prickled. "You won't tell me the plan."

"For a reason," said Tedros. "I know what's at stake. Not just a test. Your *life*."

"And what about the thousand men chasing us?" Agatha hounded.

"Choo-choo! Choo-choo!" said a voice.

Agatha looked down at Merlin, mop-haired and up to her ribs now, scampering beside her. The young wizard smiled.

"Big job for Tee Tee," he piped.

Agatha peered at him.

"Like I said. We have a plan," Tedros clipped, sprinting ahead. "Follow the others!"

Despite the Snake bearing down, he felt unshackled and *free*. Finally he'd taken control, having learned from the first test. This time, he'd handle the Snake himself, keeping Agatha in the dark. Not to punish her, but to protect her. If she knew what he and the Knights were planning, she'd jump into the fray. And with the Snake hunting her, that was the *last* place she should be.

And yet, he still had misgivings about the Knights' plan. Japeth relinquish the throne by choice? The Snake surrender . . . for *love*? Only women could invest in such a plot. But he didn't have a better one and the more he thought about it, the more his heart pulsed with hope. If he played his cards perfectly, then maybe . . . just maybe . . .

He picked up speed, looking back to see his princess fall farther behind, while the Snake and his army vanished into the valley of a dune. The idea of leaving Agatha outside the cave when Japeth attacked made Tedros sick. The Snake would go right for her to win the second test. Would Merlin stick to the plan . . . ? Tedros' gut knotted tighter. He'd entrusted a six-year-old with Agatha's life. A six-year-old who still peed his pants and had to be bribed with chocolate cake. *No going back now*, the prince thought, burying his doubts. He ran harder, tracking the compass girl's hips . . . *200 feet . . . 100 feet . . . 50 feet . . .*

A storm of sand erupted in front of him, a towering wall rising so high, it obscured the moon. Wind whittled this wall like a sculptor, Tedros covering his eyes, his lips and tongue coated in hot dust, before he squinted through his fingers and glimpsed the cave's shape: a colossal magic lamp made out of sand, the tip of the lamp the opening to the cave, its portal of gold glow piercing the night.

Behind Tedros, the others arrived and flanked him like a shield: Agatha, Sophie, Uma, Hort, and the Knights of Eleven.

It was one thing to hear Kaveen tell a story. But to see the cave now, a real place, with the magic lamp sealed inside, the lamp that made Aladdin a legend . . . *This is what Readers must feel like*, Tedros thought. The prince's palms started to sweat, his mouth dry.

"H-hi," he said, inching towards the cave, "I'm Prince Tedros of—"

A voice thundered from deep within: "Many a man has disturbed me, seeking my Cave of Wishes. But none with so *feeble* an army."

Tedros could hear the rumble of Japeth's horses. There was little time for negotiation. "I come for the lamp," he declared.

"All fools do," the cave taunted, low and resounding. "But to enter the cave, you must bring me something in return. And as far as I can tell, you don't even have a *sword*, feckless prince. So go. Before I feel offended enough to deal with you."

The sand under Tedros' boots thickened, as if to swallow him whole. By the time he looked up, the cave was collapsing back into the desert—

"I don't come empty-handed," said Tedros. "I bring your true love."

The cave instantly re-formed.

"Show me," it commanded.

Princess Uma stepped forward, taking her place next to the prince.

The cave seemed to shudder at the sight of her, the light of its portal burning red-hot, like a stoked fire.

Tedros could see Agatha grinding her teeth, as if she'd already decided this was the worst plan ever.

"Give her to me," the cave ordered. "Then you may enter."

"You'll get her once I enter and exit your cave safely," Tedros countered. "Otherwise, I have no assurance you'll let me leave alive."

"And what of my assurances? You may use the lamp to wish my true love out of this deal. Or she may flee while you are inside."

"Neither of those will happen," Tedros vowed. "I will deliver her as promised."

"Your promises mean nothing to me," said the cave. "What happens if you take what you now say is mine? What happens if you cheat?"

"Then you can have me," spoke a voice.

Guinevere stepped forward.

"His own mother," she said.

Tedros showed little reaction, as if this too was part of the plan.

"I'll enter the cave with him," the old queen explained. "If he fails to deliver the princess, then you may keep me as punishment."

The cave's light shone upon Guinevere, as if verifying she was who she said.

"What do I want with you, old bones," the cave mocked. "Better fed to vultures."

"Which is why you can trust me to deliver your true love,"

said Tedros. "No boy would sacrifice his mother to certain death. The terms favor you."

The cave paused, considering this.

Smoke fogged the sky, the smell of torch flames rising. The cave beamed its light into the distance, on the twin armies riding towards them.

"I suggest you make your decision quickly," said Tedros, with an eye towards Uma. "Given impending company, your true love may not last long enough to see the end of our bargain."

The cave's sands hardened.

"Enter," he snarled.

Tedros clasped his mother's hand, pulling her into the Cave of Wishes. The moment he stepped into the portal's light, he felt the drop in temperature, the air cool and sharp. From inside the cave, he glanced back one last time, at Agatha, his princess looking helpless and scared, the same way Tedros looked whenever she went chasing after his quests without him.

Sand poured over the door like a tomb being sealed.

Then he and his mother were alone.

FIVE MINUTES, TEDROS thought.

Any more than that and Agatha and the rest would be at risk.

Guinevere stumbled, gripping on to Tedros' arm. "Careful," she breathed, "there's a step."

Tedros lit his fingerglow. "*Lots* of steps."

A crooked staircase made out of sand spiraled down into darkness, beyond what the prince could see. He slid his boot onto the first step, sand crumbling. With each step, the footing seemed more uneven, like a rocky shoreline. Guinevere tripped again.

"You okay?" Tedros said.

"Go ahead," she said, limping. "I'll meet you at the bottom."

Tedros put his arm around her and guided her, step by step.

It was strange to be here with her. When they'd made the plan at the pub, she'd seemed the right choice to brave the cave with him. If he'd taken Agatha, she would have questioned his every move. Sophie would have been worse. And everyone else, he didn't feel comfortable with, not the way he did with his mother, which was ironic, given he'd spent the last ten years thinking her a disloyal witch. And yet, now that he was alone with her, there was an odd tension between them. Not anger or resentment. That was gone from his heart, his mother's sins forgiven. It was something else. Vacancy. Emptiness. As if they were two strangers, any bond between them imagined.

Then, in the cast of his glow, Tedros glimpsed something embedded in one of the steps: a gold coin. As he swept his glow downwards, he saw why the stairs were so uneven, each of them laden with treasures: polished jewels, glinting rings, at least four crowns, and more gold than Tedros had ever seen, coins and talismans and goblets, scattered and fossilized deep into the sand. For a second, Tedros was baffled . . .

Then he saw the skulls.

Scores of them, hanging off the staircase by ropes of tightly packed sand, some attached to their skeletons, others severed at the neck or shoulders or ribs, like a gallery of warning. These must be the seekers who'd come to this cave and hadn't made it back out, leaving the treasures from their wishes behind.

"They made mistakes," said Guinevere nervously.

How? Tedros wondered. It was the Cave of Wishes. You ask your three wishes and hurry away with your plunder.

Then again, when it came to magic, there was always a catch.

They went faster now, Tedros moving his glow off the remains of wishers past and keeping the light on the bounties of each step, one by one, until they reached the bottom, a small cellar of sand. Given the corpses along the way and the famed power of the lamp, Tedros was expecting obstacles to finding it or at least some kind of test . . . but instead, there it was, lying on its side on the floor of the cave, copper in color, tarnished and scratched up, like an old trinket in an attic. There was nothing else down here except a dirty, broken mirror, leaning against a wall.

Tedros studied the lamp, its tip poking out of the sand, like an elephant's trunk. "Doesn't look like much, does it?"

A thunder of hooves echoed outside.

"Hurry, Tedros," said his mother, watching the cave walls quake.

Tedros grabbed the lamp, rubbing sand off its surface with his palm.

Nothing happened.

Isn't that what you're supposed to do? Rub the lamp? Tedros rubbed it harder, against his elbow, his chest, then with both hands at the same time—

The lamp glowed fire red, scalding his fingers; Tedros yelped and dropped it to the sand. In the lamp's reflection, he spotted a pair of yellow eyes glaring right at him. Red smoke lashed out of the lamp, building high over Tedros' and his mother's heads, a thick mist, murky and ragged at the edges, a man's torso with a tiger's head and the golden eyes Tedros had seen in the reflection, now fixed on him and Guinevere. In fairy tales, genies were friendly, comforting creatures, solid in body, but soft in spirit. But this genie was hazy in body, harsh in spirit, and very clearly *not* his friend.

"Three wishes," said the genie, the same stark voice they'd heard outside. "But to exit the cave, you'll need the secret word. A word I cannot speak myself without being condemned to eternal pain. So you may not use one of your wishes to procure it. And if you die in this cave by your own incompetence . . ." He glanced at the skulls of all the men who had. ". . . then the princess you've brought as my gift is still mine."

The catch, Tedros thought. He knew it seemed too easy.

Guinevere frowned. "But how do we—"

"One question. That's all you get, plus your three wishes," the genie cut off. "Use your question wisely. Any further questions will be taken out of your wishes."

Guinevere bit her tongue.

"Tell me what you were going to ask," Tedros whispered, careful not to phrase it as a question.

"How to find the secret word," said his mother.

"That's your question, then," the genie prompted.

"No. Everyone must ask how to find the secret word," said Tedros. "And yet, there's a hundred dead bodies hanging in this cave? It's a trap. We need to ask something else."

"Cleverer than you look," the genie remarked, tiger eyes gleaming. "If you had asked, I would have told you 'it's a *secret*' and you'd be no better off than before. Now ask your question. I care little about what becomes of you. Only your friends outside. *One* friend, rather, soon to be mine."

For a split second, Tedros wanted to ask the genie what was happening to Agatha . . . then stopped himself. The last thing Agatha would want was for him to waste his question on her. He needed to focus on why they were here: the plan to beat Japeth and keep his princess alive. He glanced at his mother, hoping she was working out the secret word—

Guinevere wrung her hands. "What would Lance do?" she whispered to herself.

Tedros almost laughed. He'd forgotten who his mother was. She'd dumped his gallant father for the chauvinist brute that was Sir Lancelot. Lance, who swept her off her feet and let her live a highland fantasy, devoid of real responsibility. Now his mother was still lost in the fantasy, waiting for her knight to save her.

It's why Tedros had chosen the girl he did. He didn't want one like his mother. He wanted an equal.

That free feeling he'd had on the dunes evaporated. Suddenly he missed his princess.

What would Agatha do?

Tedros stifled a smile. Maybe he was more like his mother than he thought.

And yet, Agatha wouldn't be distracted like he was. She'd be thinking about those who escaped the cave . . . the ones like Aladdin, who'd made their three wishes and gotten out alive . . .

The wishes, Tedros realized.

Agatha would tell him to focus on the wishes.

He looked up at the genie. "What were Aladdin's three wishes? Consider that my one question."

The genie's eyes flickered in surprise, before he answered: "His first wish was to be Sultan of Shazabah. His second wish was for Princess Asifa, the Sultan's daughter, to fall in love with him. And his third wish was for that mirror over there," he said, nodding at the cracked slab of glass against the wall.

The prince picked up the mirror, a piece of misshapen glass, veiled in dust. Aladdin had used his last wish to have *this*. And he hadn't even taken it with him. Not a surprise: magic mirrors had pitiful powers. Even the queen who hunted Snow White could only use hers to assess her rivals' beauty from afar. Yet Aladdin had invested his last wish to have a mirror of his own. Why?

Tedros took a deep breath. Only one way to solve this mystery. He blew the sand off its surface and was faced with his own reflection.

Instantly, the eyes of his mirror twin glowed yellow, like the genie's—

Then Tedros was falling into them like a hole.

He could see the Tedros left behind in the cave, as if he'd split into two selves. Gold light blinded him, like he'd dropped into the sun, before he came out the other side, floating without gravity through a hall of mirrors, each mirror playing a scene from his life.

Young Tedros, writing a message to his mother . . . then stuffing it into a bottle and setting it into the Savage Sea.

Tedros, crying alone in his dorm room at school.

Tedros, stiffening as Aric came towards him in a prison cell, a whip on his belt.

Tedros, lost in Filip's gaze on a window ledge, he and the boy about to kiss.

Tedros, gouging out the eyes of his father's statue in King's Cove . . .

These weren't just scenes, Tedros realized.

These were his *secrets*.

Suddenly, he was back in the genie's cave, turning away from his reflection, sucking in air.

"Tedros?" his mother asked behind him.

He didn't answer. He didn't think.

Instead, he held up the mirror and reflected her.

In the glass, Guinevere's eyes burned yellow and now Tedros was falling into them.

Into her secrets.

Guinevere in her wedding veil, walking down the aisle towards Arthur . . . but behind the veil, she looked racked with doubts . . .

Guinevere, embraced with Lancelot in a forest, the two disguised by the night.

Guinevere, in a dark hood, sneaking into young Tedros' room . . . kissing him goodbye . . . then seeing him wake . . . and hurriedly closing the door to lock him in.

Guinevere, on the shores of Avalon's lake, receiving Tedros' message in a bottle . . . and crumpling it as she saw Lancelot coming, clutching freshly picked flowers.

Guinevere, years later, glimpsing teenage Tedros arrive with his friends on the moors of Avalon . . . her face clouding over . . .

Tedros ripped himself out of his mother's secrets, reeling from the mirror—

"What's wrong?" said Guinevere, as if she'd been frozen in time. "What are you seeing?"

"You never wanted me to find you, did you?" her son asked. "After you ran off with Lancelot. You would have been happy never being with me again."

The flush in his mother's face told Tedros all he needed to know.

This mirror spoke the truth.

The darkest truths, locked away in each person's heart.

And his mother's was what he'd known all along: her heart was with Lancelot, only Lancelot, whether the knight was alive or dead. That's why Tedros felt that empty feeling around her. She was here in body, but no longer in soul.

Hooves pounded the desert outside, shaking the cave harder.

He was running out of time.

Tedros focused again on the mirror, keeping his face out of its reflection. What had Aladdin used it for? How did it help him get out of this ca—

Of course.

Slumdog, street rat . . . but a legend for a reason.

The prince tucked the mirror into the back of his pants. Then he gazed up at the genie, his blue eyes aflame.

"I'd like to make my first wish, please," said Tedros.

THE GENIE GAVE the mildest swish of his hand.

"Done," he declared. "Won't last more than an hour. Even my magic has limits."

Tedros inspected his body, unchanged on the outside. But inside, his blood tingled with bubbling heat, as if his veins were growing wider. His skin felt looser on his bones, more elastic. He held up a hand and with a simple focus of mind, he watched the hair on the back of it recede, the skin turning paler, more feminine . . . Then he stopped the transformation just as he'd started it, his hand reverting to a golden, sinewy fist.

"An hour is all I need," said Tedros.

He glanced at his mother, who was surely thinking the same thing as her son. That the genie had given Tedros precisely what he'd asked for. But whether this first wish was well-used . . . only time would tell.

"And your second wish?" the genie asked.

"Same as the first," Tedros answered. He pointed at his mother. "But do it to *her.*"

Tedros could see her clutching her arms over her chest, as if trying to block the sensations she was feeling inside. Mother and son shared the same powers now. But where these powers emboldened Tedros, they seemed to make his mother shrink deeper into her skin.

Will she be able to do the job when the moment comes? the prince wondered. *Did I make a mistake in picking her?*

"And your third wish?" the genie asked.

Tedros' heart thumped harder, drowning out the sounds from beyond. This last wish was the rub. He kept his face steady, trying to give nothing away.

But his mother had no such restraint. He could see her chewing on her lip and picking at her nails, glancing worriedly at him.

The genie noticed.

"And your *third wish?*" he repeated, with suspicion.

The prince looked hard into the genie's eyes. "My third wish is that you become deathly allergic to ladybugs."

"What?" the genie snorted.

From the ceiling of the cave, a big pink ladybug dropped onto his shoulder.

Instantly, the genie broke out into bright pink pox and

clutched his throat, gagging for breath. He flung the beetle to the ground, about to stomp on it—

"Wouldn't do that, considering it's your princess," said Tedros.

The genie ogled him, confused. Then he looked down at the pink bug, blinking up at the genie with almond-shaped eyes, before it began skittering around him, making him erupt in a fresh riot of blisters. Panicked, the genie punted the bug across the cave, straight into Tedros' hands.

"You said to deliver your princess to you. You didn't say in what *form*," the prince smiled, petting the beetle. "And it turns out a teacher of Animal Communication enjoys mogrifying into the precise insect that now kills you to be near. Doesn't sound like this tale will end in Happily Ever After, will it?"

The ladybug whispered in Tedros' ear.

"Besides, Uma says she might be your true love but you're certainly not hers," he relayed.

The genie's mist went redder, his eyes poisonous yellow. "We had a deal! You made a promise!"

"Which we fulfilled," Tedros pointed out.

"You think you'll get away with this!" the genie shouted. "You cheat! You *thief*!"

"Says a genie who makes a sport of stealing men's lives," Tedros reproached. "The genie who thinks he can cheat his way to love."

The genie lunged for him, but Uma's bug bounced onto his face and the genie recoiled in horror. He smacked her away, except the ladybug kept scuttling towards him, cornering him

against the lamp, choking him with her mere presence as he
contorted with pain. Desperate to stay alive, the genie pulled
back into his lamp, leaving only his scared face exposed . . .
Then his expression changed, a triumphant leer growing, as
he extended his neck like a snake's and confronted Tedros, eye
to eye.

"You're forgetting something, failed prince. You don't
know the secret word. You're trapped here forever. You idiot.
You arrogant fool!"

"I don't know the secret word," Tedros confessed. "That is
true."

He looked up at the genie.

"But you're forgetting something too."

Tedros pulled Aladdin's mirror out of his pants and held it
up, reflecting his stunned opponent.

In a flash, the prince was falling through tiger eyes . . .

But only one secret played in the genie's soul, again and
again and again.

A single, shining word, carved in darkness, like a wish
against the night.

Tedros yanked himself back into the cave, just as the genie
surged out of his lamp with the last of his strength, claws out
for the prince—

Tedros put his nose to the genie's. "The secret word is . . .
human."

"*NO!*" the genie screamed, dragged back into the lamp.

All at once, sand swelled under Tedros' feet, lifting him
and his mother out of the cave, Uma's bug scrambling after

them. Soaring upwards, Tedros smelled the heat of the desert above him, sweat beading on his skin. He could hear the confused cries of Japeth's army, the first part of the plan surely complete—

His mother snatched at the mirror, still in his hands.

"Leave it!" Guinevere said. "Bad things happen to thieves!"

Tedros ignored her, gripping the glass, the desert surface coming closer. Taking the mirror wasn't part of the plan, but no way was he leaving it behind.

Not because he was a thief.

Because he was the *king*.

And the mirror his new weapon.

Secrets this time, instead of a sword.

Tedros grinned, rising out of the cave.

Oh yes.

There were more souls he'd be looking into.

20

Conversations with Friends

Ten minutes earlier, Agatha panicked as Tedros and his mother disappeared inside the Cave of Wishes.

The moment the door sealed, Agatha whirled to face Merlin.

"Merlin. What 'big job' did Tedros give you to do?"

The six-year-old clasped his hands under his bottom, as if unsure how much to share. Then he pointed at the armies charging across the dunes. "Tee Tee said wait 'til horseys."

"Wait 'til *horseys?*" Sophie frowned, sidling beside Agatha.

"Then what?" Agatha hounded the wizard.

Merlin beamed up at them. "Choo-choo! Choo-choo!"

Agatha and Sophie exchanged looks, while Hort, Princess Uma, and the Knights of Eleven clustered together, the Snake and a thousand men storming closer, closer . . .

"Are we really going to stand here and let him kill Agatha?" Sophie demanded, her dress morphing into white armor, mirroring the steel in her voice. "Didn't you all say you had a *plan?*"

"We do," clipped Maid Marian, nodding pointedly at Merlin.

"Knights, take your position!" Jaunt Jolie's queen ordered, eleven armored females fanning into a frontline.

Sophie grabbed Merlin. "You little brat, tell Auntie Sophie exactly what Tee Tee told you—"

"Choo-choo!" the young wizard repeated.

"I'd give him a spanking but we're about to die," Sophie growled. Both girls sparked their fingerglows, pink and gold strobing weakly, fear the only emotion fueling their magic. Over Sophie's shoulder, Agatha watched Japeth riding for her, an arrow to a target. "How could Tedros just leave you here?" Sophie hissed, sheltering her friend. "He should have taken you into the cave instead of his useless mother! What kind of prince is that?"

"He said to follow the others. That he had a plan," Agatha insisted as Japeth drew closer. But deep down, she had the same questions about Tedros, while also feeling guilty about them, as if it wasn't a boy's job to play bodyguard for his girl. And yet . . . if their positions were reversed, she never would have left her prince alone to fight. Nor would she have trusted him to survive Japeth without her. Then again, it was exactly this lack of trust that had put them in this mess to begin with.

"Well, he has a plan and we don't," Sophie conceded, squinting back at the cave. "For once in our lives, maybe we should give him the benefit of the doubt."

But she didn't look convinced.

Neither did Agatha.

"Remember this . . ." Hester exhorted her fellow knights, her eyes glinting through her pearlescent veil. "None of those bastards *touches* Agatha."

The Knights of Eleven grabbed swords off their belts, brandishing them to fight.

"Because that's how you beat an unkillable Snake. *Swords*," Hort groused, exploding out of his clothes into a hulking man-wolf. "Not just Agatha we have to keep him away from. Keep him from Sophie too."

"But by all means, let him kill me," Nicola snapped.

"Not being your boyfriend means your bad attitude is *your* problem now," Hort retorted, cocking his massive biceps as he shielded Sophie. "And you missed my point. We can't let Japeth get Sophie back. Her blood *heals* him."

"Not anymore," said Sophie, feeling safer now that wolf-Hort was protecting her. "Rhian told me of a pen's prophecy. About him and Japeth. One would marry me and be king, the other would be healed by my blood. But not both. Once Japeth killed Rhian and stole the crown, he lost my blood's powers."

"Pen's prophecy?" said Agatha, the trampling horses and camels so loud she could hardly hear herself. "Which pen? Lionsmane or the Storian?"

"Doesn't matter," Sophie dismissed. "What matters is Japeth's mortal now. He *can* be killed."

"Plus, the Sultan's army still thinks Japeth is Rhian, so Snake can't use his scims. Not without giving himself away," Nicola surmised. "This is our best chance to beat him."

"Only thing standing in our way is a thousand pirates and armed soldiers and fire-spitting camels," said adult Dot, fatally.

"And our best weapon is a six-year-old," Anadil echoed, "who seems to have *disappeared*."

Agatha scanned the desert. "Where is he?"

"*30 seconds . . .* ," Dean Brunhilde called as Japeth led two armies straight at them.

"What about Uma?" Sophie said to Agatha. "Maybe she can stop the camels—"

The girls whirled to the Princess, hoping her animal skills could save them . . . Instead, Uma mogrified into a pink ladybug, which plopped in sand near the cave's door.

"*20 seconds . . .* ," Anadil warned, her two rats leaping off her shoulders, starting to swell bigger and bigger, like twin mastiffs.

Hort roared across the desert, crouched in fighting position. "Come at me, mate!"

A camel spat a ball of fire, scorching his palm, sending the man-wolf shrieking to the ground before he snuffed the flames in sand. More fireballs slammed into Anadil's rats, rocketing them into the night.

"*10 seconds!*" Beatrix cried.

Men and beasts flew towards them, about to obliterate them with fury and fire.

"Your scream," Agatha gasped at Sophie. "Your witch's scream."

Sophie shook her head. "That was the *old* me—"

"Bring the old you back!" Agatha begged.

"*5 seconds!*" Reena shouted.

Sophie bore down, teeth gnashed, chest swelling. But then the two girls glimpsed Japeth, swerving around the Knights of Eleven, the Snake rising tall on his horse's back, double-fisting his sword, aiming it right at Agatha.

The scream seemed to catch in Sophie's throat, as if Evil couldn't beat Evil. Not this kind, darker than anything inside her own heart.

Agatha retreated from the Snake in terror, Sophie too late to stop him. Japeth's sword gleamed by moonlight as he raised it over Agatha's head like an axe—

Something swooped in front of him.

A young boy on a magic carpet, looking clear into Japeth's eyes, then twirling to Agatha with the brightest of smiles.

"Choo-choo, Mama!"

Merlin swept his hands like a magician as the Snake slashed his blade across Agatha, cutting full-force into—

Thin air.

She was gone.

Merlin too.

All of Tedros' army was gone.

Except for a pink little beetle, peeping through a vast, empty desert, before it set its sights downward and began burrowing into the sand.

ONCE, BACK IN Gavaldon, Agatha had asked her mother what happens to people when they die. "The nun at the schoolhouse says our bodies go into the ground but our souls go up into the sky, where we reunite with all our friends. But Sophie says that's nonsense and the dead have no friends."

Callis had continued to stew her frog-skin soup. "Lovely girl, that Sophie."

So when Agatha spun from the Snake, waiting for the pain of steel and the shock of her head flying off her body, but instead opened her eyes to find herself reunited with all her friends on a cloud in a strange-colored sky . . . she immediately looked at Sophie.

"Merlin, sweetie . . . ," Sophie rasped. "What did you *do*?"

The little wizard giggled from atop his magic carpet, breezing through a night full of silver stars, two-dimensional and five-pointed, as if he'd drawn them himself.

They were in the Celestium, Agatha realized. Tedros must have told Merlin to hide them here . . . to wait until the "horseys" were close and whisk Agatha and her friends to safety . . .

The same way Merlin had brought her here to help with the first test . . .

Only the Celestium was *different* now, Agatha realized. Instead of the pure, meditative sky she was used to, it was a hodgepodge of purple shades, like a poorly made quilt, filled with fast-moving clouds, comets, and constellations of fantastic shapes—dragons and castles and goblins and ships—as if instead of a wizard's place to think, it'd become a wizard's place to play. Together, they'd been transported *inside* Merlin's imagination, a six-year-old's hectic dreamscape, mirrored by the dreamer himself, whizzing around on his magic carpet, gibbering incantations, whereby new comets and clouds burst into being, streaking past his startled guests.

"Merlin! Come down at once!" Sophie demanded. "Nightwind, you too!"

"Faster, choo-choo! Faster!" Merlin tooted, buzzing his carpet around so wildly it blew the veils off Hester's and Anadil's heads.

"*Merlin!*" Sophie shouted.

"Not the Mama!" Merlin heckled, all the clouds morphing into bald, warted Sophies, complete with witches' hats—

Agatha shot a spell, tying Nightwind's tassels, sending it crashing to their cloud.

Merlin looked at her grumpily. "Tee Tee said I could have playtime. Once I finished Big Job. Tee promised."

"You can have all the playtime you want, after you explain a few things," said Agatha. "Tedros told you to bring us here?"

"Wait 'til horseys and bring Mama and friends to secret

place. That's what Tee said," Merlin nodded, subtly untying his carpet's tassels. "Then have playtime with choo-choo and stay in secret place until . . ." His voice trailed off.

"Until . . . ?" Agatha asked.

"Until when, Merlin?" Sophie tag-teamed. "Stay in the secret place until *when*?"

Merlin chewed on his lip and Agatha realized he didn't have the answer because he didn't *know* the answer.

"Until we can't stay no more?" Merlin guessed.

"How long is *that*?" said Hort, popping out of a cloud, back to his pale, weaselly body, his waist wrapped in downy white fluff. He rubbed at his scalded right hand. "How long until we 'can't stay no more'?"

But the young wizard was back in the air, Nightwind untethered and taking him higher and higher, Merlin's hoots echoing through his private galaxy.

"Tedros warned me once: that we couldn't stay here long," Agatha remembered. "Back when we were looking for a spot to hide from Rafal. He said the air was too thin. Eventually we'd lose our breath and be forced back down."

"We're alive for now. That's what matters," the Queen of Jaunt Jolie sighed, sitting gingerly on a cloud.

"The plan is only half-done," said Dean Brunhilde, settling beside her. "We'll have work to do once Tedros and Guinevere return if we're to defeat the Snake for good."

"What work?" Agatha asked, trying to suss out the rest of the plan.

"And how can we beat the Snake without killing Aggie?

That's the second *test*," Sophie badgered, but the Dean was lost in thought.

"He was the same RJ I've always known," she shuddered. "I could see it in his eyes."

"Are you sure they can't find us here?" Maid Marian asked nervously.

"Only those with wizard blood can find other wizards' thinking places," Jacinda reassured. "Presumably so wizards can meet one another in private. But mostly wizards stay out of each other's heads. That's what my own wizard tutor, Joffrey, told me. I attempted to find his thinking place on several occasions, but each time, I'd wake up high in a tree with no way down."

Merlin chuckled somewhere in the sky.

Agatha sat next to Anadil and elder Dot, the two witches in pearly armor, sharing cloud pieces Dot had turned to chocolate.

"Can't believe the idiot's plan worked," Anadil mused. "Who knew Tedros could *think*?"

Agatha snatched the chocolate out of her hands. "He's not an idiot, first off," she said, eating the cocoa cloud puff. "Second of all, you heard the Dean; the plan is only half-done, so don't speak too soon. Third, I don't know why he kept the plan from me or why none of you will tell me what it is, especially since I'm the one the Snake is supposed to kil—oh, this is *delicious*."

"I filled the holes in the cloud with peanut butter," said Dot, tossing her frumpy curls. "And pretty sure Tedros didn't tell you about the plan because then you'd nitpick and take command of it and end up making a mess, like you did with the first test."

Agatha's neck went red. "He said that?"

"No, but that's why *I* won't tell you the plan," Dot explained. "You'd think it was *your* plan and act like you could do it better than us, even if you can't. It's what you always do. Goodness, being old makes you honest."

"So that's why Tedros' plan worked. Because his princess couldn't bungle it. He should keep secrets from you more often," Anadil needled Agatha, while holding up more white fluff, which Dot zapped into chocolate.

Agatha stared at them, hurt.

"Your rats, Anadil! I saw what happened!" Beatrix cut in, armor jangling as she jammed between Agatha and the witches. "Think they're still alive?"

"My talent is making them grow. Their talent is finding a way back to me, even when there's no hope," Anadil said, forlorn. "But thank you for the concern, Evergirl."

She gave Beatrix a smile that was halfway sincere and Agatha wondered if in the process of bonding as Knights, old enemies had become new friends.

"That's what I say about Tristan too," Kiko spouted, plopping next to Agatha.

"Here we go," Beatrix groaned.

"That even after he died, he would find his way back to me. And then suddenly Willam appears, who looks so much like him, but every time I try to talk to Willam, that other boy is in the way, the one with the big head, Boston or Bojangle or whatever his name is. But I can be patient. It wouldn't be a fairy tale if there weren't things in the way. And imagine if Willam and I end up together. That means Tristan sent Willam to me himself. Or maybe he *is* Willam. Like a friendly ghost in a different body, who came back to take care of me. So don't worry." She kissed Anadil on the cheek. "Your story will take care of your rats too." Kiko flounced off as Hester sat down.

Anadil eyed her friend. "Do we tell her what Sophie told us?"

"That the boy she thinks is a reincarnation of her dead 'true love' who had no interest in girls is the brother of said dead boy who also has no interest in girls?" Hester paused. "No."

"Cheers to that," said Anadil.

Soon, they all dispersed into separate clouds—Sophie chatting with Hort, Hester with Beatrix, Reena with Anadil, more friends coupling up—leaving Agatha on her own, watching Merlin zig and zag on a drooping Nightwind, the young wizard carving his name in bright lights across the sky with his fingertip. Agatha fidgeted, her clump tapping restlessly. She was so used to playing peacemaker, shuttling between conflicts, bridging divides, that to see the Knights of Eleven getting along without her—Good and Evil, old and young, friends and strangers—while Hort and Sophie continued their conversation on a far-off cloud . . . It made Agatha feel uncomfortable, like she was Graveyard Girl again, forgotten by the world. Then she remembered this wasn't Gavaldon. That in this world, she was surrounded by friends, each as capable and strong as her, each as important to this story—including her true love, who at this very moment was trapped in a cave trying to save her from a Snake.

Dot's right about me, Agatha thought. She'd convinced herself this was her fairy tale to win. Her mountain to conquer. As if she wanted everyone to look to *her* to lead them. Why? Why couldn't she let her prince lead? Why did she have to have all the answers?

Her soul whispered back.

If I don't . . . what am I worth?

It was the same crisis that haunted Tedros. Who was he without his crown? Who was Arthur's son, if not the king?

And here Agatha was, letting her own insecurities thwart his every attempt to answer these questions for himself.

Her heart wrenched. She'd put her prince in an untenable position. Not just with having to kill her to win the second test. But now having to keep secrets from her in order to do his duty and prove himself a king.

They were different in so many ways, she and Tedros. But in their hearts, they were afflicted by the same malady: each of them needed proof that they were good enough. That they were worthy of love. The same way Agatha had needed proof from Professor Dovey that she could be beautiful. But then, as now, the only cure could come from within. And as long as she and Tedros searched for the answer outside of themselves, they would continue to stand in each other's way. Like two rival kings having their own tournament.

Maybe that's why Arthur made this the second test, Agatha thought.

Because he saw a future where she held his son back, instead of helping him.

So he put their love to the fire.

Three tests.

Three answers to find.

Was Agatha the right queen for Tedros?

Or would she be another Guinevere, another curse for Camelot?

That was the king's question.

Now it was up to Agatha to answer it.

This is my test as much as Tedros', she thought.

To survive it, she had to trust him.

They had to be a team.

A real one.

If Tedros made it out of the cave alive, that is.

Agatha's throat tightened.

He'd come back. He had to.

Any minute, he'd fall through the sky and land on her cloud, with those gorgeous eyes and a cocked grin.

In the meantime, to distract herself, Agatha did what old Graveyard Girl used to do: lurk around in darkness and eavesdrop on the living . . .

"That's what he said to you?" Maid Marian was asking Dot. Marian looked off guard and stiff, as if she'd been cornered by the age-hexed witch. "That he and your mother were . . . 'love'?"

Dot nodded. "Funny to think he loved someone else besides you, isn't it?"

Marian's eyes widened.

"Oh please, even the town fool knew Daddy was obsessed with you," Dot teased. "It's why he hated Robin so much. But you were always so kind to Daddy, even with him intent on killing your true love. Sometimes I wondered if you and Daddy had a secret friendship. A moment when you and him were more than enemies."

"Only a moment," said Marian quietly. "Your collar. The stitching's come apart. Let me fix it."

Marian used a pin from her hair to rethread Dot's armor.

"You smell nice," Dot said.

"Like beer and chicken wings?" Marian laughed. "That's what I smelled like working at the Arrow."

"No . . . like a homey blanket or pillow."

"Oh," said Marian tautly, continuing to sew.

Dot looked up at the Celestium's moon, made out of cheese, which Merlin took bites out of between rounds of mischief. Dot's brown skin glowed under the half-eaten orb. For a moment, she seemed ageless. "Daddy never told me about my mother. Said she died when I was young. A few other things here and there. That she was so beautiful that Good and Evil both loved her. That she had a kind heart, even to those who treated her poorly. That she was a good tailor. Not much more than that. But it doesn't matter, does it? If it was love, *real* love, like he said . . . then that's all I need to know."

Marian let go of Dot's collar, putting the pin back in her

hair. Her hand trembled. Her throat bobbed. Tears slipped down her cheeks.

"What is it?" Dot asked, confused.

Marian hugged old Dot tight. "Your mother would be so proud of you."

Agatha gasped audibly and dropped to another cloud before Marian or Dot spotted her.

The emotions hit her hard.

Marian is Dot's mother.

The clues had always been there, but she hadn't put the pieces together until now. The way Marian skirted tensely around Dot and her friends. The way the Sheriff treated Dot, his pent-up fury and cruelty borne of unrequited love. The way Robin had a soft spot for Dot, as if he knew Marian's secret. Dot's warmhearted charm, inherited from her mother, balanced with the dark edge of her father. Agatha peeked up to see Dot, joined by Anadil and Hester, with Marian studying the latter's tattoo, mystified by how it worked. From Dot's relaxed pose, it was clear Dot didn't know the truth about her mother. Or didn't *want* to know. Young or old, Dot had a new family now. A family that, unlike her own, had been there for her from the beginning.

Agatha heard a loud sigh and turned to find Nicola in the shadows of the cloud.

"If you've come to tell me to be more social, I'm perfectly fine on my own," Nicola said. "Always have been."

"Actually I didn't even know you were here—" Agatha started, but Nicola was already unburdening herself.

"In the pub, I felt okay at first, because it was *my* decision to break up with him. He needed to know he wasn't treating me right. That I deserved to be more than second best. But now he doesn't even seem upset about it"—Nic swished a hand at Hort and Sophie on a faraway cloud—"as if he and I never were together. He hasn't even come to check on me. I know I broke up with him, but still! He should see how I'm feeling! He was my first boyfriend. My first kiss. And now he's talking to her. *Again.*"

"To be fair, he's been talking to 'her' since the first day of school," Agatha pointed out. "And if Tedros ever broke up with me, I would bomb his castle before I ever checked in on him."

"But Hort *did* like me," Nicola barreled on. "We had time together in Sherwood Forest and Foxwood when Sophie wasn't around . . . We were *happy*. But when she's there, it's like I don't exist. Because of how I look. Because I don't look like *her*."

"No," said Agatha. "It's not about that."

"She's blond and thin and has a small nose and no pores and I'm—"

"It's *not* about how you look," Agatha repeated.

She said this so sharply that Nicola stopped her monologue.

"And as long as you have doubts about the way you look, you'll never be able to truly love someone," Agatha preached. "Take it from me. Even if you have the most loving, doting fairy-tale boyfriend, you'll reject his love if you don't believe you deserve it. And then it's only too easy to blame it on looks or something else that you can't possibly control, because the one thing you *can* control—how you feel about yourself—you were too afraid to change."

Nicola grimaced. "But—"

"Let me finish," Agatha said. "Yes, Sophie is beautiful. Yes, Hort has always been fond of her. But Hort also believes in true love, even though he's a Never. And he wouldn't have kissed you and been your boyfriend if he didn't think there was a chance that *you* were the one. Period. Hort is too kind and honest and real to settle for anything less. Maybe he wasn't ready in the end. Maybe you're not ready. Maybe you two just aren't right for each other. But this isn't about you not having blond hair or a princess figure or anything else. This is about letting yourself take chances at love and not giving up. That's why love is the ultimate test. It forces us to grow, to be better, and even then, sometimes it's not enough. We get in our own way. We're our own worst villains. But only a *true* villain believes he can control love. Love can't be controlled any more than a wildfire can. It lives in the balance of fate and free will, Man and Pen. We do our part, we hope, we wish . . . but it writes its own story in its own time, the way it's meant to be. For you. For Hort. For everyone who believes in Ever After. For me too." Agatha clasped Nicola's shoulder. "Love makes fools of me and Tedros each and every day."

Nicola didn't say anything for a long while. Then she peered hard at Agatha. "I can't believe I'm taking advice on boys from the girl who hung skulls in Gavaldon Square on Valentine's Day."

"You knew that was me?" Agatha said, surprised.

"*Everyone* knew it was you."

The two girls cracked up.

"Nic!" a voice called.

It came from above: Hester, Beatrix, and Kiko crowded onto Nightwind, which had left Merlin asleep on top of the moon and now seemed enthused about new riders.

"Room for one more!" said Kiko.

Agatha smiled at Nicola. "Go."

Nic was already running.

Agatha couldn't leave Merlin teetering on the moon, so she hopped up clouds, like a frog jumping lily pads, but still found herself too far away to retrieve him. Only then did she realize she was hovering directly above Hort and Sophie, who were on the cloud below, the weasel looking scrawnier than usual in his fluff diaper.

"So out with it, what did you and Tedros *really* talk about when you were flying on that stymph?" said Sophie.

Hort's eyes roved around. "I should find some clothes—"

"Do you think anyone here hasn't seen you without your clothes on? Even when you were the History Professor. And don't think of lying to me," Sophie hectored. "First of all, you're not good at it and second, you and I are too close for you to keep secrets from me—"

"I was asking him for girl advice, okay," Hort blurted.

Sophie hesitated. "What *kind* of girl advice?"

"Like . . . what it was like to, you know . . ."

"No, I don't know."

"What it was like to kiss you."

Sophie stared at him.

"Versus kissing Agatha. Like how he felt kissing you in comparison," said Hort. "Because when I kissed Nic, it was amazing and fun . . . and yet, something was missing. And I just wanted to know what kisses feel like to him because he's probably kissed lots of girls."

"So let me get this straight," said Sophie. "You asked Tedros what kissing me was like versus Agatha so you could figure out whether your kisses with your girlfriend—"

"Ex-girlfriend."

"—were good kisses or bad kisses."

"Essentially."

Sophie looked so galled that Agatha wondered for a moment if she might clobber the poor boy, before Sophie flattened her lips and squinted hard at him. "What did Tedros say about kissing me versus—actually, forget it. I don't want to know."

"Not that I take anything that lump says seriously," Hort offered. "Can you imagine kissing Tedros? He's slobbery and smells like grass." He shivered. "Bleecchh."

Sophie cackled so loud it woke Merlin up. "Oh, Hort. You really are a goon."

"Better than a sad, soft boy," Hort muttered.

"Why are those bad things?" Sophie came back, exasperated. "Why can't a boy show his emotions? Why can't a boy just be himself?"

"Because girls like you won't go for us," said Hort grimly.

"Have you considered that it's because you are a *real* boy, in all your softness and sadness, that I am having this conversation with you to begin with?" Sophie asked. "I can have any handsome boy in the Woods, but they're insufferable like Tedros or possessive like Rafal or maniacal like Rhian. But I had to learn that they wouldn't make me happy, didn't I? The same way you had to kiss Nicola to learn there was something missing. The same way I had to spend time with you again and again to learn that you weren't creepy, useless Hort at all, but Hort who is open and true—and yes, sad and soft—but altogether, sweet, steadfast, and the strongest boy I know."

Hort's whole body seemed to blush. "Uh, so . . . what are you saying?"

Sophie crossed her arms. "What I am saying is . . . what I'm saying . . ." She looked up at Hort. "I don't know what I'm saying."

The two of them stared hard into each other's eyes, the silence as thick and wide as an ocean. Agatha tipped over the cloud to get a better look—

Her shadow cast over Sophie, who glanced up. "Agatha, darling!"

Agatha toppled in surprise, crashing down and landing hard on Hort, kneeing him in the groin.

"*Aggaaaain!*" Hort wheezed. "The witch strikes *agaaaain!*"

"I'm assuming you're the witch, this time," Sophie said to Agatha.

Wails echoed above them.

Merlin, crying from atop the moon. "Naughty! Naughty!"

"Yes, Merlin, yes! Very naughty!" Sophie called out. "Go back to sleep!"

Merlin wailed harder.

"Strange," said Agatha. "Never cried before. Puts himself to sleep and eats from his hat when he's hungry—"

"Guys?" Hort said quietly.

The girls followed his eyes.

To the corner of the Celestium.

A tear had opened up in the purple canvas, a rip in the night. Stars tumbled out of the sky as the sky pulled apart, a shadow coming through.

Agatha smiled at the firm chest and lean silhouette, her heart surging. "Tedros . . ."

Then moonlight hit the shadow and Agatha stumbled back into Sophie's arms.

Merlin cried harder, pointing at the sky. "Naughty! Naughty!"

Agatha choked on her scream.

Naughty.

Nottee.

Not Tee.

21

AGATHA

The Second Half of the Plan

"Impossible . . ." Sophie rasped to Agatha. "He's not a wizard . . . He can't be here . . ."

But he *was* here.

He was inside Merlin's Celestium.

Japeth stared hard at Agatha, his face in shadow, the whites of his eyes glowing in the dark. He slithered through the tear in the sky and leapt down onto a cloud, landing in a crouch. Then he rose, his blue-and-gold suit rippling in the moonlight.

Slowly, his king's suit melted

pitch-black, the Snake returned, scims shrieking and sliding all over his body.

His eyes never left Tedros' princess.

Sophie shielded her best friend. "Run. *Now.*"

Scims spiked for Agatha's head and she and Sophie dove off the sides of the cloud, with Sophie crashing on a puff below. But there was no cloud for Agatha to land on; she tumbled into oblivion—

A red horn hooked through her collar, Hester's demon slobbering in her face—"*nogoodverybadday*"—before it flung Agatha onto a thick cloud with its master. "Stay behind me," Hester hissed, blocking her. "If you die, we *all* die."

"Merlin!" Agatha pointed at the wizard, howling on the moon. "We have to get Merlin!"

Hester's demon soared for the ball of cheese, snatching the six-year-old in its claws and flying him higher and higher. But the Snake had no interest in Merlin. He stayed locked on Agatha, his chest exposed where the scims had peeled off him.

Scims still on the loose.

She spun just in time—

They speared for Agatha's face and she plunged into the center of her cloud, barely eluding them. She popped her head through, spitting out fluff. "Up there!" she said to Hester, pointing at the rip in the sky.

The scims circled around, angling for Agatha harder, faster. Hester yanked her back into the cloud—

"I'll use that portal," Agatha panted. "Scims will follow me out . . . All of you will be safe . . . I just need the magic carpet to get there . . ."

She peeked up, searching for Nightwind . . . then saw the carpet veer sharply, Beatrix, Kiko, and Nicola aboard to ambush the Snake, swords aimed at his open flesh—

Scims launched off Japeth's shoulder and slammed into Nightwind, obliterating it to shreds, sending the girls scattering to clouds.

"Agatha, look out!" Sophie cried from below.

Eels whizzed upwards, nicking Agatha's and Hester's ears, before both girls dodged into the cloud, tunneling through fluff. They hit the end of the cloud, nearly plummeting over. Scims slashed down on either side of them, cutting holes into white. Agatha spied through one of these holes, tracking the cloud path to the gash in the sky. "I have to make a run for it . . ."

"You'll be dead in a second!" Hester said. "You won't make it one cloud!"

"Watch me," Agatha steeled.

Like a gazelle, she sprung for the next one up—

Scims blasted for her; Agatha recoiled mid-jump, twisting awkwardly and flopping back onto Hester's cloud, just missing the eels sizzling past her.

"Ho hum," Hester growled.

Only now the Snake was the one moving, bounding across clouds, more scims rocketing off him for Agatha, this time from a closer distance, too fast to escape. Agatha shoved

Hester aside, saving her friend, the scims about to run Agatha through—

Dean Brunhilde lunged in front of her, hacking eels with her sword. "In all my years, did my best to turn Evil into Good! Well, killing every last one of you sounds Good to me!" Gobs of black-and-green goo sprayed onto her armor, Dean Brunhilde axing them with vengeance.

Japeth seemed weakened, the patches of flesh on his chest and shoulder bruised and bloodied, vulnerable to attack. He charged Agatha and the Dean, hurdling cloud to cloud, only to see the Queen of Jaunt Jolie block his path, sword in hand.

"How did you fake a wizard's blood, Your Highness?" she cooed. "Same way you faked a *king's*, perhaps? Nice snakesuit, by the way. And here I thought King Rhian was the one who killed the Snake. So you must not be '*Rhian*' at all."

Agatha dashed to save her, but Dean Brunhilde grabbed her back.

"Proud of your cleverness, are you?" the Snake taunted Jacinda. "Your daughter was too. Almost told my secret to the Woods." He stood tall, scims still protecting most of him. "*Almost.*"

"I need to help her," Agatha fought, battling the Dean. "*We* need to help her—"

"We need you *alive*," said the Dean, holding her fast.

Queen Jacinda stepped towards Japeth, sword pointed. "Your brother had a soul. He had the capacity to love. No one will ever love you."

"Words," the Snake dismissed, setting his sights on Agatha once more.

"Let's talk words, then," Jacinda threw back. "You say you seek the Pen's power for the good of the Woods, when in truth, you seek to raise a boy from the dead."

Japeth looked at her.

"A boy you think will admire all that you've done to have him," said the queen. "But you've mistaken him like you've mistaken me. He will reject you. He will condemn the Evil you've done in his name."

"I know the end of my story," the Snake said coldly. "And *yours*."

"You will end alone, Japeth." The queen raised her blade. "All of this Evil done for no other reason than to damn you to Hell."

The Snake struck the sword from her hand. Then he clasped her throat and squeezed. "I looked into your daughter's eyes when she knew she was going to die."

Agatha broke free of Dean Brunhilde—

Japeth's fingers dug into the queen's neck. Jacinda fell to her knees, choking for breath. Japeth bent over, strangling the life out of her. "And I see the same thing in you that I saw in her. Not courage. Not conviction. Just *fear*—"

A clump crushed him in the face.

Japeth reeled, releasing the queen. He looked up at Agatha standing over him, his face a spatter of blood.

"It's me you need to win the second test, *coward*," she lashed.

Agatha started running, jumping across clouds.

Japeth exploded after her, his legs so strong that he was already closing in, Agatha cornered on the last cloud—

A sword impaled the Snake's bare shoulder.

Japeth whirled, facing Dean Brunhilde, who punched him in the throat.

"You killed Rhian. Your one hope for love," she condemned, crushing him in a headlock. "Why? Because he was your better half? Or did Rhian know what I do? That you're a monster. Because only monsters kill those who love them."

"You who took love away from me?" the Snake seethed, thrashing in her arms. "The only monster I see is *you*."

"Your mother told me something when she left you in my care," the Dean said, struggling to restrain him. "That you have none of her blood. That you must be all your father's." She held him close. "Because she saw nothing in you she ever wanted back."

The Snake roared, elbowing her in the face. He dragged the sword out of his shoulder and slashed it across the Dean's neck.

"Say hello to her for me," he said, gripping her collar. "And my '*better half*.'"

He threw Dean Brunhilde off the cloud.

Agatha's heart jolted, watching her body fall into purple night.

Until today she hadn't known Dean Brunhilde. Yet the Dean had protected her with her life. The same way she'd protected students from their own Evil. Dean Brunhilde was brave, strong, and Good, all the things she'd tried in vain to help Japeth become. Now, she too had been lost to him. What chance did the rest of them have?

Even so, the Dean had left her mark. Japeth wasn't moving. He struggled for breath, his shoulder dripping blood, the scims left on him dulled and limp.

The cold green pits of his eyes rose to Agatha's cloud. His cheeks reddened, as if the mere sight of her rekindled his fire. Then he charged her like a lion—

His cloud jerked suddenly, knocking him off his feet. Japeth rebounded, launching for Agatha. This time, Agatha's cloud shifted, dragging the princess out of reach.

A child's giggle echoed overhead.

Both hunter and prey looked up at Merlin, hoisted by Hester's demon, as the child swished his arms, magically swinging Japeth's and Agatha's clouds away from each other like chess pieces. "Naughty hurts Choo-Choo! Now I hurt Naughty!" the child wizard promised, watching Japeth leap for Agatha and miss. Merlin puppeted the other clouds and surrounded the Snake's with them. Japeth was trapped, nine sword-wielding females prowling at him. Beatrix. Kiko. Reena. Anadil. Hester. Dot. Nicola. Maid Marian. Jacinda. The Snake froze, his scims too sapped to ward off this many knights.

Slowly he looked up. His eyes slitted with purpose. Agatha realized the move he was about to make—

"Merlin!" she screamed.

Scims shot off Japeth's arm for the child—

A big, hairy hand caught them and crushed them to slime.

Hort's man-wolf glowered at the Snake.

"No one touches the kid," he snarled.

Hort turned his gaze on Agatha. *"Go."*

Agatha read his intent. She sprinted for the rip in the sky, the one Japeth had come through, Merlin hastily arranging a ladder of clouds for her to get there. The Snake would chase her to win the second test. Her friends would be spared—

But Hort had no intention of the Snake chasing Agatha. He had no intention of the Snake leaving his cloud alive. Hort slapped Japeth hard in the face, sending the Snake flying backwards. "That's for the Sheriff." He slapped him again. "That's for Lancelot." He smacked him more. "And this is for Dovey and Dean Brunhilde and Millicent and Betty and Robin and Tink and your lying, sack-of-crap brother." Blood gushed from Japeth's mouth, Hort's wolf cuffing him to the edge of the cloud.

Agatha was almost at the portal. She glanced back—

Hort reached his paw and snatched a star out of the sky, its silver point as keen as a knife. "And this one . . ." He raised it over Japeth's pale chest. "This one's for *me*."

He stabbed it down—

"Hort, watch out!" Agatha yelled.

A single scim flew off Japeth's neck, slipping between Hort's fingers. He dropped the star in shock, the eel aiming straight for his eyeball, about to gouge it through—

It stopped short.

Because there was a pink flare to Japeth's throat.

Sophie stood behind the Snake, her hand against the

scimless flesh on Japeth's neck, a six-year-old wizard having stealthily snuck her cloud behind his.

Agatha blanched. *No, no, no, no.* She turned back, jumping downwards to rescue her best friend from sure death, but Merlin magically swerved Agatha's cloud higher.

Japeth withstood Sophie's grip, her glow hot against his skin. "I remember how you and I first met," he said. "We were in a room. Our bodies this close. You thought I was Rafal. You thought I was a ghost, come back to be with you . . . Fitting, isn't it?" He leaned back, whispering into her ear. "Now it's *you* who'll be the ghost."

The eel at Hort's eye reversed like a missile, cutting across the cloud, skimming Japeth's body, about to rip into Sophie's neck—

"You need me," Sophie said sharply.

The eel stalled midair.

"You need me as your queen." Sophie spoke crisply, unafraid. "That's how you become the One True King. A pen told you that. Marry me and only then can the power be yours. The power to bring back your *real* true love. That's why you don't know whether to wed me or kill me. Kill me and you can't claim the powers you seek. Kill me and you'll never have your precious Aric again. And yet, leave me alive and I will kill *you*. So I'll give you one chance. Surrender the tournament. Tell the Woods that Tedros is the true king. Or . . . you can fight for your Aric and die. So what is it, Japeth? What do you choose? Love . . . or *life?*"

Agatha saw Japeth hesitate, the scim in front of Sophie wavering.

Then, slowly, it settled back into his body.

The Celestium was quiet, all eyes on Sophie and the Snake.

Japeth spoke, his voice soft. "I choose . . ."

He went slack in Sophie's arms.

"*Love.*"

He broke free and sprinted across his cloud, kicking against Hort's chest, running up the man-wolf like a wall and vaulting high for Agatha, the Snake blacking out the moon like an eclipse, scims flying off him too fast for Agatha or Merlin or anyone to stop.

Agatha thrust out her hands in terror, eel tips grazing every part of her—

Then a scream.

A scream so terrible and piercing that it shattered the scims to pieces against Agatha's skin. Agatha quailed, fingers in her ears. So did Merlin and Hort and all the knights, defending themselves against the sound.

Only one was powerless.

Japeth crashed down in front of Sophie, the exposed flesh of his torso tightening against his ribs, cracking at the edges.

Sophie screamed louder, lording over him, fists clenched like stones, eyes pooling with blood, her veins throbbing red.

The Snake crumpled at her feet.

Sophie screamed with the power of a thousand lives, mist rising into her pupils, as if her whole body might burst into flames.

Blood spilled from Japeth's ears and nose, his skin flaying off his bones.

Agatha watched, shell-shocked.

He was dying.

The Snake was *dying*.

Sophie was killing him.

Not to save Camelot or make Tedros king.

But for *her*.

For Agatha.

Evil fueled by love.

Real love.

Japeth curled to a fetal ball, blood pooling under him. Sophie's scream only got louder—

Agatha's heart lifted.

They had won.

The story finished as it began.

No prince needed.

Two souls, bonded forever.

Two friends, at the End of Ends.

Two girls, the One True King.

But then . . .

Sophie's scream stopped.

She clutched at her throat, as if she couldn't breathe.

Agatha, too, couldn't find air. She heard her friends choking, wheezing—

The Celestium.

They'd been up here too long.

In a flash, the purple sky began to vanish, like a scene being erased.

She felt a blast of hot, thick air . . . smelled the dry, dune dust . . .

The desert. They were going back to the desert—

Except Japeth was still moving.

Japeth was still *alive*!

Sophie looked at Agatha in horror. She tried to force out a scream, to gasp a fatal blow—

Too late.

The Snake looked up at them with his last ounce of life . . .

Then the sky and everyone in it was gone.

Sand whipped Agatha's face, her feet back on the ground. She couldn't see, the dust storm too strong to yield more than glimpses of ink-blue night. But she smelled tones of lavender and vanilla, swirling somewhere near.

"Sophie?" she croaked, her throat filling with dust. "Are you there?"

A warm hand gripped her wrist.

The two girls endured the punishing wind, palms at their faces, until all at once the storm dispersed. They lowered their hands from sand-caked cheeks.

"Agatha?" a boy's voice called.

The last veils of sand swept away, revealing her prince and his mother, standing in the open desert, the Cave of Wishes disappeared.

Tedros smiled at Agatha—then his eyes flared. "Wait . . . you're not supposed to be here!" He glimpsed the cuts and welts on her arms and saw Sophie on the verge of tears. Behind the girls, the other knights were silent and shaken. Witches. Jacinda and Marian. Hort and Nicola. Merlin, too.

"Where's Dean Brunhilde? Where's Nightwind?" Tedros questioned. "This isn't what we planned. You were to hide in the Celestium until I made my wishes and called Merl—"

"He got in, Tedros," said Agatha.

Tedros blinked. "What? Who?"

"The Snake," she said. "He got *in*."

Shouts echoed in the distance.

Tedros turned sharply to the north. Miles downhill, the twin armies of Shazabah and Camelot were circling around. Agatha's heart stopped. The Snake's men must have ridden on when she and her friends disappeared . . . but now they'd been spotted. Camels and horses thundered back towards them.

"Tedros?" Sophie rasped.

The prince tracked her gaze in the opposite direction.

From the south came a lone figure in the night.

Limping, blood-soaked, his blue-and-gold suit shredded.

Japeth picked up his sword from the sand.

Then he set his sights on Agatha.

"At the ready!" Queen Jacinda called.

Her knights fanned out, covering Agatha and her prince from the north, while Tedros shielded his princess from the south. Sophie rushed to Agatha's side, trying to summon another scream, but mustered only a hacking cough. She lit her fingerglow, but it, too, was weak. Hort's wolf snatched Sophie onto his back. "Put me down!" Sophie demanded. "And watch you die? Not a chance," said Hort. Behind them, a pink beetle scampered to Uma's piled clothes and instantly reverted to the lithe princess, who joined with the knights.

The Snake and his armies closed in, Agatha suffering a dark sense of déjà vu.

"How could Japeth find the Celestium? He's not a wizard!" Tedros pressed her. "And why isn't Brunhilde with you—" The prince went rigid, reading his princess's grief. "I don't understand. I sent you all there to be *safe*. Until I could finish the plan to beat him. The second half of the plan . . ."

But Agatha knew better.

Death cared nothing about plans.

The Snake moved across sand like a shadow, picking up speed, what strength he had left focused on killing her. Behind them, two armies swarmed the knights, faster, faster, about to smash through them—

Six dunes erupted under the Snake's armies like volcanos—camels buried in sand, now launching to their feet. Familiar camels. Faithful camels, who'd had their own plan to help their friends. The camels jammed straight into the stampede, bleating calls of alarm, sending enemy steeds bucking in confusion. Instantly, Shazabah camels and Camelot horses began dumping their riders and fleeing to the north. In the chaos, Tedros' knights saw their chance and escaped south. "Hurry, Aggie!" Sophie yelled as Hort wolfed her away—

Agatha grabbed Tedros, but her prince didn't move.

He was still watching Japeth, stalking right at them. Tedros gripped Agatha's palm. "Whatever you do, don't let go of my hand."

Her prince faced the Snake dead-on.

Tedros had no weapon.

He had no defense.

Whatever his plan to beat Japeth, it couldn't work.

Tedros felt her resisting. "Trust me, Agatha."

Agatha knew she should. That was Arthur's test. To trust his son with her life. But she couldn't. Not like this. "We have to run!" she fought, pulling Tedros away.

Her prince held her in place. *"Trust me."*

Japeth started sprinting at them.

"He'll kill us, Tedros!" Agatha cried. "We have no move to make!"

"Except this one," said her prince.

Tedros pulled something from his coat. Agatha anticipated a dagger, a sword—

Instead, the prince produced a dirty mirror.

"That's your plan?" Agatha gasped.

"Consider it a detour," said Tedros.

Japeth raised his sword to kill them. *Both* of them—

Tedros flashed the glass at the Snake.

Moonlight reflected between Japeth's eyes, his startled face caught squarely in the mirror.

Then Agatha felt herself falling, her prince's arms wrapped around her, like two rabbits down a hole.

22

TEDROS

Snake Eyes

"**W**here are we?" Agatha asked.

Tedros couldn't see anything, his arms still around his princess. There was no sun-gold light this time. They'd fallen straight into darkness before sliding into dry, scratchy earth. It smelled oily and rank, like fish gone bad.

"We're inside his secrets," said Tedros.

Agatha pulled away. *"What?"*

She sparked her glow, casting it around—

They were in a tunnel.

Made of scims.

The ceiling, the floor, the walls . . . all of it was a mass of dead, desiccated eels, black and briny, packed like mulch.

Tedros rose, shining his own glow behind them. No visions or clues. No window into the Snake's heart. Just more endless tunnels. More darkness and scims.

Is something wrong with the mirror? Tedros worried. Did it not work outside the cave? Was that the genie's revenge? Trapping them inside someone else, with no way out? A someone else that just happened to be their nemesis?

"How are we *inside* his secrets?" said Agatha, still in a fog.

"A magic mirror I picked up from the genie's cave," Tedros said quickly, masking his panic, trying not to tell his princess that he just locked them inside the Snake's soul. "Supposed to show you a person's greatest secrets. Things they want to hide."

"Supposed to?" Agatha said, eyes narrowing.

"Like it showed me the genie's secret word to escape his cave, and it showed me my mother so happy with Lancelot that she never really wanted me back in her life," Tedros rambled. "Explains a lot, actually—"

"But where *are* his secrets, then?" Agatha pressed. "According to you, we're supposed to be seeing the Snake's, but there's nothing here."

Tedros swallowed. "Right."

"So how do we get out?"

"Uh . . . not sure."

Agatha waited for him to say something else.

He didn't.

Her cheeks flushed, as if about to unleash on him, for his foolishness, for his failure to think through things, a big, fat I-told-you-so speech that she surely was holding in about his impetuousness and poor instincts and all his other shortcomings as a man, the same speech Tedros had waited so tensely for his dad to give him before he died, the speech that never came, but instead lived in the prince's own head day after day, now at last to be spoken out loud by his princess . . .

Instead, Agatha smiled at him. "Still alive, aren't we?"

Tedros watched her sleuth around the cave. "How did you see your mother's secrets?" she asked.

"They were just there, clear as day—"

Her gaze fixed past him. "What's that?"

Somewhere, at the end of the darkness, a tiny green light beamed.

Agatha moved towards it, but Tedros cut her off. "Stay behind me."

His princess hesitated, then followed. Tedros could hear her holding her breath. If there was one thing about Agatha, she *really* didn't like being led.

"The others," she panicked. "They're still up there—"

"When I went in the mirror before, I returned without losing time. The same way time stops in the Celestium. Which means our friends are safe as long as we're here. Speaking of which, Japeth looked like he'd been boiled to a pulp. Your doing?"

"Sophie's. He tried to kill me . . . and she screamed."

Tedros simmered. That Japeth tried to kill Agatha and he wasn't there to save her, leaving Sophie to do the job . . . He forced a light tone. "Vintage move! Not surprised she still had it in her. Once a witch, always a witch. Wonder what would happen if we went inside Sophie's secrets. Better not. Might find out she's still in love with me."

"She'd rather marry Japeth." There was no levity in Agatha's voice. Instead, she looked crestfallen. "We were so close to killing him, Tedros. To all of this being over."

"It wouldn't be The End, even if you did," said the prince. "Killing Japeth might have made *you* the hero, Agatha. You and Sophie. But it wouldn't have made me king. You said it yourself at the palace. I need people to believe *I'm* the Lion. There's only two ways to do that: win the tournament or expose Japeth as a fake. Thought I could win the tournament, but I'm trapped at the second test. So we need to expose Japeth. To make him give up the throne. That's the plan the knights and I came up with. But maybe there's an easier way . . . Which is why I brought us here, inside his secrets. Hoping to find the secret that can show the Woods who he really is."

"Makes sense," said Agatha flatly.

"What are you really thinking?" Tedros asked.

"Both of us are being fools, thinking there's an easy way out. Your father made the tournament for a reason. He wants you to finish the tests, not find some way around them."

"But I can't get past the second test—"

"Why would your father make a test you can't pass?" Agatha

pushed. "You who he gave his ring to? You, his true heir?"

Tedros thought about this. "What if these tests aren't just meant to prove I'm king? What if they're meant to make me a *better* king than my dad? The first test was about the Green Knight. Why? To learn there were two Japeths and a connection between them, yes. That strange vision of Evelyn you saw in the pearl. But the test was more than that: to see that the Green Knight was one of my dad's *mistakes*. He lost his brother to anger and pride. He lost Merlin too. He knew I could be just as angry and prideful, like when I refused to hear the story of the Green Knight. He feared my emotions would get the best of me. So the test was a lesson. Swallowing Merlin's beard meant swallowing my pride and letting the grudges against my father go. It meant accepting him as fallible and forgiving him for it. The first test of being a good king."

"Only I messed it all up," said Agatha.

"Did you?" said Tedros. "Or did Dad *want* the second test to be about you? Maybe Dad had a glimpse of the future, like you and Sophie guessed. The more I think about it, the more I think he wanted to put you to the test. The next Queen of Camelot. Because Dad chose the *wrong* one. My mother ruined him and nearly brought down the kingdom. Everything that's gone wrong in Dad's story can be traced to the Guinevere Mistake. Dad wanted her to die for the pain she caused him. He even put a death warrant on her head. Not because he truly wanted her to die. Because he wanted her to come back to him. That death warrant was his last cry of love. So now he's putting the same warrant on *your* head. Daring us to find a way out.

Maybe this is his way of forgiving my mother—*if* I can learn from her sins. If I choose the right queen *because* of her. That's why I think Dad moved the bounty to you. To test our love. To redeem Guinevere. To finish his and my mother's story."

Tedros exhaled. "Only I have no idea how. Which is why we're inside a Snake, looking for something to help us." He walked taller, his voice steeling. "But we will win somehow. I promised you that from the beginning. You are the queen, Agatha. *My* queen. We're unbreakable in a way Arthur and Guinevere never were. Which means we're not going to die from this. We're going to come out *stronger*."

He waited for her to say something. When she didn't, he looked back at her, silhouetted in their twin gold glows, his princess quiet and thoughtful, her head bowed. She clasped his hand, letting him lead her. Soon, their glows faded, neither able to sustain them. But the green light paved the way, throbbing bigger, brighter ahead, like an emerald in a mine.

"Your wishes," Agatha remembered. "What did you ask the genie for?"

"Powers," said Tedros vaguely, still feeling the genie's magic pulsing in his blood.

"Powers that can help us?" Agatha probed.

Tedros didn't answer. Because he didn't know the answer. The genie's powers wouldn't last much longer. Would they work against the Snake when the time came? Tedros still had doubts about the Knights' plan. Which is why he needed to find something here fast . . . something else to use against Japeth . . .

"Suppose he can see us?" said Agatha, eyeing the glow

ahead. "Suppose he knows we're in his secrets?"

"We're safe here," Tedros reminded. "It isn't real."

"I thought the same thing when I went into Rhian's blood," she pointed out. "Japeth saw us, remember? Almost killed me and Sophie."

The blood crystal, Tedros thought. It was inside Rhian's blood that Agatha had learned that Rhian and Japeth were Arthur's sons with Evelyn Sader.

And yet . . .

"What about Japeth's blood?" Tedros mulled. "To get into the Celestium, he had to have wizard's blood. There's no other way in."

"But how could Japeth have *wizard*'s blood?" Agatha asked. "Rhian's blood said he and Japeth are Arthur and Evelyn's sons. Neither parent is a wizard or sorcerer. There must be another explanation."

"Like what?"

"How could Rhian pull Excalibur the first time? Why did the Lady of the Lake kiss Japeth, thinking *he* was the king? Why did Rhian have a fingerglow and not his brother? Why did I see Evelyn Sader in the pearl? There's so many questions *without* explanations, Tedros. As if we not only have the story wrong, but don't even know the story *at all*—"

Tedros stalled, Agatha bumping into him.

"What is it?" his princess said. Then she stiffened. "There's . . . two?"

Two green balls of light, as big as globes, each a distance from the other.

Which meant the tunnel had to have gotten wider while they were walking.

A lot wider.

Slowly, the prince and princess shined their glows.

Tedros' blood ran cold.

They weren't lights.

They were *eyes*.

A colossal black snake glared right at them, as big as a whale, floating over a pit of dead scims that extended infinitely in every direction, like the darkest of nights.

Agatha recoiled, expecting it to attack—

But the snake didn't move.

It was at once alive and dead, green eyes glowing, its mouth wide open around knife-sharp teeth, but otherwise lifeless in midair, as if frozen in time.

There was nothing else in sight.

Nowhere else to go.

This was where the mirror had led them.

Which meant they had only one choice.

Tedros took a deep breath.

"No, don't!" Agatha choked.

But her prince was already climbing into its mouth.

IT WAS SURPRISINGLY cool inside, the air crisp and dry, the passage ink-black. Tedros tried to light his fingerglow, but it didn't work this time. Neither did Agatha's apparently; he heard her dress rip as she stumbled over the snake's bottom teeth, his princess mumbling un-princess-like words, before she found Tedros in the dark.

"Magic must not work in here," he said.

"Maybe because we are inside a snake's *mouth*. Why are we inside a snake's mouth!"

Tedros squinted ahead. "To find *that*."

Deep inside the snake, the prince spotted something blocking their path.

A door.

He led her closer, the door growing sharper in its details, smooth and luminescent, as if under a spotlight. But it was only when they came within a few feet of it and spotted the lion pattern on the moldings, the distinctive orange-gold of the knob, that Tedros and his princess both realized something.

"White Tower," said Agatha, glancing at her prince. "Isn't this what the doors look like?"

Exactly like this, Tedros thought. The White Tower, where Tedros rarely ventured in his time at Camelot's castle, whether during his father's reign or his own. There was no reason to: it was mainly staff quarters and storage. But there was one room in the White Tower that Tedros knew well. A room that kept pulling him back, like a ghost out of a grave. A room where all the darkness in this story had been born. And as Tedros turned the knob, moving deeper into the Snake's secrets, he was quite sure this was the room he was about to enter . . .

He opened the door.

Immediately he smelled the familiar thick, unwashed scent.

The Guest Room.

That strange suite his father had built soon after he became king. It was a room for visiting friends, his father would tell him as a child, but Arthur never used it for guests as far as Tedros knew. Arthur hadn't even let maids in this room (hence the smell), nor his wife or son. Indeed, only Arthur had the key to it. And Lady Gremlaine, Tedros remembered. She'd had a key too, since her private quarters adjoined this one. In later years, Tedros' father would lock himself in here during his drunken hazes, but it never explained why he'd built the room in the first place. Tedros himself had only been inside a few times since his father died, and each time, it gave him a dark, seedy feeling.

Except the room was different now, Tedros realized.

The brown-and-orange rug was bright and fairly new, the leather sofa fresh and unstained, the beige walls unblemished. There was even a brass flowerpot in the corner, with blooming seedlings—

"Tedros?" Agatha rasped.

He followed her eyes to the bed in the corner.

Someone was sleeping on it.

A young man with gold curls, rosy cheeks, and a coat of light, patchy stubble. For a moment, Tedros thought he was looking at *himself* . . . then saw the man was taller, ganglier, and at least a few years older . . .

The prince's eyes flared. *"Dad?"*

He moved past Agatha, thrusting a hand out for the young Arthur, but it went straight through, as if Tedros was a phantom. King Arthur remained asleep.

Tedros could see Agatha's fists tighten, her throat bobbing, and only then did he understand.

"This is it, isn't it?" Tedros said, tensing. "The scene you saw in Rhian's blood."

Voices rose from next door.

Lady Gremlaine's room.

"That's them," said Agatha. "Lady Gremlaine and Evelyn Sader. They're about to come in."

And indeed, now Tedros could hear Gremlaine's voice on the other side of the wall—

"Only Arthur and I have the keys," she was saying. "When he came from school with that *tramp*, acting like she was already queen, I tried to leave. He begged me to stay. Built this room as a place for us to meet without Guinevere knowing."

A secret door in the wall pushed open, two figures entering from Lady Gremlaine's room. Tedros broke into a cold sweat. Agatha had already described this scene to him, but now it was real, the prince witnessing the younger Grisella Gremlaine in lavender robes, her tan face unlined, brown hair loose to her shoulders. At her side was a hooded figure in a black cloak, gripping a knotted piece of rope in her hand. A rope that looked like it was made out of human flesh.

The spansel, Tedros thought.

Beneath the hood, he could make out Evelyn Sader's forest-green eyes, glinting like a snake's.

Nausea coated the prince's throat.

"I put hemp oil in his drink like you told me to," Lady

Gremlaine said to Evelyn. "Fell straight to sleep."

"We must move quickly, then," said Evelyn, holding out the rope. "Place this spansel around his neck."

Lady Gremlaine swallowed. "And then I'll have his child?"

"That is the power of the spansel," Evelyn replied. "Use it and you will be pregnant with King Arthur's heir long before Guinevere marries him."

Tedros felt light-headed, hardly able to listen.

The Evils of the present were seeded in the past. *This* past. Right here, in this room.

He looked up to see Lady Gremlaine standing over his father as he slept, her shoulders stiff, her lips quivering.

With a choked gasp, she spun to Evelyn and grabbed the rope into her hands. Her shadow stretched over the sleeping king, her fingers firm on the spansel. She stared down at Arthur, cheeks pink, breaths rushed, her thirst for him fighting the sin of what she was about to do. Fingers shaking, she reached the spansel for his neck.

Tedros averted his eyes, even if he knew how this played out. The idea that this was happening at all . . . that Lady Gremlaine and Evelyn Sader were in cahoots . . . that Grisella Gremlaine, his father's once-steward and lifelong friend, had drugged him asleep and wanted to have his *child*—

"I can't," she whispered.

Tedros looked back at her.

"I can't do it," Lady Gremlaine sobbed. "I can't betray him like this. I love him too much."

She dropped the spansel and fled the room.

Tedros exhaled . . . until Evelyn Sader picked the spansel up. His blood rushed so hard he could feel it in his teeth.

"I won't watch this," he said to Agatha, spinning for the door from which they came. "We have to leave—"

"This is where the Snake's secrets led us, Tedros," said his princess, not moving. She held him in place the way he'd held her when the Snake charged them across the desert. Each one strong for the other when they needed it.

Tedros let her hold him, his legs steadying. Slowly, he lifted his eyes to Evelyn, pulling back her hood, the spansel pinched between red-painted nails, as she skulked towards Tedros' father. She had Rhian's tan and Japeth's cold leer, so clearly their mother, Tedros could see now. She smiled down at the sleeping king. Then Evelyn hooked the spansel around Arthur's neck . . .

"This is where the scene ends," Agatha told Tedros. "It disconnects here—"

Only it didn't this time.

The scene continued, Evelyn releasing her hands from the spansel, leaving it noosed on the sleeping king's throat.

Arthur's eyes opened.

They fixed upon Evelyn Sader, his big blue pools brimming with lust.

Agatha pulled away from Tedros, her face pale.

"What's happening?" said the prince, watching his father and Evelyn draw close.

"I—I—I don't know," Agatha sputtered. "I didn't see this!"

Tedros wanted to rip the spansel off his father's neck, to

fight the horrors of the enchanted rope, but he was as powerless to stop its magic as his father had been—

From behind Tedros came a whirl of motion, flying past the prince, swinging something down—

Straight into Evelyn's head.

She fell without a sound, onto the startled king, before she slumped to the floor, unconscious.

Arthur looked up at Lady Gremlaine, hunched over Evelyn's crumpled body, a brass flowerpot in her hands.

Her eyes spilled tears, her face ghost-white. "I didn't know . . . I didn't know what she was doing . . . I had to stop her . . ."

Arthur looked startled for a moment, like a child shaken from sleep. Then his gaze set upon Lady Gremlaine, kindling with the same lust he'd just had for Evelyn—

Lady Gremlaine yanked the spansel off his neck.

Instantly, Arthur snapped out of his trance.

The young king gaped at his weeping steward . . . then at Evelyn on the floor.

Arthur lurched off the bed, backing towards the door. "What's happening!" he panted. "Guards! *Guards!*"

"Arthur, I—I—I can explain," Lady Gremlaine stammered. "It was m-m-me . . . I asked her for the spell . . . I—I—I'll explain everything . . ."

The color went out of Arthur's cheeks, his eyes darting between his steward and the flesh rope and the stirring body on the carpet. "Grisella . . . ," he breathed. "What have you done?"

The room vanished, returning Tedros to the coolness of a dark passage, inside the body of a snake. His heart was leaping out of his ribs, his body vibrating with fear . . . horror . . . *relief*.

He glimpsed his princess's eyes shining through the dark with the same emotions.

"Agatha . . . Arthur's not his father."

"Or Evelyn his mother," she said.

Neither prince nor princess finished the thought they were both sharing, but it hung over them like a dagger.

So who are his parents?

"Tedros, look!" said Agatha.

Ahead, an emerald flare of light blinded them. Then two. A new pair of eyes. Only these were *moving*, racing towards them like green fireballs, a black body attached. A snake within a snake, hissing and flashing massive fangs. Tedros grabbed Agatha to run, but it was coming too fast and too big to dodge. Tedros dove, sheltering his princess with his body. The snake swallowed them whole—

Then it was muggy and hot, like a jungle in summer.

They were in Sherwood Forest.

Marian's Arrow lay ahead, couched against lush, dewy trees, growing so wild that all the branches had wrangled around each other, giving only peeks of a red sunset.

"Another secret," said Agatha. "Something the Snake doesn't want us to see."

"In Sherwood Forest?" said Tedros, dusting himself off. "What does Sherwood Forest have to do with the Snake?"

Whistles and hoots echoed behind them, along with men's chants—

"To the three rings of marriage!
The Engagement Ring,
The Wedding Ring,
and the Suffering!"

Tedros and Agatha turned to see a parade of Merry Men, carrying a fresh-faced Arthur on their shoulders towards the Arrow, the young king wearing a donkey-skin cape and a paper crown with the word "BACHELOR" scrawled in red, while he gnawed on a charred turkey leg and responded with a chant of his own.

"Guinevere, Guinevere,
My heart, my love, my dear,
These men are just jealous
For life without you is hellish!"

The men booed.

"Can't boo a king!" Arthur scoffed.

"In Sherwood Forest, we boo any prat who deserves it, *especially* kings," said the leader of the pack, boyish and muscular, with strawberry-blond hair and a dashing smile. *Robin Hood*, Tedros realized, handsome as ever, carrying young Arthur towards the Arrow.

"It's your last night as a single man, Arthur!" Robin crowed. "Better make good use of it!"

Tedros smiled, seeing his dad and Robin alive and together, a lump rising in the prince's throat . . . Agatha pulled him towards the pub. "Come on. Must be a reason we're here."

Together, they piled into the Arrow. A boisterous party was at its peak, a dozen women to every sweaty, red-faced man, servers splashing beer and tipping plates of chicken wings, all those present chanting *"LION! LION!"* as soon as they spotted the king. A band of Sherwood fairies streamed through the window playing a jaunty tune on willow violins, whereby three Merry Men took to tabletops, danced a jig, and promptly fell off, before two more swung from the cheap chandelier with the same result. A gaggle of women crowded around a young Maid Marian in the corner, who gave Robin a cheeky grin, as if at once happy to see him and warning him away from other girls. He saluted Marian across the bar, like an obedient soldier.

"Sheriff was in here earlier," one of the servers whispered to Robin. "Thought he was here to make trouble, but he wanted to talk to Marian."

"About what?"

"Tried to listen in. Something about Marian going to visit her folks for a few months in Ginnymill?"

"Maidenvale. And yeah, I know. Leaving next week. Wait. Few *months*? Didn't tell me that. What else?"

"Sheriff said he wanted to visit her there."

Robin laughed. "Get your hearing checked, mate."

He strutted into the mob and swung an arm around Arthur, who was dancing poorly, a chicken wing in his mouth. Robin nodded towards Marian' friends. "Fine flock of women, Your Highness."

But Arthur wasn't looking at them. He was eyeing a woman at the bar, sitting alone, near a couple of brown-hooded Merry Men. A woman with long hair, tan skin, and a lavender dress. Arthur's face tightened. "Excuse me," he said, heading over to her.

Robin shrugged. "Bring him a pub full of women and what do you know, goes for the one he already knows."

Tedros and Agatha were already huddling behind Arthur as he sat beside Lady Gremlaine, the prince and his princess listening close in the raucous pub.

"What are you doing here, Grisella?" Arthur asked.

His steward couldn't look at him, her hand gripping a full glass of cider.

Arthur exhaled. "I'm assuming you followed me—"

She spun to face him, splashing her glass. "It's been three months, Arthur. Three *months* you haven't said a word to me. Every night I listen for the knock from the guest room and it never comes. And you won't talk to me when you see me in the castle. What was I supposed to do?"

Arthur drank from her cider. "Forgive me if I haven't come knocking, Grisella. I don't especially feel like going into that *room*."

"I know you hate me," said Lady Gremlaine, reddening. "I know you'd have me jailed or punished or killed if you could without Guinevere finding out what I've done. That's why you're avoiding me. You're trying to shame me out of the castle. To force me to run away. But I won't. Not without trying to repair things between us."

"I don't hate you, Grisella. I just don't know what to say to you," said Arthur. He paused, looking at his hands. "There's no ill will. I'm nothing but grateful. You've been my friend since I was six years old. When I was Wart and you were my Grizzle-Grazzle. You know me as I really am: flawed, restless, impetuous . . . and yet you never make me feel unworthy of my new place. If it wasn't for you, I wouldn't feel at home in that castle. I wouldn't feel like myself, let alone a king. And if it wasn't for you, that Sader witch would be pregnant with my heir, instead of deep in the Woods, wherever my guards dumped her. Told her if she came within a hundred miles of Camelot, she'd be shot full of arrows at first sight. Put out word to the Kingdom Council that she wasn't to be allowed in their lands either. Quite quickly Evelyn Sader discovered she's no longer welcome in these Woods. Hasn't been seen since."

"But I was the one who brought Evelyn in! It was me who wanted to use that spell!" said Lady Gremlaine. "*I* wanted your child, Arthur. *I* was in love with you."

"And it's my fault that you were," Arthur sighed. "Because I loved you too."

Grisella stared at him. "What?"

"Boys are just better at hiding it," Arthur said wryly. "I loved you before I even knew what love was. Maybe because deep down, you and I are the same: perfectly happy with a small, ordinary life, and yet fated for a life that's neither of those things. Why do you think I wrote you every week during my years at school? Because you remind me of who I used to be and who I can't be anymore. The real Arthur. You don't know how much I missed you while I was gone, Grisella. How much I missed our old days, before I ever pulled that sword from the stone. Perhaps you sensed my love in those letters, because I sensed yours, growing stronger and stronger, and yet I kept writing you back—" A beer mug shattered somewhere, followed by a chorus of boos. Arthur took a deep breath. "But then I returned with Guinevere as my wife-to-be. How confused you must have been. Nearly four years of letters. Nearly four years of waiting for me. And then I arrive at the castle with a pretty, strong-willed Evergirl, who insults you in front of your staff at your very first meeting. No wonder you hated her. No wonder you hated each other. She must have known there were feelings between us. But it's neither her fault, nor yours. It's my fault for not telling you the truth."

"That you love her more," Grisella said starkly. "That you don't love me as you thought you did."

"That I *can't* love you," the young king contended. "Now I'm the King of Camelot. The leader of our world. Whoever I marry doesn't belong to me. She belongs to all the Woods. A queen who must play the part. A queen for the people."

"Which isn't me," Grisella admitted.

"Which isn't you," Arthur agreed. "Guinevere is from the right family, the right upbringing. She was top of our class at the School for Good. You should have seen the way Everboys looked at her, Lancelot included. Everyone knew Gwen was meant to be a queen. I had to make her mine. Especially since there's a good many people who aren't sure of me as king. But with Guinevere, I look the part . . . like I deserved to pull Excalibur from the stone. Marrying her means I can start my reign the right way. She's who my kingdom needs. She's who I need."

"And do you love her?" Lady Gremlaine asked.

"With her, I *believe* I'm a king," Arthur answered.

Grisella teared up.

"Please don't cry," said Arthur.

"You might be king, but I only see the boy I knew. You're as pure a soul now as you were before," Lady Gremlaine said softly. "Thank you, Arthur. For telling me the truth. For being so decent when I've been nothing but lying and deceitful."

"You're guilty only of being human, Grisella. Something neither a king nor a queen is allowed to be," said Arthur, touching her. "Your story isn't over. You'll find love one day."

Grisella shook her head. "Your story *is* mine, Arthur. You were my one love. Maybe I wasn't worthy of you. But loving you was enough. The real you."

Arthur's eyes misted. "It is I who am not worthy of you," he spoke. "I chose Guinevere so that I can erase who I used to be. The Wart who was nothing, a nobody, completely insignificant. But you loved that Wart with your whole heart. The way I loved you. And tomorrow that boy will be gone for good. I only wish our story had a different ending. One that let us forever remember what we were to each other."

Arthur gazed deeply at her, lost in his thoughts. Grisella noticed his hand on hers, warm and soft.

She sighed, pulling her palm away. "One last night as Wart and Grizzle-Grazzle. Better enjoy our time together."

Through the empty glass, she saw Arthur still watching her. "What?" she asked.

"Is there somewhere we could go to talk?" he said.

"We are talking."

Then she saw the look in his eyes.

"Course there is, laddie!" Robin chimed, swooping in, shunting Arthur and Grisella out the front door. "Use my tree-house. Perfectly empty!"

"Follow them! Hurry!" Agatha hastened Tedros, guiding him to the door, but the prince didn't move. "Tedros, what are you wait—"

But now Agatha saw what he did.

A blue butterfly tailing behind Arthur and Gremlaine as they went into the forest.

Slowly Tedros and Agatha turned, looking back in the direction from which the butterfly came.

Those two strangers in the corner. The brown-hooded ones near where Grisella had been sitting. Tedros had thought them Merry Men. But now they slipped off their hoods, watching Arthur and Lady Gremlaine leave together.

They weren't Merry Men at all.

"Funny what you see in Sherwood Forest," drawled Evelyn Sader, eyes on the door.

"Everyone here has their secrets," her male companion

replied. "It's why both of us found our way here too. In Sherwood Forest, we're all sinners."

He was thick and muscular, a few years older than the young Arthur. But that's not what made Tedros recognize him.

It was the green tint to his skin.

As if Sir Japeth Kay had only begun his transformation into the Green Knight.

"The spansel was *her* idea, of course. And now he acts like I'm the villain, while those two serpents cozy up," Evelyn groused to Sir Japeth. "And to think they call him the Lion! I see a Snake, through and through. Had me banished from every kingdom, that coward. I managed to find a home at the School for Good and Evil—School Master doesn't answer to Camelot—but ended up expelled from there too, thanks to my traitorous brother. For months, I skulked around in pits and caves, a homeless hag. And then to fall ill . . . terribly ill . . . and to be in my condition, while winter raged . . ." She shifted in her chair, looking uncomfortable. "If it wasn't for you, coming upon me and shepherding me here, I'd have been food for rats."

"Was on my way here anyway after leaving Camelot myself," Sir Japeth admitted. "And truth be told, you offered me friendship at a time when I had none."

"Two fair souls, equally cursed," Evelyn cracked.

"We do share a bit in common," Sir Japeth remarked. "Betrayed by our families. Forced to watch our brothers steal our fate. *Our* glory. And they say the Storian is balanced! Bah. The Pen favors them with impunity and leaves us to rot. No wonder our brothers fight to protect it. When there is no other pen to fight for the likes of us."

"August and Arthur. Even their names sound alike, dripping with self-importance," Evelyn mocked. "No doubt they'll be bosom buddies soon enough. August finds every way to suck up to power."

"And to think, all that power blessed on a *wart*," Sir Japeth said grimly, as Evelyn's butterfly spy returned from the forest, whispering to the Dean. "If only there was a way to humble them both . . ." He sighed ruefully. "Sherwood Forest, home of outcasts and dreamers."

But now Evelyn's face was changing, the butterfly at her ear . . .

"My dear Sir Japeth . . . ," she said, peering up at him. "Perhaps there *is* a way."

She slipped open her hood, letting her tiny spy flit back into her dress of blue butterflies, nestling amongst the ones near her stomach—

Tedros' eyes bulged.

Agatha choked.

She was pregnant.

Evelyn Sader was *pregnant*.

"Yes . . . there might be a way after all . . . ," she mused, thinking it over.

She whispered to Sir Japeth, who cocked a brow, listening.

"Oh, how I love your wicked little mind," he said, when she finished. "And the surest sign yet that you've returned to full health."

"I have only you to thank, Sir Japeth," Evelyn pointed out. "You could have left me to die. Instead, you've given my child a path to a throne. The throne of a king who hurt us both."

"And you've given me a chink in my brother's armor," said Sir Japeth.

"Sounds like we both have work to do, then," said Evelyn. "Our time together may soon be at an end."

"Wherever our travels take us, know that you'll always have a knight at your service," said Sir Japeth.

"My Green Knight," Evelyn anointed him. "My child will know your story."

"Then let me bless it with all the love I have left." Sir Japeth put his hand on her pregnant belly. Evelyn closed her eyes. For the briefest of moments, her skin tinged green, before it restored milky smooth. Her eyes fluttered open.

"The Green Knight . . . I quite like that . . . ," Sir Japeth said. "You've given me a name, my lady. Perhaps I can give your child mine?"

Evelyn smiled back at him. "Perhaps."

The lights in the bar went out, plunging Tedros and Agatha into darkness.

Crisp air chilled Tedros' skin. He could smell the oily hollow of the serpent, he and his princess returned inside its body. Agatha's eyes pierced through the dark.

"So the Snake *is* Evelyn Sader's child," she said, with certainty. "Only not her child with Arthur."

"He's the son of Sir Kay and Evelyn," Tedros agreed.

"Explains the connection between the Green Knight and the Snake. And the vision you saw in the pearl. Plus, Sir Kay and Arthur were brothers. If Sir Kay was their father, Rhian and Japeth would have had Arthur's blood. It explains everything—"

"No it doesn't. Kay and Arthur were *foster* brothers, remember? They weren't related by blood," said Agatha, the confidence in her voice fading. "Lady of the Lake wouldn't have mistaken Kay's blood for Arthur's. And it doesn't explain how Japeth would have *wizard*'s blood to get into the Celestium. And Evelyn's tone with him . . . she called it 'my' child, not '*our*' child—"

"We have our proof Japeth isn't my father's son, Agatha. We have the Snake's secrets. *All* of them," Tedros disputed. "We can use them against him. We just need a way out of here—"

"Tedros?" Agatha said.

"What?"

Then he caught the green glow reflecting in her pupils.

Slowly, Tedros turned.

Just in time to see a new snake about to swallow them.

CRIES OF A baby.

Two babies.

That's what they heard first, suspended in a wash of white, before the scene filled in, like the Storian inking a page.

On a rumpled bed, stuffed in the corner of a cluttered one-room house, Evelyn Sader swaddled her twin boys in her arms, the Dean's face ashen and sweat-soaked, the sheets around her stained with blood. The babies were almost identical; one had a rosier complexion, with sea-green eyes, the other milky pale, his eyes ice-blue. A woman with long gray hair bent over her— the midwife, Tedros assumed—patting her forehead dry and wrapping the boys in fresh blankets.

"Is he coming?" Evelyn said weakly.

"Soon," said one of two more midwives in the corner, rinsing bloody towels and boiling tea, both of whom had the same stringy gray hair, high foreheads, and—

Tedros balked.

"Mistral Sisters," Agatha said, her eyes shifting between the three women, who looked just as old nearly two decades into the past as they did in the present.

What were they doing here? Tedros wondered. As far as he knew, Evelyn Sader and the Mistral Sisters had never crossed paths . . .

"I need to see him," Evelyn insisted, trying to soothe the paler boy, who was wailing, while the ruddier boy smiled and cooed on her arm. "You promised he'd come."

"Patience," said the Mistral named Alpa.

"You did a wise thing writing us," said Bethna. "Your brother, August, has spent years maligning our efforts to find the One True King, who can bring the Storian's reign to an end. We've had few allies in our search. Even our own brother doesn't believe the One True King exists, despite his continued efforts to control the Storian."

"But now we can all work together for the same goal," hissed Omeida next to her, pouring a cup of smoky tea. She brought it to Evelyn. "Drink this, dear. It will give you strength to nurse them." She held it to Evelyn's lips and the Dean took a sip, still trying to calm the pallid, unruly child.

"They'll be safe here in Foxwood, won't they?" Evelyn asked, anxiously cuddling the newborns. "Couldn't stay in Sherwood anymore. Too many high-ranking leaders coming in and out. Needed a place where we could blend in. Especially with *two*."

"No surprise that you'd have twins," Omeida chuckled. "They run in the family, after all."

"Have you given any thought to their names?" said Alpa.

"*I* have," a voice said.

A man's voice.

Tedros' heart stopped.

A voice he knew.

Slowly the prince and Agatha turned to a shadow in the doorway. Behind him, an empty street of cottages swirled with autumn leaves, as if he'd arrived by wind. He glided inside the house, hooded silver robes billowing over his slender frame. A silver mask covered his face except for puckish blue eyes and full lips, pulled into an impish smile.

"No . . . *way* . . . ," Agatha gasped.

His eyes flicked to the prince and princess, as if even from the past, he seemed to know that they were standing there.

"Hello, Evelyn," he said, his focus turning to her twins,

his lithe fingers touching the head of the pale, crying child. Instantly its wails ceased. "*Two* boys. Imagine that."

"Past is Present and Present is Past," said Evelyn, peering up at him.

"Indeed." The man's eyes moved to the rosy, genial child. "But you only need one to complete your plan. Let me take this one to school. Spare him the indignity of growing up in Foxwood. Hello, little cub. Should we make you an official student?" He put his finger to the boy's, as if to unlock a spell, and the child's fingertip suddenly glowed gold, alive with magic. "Sweet nature . . . dashing smile . . . and now he has a fingerglow too . . . My precocious Everboy, soon to walk the halls of Honor Tower. Proof I'm as Good as people think." He winked at the child.

"I know you well enough to know you're joking," said Evelyn, though she pulled the boy closer to her, out of his grasp. "If I was still a teacher at your school, you would have the right to see them whenever you wish. Your school that took me in when Arthur banished me from the Woods. You saved me in a time of need. You, my true love. But then my brother convinced you I *wasn't* your true love. And you listened to that lying fool, expelling me like I was nothing, despite my loyalty to you . . . Well, disown me and you disown my children too. After today, you will never see them again. Nor me."

The man's eyes twinkled through his mask. "And yet, a part of me lives inside you forever . . ." He pulled aside the bedsheets and put a hand to her chest, a subtle blue glow lighting up at the heart of her butterfly dress. "I never questioned your sincerity, Evelyn. I believe you loved me. Yet I also believe your brother: that I will love someone *more* in years to come. Even so, I can't discount the possibility that you are right. It's why I imparted a piece of my soul into you before I expelled you from school. And if you are correct that you are my true love and that August Sader will destroy me . . . then one day you will use that piece of my soul to bring me back to life. Wouldn't that be something? You and me together again." He looked down at the boys. "This time, a *family*."

Evelyn stared at the masked man, their eyes meeting, and for a brief moment, her face blushed with hope. Then she hardened, drawing away. "Go and make your *own* family. I almost died in the Woods because you betrayed me. Because you threw me out like Arthur did. If it wasn't for a kind knight named Japeth, these boys never would have been born. A man like that should be my true love."

"Except he isn't. Otherwise he would be standing here instead of me," replied the visitor. "Your heart only loves me, Evelyn. We both know that."

Evelyn glowered. "I don't need you. Nor will my children. They're mine now."

"You summoned me here, Evelyn. And not just to insult me, I presume," said the man coolly. "Your letter proposed a plan that I found compelling. A plan to rule Camelot. A plan for which you need my help."

"To be fair, brother, you will benefit as much as she will," Alpa chirped, alongside Bethna and Omeida in the corner.

"As will you, Sisters. All of us will benefit," said the masked man, without a glance. "And you're sure of what you saw, Eve-lyn? Arthur and a woman not his wife . . ."

A butterfly fluttered off Evelyn's dress into the visitor's hands. A scene magically replayed across its wings for him. His eyes grew bigger as he watched.

"Quite sure," said Evelyn.

The man let the butterfly return to her.

His gaze moved back to the paler child, silently studying the visitor. Next to him, his sunnier brother fixated on his new fingerglow, making it beam on and off.

"Very well, then. The boys can stay with Evelyn," spoke the man, as if the matter was still in question. "Let them grow up together, the way my brother Rhian and I once did. Only one can be the King of Camelot, of course. But they can fight it out for themselves, Good versus Evil, brother against brother. Like two School Masters did, before one rose to power . . . But this time, it is a *King* who will rise. A King who can ensure that Camelot is in the hands of our bloodline, as much as the school is. The two great forces of the Woods fully under our control."

"Provided you stay alive," Evelyn observed. "Your alliance with my brother certainly limits those odds."

"Then you would bring me back to life, wouldn't you?" the masked man needled. "My brother was a far more deadly opponent and I put Rhian in his grave. Wizard blood runs through my veins. A blind seer hasn't a chance against me. Besides, from what I can tell, your brother has done nothing other than tell you the truth: that he does not see you as my true love."

"Whoever he does see as your true love will kill you,"

Evelyn scorned. "And knowing my brother, she'll kill me too. And who will bring you back to life *then*? My brother is a greater threat than you realize. He may play the friend to both Good and Evil, but he is as surely on the side of Good as your brother Rhian once was. August won't rest until you and I suffer the same fate as Rhian. Why do you think August came to teach at your school in the first place?"

The man could see Evelyn's conviction. Doubt flickered in his pupils . . .

He turned to the Mistrals. "In the *unlikely* case that Evelyn and I *both* perish, then it will be up to you, Sisters, to guide the boys to Arthur's throne. To make them believe they are King Arthur's sons, so that they may seize control of the Woods. With a little help from me, of course . . ."

He reached down and lifted a single butterfly from Evelyn's dress. On his finger, it morphed into a small, scaly, black eel, which he raised to his ear, before the tiny eel slithered inside. The masked man closed his eyes, as if imparting his thoughts to the creature, before he gently drew it out the other ear.

"Everything they need to know is here for them to find."

He held the eel up on his finger, twisting and gleaming in the house's dull light.

"Including how to bring me back if I die?" asked Evelyn. "Including how to take the Storian's power?"

The masked man hesitated.

In the corner, the Mistral Sisters smirked. "She believes in the One True King, brother," spoke Alpa. "It's why she's brought *us* here, too."

"I'll leave specious theories to my sisters," the man said sourly. "But even if the myth of the One True King *is* true, it would not be enough to claim the powers of the Storian. These boys have my blood. And the Pen *rejects* my blood, ever since I killed my brother. Even if my sons make all the kingdoms burn their rings, even if they sever the bonds between Man and Pen . . . the Storian's powers will not be theirs. For the same reason I'm unable to control the Pen. Good is too strong. The balance still intact. But there is a cure, says August Sader. Marrying a queen whose blood is as Evil as mine. A queen whose blood bonds with ours to tip the balance. A queen your brother promises me I'll find."

"And if my brother betrays you? If this queen *kills* you instead?" Evelyn pressed. "Then what?"

The masked man considered this. He whispered to the eel, a wizard making a prophecy: "Then my son will have my revenge . . . by making that queen his *own*."

He let the eel morph back into a butterfly before returning it to the rest of the butterflies on Evelyn's dress. "In the event of our deaths, give them this dress, Sisters. It will lead them to a pen that shows them their future. A *new* pen. A pen that ensures that even death cannot stop our blood from ruling the Woods."

"Which pen?" Evelyn asked, unsure.

"The better question is: Which son?" the man spoke, watching the boys. "Which will succeed if we fail?"

He honed in on the ruddier, cheerier boy, still playing with his new fingerglow, Evelyn trying to keep him from squirming off her arm. But then the man noticed the other boy grinning at him. In a flash, the skin on the boy's face coated with scales, like a snake's, before it reverted milky and smooth. He saw the man's eyes widen and the boy giggled, his mother none the wiser.

"But I have my suspicions . . . ," said the man.

The rosier boy began to whimper, showing distress for the first time. "Shhh . . . my good boy," Evelyn whispered. "My sweet Rhian."

She didn't look at the masked man, her lips curled with triumph, as if she knew the name had made an impact. As if she knew that he was glaring right through her.

"And *his* name?" the man said, pointing at the paler child.

Evelyn held the second boy close, kissing his face that had just been a snake's only a moment before. "For a middle name, Japeth, after the knight who saved him. That's what I'll call him."

"And his birth name?" the man asked, stone-cold.

Evelyn finally looked up at him. "Rafal," she breathed. "For his father."

The man pulled off his mask and hood, revealing young, frost-white skin, a shock of silver hair, and a smile as wide as the devil's.

Tedros heard himself scream, Agatha's own scream slashing into his—

But they were already falling into darkness, the cool insides of a snake opening up into a vast, strange sky.

~✦ 23 ✦~

AGATHA

Flesh and Blood

Past is Present and Present is Past.

The Snake.

Son of the School Master.

Son of Rafal.

Pure-blooded Evil.

Following them across time.

Across death.

To the End of Ends.

No more time to think—

Agatha's feet sank into softness, her eyes flying open to a fluorescing green cloud, Tedros landing on a green cloud above her. A black sky expanded around them, with a glossy sheen, as if its surface was wet. Stars pinned against this sky, not childish five-pointed stars but steel snowflakes, edges deadly sharp like a handblade's, the center of each star a glowing green marble, like an all-seeing eye. In the stars' dim light, Agatha glimpsed etchings in the black sky, like tree carvings, but Agatha couldn't make them out, the darkness too thick.

"Help me up," said Agatha, reaching for her prince.

"The Celestium," Tedros surmised, hoisting her to his cloud. "Must be reflecting Merlin's mood, wherever he is . . ."

Except Agatha was on her toes now, shining her finger-glow at the sky's carvings.

Agatha skin crawled. "No. Not Merlin's." She lit up the sky—

"Japeth & Aric." Tedros shrank backwards. "Agatha . . . this is the *Snake's* place to think."

"Rafal's blood . . . ," Agatha rasped. "*Wizard's* blood . . ."

"Which means he knows we're here," her prince said. "He *brought* us here."

Panicked, they scanned the Snake Sky, but found only more glowing green clouds, razor-sharp stars, lovesick carvings.

A noise scuffed behind them and they whipped around—

Guinevere and Merlin appeared on a cloud.

"Big Mama!" Merlin piped, pointing at Guinevere.

Tedros' mother stared down her son. "Told you that mirror was trouble, Tedros. Japeth must have known you went inside his secrets. Moment you did, Merlin felt Japeth's spirit vanish to his thinking place. Luckily, wizards can access other wizards' thinking spots."

"Tee Tee needs Big Mama . . . for big job . . . ," Merlin said, winking at Tedros.

Agatha could see Tedros and his mother eyeing each other, as if they knew what Merlin meant. Whatever plan Tedros and his knights had made to defeat Japeth, the old queen was most certainly involved.

Powers, Agatha recalled. That's what Tedros said he'd asked the genie for. That's why he'd gone into the Cave of Wishes. *What kind of powers?*

"If this is Japeth's thinking place, then where is he?" Tedros growled. "Watching us, no doubt, like the creep he is." He bellowed to the sky. "You slithering fraud! Rhian really thought he was my dad's son. But you? You knew the truth. You knew you were Rafal's son with that witch—"

"*What?*" a voice gasped.

Tedros and Agatha turned.

Sophie was alone on a cloud, her face ashen.

"Couldn't remember if Tee Tee needs Big Mama or Not-the-Mama, so I bring both," Merlin squeaked at Tedros.

Agatha was already leaping to Sophie's cloud.

"I d-d-don't understand," Sophie spluttered in her friend's arms. "Rafal's son? Japeth is *Rafal's* son? With Evelyn Sader?"

Her eyes brimmed with horror. "RJ. Isn't that what Dean Brunhilde called him? R for Rafal, J for Japeth . . . Rhian and Rafal . . . The names of twin School Masters, passed down from father to sons . . . That's how he has wizard's blood, isn't it? . . . His eyes . . . they're like his father's . . . and that ice-cold touch . . . Oh, Aggie . . . The answers were there all along!"

"That's why you could heal them. That's why they had to marry you," Agatha said. "Because your blood gave Rafal's blood power. The same way it gives power to his sons'."

"So they aren't Arthur's sons for sure?" Guinevere asked. "Then Arthur would have known Tedros was his only child. Why would he create a tournament giving an impostor a chance? Why would he risk his true heir?"

Agatha and Tedros glanced at each other, still without an answer to the question they'd asked themselves.

"Mer Mer knows story," the wizard offered. "Rafal old . . . ooga booga . . . then young . . . still ooga booga! . . . kiss Not-the-Mama . . . hurt Mama and Tee Tee . . . then Rafal die . . . then not die"—he mimicked stiff-armed zombies—"then die again. Now small Rafal. With snakes."

Tedros blinked at him.

"Yes, Merlin, small Rafal with snakes," said Agatha, anxiously searching the sky. "Where is he, Tedros?"

"Sophie's scream hurt him badly. Maybe he can't last up here," Tedros guessed.

Sophie was still mewling: "Once upon a time, I wanted to marry a prince. Now I'm the bride of Father Evil and his two sons!"

"You didn't marry Rafal, you didn't marry Rhian, and you haven't married Japeth," Agatha countered. "They all thought your blood was the one. But you're not the one, because you're here with *us*."

"And how long will '*us*' last?" Sophie asked fatally. "He's made us the villains. He's turned the Woods against us. With no consequence."

"*We* are the consequence," said Tedros. "The Storian believes in us. Our school believes in us. My father believed in us. That's why I wear this ring. I'm his son. *I'm* the king. Not Rafal's spawn. The only place scum like that can be king is in *hell*."

"Welcome to hell, then," came the reply.

Dread snaked up Agatha's spine.

Slowly, she and Tedros turned.

Japeth waited on a cloud in the sky.

He wore his blue-and-gold king's suit, his sword strapped to his belt. His face was flecked with blood, his skin frayed at the edges, like a mask about to fall.

Tedros shot a spell, severing Japeth's sword strap, the blade plunging into darkness. Japeth looked up to see the prince bullrushing him across clouds, Tedros' fists raised—

Japeth waved a hand, magically sweeping a cloud out from under him. The prince flailed, crashing to Sophie and Agatha's cloud, knocking the two girls down.

Agatha lurched up, expecting the Snake to attack—

But Japeth hadn't moved. "You cheat your way into my brother's blood. You trespass into my secrets. You attack and hate, while I defend and fight for the one I love. So who's Evil now? There is no limit to the wickedness you'll do to win. Even raid my soul. Fitting, then, that you'll all die inside it." He paused. "But not quite yet."

He sat down on a glowing green cloud.

"You have most of it right, whatever that cheap mirror revealed," said Japeth. "Rhian always believed King Arthur was our father, but I knew the truth about our parents. Because it was I who found the pen my father spoke of. I know: '*Which pen?*' Now I'll show you." He set his sights on Sophie. "After our mother's death, the Mistral Sisters brought us that dress you're wearing. My mother's dress."

Sophie's white gown morphed to blue, birthing a thousand blue butterflies, matching the Dean's signature gown. All at once, the butterflies flew off it, lighting up the Snake Sky with rich blue glow. They huddled like Wish Fish, their wings turning colors, the butterflies painting scenes in brilliant mosaic . . .

"The butterflies from Mother's dress led us to the Garden of Good and Evil. An unmarked grave. There, the Mistrals said we would find Mother's will."

The butterflies painted a grave and two copper-haired twins digging into it—

"Instead, we found something quite unexpected . . ."

The grave opened, revealing dozens of metal slabs, long and thin, sharp at both ends, like knitting needles.

Agatha's eyes widened.

Pens.

A grave full of them.

Identical to the Storian, but gold instead of silver. Each pen slightly different in size, shape, and carving.

"This is what our mother wanted us to have. Pens that once belonged to King Arthur, the Mistral Sisters explained. Mother and the Mistrals had become friends—the same sisters who came to advise King Arthur after Guinevere and Merlin left him. Arthur had turned to drink, his mind dulled and judgment soft. The Mistrals wormed into his court, telling him what he wanted to hear. That he wasn't to blame for his queen leaving. That it was the Storian's fault. That he was the fated One True King, born to take the Storian's place . . . Overthrow the Pen, they urged. Claim its powers. Become the One True King. Then he could write destiny as he wanted it. Then he could bring Guinevere back to him! All he had to do was get the Woods behind a *new* pen. A rival Storian he would control. The King's Pen. 'Needs a better name,' Arthur considered . . . '*Lionsmane*.' Tedros might like that. And yet, when the Mistrals tried to bring 'Lionsmane' to life, Arthur rejected each pen made for him. Too thin. Too thick. Too pompous. Too humble. Looking for every excuse not to follow through."

More and more pens heaped into the skylit grave, Lionsmanes discarded.

"No matter how much he loved your mother, he wasn't willing to destroy the Storian to have her back. A weak king. An even weaker *man*," said Japeth.

Tedros snarled: "You, who pretended to be his *son*."

"For good reason," said Japeth, unfazed. "After Arthur drank himself into the grave, Rhian and I learned of our own mother's death. Our mother had planned to tell us we were King Arthur's sons once we came of age. But in the case of her death, she'd trusted the Mistrals to find us and give us her dress. The butterflies would tell us what we needed to know. Butterflies that had my mother's spirit."

Across the Snake Sky, butterflies drew more scenes . . .

"These butterflies filled in her version of the story. How Arthur abandoned us. How to assume his throne. There would be steps to take. A carefully made plan. Sabotage Tedros, the false king. Pull Excalibur from the stone. Use Lionsmane to win the people and make leaders burn their rings. Marry the queen named Sophie, whose blood bonded with ours. Do these things—burn the rings and wed Sophie—and we would become the One True King. Immortal, invincible, with the power to bring Mother back to life . . . Only one brother could marry Sophie, of course. Only one could be king. But as long as Rhian and I loved each other, we could share the powers of Sophie's blood. One of us made king by it. The other, magically healed by it. My mother's dress would bind her and keep her loyal. All Rhian and I had to do was stick together. Two brothers, Lion and Eagle, against Tedros the Snake."

Japeth watched the butterflies in the sky. "Rhian believed every word. He loved my mother. He trusted her. He longed to have her back. But I didn't. I knew she disowned us the day she dumped us at Arbed House. Because she wanted to be rid of me. Because she wanted to find our father and be with him instead . . . But King Arthur that father? Uptight, do-gooding Arthur with my viperous mother? Psssh. I didn't trust her story one bit . . . In the shimmer of the butterflies' wings, I began to glimpse secrets hidden in my mother's spirit . . . a Green Knight who was Arthur's brother . . . a plot to steal Arthur's throne . . ." His blue eyes narrowed. "Then I saw it."

All the butterflies in the sky darkened except for one.

"The butterfly that the others were obeying. The leader amongst them. The butterfly that knew I'd found it out . . ."

The butterfly fluttered down into Japeth's hands. Cupped in his palm, the insect began to shrink and shrivel . . . black scales coating its body . . . until it was no longer a butterfly at all . . .

. . . but an eel.

It sharpened at both sides like a pen, its color coal-black.

The slimy pen floated out of Japeth's hand and slipped into his ear.

"This pen told me the true story. King Arthur wasn't our father at all. We were the School Master's sons. *Rafal's* sons. That's why Sophie's blood bonded with ours, like it did with our father's. If I was hearing this message, then Rafal's queen had killed him and likely my mother too. We must punish his queen. Follow my mother's instructions, the pen said. Take Camelot and bring Mother back to life. That's how we could avenge my mother *and* father. This pen would help me, made of my father's spirit. This pen would be our weapon, more than any sword. But the pen warned: I must never let Rhian learn the truth about his father. He needed to believe he was King Arthur's son. Because he was Good inside. And I was Evil. I must always put my brother first. That's where Rafal had cursed himself. He'd killed his twin believing he would find truer love. *Evil's* love. Only to be killed by that love in return. I couldn't repeat my father's story. I had to stay Rhian's faithful liege to the end. That's why my father left this message for me to find. So if Rafal failed to find true love, he could be redeemed by his son. Just as I suspect King Arthur left three tests for his son to redeem him."

The pen flew out of Japeth's ear, a butterfly once more.

It landed on Tedros' shoulder.

"Except my father miscalculated," he said, rising to his feet. "Because he believed love for my brother would satisfy me. Our bloodline, ruling the Woods together. But it wasn't enough for my *father*, was it? And it wasn't for me. Because *I* found truer love too. Someone who cared for me more than my own blood ever did."

The ghost of Aric appeared in the sky, made out of butterflies. The butterfly on Tedros' shoulder fluttered up and joined them, adding the violet sparkle to Aric's eye.

"Strange that Tedros and I are enemies, when we share so much in common," said Japeth, as the sharp-haired silhouette glided towards him. "Abandoned by our mothers. Our fathers destroyed by love. No wonder Tedros and I quest to find love for ourselves. Real love. But Tedros trusts the Storian with his fate. Fate which *stole* love from me, just like it did from Tedros' father. But unlike Arthur, I won't shrink from fixing fate's mistakes. Soon I'll be fate's master, with the power to take love *back*."

Aric landed on his cloud and Japeth put his arms around

him . . . Aric's glowing outline crumbled, butterflies flying away.

Japeth was alone once more.

He smiled bitterly, his king's suit blackening to eels. "But first there is a tournament to win," the Snake said. "A last ring to burn."

His eyes shot to Agatha.

"Which means killing *that*."

The Snake's scims sharpened, about to attack—

The light in the sky went out.

Every hint of green glow swallowed by hard, flat black.

Agatha whirled around, expecting to be stabbed in the dark—

But then she noticed Tedros gone from her side. And she could still see the shine off Japeth's suit, the Snake frozen on a higher cloud, like he'd been taken by surprise. Agatha held her breath, trying not to move. If he hadn't put out the lights, then who? The glint of his eels rippled as if he was turning in place, hunting his prey. It was clear he couldn't spot Agatha in her cloak. She was too far away, the sky too dark.

Agatha smelled silky fragrance as soft wings closed around her: Sophie, her once-white dress now turned to black feathers, lifting her friend from the cloud and silently flying her down to a lower one, farther away from Japeth. "The dress did it," Sophie whispered in Agatha's ear. "It killed the lights. So he couldn't kill us. It's helping me, Aggie. It's *been* helping me."

The dress? Agatha thought. *But Evelyn left it to bind Sophie to her sons. Why would it help Sophie?*

"Tedros. Where is he?" Agatha whispered, unable to see in the dark.

"Thought he was with you," said Sophie.

Agatha's stomach knotted—

Tiny hands snatched the girls and yanked them into the cloud. Merlin was huddled in fluff, a finger to his lips. He poked a hole in the cloud so Agatha and Sophie could peek out.

For a moment, the Snake Sky was quiet.

Then the night ripped open, heavenly light pouring forth, radiant and gold.

A shadow appeared in the glow, an imposing silhouette.

Light caught his purple eyes, his ivory skin, the sharp barbs of his hair. He wore sleeveless red leather and black breeches, his legs and arms pumped with muscle.

Agatha broke into a cold sweat.

"Impossible," Sophie breathed.

He was dead.

They'd *seen* him die.

But here he was.

As if he'd never died at all.

Agatha looked around for Tedros or Guinevere, but the sky was empty.

Just the Snake and the boy.

"Japeth?" the boy spoke, strapping and deep.

The Snake gave him a dead, chilly look, then continued

to search the sky. "Cute trick, Merlin," he called out, looking everywhere but at the boy. "A mimicking hex? Or transmutation?"

Agatha glanced at the six-year-old between her and Sophie, nervously biting the end of his hat. The most Merlin could do was conjure shapes and play fleeting pranks. No way this was his spell.

"Or perhaps just good old-fashioned black magic," said the Snake, his eyes pausing on Agatha and Sophie's cloud.

"I thought you'd say that," the boy replied, hopping smoothly from cloud to cloud until he reached the one across from Japeth's. "That's why I veiled our meeting from the others. They can't see us and we can't see them."

"Right. As if in addition to rising from the dead, you also acquired the power to enter a wizard's thinking place without wizard blood," Japeth mocked. His scims peeled off his suit and circled the boy menacingly. "No, I'd say you're purely the figment of my enemies' creation. Enemies who think I'll engage a fake ghost."

"Well, I am a ghost. That is true. Thoroughly as dead as I was yesterday," the boy acknowledged, petting the eels with no fear. "Which means I have the power to haunt where and how I choose, including a wizard's thinking place. To be honest, I thought you'd be happy to see me."

Finally, Japeth looked at him. "Even sounds just like you." His eels probed the boys' muscles. "Feels like you too. Any idiot can fake a ghost. But to fake a dead boy in a real body . . . I have to say I'm impressed, Merlin. If it's indeed you hiding under there. Or is it one of your friends who took on the task? Knew we should have killed the wizard when we could, precisely to put an end to his games. But Rhian thought if he could regress Merlin to a child, then he could remake his loyalties . . ." Scims pried the boys' eyes open, assessing his purple irises. "Amazing work, really. Too bad I have to kill you to see who you really are. Maybe Sophie, now that I think about it. She does like to get too close to the fire." His eels dropped to the boy's throat, about to tear him apart—

"Go ahead. I won't feel a thing. I'm dead, remember?" said the boy, unruffled. "The moment you kill me—*poof!*—I'll be gone forever and your enemies will be right where you left them, ready to fight. I hid them so I could *help* you, Japeth. So I could warn you what Tedros is about to do."

"I see," Japeth said, suddenly amused. "And what secret plan have you managed to catch wind of? What is it that the idiot prince plans to do, hmm?"

"Disguise himself as me," the purple-eyed boy replied. "He went into the Cave of Wishes. The genie granted Tedros the power to turn into whoever he wants. The genie's magic lives inside his blood long enough for Tedros to take on my body and warp your mind. To fool you and make you believe he's the real thing. See, that's him over there, waiting for his moment." A spotlight appeared, on a second clone of the boy, posed atop a distant cloud, looking fidgety and anxious, before the spotlight abruptly went dark. The boy turned back to Japeth. "I wanted to be with you before Tedros tries. So you can remember what's true."

Japeth's grin lost its shape. "Let me get this straight: you will disappear and be replaced by a *new* you, who is Tedros in disguise. And *that's* who I should kill." He snorted, but it was half-hearted, the Snake increasingly wary of the boy. "Well, whatever magic he's using, it can't be better than what is in front of me."

"This isn't magic," the boy replied. "It's me, Japeth. As me as a ghost can be."

The Snake inspected him closer, trying and failing to see through him.

"It isn't you if you're not flesh and blood," Japeth taunted.

"Try me," said the boy.

Japeth stared hard at him. Slowly, one of his scims moved from the boy's throat up to his mouth . . . and pricked it with its tip. Blood seeped from the boy's lips. He didn't flinch.

Agatha's eyes bulged.

So did the Snake's. "You're . . . you're . . . *real*?"

"More real than the real thing," said the boy.

Japeth's face warmed with color. He leapt onto the boy's cloud. "Aric?" He put his nose to Aric's neck, inhaling his skin, touching his nose, his cheeks, before his arms clasped hard around the boy's chest. "It's you. Exactly you." Tears flooded Japeth's eyes.

From her hiding place, Agatha watched a murderous Snake embraced with a murderous savage, the two of them so close and bonded, their love almost . . . human. Emotion tickled her throat, which she instantly shoved down. She couldn't let herself feel. Not for these two. Even her, with a heart so stubbornly Good.

"What's happened to you?" Aric whispered, holding the Snake tight. "Changing yourself to look like Rhian. Pretending to be your own brother. The Japeth I know wouldn't have done that. Kill Rhian, maybe. But not *become* him," he smiled wryly. "Not lose wild, beautiful Japeth along the way."

"I did it for you," Japeth said tensely. "Everything I've done is for you. To get you back."

"And then what? I have to be with 'Rhian' in my new life? And his terrible haircut and fake tan? I have to join your charade?" said Aric.

"I'll tell the people the truth. About who I am. You'll be my new liege—"

"Ah yes. Japeth the Snake, who attacked their kingdoms, murdered his brother, and pretended to *be* his brother, now forgiven and welcomed as Camelot's new king. More than that: the One True King, who controls all their lives with his new Pen. And oh, he's bringing his love back from the dead with him, who just happens to be a boy."

"Then I'll give up my crown—"

"They'll kill you, Japeth. They'll kill us both. I don't want to be brought back to life, just to die a more ignoble death than I suffered the first time."

Japeth was shivering now. Utterly overwhelmed. "You don't know what I've done for you. Are you really turning down the chance to come back to life? To have a second chance with me? It can't end this way. With you just . . . *leaving?*"

"This isn't The End," Aric promised. "But I'm at peace

now. If you love me, Japeth, you'll let me go. The time will come when we'll be together again. But not like this. First you have to be who you are. Who you really are, not some Snake out to get revenge on my behalf. Surrender the crown that isn't yours. Admit your deception to the people. Even if you're punished for it. Even if Excalibur takes your head. Tell the truth and it will set both our souls free. We'll be together forever, then . . . But fight too hard against fate and your spirit will never find mine. Because you can't escape your fate, no matter what you want to believe. I learned that the hard way."

Japeth nestled into him. "Where was this Aric when you were alive? Who is thoughtful and loving? Who speaks so tenderly to me?"

"Do what I tell you, dear Japeth," Aric pressed. "Give us a second chance beyond this world. I'll be waiting for you."

Japeth gripped his shirt. "No. Not yet. Please . . . stay with me."

"I don't have that power, friend."

"Then let me ask for one thing. Before you go." Gently Japeth reached a hand to Aric's gashed mouth, wiping away blood with his fingers. "The one thing I need from you to have peace."

"Anything you wish," said Aric.

Japeth held his gaze. "Can I kiss you? Like we used to?"

Aric hesitated, taken aback. He stood straighter, his lips pressing together. "Oh." He nodded with a smile. "Of course."

Japeth's face sharpened. "Well, in that case . . ." He stepped back just as Aric leaned in. "Let me reconsider. Because we never kissed when you were alive. *Your* rule." His fingers were shiny with Aric's blood. "The real Aric would have known that. The real Aric was ashamed of our love. Which means you must not be Aric at all. You're exactly what you warned me about. Tedros, with the power to turn into whoever you wish. And that second Aric over there was just a trick to make me believe what you were saying—your mother, I'd bet, from her bumbling pose. She must have the genie's magic too, a decoy made to sell me your plan. So close, Tedros. So close to getting me to give up. Only one wrinkle in your plan, arrogant prince. I have your blood on my fingers. Your genie-hexed blood with shape-shifting powers . . ."

The Snake bit his own lip, splitting it open. He licked his fingers, letting his and Aric's blood mix.

". . . and now that blood is in *mine*," said Japeth.

Aric's irises suddenly went blue—Tedros blue—the prince's eyes bright with panic.

The Snake smiled at him. "Let the games begin."

In his sky, the light snuffed out, like a door slammed shut.

24

The Agatha Quartet

Tedros had his plan.

But everyone has a plan until they're kicked in the face.

Then the plan isn't worth very much, is it?

But it's not only the prince who is in danger . . .

At the moment, the Snake Sky was black-out dark. Agatha and Sophie remained huddled inside their cloud, Merlin

whimpering between them. They couldn't see Tedros anywhere. Or the Snake. Just the ragged shapes of clouds and
the glint of steel-edged stars. Japeth was out there somewhere.
And now with Tedros' blood in his veins, he'd also absorbed
the genie's powers . . . the power to become anyone he wished.

"Tee Tee need help," Merlin squeaked, eyes wet.

"Shhh," said Sophie, but the six-year-old was distraught,
blubbering louder.

"Tee Tee!" Merlin fretted, poking his head through the
cloud hole. Agatha grabbed him back.

"Merlin, stay still!"

But the wizard was already lurching out of their hiding
place, Agatha and Sophie scrambling with him, the little
wizard wildly swishing his hand—

The sky flooded with blazing white light, like a storm
paused during a lightning strike.

"Tee Tee!" Merlin smiled with relief.

Then his smile vanished.

Because there were *three* Tedroses in the lit-up sky.

On three different clouds.

Each armed with a sharp-bladed star from the sky.

"Aggie . . . what's happening . . . ," Sophie croaked.

"One is Tedros. One must be Guinevere," said Agatha, pale
with terror. "So the third is . . ."

Merlin gaped at the two girls. "*Hiss.*"

All three Tedroses looked at each other.

Then at Agatha.

Instantly, they sprinted for her.

"Agatha, it's me!" cried one.

"No, it's *me*!" yelled the second.

"Don't listen to them!" shouted the third.

Three princes with gem-blue eyes, golden waves of hair, and a torn black cloak. Each as Tedros as the other.

"Which one's real?" Sophie gasped.

But Agatha was already running, diving off her cloud and burying into one far below. Sunk in cold green puffs, she closed her eyes and tried to focus. In that split second, she'd scouted the Tedroses closely. The way they carried themselves, the way they targeted her . . . The real Tedros wanted to protect her; the Snake's Tedros wanted to kill her; while Guinevere had surely taken Tedros' form to throw off the Snake. And yet, they all looked the *same*. Sounds of chaos echoed above; no doubt they'd seen where she landed. She had to keep moving. But where to? Her only hope was to pick a Tedros: a two-in-three chance of being saved; a one-in-three chance of being gutted . . .

A body plunged into fluff next to her. Agatha turned to flee—

"It's me," Sophie panted, blinking emerald eyes, her black-feathered dress bunched in the cloud. "Stay with me. Don't move."

Agatha exhaled. Then her heart kick-started. "Wait . . . how do I know you're . . ." She backed up. "What's the name of my cat?"

"Aggie—"

"What's its name!"

"Reaper."

"And he's King of the—"

"Gnomes. Agatha, listen—"

"What's the name of the runty, bucktoothed boy in Gavaldon who was obsessed with you?"

Sophie stared at her blankly. "Ummm—"

"Stay back," Agatha choked, crawling away, before she felt Sophie's arm grab her. Agatha whirled around, finger lit, about to shoot a spell—

Only to see Guinevere, where Sophie had just been.

"It's me, Agatha. I thought you'd trust me if I took Sophie's form. Listen to me: the Snake is out there, looking like Tedros. You and I have to stick together or he'll—"

But Agatha was in a blind panic, questioning if Guinevere was really Guinevere, her body already lunging out of the cloud and dashing into open light with no direction or plan. Guinevere chased her. "Agatha, wait!"

"You're supposed to protect her, Mother!" one of the Tedroses barked at Guinevere veering towards Agatha.

Agatha whirled to this prince, the *real* Tedros . . . but then she glimpsed the *other* Tedros throttling from the opposite direction, closing faster, faster, the blade-sharp star raised in his hand, both Tedroses about to flying-leap onto her cloud, with Agatha trapped between them—

A third body cannonballed from above: Sophie with young Merlin piggybacked to her, crashing on top of Agatha. By the time Agatha recovered, Sophie's dress of feathers was sweeping the two girls upwards like a black swan, away from the twin

Tedroses, both princes receding and indistinguishable, before little Merlin swished his hands and doused the sky's light.

Pure darkness reigned once more.

Sophie's black dress magically expanded, hiding her and Agatha in a round cocoon that floated midair, while Merlin perched atop the cocoon, keeping watch.

"Please tell me it's you," Agatha rasped to Sophie, huddled in feathers. "The real you."

"As real as the bran biscuits I generously made you in Gavaldon that you used to dump in your graveyard when I wasn't looking. Listen, there's two Tedroses. One is Teddy. One is the Snake. And yet, somehow I can't fathom which is *him*. Teddy did a magnificent job playing Aric and now is doing an odious job playing himself. Maybe if Teddy had more substance or character, he'd be easier to recognize—"

"Now I know it's you," Agatha snapped. "Can't Merlin tell them apart?"

"Tee Tee Tee Tee. Two Tee Tees," a child's voice pipped.

"That's a no. Aggie, what's something only Tedros would know about you? Something Japeth *can't* know."

"Snake's read *The Tale of Sophie and Agatha*, inside and out. Everything you know, he knows, and you know everything." Agatha paused. "Except . . ."

"Except?"

"How Tedros proposed to marry me."

Agatha's big eyes sparkled in the dark, so intensely that Sophie turned away. "Well, heaven forbid your best *friend* know how your prince asked to marry you! Seems like something a best *friend* might share. But seeing you haven't, you should use your little secret to suss out your groom," said Sophie. "As soon as you find who the real Tedros is, we'll know who the Snake is and attack him. I don't care if killing him isn't the Good thing to do or won't make Teddy king. If he's Rafal's son, the sooner he's dead the better. I'll stay up here until you find him. This way, I can shoot spells at anyone who dares comes near you, since I'm the only one who knows you're actually you."

Agatha's neck rashed red. "I can't leave you here—"

"If I'm with you, the Snake will know who you are. I'm not letting him kill you, Agatha. I'm not letting him win. Find Tedros. Kill the creep. Got it?" Sophie's dress opened like a flower and she brought Merlin down into her arms. "I'll keep this one with me so he's safe. Now *go*."

Before Agatha could speak, Sophie shoved her from the cocoon. Agatha flopped onto a cloud down below. Above her, Merlin swished his hands—

Light returned to the Snake Sky.

Agatha braced herself, ready to pick Tedros from his impostor, confident she knew how to find the answer . . . then saw the answer no longer matched the question.

Because where Agatha expected two Tedroses to choose between, now there were *none*.

Instead, there were three *Agathas* on the clouds surrounding her, each dressed in the same pink dress and hooded black cloak that she was wearing.

A quartet of Agathas, which included the real Agatha since now the other three were inspecting her and each other, with no inkling yet as to who was who.

Until this very moment, I've told this tale through Agatha's eyes as if it were her story to tell. But where Agatha no doubt thinks she is the main character of her story, as any Man in the throes of life does, the Pen has a wider view of things. Which is why we must turn to Sophie, high on a cloud, entrusted with protecting her best friend, but suddenly confused as to which was the real Agatha and which were the fakes.

"Merlin, who's Aggie?" she asked the child with her.

But the wizard too had lost track.

All Sophie knew was that she had to find the real Agatha before Japeth did.

Think, Sophie coaxed herself.

Why had they all taken Agatha's form?

Each had good reason.

Tedros and Guinevere wanted to confuse the Snake, who was hunting Agatha to win the second test. Meanwhile, the Snake wanted to confuse Tedros, who was determined to protect his princess.

At first, Sophie assumed Japeth's Agatha would attack the others, believing he'd slay the real Agatha in the process and win his test. And yet, this would also give the Snake away, enabling Tedros, Agatha, and Guinevere to team against him and Sophie to snipe him with a spell from above . . . which is precisely why the Snake's Agatha *wasn't* attacking and instead hanging back like his fellow Agathas, waiting for someone else to make the first move.

Sophie realized that someone had to be her.

"Attention, friends and *filth*," she called crisply, her dress of black feathers holding her in the sky, like an extraterrestrial bird. Four Agathas craned their heads up. A spotlight appeared on Sophie out of nowhere (Merlin trying to be helpful). "Allow me to ask some questions. Think of it as a test. The Tournament of *Stings*. Each of you will take a turn answering and if I sense a certain serpentine quality to your answer, you will be *stung*." Sophie lit her fingerglow, a smoking-hot pink. "A well-aimed stun spell to the head, reserved precisely for Snakes pretending to be my best friend. And I'm not sure you'll wake up alive, given that as much as you want Agatha dead, my friends and I want you dead *more*. Shall we begin?"

She glared down at the Agatha Quartet lined up left to right, still hoping Japeth would snap and show himself, but the four Agathas stared right back, willing to engage.

Clever Snake. He's looking for Agatha the same way we're looking for him, Sophie thought.

She had to be careful with her questions.

"What is Agatha's favorite food?" Sophie asked, starting with the Agatha on the left.

"Candy," said Agatha #1.

"Honeycake," said Agatha #2.

"Cinnamon rolls," said Agatha #3.

"Jellybeans," said Agatha #4.

Sophie frowned. Agatha's taste for sweets preceded her, it seemed. Worse still, Sophie had assumed the answer would be salted peanut crunch, since Agatha used to consume mounds of it in Gavaldon, but apparently it wasn't, since whoever the real Agatha was didn't agree. The responses weren't entirely unhelpful, though. Only Guinevere, Tedros, and Agatha had been in the Mirage Pub, where Agatha had discovered honey-cake, meaning Agatha #2 wasn't the Snake. And Agatha #4 wasn't Tedros or Agatha, because anyone who knew Agatha would know she found jellybeans infantile. So who was who? It felt like a math problem, and Sophie had always found math a poor use of time, so she gave up and asked another question instead.

"Who is the One True King?" Sophie asked.

Come out, come out, little Snake.

"Tedros," said Agatha #1.

"Tedros," said Agatha #2.

"Tedros," said Agatha #3.

"Whoever wins the Tournament of Kings," said Agatha #4. "Just as Arthur willed."

Agatha #1, #2, and #3 all peered at Agatha #4. So did Sophie.

Has to be the Snake, she thought. *Can't even stomach the idea of saying Tedros' name.*

Sophie bit her lip. *And yet . . . would the Snake give himself away so easily? Isn't Japeth smarter than that?*

She could see Agatha #3 studying the fourth Agatha, fists curling as if itching to attack, but also struggling with the same doubts Sophie had.

Sophie focused harder—

Agatha #2 isn't the Snake.

Agatha #3 is Tedros or Agatha.

Agatha #4 isn't Tedros or Agatha.

She was getting closer.

One more question.

The question.

"Tell me. How did Tedros propose to you?" Sophie asked.

Agatha #4 gave Agatha #3 a coy glance, which Sophie noticed. Agatha #1 noticed too and gave Agatha #4 a probing look. Agatha #2, meanwhile, glowered hard at Sophie, though Sophie didn't know if it was because she was offended or stumped. All in all, Sophie felt more baffled than ever.

"Well?" Sophie hounded. "How did the prince ask you to marry him?"

"It's a secret," said Agatha #1.

"Kept it to myself for a reason," said Agatha #2.

"No one's business," said Agatha #3.

"He did it at Camelot," said Agatha #4. "The first night we arrived after we left school. Tedros arranged a romantic dinner and proposed during dessert, exactly as you'd expect."

The air seemed to drain out of the sky, a thick silence hanging between Sophie and the Agathas like a curtain about to drop.

Agatha #1 and Agatha #3 prowled forward, each looming towards the Agatha that had just answered.

Agatha #4.

Then, in tandem, as if they were one and the same, the first and third Agathas drew something from their cloaks. Something each of them had been hiding.

A sharp-bladed star.

Agatha #4 began to retreat, her twin assailants closing in.

In a flash, Sophie understood.

Agatha #1 and #3 were Tedros and Japeth. Or Japeth and Tedros.

Together, they were about to kill Agatha #4.

Because each thought they knew who this Agatha was.

Tedros thought it was Japeth.

Japeth thought it was Agatha.

Agatha #4 stepped back, hands up, her clumps teetering at the edge of the cloud. She looked at her star-armed hunters. "Caught me," she said.

Her assailants raised their stars like daggers.

Sophie realized what was about to happen. So did Agatha #2, the last Agatha left. "*No!*" the two girls gasped.

Agatha #4 turned to jump—

Steel-edged stars impaled her back and neck.

She collapsed onto her cloud.

Twin Agathas rushed towards her, both believing they'd won, both believing they'd slain their enemy . . .

. . . only to recoil in shock.

Guinevere lay on the cloud, blood soaking the cotton softness at her wings.

Agatha #3 melted back into Tedros' body, the prince lunging to her side.

Agatha #1 reverted to Japeth, the stunned Snake swiveling to Agatha #2, the *real* Agatha, already far away in the sky, rescued by Sophie's magical dress.

"Mother . . . ," Tedros breathed.

"One more test left." His mother held on to him. "You killed your princess."

Tedros' eyes widened.

Guinevere smiled weakly. "You had your plan and I had mine."

"This can't be the end . . . ," Tedros wept.

"Make no mistake. *You* won this test, Tedros," his mother said. "By getting us here. By loving Agatha so strongly. Somewhere Arthur must have known. That your love would set all of us free." Her grip loosened. "Your father and I will meet again. And he will forgive me. Because we made you. Our son. The King. This is how it's meant to end. It always was. With me finally a mother to you . . . With Lance waiting for me . . ."

She drew a breath and let him go, the cloud swallowing her up, staining red, like a rose dipped in color. Tedros hunched over, head in hands, letting out a ravaged howl. He raised raw eyes to the Snake, the prince breathing fire. Japeth's face hardened, his scims turning to spikes. Both boys surged for the other, enemies primed for war—

From within the cloud, red smoke shot up into the sky, smashing the two apart. The red smoke roiled higher, thicker, as if the once-queen's blood had become air, expanding into a storm cloud over the Celestium, taking the shape of a Lion. Arthur's voice thundered:

"You have done what I asked.
Both of you.
The second test done.

One more test remains,
Two kings still in the race.
The final trial awaits."

Beneath the clouds on which Tedros and Japeth lay, the sky broke open like a portal, revealing a familiar landscape.

The royal gardens of Camelot.

A mountain of rubble where a statue used to be.

Arthur's sword trapped in the stone.

"Excalibur," spoke the king. *"The Lion's Grail."*

The blade glowed gold with magic, vibrating faster, harder, before it shattered the stone with a thunderous *crack!* and vaulted high into the night like a beacon. But then another Excalibur appeared next to it . . . then another . . . glowing just as gold, just as brightly, then more and more and more, repeating infinitely across the sky, again and again, until the galaxy was nothing but the king's sword.

"Find the grail," Arthur ordered.
"Find Excalibur.
Free it once and for all.
He who does will be king.
He who fails . . . will pay with his head."

A million Excaliburs shined in the dark, each perfection, each the same.

Lording over five small shadows.

One who would be King.

The Lion roared—

Swords stabbed down like Pens to a page, slashing open the sky with blinding light and swallowing all of Man's fate with it.

Game of Swords

"How are you going to propose?" Lancelot had asked him. They were swimming in the ice-cold sea a few miles from the castle, just the two of them, while Guinevere accompanied Agatha to dress fittings for the coronation. It had only been a few days since they'd all come to Camelot from the School for Good and Evil. Only a few days since the war against Rafal had

ended with the School Master dead and a new alliance between Camelot and the School, the Woods' two greatest powers. The future seemed filled with hope and promise. So much so that when Lance had barreled into Tedros' chambers at the crack of dawn, demanding the prince come swim with him, for once Tedros decided to be agreeable and tagged along.

"Well?" Lancelot pressed, now that they were deep in frigid waters, the winter sun doing nothing to warm them. "If you're going to ask her to marry you, you better have a plan."

"A plan I'll keep to myself, thank you," the prince replied, trying to stop his teeth from chattering, given Lance looked perfectly comfortable. "I hope now that you and Mother are going to live with us, it won't make you think I care about your opinion. You're not my father and you never will be."

Lancelot grinned a dirty smile. "Haven't thought about how you're going to do it, have you."

Tedros glanced at the wild-maned brute with a hairy chest, all leathered and brawny where the prince was smooth and lean, his skin pinking at every stab of cold. "What do you care? You never asked my mother to marry *you*."

"Your mother had the choice to marry me, but chose Arthur instead. In the end, it wasn't what she was looking for," Lancelot replied. "So we had to find something else to call what Gwen and I have."

"Like what?"

"Love."

Tedros looked at him.

"That's why it matters how you propose," said the knight.

"Because if it's marriage you're trying to get her to agree to, well, then that's easy enough. Any king can make an offer a girl can't refuse. The pull of duty and honor, the promise of riches and fame, the carving of a name into history. It's why Gwen couldn't say no to your father and why any girl won't say no to you. But if it's *love* you're offering, love bigger than marriage, love that will last forever . . . well, that's a very different proposal indeed. Because a girl can only say yes to that once. Like your mother did to me."

Tedros took this in, so lost in his thoughts that he didn't see Lancelot's big, meaty hand reach up behind him and dunk his head into the sea.

"Why are you *such* an ass?" Tedros spewed, spitting salty water.

"Someone needs to teach the cub how to be a lion, don't he?" Lance chuckled.

By the time they swam back to shore, Tedros had scrapped his original plan for asking Agatha to marry him. Soon, a new proposal brewed in his heart: one that he didn't second-guess. He didn't share it with anyone. Not Lance. Not Merlin. Not his mother. Not a soul, until his princess on the day he chose. Since that day, neither he nor Agatha had spoken of it to each other or anyone else. What had happened was too sacred, too private to live outside their own hearts.

It's why when Tedros watched that fourth Agatha lie about the proposal, telling a version that resembled nothing of the truth, he'd felt so offended, so violated . . . that his mother had known he would confuse her for a Snake.

⟨⟩

"TEDROS?" HIS MOTHER's voice spoke.

He opened his eyes to a wet, glacial darkness, as if he was trapped deep under the sea.

"Tedros?" the voice spoke again.

Not his mother.

Someone else.

A body climbed on top of him, light but bony, before thin, warm fingers touched his eyes, pulling away a cold veil. Sun blinded him, blotting out everything except his snow-dusted princess, panting softly, pink cheeks tinged blue, her cloak crusted with ice as if she'd been buried in it. More snow fell from the sky, filling Tedros' eyes where Agatha had just scraped it away. The prince turned his neck and saw heaps of snow blocking his view, as if he, too, had been buried before his princess dug him up.

A short while ago, they'd been in the hot fog of the desert. Tan lines peeked from under his father's ring. Sand was caked to his chest and armpits under his lace-up shirt, no defense against this cold. One thing was for sure: they weren't in Shazabah anymore.

He looked at Agatha. "What is this place?"

Her throat bobbed, her big brown eyes lifting beyond the prince, as if Tedros was asking the wrong question.

Tedros rocked to his knees, craning over the mounds of snow—

He fell backwards in surprise.

Everywhere he looked . . .

Swords.

The *same* sword.

Excalibur, trapped blade-first in snow, again and again, the lion-carved hilts jutting out of the white landscape, every six or seven feet, thousands and thousands of them, as far as the eye could see.

Tedros stumbled to his feet, lurching for the nearest one. He grabbed it—

The sword crumbled to black dirt.

He tried another one. Another. Another.

All withered.

Suddenly Tedros understood. That vision in the night sky. Arthur's prophecy of Excalibur hidden for him or the Snake to find . . .

It was here.

The third test had begun.

"Where is it?" said Tedros, yanking more and more swords, his shirt and breeches spattering with dirt. "Where's the real one?"

But Agatha was gazing out at sunlit snow, as if these too were the wrong questions. She looked back at her prince.

"Where's Sophie?" she asked.

Silence hung between them.

Pink lightning shocked the sky, followed by a puff of pink smoke, somewhere in the distance.

Tedros and Agatha glanced at each other.

Then they started running.

NEITHER SAID A word as they sprinted across snow, Tedros sweeping his hand across hilts and turning them to dust. He knew in his heart that the final test couldn't be won by luck, but still, he touched as many as he could, watching swords vanish as he tried to keep up with his princess, who was heading straight for where they'd seen the pink smoke. He heard Agatha holding her breath, which reminded Tedros to keep breathing, even if every breath brought with it thoughts of Rafal and Japeth and Aric and how Tedros had played the part of the last, the prince willing to kiss his own enemy to send him to hell . . . only to kill someone else instead . . .

My mother.

I killed my mother.

He buried his guilt and anguish, holding on to the peace in Guinevere's face as she let him go.

"Lance is waiting for me . . ."

It was what his mother wanted. To be reunited with her knight.

But not before protecting her son. Not before sacrificing herself to get him to the last test.

To Excalibur.

The Lion's Grail, his father called it.

The sword that once rejected Tedros as king.

The sword he now had to find and claim.

Not that he had the faintest clue how. He couldn't possibly touch every impostor blade in sight; nor did he know how far this gameboard of Excaliburs would go on or whether the Snake had a better plan to win or where the Snake even was . . .

Or where I am, Tedros reminded himself, still flummoxed by the terrain. The Frostplains, maybe? But the snow was too soft, the land too rugged . . . He considered other options— Maidenvale, Altazarra, even Netherwood—but there was nothing to orient him, no town or castle or sea or *something* that might clue him to where they were . . . just more swords and more snow, as if they were stretching the bounds of the world, into the Endless of the Endless Woods.

"Hurry, Tedros!" Agatha urged, outpacing him.

"What happens if *you* touch one?" Tedros called out.

"Nothing happens! It's your test!"

"Just try it!"

Agatha seized a sword by the hilt—it resisted her pull, staying trapped in the snow as if it were stone. "See? Worry about them later! We need to find Sophie!" she harped, running faster.

"We need to find my *sword*!" said Tedros.

But unless the real sword glowed like a beacon or sent up a flare or sang to him like a siren, this hunt would take a very long time.

And what if I do find it somehow?

Excalibur rejected me as king.

Will it reject me again?

Another bolt of pink lightning jolted the earth in front of them, sending a shockwave of pink light across a swathe of swords, disintegrating them into smoke. The pink mist fogged Tedros and Agatha in, the prince following his princess's coughs before he found her, taking her arm and waving away smoke, until it finally cleared.

A boy peered back at them.

He was stringy and mop-haired, dressed in a purple velvet suit, his hands cupped around an orb of pink lightning.

Instantly Tedros shielded his princess and grabbed the nearest sword, only to turn it to dust. "Damn things!" Tedros lit his fingerglow, pointing it haphazardly at the stranger. "Stay back, whoever you are!"

But Agatha was already moving towards the brown-headed lad, with full eyebrows, high cheekbones, and green eyes that blinked behind spectacles.

"Merlin?" Agatha said.

"I was wondering when you two would wake up," the young wizard spoke with a singsong tone, before casting the ball of lightning and clearing more swords.

Tedros goggled. "But . . . you're . . . you're *tall* . . ."

"That's the Tedros I remember. I'm finally past the age of wetting the bed and calling you Tee Tee and the first thing you talk about is height," said the boy. "Maybe it's because most princes the Storian writes about are tall and you are . . . not."

Tedros looked like he'd been slapped.

"Oh, Merlin, we missed you," Agatha breathed, hugging him.

"I'm still the same boy who thought you were my Mama. Just capable of full sentences now," the young wizard chuckled, smoothing his purple suit. "First night was terrible. A six-year-old on his own? I was scared out of my wits. Then I shot up a foot overnight and my whole body felt like it might rip apart. Kept trying to wake you, but the magic that dropped us here affected you both more than me. After a while, I was just plain bored, waiting for you to get up. Tried to use the time to recover my own magic. Only figured out this sword-clearing spell just now. Puberty will probably start tomorrow. Oof. I don't remember loving it the first time. At least it'll only last a few days instead of a few years."

Tedros was still gawking at him. "But how did you—"

"Hester's potion," Agatha realized, her hand in her coat. "Where is it?"

Merlin's blue hat flounced up from the snow, raggedy and dented, and belched out the vial from its mouth.

"Nicked it off you and took it each day on schedule. You missed the worst of it: at eight, I had a bout of chicken pox and spent most of the day mummified in snow to stop from itching . . . at nine, I rebelled against my hat's ruthless insistence I eat vegetables and nearly beat the thing to death . . . then at ten, all my baby teeth fell out," said the wizard, pointing at a pile of white shells in the snow. "Tomorrow I'll officially be a teenager. Bet Hat's excited about that." (Merlin's cap made a loud fart noise.)

Agatha blanched. "So that means we've been asleep for . . ."

"Six days, eight hours, and twenty-three minutes," the boy wizard chimed.

"*Six days?*" said Agatha.

"Wait! If you're almost thirteen, surely you remember your old life now!" Tedros jumped in. "You can tell us why my father made the tournament. You can help me win the third test! You can fix everything!"

"I'm *twelve*, Tedros. I can barely concentrate on anything other than growing pains, how badly I need a bath, and the first pimple I got an hour ago, which magic won't make go away," said Merlin, puffing at his hair. "I remember most of my old life before I turned into a baby, along with my usual command of language, thank heavens, because if I had to speak in the stunted gargles of an adolescent, I'd gag myself with my hat. And yet, my command of magic *is* juvenile, my best spells erased from my memory. Maybe with each day I'll remember more, but who knows? And no, I don't have a clue where the real Excalibur is or how to find it or what your father was up to when he made this tournament, because as far as I can remember, he kept the details secret from me. I don't know much of anything about his tests at all, other than that your enemy seems to be struggling as much as you are."

Tedros followed the boy's gaze to the blinding glare of sun. The prince shielded his eyes and made out gold letters where he hadn't seen them before. They were small and far away, as if he and his princess were on another planet, Lionsmane's words faint against the sky.

Your king has returned to Camelot, only to find Excalibur missing and hidden in the Woods. King Arthur's final test. Help me find it. Help the Lion win, so that Excalibur takes the head of Tedros the

Snake. All of you are my Eagle now. He
who finds the real sword shall be rewarded!

"Message has been up for five days, so clearly no one's found
it," said Merlin.

"Japeth's at Camelot?" Agatha asked. "Must have been
dropped there, then."

"Wait. So he gets dropped at Camelot. *Rafal's* son. At *my*
castle. By *my* dad," Tedros growled, "and we get dropped in a
middle-of-nowhere snowhole?"

"Not exactly nowhere," said Merlin. He flicked his fingers
and magically swelled the snow beneath his and Agatha's feet,
raising the mound higher and higher, until the wizard and
princess were fifty feet above ground.

"What about me?" Tedros shouted below.

"Oops," said the young wizard, flicking fingers quickly—

The snow ruptured under Tedros' feet, sending him plummeting ten feet into ice. "MERLIN!"

"Still rusty!" Merlin called, with a wink at Agatha, before
springing Tedros up on a spout of snow.

"This is pointless. I just see more swords," wet Tedros
groused, glaring into endless white—

Only it wasn't endless, he realized now.

In the distance, he could see a house on a hill.

A small farm cottage, breaking up the sweep of snow.

The same farmhouse where he and his princess once came
to hide from the same School Master whose son threatened
them now.

"Agatha?" he rasped.

But she was looking upwards, straight into the gray sky, which upon closer inspection had a flat, undulating sheen as if it was a glass wall, hiding waves of water behind it . . .

Not just water.

Hiding something else too.

A face.

Spying on them from behind the sky, before it vanished back into the lake from which it came.

"Always summer here when the Lady was in good spirits," said Merlin. "Her mood has changed, it seems."

"But why are we here?" Tedros asked Merlin. "Why would Dad drop us in Avalon and Japeth at the castle?"

"Who's to say it was your dad and not *you* who decided that we be dropped here?" said Merlin, cocking a brow, suddenly looking like the wizard Tedros knew, despite his twelve-year-old form. "Japeth would have wished to return to the castle where he could seek the people's help to win the last test. Maybe deep down, you knew coming here would be your best chance to find the sword."

Tedros crossed his arms. "Doesn't make sense. Why would I come to the Lady of the Lake? What does she have to do with Excal—"

His eyes widened.

Merlin grinned crookedly. "Everything to do with it, Tee Tee. She did *make* it, after all."

The prince swallowed. "We have to talk to her, don't we?"

"*You* need to talk to her," said the wizard boy. "Can't

remember the specifics, but I have the vague feeling she hates me. Old me, I mean."

"While you were gone, she tried to kill me," said Tedros.

"Mmm, maybe Agatha, then," the wizard murmured.

They turned to the girl between them.

She was still looking into the sky.

"So let me get this straight," Agatha spoke finally. "Japeth wished to return to Camelot. Tedros wished to come to Avalon . . ."

She leveled with the two boys.

"So where did *Sophie* wish to go to?"

26

Don't Talk to Strangers

"Yoo-hoo! Boys!" Dean Rowenna sang at the bottom of the staircase, smacking a ruler against her palm. "Hurry up or someone else will find the sword first!"

Sounds of commotion echoed from the top floor.

"Emilio! Arjun! Pierre-Eve! And the rest of you whose names I haven't learned yet!" She rapped the ruler on the banister. "Get your bottoms down- stairs at once!"

Eight boys trampled down the steps of Arbed House, uniform shirts half- buttoned, boots untied, faces in various stages of cleanliness, all with Lion pins on their lapels. Arjun tripped on the last stair, toppling the others in a domino fall.

"Now I see why Arbed boys are kept separate from the rest of the school," said Dean Rowenna.

"Sorry, Dean Rowenna," Arjun panted. "Dean Brunhilde said we have to say our prayers and brush our teeth and step in the bath for at least five seconds every morning or the Evil will get in."

Dean Rowenna lowered her spectacles, revealing emerald eyes, her lips painted matching green, her black hive of hair speared with a pencil and her nose anointed with a big brown wart. She wore a black whipstitch skirt, a green ruffled blouse, and long green boots that shined against black stockings. "Well, Dean Brunhilde isn't here, is she? Gone to help the Lion find his sword. Called upon by King Rhian himself, since he used to be her student right here, in this very house. Which is why Rhian sent me, his beloved cousin Rowenna, to take Brunhilde's place as your Dean. And now we, too, will assist the Lion in winning the tournament's last test." She leaned in, green eyes sparkling. "Because I know for a *fact* Excalibur is somewhere here in Foxwood. Which means we're going to find it, aren't we?"

A dark-skulled boy looked suspicious. "Whole Woods is covered in swords. How do you know the real one's in Foxwood? If that's true, wouldn't *everyone* be searching here?"

"Emilio's right. How would you know where King Arthur hid his sword?" said a boy at once bald and littered with dandruff.

"No one can *know* where the sword is. They all look exactly the same," a boy said, dark skin still damp from his bath. "And it's not like we'll even know if we find it. Every time I grab one, it stays stuck in the dirt."

"And if we *do* find something suspicious and write the king, he sends his guards to investigate and they probably have a thousand false leads already," said Emilio.

"Plus, why would King Rhian ask Dean Brunhilde to help him instead of a wizard or sorcerer?" Arjun peppered. "And why didn't Dean Brunhilde say bye to us? And why is the wart on your nose a different size every day?"

"Questioning your new Dean with such arrogance! Speaking so rudely to the blood cousin of the king! All of you!" Dean Rowenna chided. "I see why your households sent you here to be reformed. No matter. I'll have the Evil out of you soon enough. As to how I know the sword's whereabouts, let's call it a Dean's intuition. And since I'm Rhian's cousin, there's no need to piddle with guards. I have a direct line to the Lion himself! Come, my loves. Whoever finds Excalibur will accompany me to tell the king!"

"I'm gonna find it!" Arjun yelped, bolting out the door.

"No, I will!" cried the bald boy.

"Wait for me!" shouted another, and another, until all eight were gone, even stink-eyed Emilio.

Dean Rowenna watched them go, her smile tightening, before she followed them out to the courtyard, packed with autumn leaves and swords fallen from the sky, her boys yanking uselessly at the hilts.

They were right, of course.

There *was* no way to find Excalibur.

But she was a witch, after all.

And witches always find a way.

SOPHIE COULDN'T BE sure how she ended up in Foxwood, but she had a pretty good idea.

It was that moment in the Celestium.

After Arthur had revealed the third test, when a thousand Excaliburs stabbed through the night and ripped open the sky. As she fell, two portals appeared: one to Camelot's castle, taking Japeth . . . one to Avalon's lake, taking Agatha and Tedros . . .

Sophie could feel herself wanting to chase Japeth, to kill him and finish the job this time. In a flash, she was pulled towards the Camelot portal. Then her heart jolted, wishing to be with Agatha, and her body swerved towards the Avalon portal. She had a split second to choose who to follow, to wish for where she wanted to go next . . .

Which is how she'd ended up falling into bushes near shirtless lads playing rugby, a second before swords rained down from the midnight sky, sending the boys scattering for their lives.

As Sophie caught her breath in the bushes, Evelyn Sader's dress magically camouflaging her, one might think this is precisely where Sophie had asked the universe to send her— a harem of athletic, teenage males—but it wasn't.

To Sophie's own surprise, she'd forgone her wish to kill Japeth or stay with Agatha and made a third wish instead.

A wish to help Tedros win the last test.

Right then and there, a new portal had opened, and this is where it had sent her.

Foxwood.

Which meant the answer to the last test must be here.

Excalibur was *in* Foxwood.

Except there were swords *everywhere*, she'd realized as she slipped out of the bushes, scanning the blades blanketing the field and streets beyond. A few night owls poked their heads out of windows and, seeing the new landscape, promptly ducked back into their houses. Hiding in the shadows, Sophie grabbed at a few hilts, but they didn't budge. Which they wouldn't, of course, until the true king pulled the true Excalibur.

She had to make sure that king was Tedros.

But there were obstacles. First off, she was a Wanted girl, with Japeth's men surely hunting her. And she was famous in the Woods, with most kingdoms still thinking she was Camelot's queen. The moment she was spotted lurking around, word would get back to the Snake. Plus, there was Foxwood's sheer size, with countless swords alone within its vast borders. To find Excalibur, she'd need help. Manpower she could supervise until there was an inkling of Arthur's grail . . .

That's when she saw where she'd fallen.

A gray castle towered above her, bright gold letters carved into stone.

THE FOXWOOD SCHOOL FOR BOYS

Boys, Sophie thought.

A castle full of them . . .

And weren't some of those boys missing a *Dean*?

SIX DAYS LATER, Sophie roamed the dead grass around Foxwood's vales, drearily inspecting another cluster of swords while her students' voices carried from cottage lanes.

"This one looks suspicious!" Arjun's voice piped. "The hilt is marked!"

"With crow poo, you idiot!" Pierre-Eve yelled.

"Emilio, where you going!" said Arjun. "Headmistress told us not to talk to strangers!"

A good Dean would go check on Emilio, Sophie thought, but she kept walking in the opposite direction of her students. Her eyes glazed over more swords, on and on and on, her fists balling with frustration. Suddenly, she kicked a blade, then kicked it harder, scuffing its steel. She slapped it with a stun spell for good measure, which ricocheted off the handle and knocked her on her rump. Sophie blinked into the murky sky, Lionsmane's message still appealing for the Woods' help.

Clearly, Japeth was having as much luck as she was.

Rafal's son . . .

And to think she'd kissed that demon at their "wedding."

Not by her own volition, but still. A kiss is a kiss.

Wherever in hell he was, Rafal must be laughing.

He'd had his revenge.

For now.

Her time was coming.

But first she had to get off the ground, her body still throbbing as she lumbered to her feet. She was tired of looking at the same sword over and over with no clue what she was looking for. She was tired of babysitting smelly boys and reading them stories where Good always won and eating their ghastly meals, which Dean Brunhilde had made them cook to learn "personal responsibility." She was tired of getting her hopes up every time a student showed her a sword, insisting it was "The One," only to find a bee nest on the hilt or steel sprayed with skunk stench or a blade caught in tumbleweeds. She was tired of disguising herself to be a Dean, tired of Evelyn's dress hiding her beauty, tired of the wart she'd conjured on her nose. Most of all, she was tired of missing Agatha.

"This is *stupid*," she growled out loud as if hoping some cosmic voice would reassure that she'd made the right wish to come here . . . that the sword was indeed close for her to find . . .

A horn blared in the distance.

It was the Headmistress's signal, herding the rest of the Foxwood schoolboys on their hunt for the sword. The horn usually sounded at 1:00 p.m., starting the hunt, and sounded again at 3:00 p.m., to signal the boys back to class. Each day, Sophie spied on their efforts, in case one of them found Excalibur, which would send her dashing off to Avalon to tell Tedros. Not that any of them did, of course—including the boys who'd bought phony "Excalibur Detectors" at the market, the sons of blacksmiths who insisted they'd know a king's sword when they saw one, or the cocky, big-talking lads who claimed to have a drop of Arthurian blood in their veins. Meanwhile, Sophie made it a point to send her own students home for these two hours so she could peek in on the schoolboys undisturbed. (That Foxwood lads tended to be deliriously handsome had nothing to do with it.) Until now, Sophie had also managed to avoid the school's Headmistress, which meant she'd eluded pesky questions about where Dean Brunhilde had gone. But today, the Headmistress's horn had come much earlier than usual. It wasn't even half-past ten.

Sophie knew she should find her group and hide them in the forest until the second horn in case the Headmistress or other meddling boys came this way. But she didn't have the energy to wrangle pesky Arjun or insolent Emilio or hoggish Jorgen, who never used a toilet he didn't miss. Why was it that her story always brought her back to being a steward of dark souls and misanthropes? Was the Storian trying to tell her something? That no matter how she wished her story would go, it would end with her being a Dean *somewhere*? Perhaps that was the original sin: leaving her post as Evil's Dean to marry Rhian. Because if she hadn't left school, if she'd stayed loyal to her Nevers and turned Rhian down, then none of this would have happened. She'd still be stalking the halls of Lady Lesso's old tower and Tedros would be on his throne.

But she didn't *want* to be a Dean anymore, Sophie reminded herself. Not there or here or anywhere else. She didn't want to be like Lesso or Dovey or Brunhilde—

Why?

All were formidable, intelligent, strong. All were leaders she admired, with honor and wisdom and conviction. What else did Sophie want from a life? Why couldn't she be happy as a Dean? What was missing?

Tears stung her eyes, the answer so obvious.

Love.

The first of the holy trinity.

Love. Purpose. Food.

As Dean, she could have Purpose. She could have Food and earthly delights. But like Lesso and Brunhilde and Dovey before her, Sophie would never have Love. For that was the rule, wasn't it? To be a good Dean in this world, you sacrificed all attachments and devoted yourself to your students. It wasn't meant to be a punishment. By the time you became a Dean, you should have had your fun. You were ready to put others' needs before your own, like a mother would for her child.

But Sophie's life had only just begun. She wasn't ready at all. True, she had Agatha, but Agatha had Tedros, who she'd likely marry and then there'd be babies (ick) and then what would become of her? The spinster best friend? The eternal third wheel? She could picture it now: giving baby Tedros a bath and pureeing his green peas while Agatha and Teddy were off at a court ball. At night, she'd hug a pillow as she slept, her substitute for love. But it wasn't being alone that was the problem. Sophie didn't fear loneliness. She'd be perfectly happy in a chateau by herself until the end of her days, feasting on caviar and cucumbers, soaking in milk baths and taking vigorous massages. Indeed, that's what most people would expect from her. Sophie, who answered to no one. Sophie, who'd learned to be happy on her own . . . But there was no surprise in that ending. Nothing that would challenge her or make her grow. Couldn't there be another end? Another chance at Ever After, even if she'd failed all her chances thus far?

As tears and feelings flowed, she looked up to a dark forest. How long had she been walking on her own? Where had she left the boys? Her stomach was gurgling, her forehead clammy. She suddenly felt faint. Was it the lingering effects of her spell that had knocked her on her bum? Or that hellish broccoli quiche the boys made last night? She knew she should turn back before she got too lost, but now she spotted a seed of light through the trees, an opening out of the forest. Perhaps she could find some chickweed or dandelion to appease her stomach . . . Her pulse slowed, her body weaker with every step. The corners of her mind drew in, but she couldn't let herself pass out. Not here, where no one would find her. She struggled between trunks and over tangled twigs, breathing shallower, shallower, before she finally limped out of the forest, stumbling into the light—

Sophie went still.

A sun-soaked wheat field stretched before her, the tall, golden reeds up to her ears. A breeze swept through, bowing the wheat to the ground, revealing dozens of swords glinting between stalks, their Lion-carved hilts shimmering. And in the middle of these swords, bent over, inspecting each one . . .

A boy.

His hair was light brown, his Foxwood school shirt slung over his shoulder, his sweat-drenched chest burly and strong. He sensed Sophie's presence and looked up with big gray eyes.

Sophie's heart thundered. Her head spun.

"Chaddick?" she gasped.

The boy rushed towards her—

But she had already fallen.

"Drink this," the voice ordered.

Sophie pried her eyes open to a blurry silhouette, holding a glass of creamy goo to her lips. She was on a bed, her head propped by pillows, her blouse scattered with wheat. Her temples spasmed, making her gaze squinty and wet. Slowly, the boy came into focus, with thick eyebrows, a commanding nose, and that surly Chaddick mouth. But he was tall. And Chaddick *wasn't* tall. So this couldn't be Chaddick. Her rescuer was someone else entirely, a thought that made Sophie sit up with a kittenish smile . . . only to remember she wasn't Sophie, but Dean Rowenna, with ugly clothes and a fat wart.

"What's in it?" she asked, pointing at the glass.

"Bananas, yogurt, and coconut," the boy replied. "Will get you back on your feet."

Sophie didn't like any of those things, but she sucked it down, ignoring the syrupy taste as her eyes roved the room: a smooth blue mural of a knight fighting a dragon, a closet full of boys' clothes and boots, and the four-post bed she was on now, with stiff navy sheets. "Where am I?"

"My brother's room. Carried you up here," said the boy. "Would have kept you downstairs . . . but it's not habitable at the moment."

"So you knew our brother?" a voice asked.

Sophie turned to a younger boy at the door, with messy ash-blond hair and sad blue eyes. "Cedric said you thought he was Chaddick," he explained, nodding at the older lad.

Cedric smiled. "This is Caleb," he said, shepherding the tiny boy in and hugging him to his side. "Chaddick is our middle brother." His smile tempered. "Was, I mean."

"This is Chaddick's . . . house?" Sophie asked, surprised.

A swaggering, gray-eyed portrait at school came to mind: *Chaddick of Foxwood.*

"That's his bed you're on now," Cedric confirmed, quietly. "Mother wanted to keep the room just as he left it."

Caleb teared up. "Don't even know who killed him."

The Snake, Sophie wanted to say. *Killed him in cold blood. While the Lady of the Lake watched and did nothing to save him.*

"Last we heard, Chaddick was going to be lead knight for Tedros. That was his quest after finishing school," said Cedric. He clenched his teeth, holding down emotion. "Doesn't deserve to be king, that Tedros. A real king protects his knights. Chaddick would tell me to forgive him. To stand behind King Tedros instead of King Rhian. But I'm not as pure-hearted as Chaddick was. That's why he made it into the School for Good."

Another family torn apart by the Snake, Sophie thought. Another fairy tale cut short. "Chaddick was so loyal to Tedros," she said, her eyes on the mural. The knight in the mural looked just like him: dark blond and barrel-chested, chasing fearlessly at dragons. "Charming, courageous in every way. All the girls loved him. Boys too. He was rock solid. The one you could count on."

She glanced back and saw the two boys gazing at her.

"Uh, how did you know Chaddick?" Cedric asked.

Sophie blinked. "From school—" She cleared her throat, sitting straighter. "Foxwood School, I mean. Where I'm a new Dean. Chaddick and I crossed paths once. A fish market in Abu-Abu. Now, if you'll excuse me, I have to get back to my students."

She rushed out of the room, stumbling down the stairs—

Sophie froze.

The bottom floor of the house had been smashed in, shattered blue tiles blanketing the living room. Sophie squinted up at a hole in the blue-tiled roof, sunlight catching the flurries of dust. The source of the roof's hole lay in the center of the room: a Lion-hilted sword, stabbed into a heap of blue, broken stone.

Sophie maneuvered through the wreckage to the front door of the house and pulled it open. Stepping onto the porch, she surveyed the quiet Foxwood streets, scattered with Excaliburs, a few young schoolboys jogging around and inspecting them. Colorful cottages lined the vales, all of them fully intact.

"Unlucky," a voice sighed.

She turned to see Cedric at the door.

"We're the only house that was hit," he said.

A horn sounded in the distance.

Sophie looked up and noticed a woman in a rose-pink turban hustling towards them.

"Caleb! Mother's coming!" Cedric called into the house, before glancing back at Sophie. "Chaddick dies, then a sword hits us . . . Caleb's too afraid to go to school. Mother has to keep checking on him. You said you're a Dean at Foxwood School? Mother will know you, then. She'll be happy we nursed you back to health."

"I better be going. Have to gather my students," Sophie replied quickly, about to take off in the opposite direction—

"Headmistress Gremlaine, I found it!" a young boy hassled the turbaned woman, pointing at a sword. "There's a dead mouse right by it. Must mean something!"

"Horn sounded, Brycin. Head back to school," Headmistress Gremlaine replied crisply, keeping on towards Sophie, who hadn't moved.

"Gremlaine? Chaddick was a Gremlaine?" Sophie asked Cedric. "Like Grisella Gremlaine?"

"Wait. You knew?" Cedric said, wide-eyed. "That Chaddick was Aunt Grisella's son?"

Sophie's heart jumped. "Grisella Gremlaine. Steward to

King Arthur and King Tedros of Camelot? *That* Grisella Gremlaine? She was Chaddick's *mother*?"

"Oh, so you didn't know." Chaddick exhaled. "Caleb and I had no idea either. Mother only told us after Chaddick died. She thought it would make us feel less sad about his death if we knew he wasn't our real brother. Only made it worse, really. No idea why Aunt Grisella didn't raise him herself. But Caleb and I were lucky she didn't. Chaddick was a real brother to us. We loved him so much." His throat quavered. "Um, how do you know my aunt? Haven't heard from her in months—"

Sophie didn't answer. She was watching the woman hustling towards her, with tan skin and sunken cheeks.

Arthur . . .

Rafal . . .

Sader . . .

Gremlaine . . .

Sophie lost her breath.

She knew where Excalibur was.

She knew how Tedros could win.

"Cedric, who's that?" Headmistress Gremlaine called out, shielding her eyes from the sun. "I told you not to talk to strangers!"

Cedric turned to his guest. "Didn't you say you were—"

But Sophie was already running.

Away from the house.

Away from Foxwood.

She surged past the vales where she'd left her students, into the forest, chasing north towards Gillikin, where she could catch a fairy flight to Avalon—

She stopped cold.

"Emilio," she gasped.

The dark-skulled boy sat on a rock, all alone, in the middle of the Woods.

"Been looking for you, Dean Rowenna," he said. "Me and some friends."

"Go back to school," Sophie panted. "I'll be there soon—"

Emilio whistled with his fingers.

Through the columns of trees, shadows appeared, sifting into dappled light.

Lion crests gleamed on their chests.

"Friends of King Rhian, actually," said Emilio. "They wanted to meet you after I wrote them about you."

Emilio stared Sophie down as Camelot soldiers surrounded her.

"You know. Since you're his *cousin*."

27

TEDROS

Ask the Lady

Tedros didn't love teenage Merlin. After trekking two miles through snow, it had been time for another dose of the wizard's aging potion, the span from twelve to thirteen condensed into a single drop. And thirteen-year-old Merlin was as imperious and grandiose as eighty-year-old Merlin but also a moody, pubescent know-it-all, despite seeming to know nothing that could be of use.

"Where are we going, Merlin? The Lady of the Lake already saw us," said Agatha. "Clearly she doesn't want to talk to us, let alone help."

"And she's the only one who can let us out of this place," Tedros added, using his hands and boots to turn more swords to dust, like a game of footie. "We're trapped here, Merlin."

"Glad it was the *witches* who rescued me. You two would have given up at the first gust of wind," Merlin replied, tossing pink lightning and clearing blades just as Tedros reached for another one. "I'm hungry *again*," grumped the wizard boy. "No wonder Hansel and Gretel's parents couldn't keep food on the table. The kids probably ate it all, just like they did that witch's house. Hat! Make me something with cheese!"

"This is ridiculous, Merlin. You have to know where Dad hid Excalibur! It was you who helped August Sader leave clues for the first test!" Tedros said, light fading over the swordfields. "We saw your white stars in the Living Library. You *gave* Sader the stars' magic—"

"Because Professor Sader asked me for it," Merlin snipped, munching on cheese-fried popcorn out of his hat, the boy's scrawny frame snug in his purple suit.

Tedros waited for

him to elaborate, but instead Merlin paused at a sword in the snow. The prince's heart swelled hopefully, only to see the wizard pulling at his face in the blade's reflection. "Wow. Young skin is so elastic."

"And Professor Sader didn't tell you what he wanted your magic *for*?" Agatha said, exasperated.

"Yes, he told me every detail of Arthur's tournament and I just enjoy the deadly consequences of not giving them to you," Merlin huffed, with a loud burp. "Like I said, Arthur kept his second will hidden from me. For good reason. If he'd told me about a tournament to find his heir, I'd have asked why he doubted who his heir was in the first place. Clearly Arthur had secrets to keep. Secrets that Rafal and Evelyn Sader took advantage of."

"What about helping King Arthur see the future?" Agatha prodded. "His will said, '*The future I have seen has many possibilities . . .*'"

"If I could see the future, do you think I would be here, decades younger than I'm supposed to be, battling my own hormones and your fruitless questions, instead of basking on the beaches of Samsara? Because that's where I'd like to spend *my* future." Merlin shoved his hat back on. "Once the work is done."

"When is that?" Tedros asked.

"With you, the work is never done," snapped the wizard child.

That put an end to Tedros' questions.

They waded into an oak glen, between more snow-buried swords, past the twin graves of Tedros' father and Tedros' knight, to the old Wish Fish pond.

"It's frozen over," said Agatha, knocking on the solid surface, the fish obscured by ice.

Tedros rankled. "Merlin, what are we doing here—"

But the young wizard was elbow-deep in his hat, rustling around, before gently extracting a single, perfect strawberry.

He laid it on the ice, seeded dimples catching the last rays of sun.

Tedros and Agatha exchanged glances. Before either could speak, a bony hand stabbed through the ice, snatching the strawberry and drawing it under. Two dark eyes glared through the hole at the boy wizard. Then they widened, recognizing him. Merlin winked. The Lady of the Lake held her stare . . . then vanished beneath, the ice resealing.

The prince and his friends were alone again, swords surrounding them, the snow hard and wet under their knees. Silence misted through the glen.

"So," said Tedros. "That was helpf—"

By the time he finished his sentence, they were someplace else.

A WHITE STONE tunnel.

They'd magically reappeared between cold, cramped walls.

"I know this place. It's her castle," Agatha remembered. "Sophie and I were trapped here once."

Tedros had never been inside the Lady of the Lake's lair.

Neither had Merlin, from the way the boy was probing around the tunnel. The few times Tedros had seen the castle within Avalon's gates, he'd taken note of its smooth white stone, laced with vines of bright green apples, the castle free from any doors or openings. Only the Lady could grant permission to enter. Yet the Lady was nowhere to be found.

"Which way do we go?" said Tedros.

They were at a fork in the passage. Four routes they could take.

"This way," said Merlin, crouching on the floor.

Agatha shined her fingerglow where he was pointing.

Strawberry juice, dripping to the east.

They followed the trail down a maze of damp, chilly corridors, halting at a dead-end wall. Only it wasn't a dead end, Tedros saw now. The wall had been propped open like a hidden door, smoky light spilling through.

Agatha took a deep breath, as if she knew precisely where they'd been led. Tedros and Merlin followed her inside.

The Lady of the Lake was crouched against the wide rim of a cave, opening to a view of Avalon's coast. Swords dotted these snow-soaked shores, the sunset glow of Lionsmane's message reflected in the Savage Sea. The Lady watched the waves, her hands under her chin, her thighs drawn to her chest. White coils of hair matted her skull, her face a shriveled mask.

"Every king or queen who wanted something from me brought me gold and silks and the rarest of jewels. But not you, Merlin. All those years ago. You brought me a strawberry. Me, the Woods' most powerful sorceress, who lives on the dew of the wind."

The young wizard smiled. "Just because you don't need something to live—"

"—doesn't mean it's not worth tasting," the Lady finished, turning to him. "How bold you were. I thought you'd come to set me free. To love me for who I am, instead of what I can give. One kiss was all I asked, a kiss of true love . . . But you too wanted something. You asked that I watch over your young ward who had become king. That I help Arthur if he came to me for protection." She took in the wizard's moppy hair and rosy cheeks. "But now look at you. Younger than even that king was, with your old wisdom intact. However you've managed it . . . I'd make a deal with that devil."

"You already have. The same devil who kissed you and stole your magic," the boy wizard cut back. "He is responsible for what I am now. And you know full well, Nimue." Merlin glared through her. "Any deal made with that devil must be undone."

Nimue. It was the first time Tedros had heard the Lady of the Lake called by a name.

She returned a fake, rotted smile. "I can't undo anything, remember? No magic. A few powers are still left, of course. I am a born sorceress, after all. Until I use my Wizard Wish and take leave of this world. That day is coming . . . 'Til then, I have nothing to help you or anyone else. It's a relief. No more visitors asking to see the future. No princes and wizards lurking in my realm to get something from me."

"That's not why we're here—" Tedros said.

"Liar," the Lady flamed. "You want to find the sword. The sword I made for your father. The sword he left for a king. And you want to know if you *are* that king. Except I cannot tell you, dear prince. The future I showed your father has many possibilities. But only that. Possibilities. The rest is your fate to find out."

Tedros' legs jellied. He could hear Agatha holding her breath. Merlin, too, looked startled.

"Possibilities," said Tedros carefully. "Possibilities *you* showed my father."

The Lady gazed out at the herd of red-orange clouds. "When I looked into your father's eyes, I saw a kindred soul. A soul blessed with great power and yet hungering for real love. At first, I thought he might be the one to set me free. But just as Aladdin saw a genie only as a path to a throne, Arthur saw me only as a means to protect his. But I believed in Arthur's goodness. It's why I gave him Excalibur, so that he could defeat any enemy from the outside. Little did I know the true enemies in Arthur's life would come from within."

She paused, the sun sliding deeper into the sea.

"One evening, after Guinevere and Merlin had deserted him, he came to me, looking nothing like himself. His hair was wild, his eyes frenzied, his breath smelling of drink. He'd made a mistake, he told me. A mistake long ago that he thought had no consequences. But someone had come to his court who'd suggested otherwise . . . a Green Knight who Arthur then killed . . . Even so, Arthur was afraid others might know what the Knight did. That Arthur's secret would come to light and destroy not only him but his kingdom and those he loved. He needed to see what would happen. He needed to see the future, so that he could fend off any harm that might be done . . . He'd already gone to the School for Good and Evil, to his friend August Sader, but a seer like Sader cannot answer questions of what is to come, not without losing decades of life as punishment. Desperate, Arthur went to the School Master too, asking if the famed wizard had a spell or a crystal ball that might reveal the future. The School Master offered no answers and yet seemed amused, Arthur recalled, as if he knew precisely what disturbed the king . . . But then, Arthur noticed the Storian behind the School Master's back. The Storian that was telling King Arthur's tale at the time—a pen that Arthur and his new advisors believed responsible for the downturns in the king's fate. Indeed, Arthur had been considering ousting the Storian and taking its powers for himself as One True King. Except now the enchanted pen was writing something behind the School Master's back . . . something only the king could see . . . *'Ask the Lady.'* By the time the School Master had turned, the words had vanished. Arthur was stunned, of course. The Storian doesn't address the reader. The Storian doesn't jump ahead. And yet, now it had, as if the story was trying to *lead* him . . . So he came to me, just as the Pen told him, asking to see the future. I didn't question the Storian's orders; I knew the Pen did not write out of turn without good reason. I pulled an apple from my breast, greenest of greens, and told the king any question he asked would be answered with a bite. I am not a seer, of course. But the Storian knew my power: to see all the routes a story might take, like an eagle from above . . . Arthur spoke his question out loud: '*Who will have my throne?*' He bit into my apple. The future flashed through his mind. *All* the futures. All the possible answers to his question, like a wizard tree bloomed from a single fruit, his eyes filling with surprise, regret, terror . . . and hope. That is what I remember most. That delicate look in his eyes, two gleaming pearls of hope."

Tedros' throat had gone dry. It was Agatha who managed words first: "You both knew all of this would happen?"

"*Could* happen," the Lady replied. "That's why Arthur made a tournament. That's why I kissed the king I did. Both of us wanted to make sure the *right* king ended up on the throne." Her face clouded, light emptying in the cave. "But the future we saw had other possibilities, too. Futures we each thought we could escape. But that was our biggest mistake. Believing we could choose our fate. Because fate's web is as vast as it is inescapable . . ."

She hunched deeper into her ball.

"Nimue," Merlin spoke, low and urgent, "but surely you know where the real sword is?"

"You *made* Excalibur. It's *your* magic," Tedros pressured.

"You can save Tedros," said Agatha fervently. "You can save all of us."

The Lady of the Lake didn't look at them. High above the snow, her eyes remained on the blades swept over her realm, each a copy of the one she forged for a king long ago. Tears dotted her eyes, her gaunt fingers trembling. Finally, she turned, half-shadowed.

"Why would you come to me? Asking me to save a king? When I failed the first time?"

Tedros didn't understand at first. But then he saw the look on her face. The same look he'd seen inside a crystal ball. It happened that last time they were in Avalon . . . He and Agatha had gone into the Lady's memories. They'd seen the Lady kiss the Snake, as Chaddick lay dead on the shore. Tedros watched the Lady with Japeth, her face blushed with love. But as her and Japeth's lips parted, her eyes gazing into his, her face changed. Love turned to fear, panic, *guilt* as if she knew she'd done something wrong . . .

Sweat trickled down Tedros' back.

The question isn't who helped Arthur see the future, Hort had warned. *The question is whether that person is on your side.*

"You made a mistake," Tedros addressed the Lady. "The king you kissed. You knew it after you kissed him. You knew he wasn't Arthur's blood. I saw it in your face."

Merlin bristled. "This is Nimue we're talking about, not some woeful first year at school. She is Good's most reliable protector. The Woods' greatest sorceress. She wouldn't smell Arthur's blood for nothin—" He swallowed his words. The wizard's young eyes shuddered. "Unless . . ."

Agatha looked right at Merlin, as if she was in his head. "Unless," she said softly.

"Unless what?" Tedros said, glancing between them.

The Lady curled her face into her hands. Outside, rain began to fall in hard, punishing drops, like tears from the sky. Darkness amassed over Avalon, Lionsmane's golden appeal for a sword the only source of light.

"What is it?" Tedros asked Agatha.

She didn't look at him.

"Tell me!" Tedros demanded.

"Two boys." Agatha met his eyes, her voice sick. "There were two boys that day on the shore."

Tedros' heart stopped.

Chaddick.

His knight had tracked the Snake to Avalon. He'd ignored all summons to come home, believing he could kill the Snake on his own. Instead, the Snake had attacked him, trailing his blood across the Lady's realm. Chaddick limped to the Lady's shores, screaming for help, begging her to save him from the Snake . . .

She didn't.

She chose the Snake instead.

The Lady sobbed into her hands. "I smelled Arthur's blood in both boys. But one had an aura of magic, an overwhelming beauty. He promised me love, freedom, everything I wished. Your friend offered me nothing. He wanted only to protect you. The choice was obvious, of course. The beautiful boy was a trap. Your friend was the one to be saved. Except then I remembered the future I'd shown Arthur. All the futures. And in one of those futures, I'd made the wrong choice. I saved the wrong boy, bringing a snake into the Woods. I couldn't let that happen! And yet, I didn't know *which* boy was that snake. An eagle on high has no view to the details, only the possible paths. I had to make a choice. Fears overwhelmed me. Fear of making the wrong choice . . . fear of being tempted by love and yet also giving up my chance at it . . . My heart and head were at war, time against me . . . So I changed course. I chose to save the boy who promised love. Even if it went against my instincts. You understand, don't you? I tried to do the right thing. I tried to avoid the fate we are living now. But in doing so, I only ensured it." She shrank deeper into the shadows. "He took my magic, left me like this . . . It's the punishment I deserved. The true blood of Arthur was dead. He was *dead*. Because of *me*, who was supposed to be his loyal guardian."

"I—I—I don't understand. What does Chaddick have to do with Arthur's blood?" Tedros questioned, his palms wet.

"That's why I haven't used my Wizard Wish," the Lady wept. "Because I couldn't leave this life . . . not until someone knew the truth . . ."

"Chaddick was my knight. My schoolmate," said Tedros. "He had nothing to do with my father—"

"I did what I could to atone. I buried him near Arthur. Where he should be . . ."

"What? You're not making sense—" Tedros fought, his chest throttling.

"Two kings, side by side," the Lady mourned.

Tedros choked, "What are you saying—"

"He's the heir, Tedros."

Agatha's voice hit like a stone.

"Chaddick was your father's heir," said his princess.

Tedros shook his head. "But . . . that's . . . that's not true," he rasped, appealing to Merlin.

The young wizard's gaze was far away. "It's how Rhian

pulled Excalibur, isn't it? Japeth knew Chaddick was Arthur's heir. He must have hidden a drop of Chaddick's blood on Rhian. And Excalibur sensed this blood of Arthur's son, his *eldest* son . . . That's why the sword let Rhian take it from the stone. That's why it denied Tedros all those months before the Snake appeared. Chaddick was still alive then. Tedros *wasn't* the king."

"That age potion's warping your brain," Tedros assailed. "You're talking in riddles—"

But his words trailed off, a memory floating back.

One he'd seen in a crystal of time.

It came from the day Chaddick left to find knights for Tedros' Round Table. Chaddick had stayed at Camelot in the week prior, Lady Gremlaine fussing and doting over him, far more than she ever did over Tedros or Agatha, as if Chaddick were the lord of the castle. While Chaddick readied his horse for the journey, Lady Gremlaine piled him with satchels with food, brushed his gray shirt which she'd had made for him that matched his eyes, a gold *C* on its collar, and again and again, she hovered over him, asking what else he needed. Agatha had remarked that it was only around Chaddick that she'd ever seen Lady Gremlaine smile.

Now Tedros knew why.

He was her son.

Chaddick was Lady Gremlaine's son.

And King Arthur his father.

A secret conceived in Sherwood Forest the night before Arthur married.

A secret Rafal and Evelyn Sader came to know.

Tedros was never Arthur's eldest.

Chaddick was.

The true heir to the throne.

Tedros looked at his hand. The carved silver ring cold on his finger. His voice was a whisper: "Dad gave it to me. Why?"

"For the same reason he made the tournament. He saw the future and all its possibilities," said the Lady. Her tears had ceased. Behind her, the rain abated over Avalon's shores. She turned to Tedros, a light growing in her eyes. "And despite all the darkness in that future, he saw one hope. That hope was *you* becoming king. Not Chaddick. Not anyone else. *You*. Because it's you who were the Lion. Only you who could have had the strength and will to rise out of the ashes of Arthur's mistakes and build a better Woods. It's why Arthur didn't fight death when it came for him. His story was the beginning of yours and your story the completion of his. Father and Son. King and King. Two fates intertwined. The true End of Ends. This was the future Arthur believed in. And he was willing to bet everything on that future." In the glow of Lionsmane's message, she looked at him like a flame against the night. "But now it's your turn, Tedros. You must finish the last test. Excalibur didn't see a king in you before. Will it see one now?"

Tedros walled off his feelings like a knight shielding dragon fire: a blast of rage, horror, shame, all the emotions of his father not being the father he knew, his liege now his brother, the throne he believed so rightfully his not his at all. But in the siege of these feelings, he sensed another wave, light and cool, washing them all away.

Relief.

As if at last he had the answer to what made a king. Not blood. Not birthright. But something deeper: faith. Faith his father had in him. Faith Tedros never had in himself. Until now. Because he was a better man than his father, loyal to his princess, loyal to his heart. Because he'd be a better king, having chosen not the queen who would compensate for his shortcomings, but would love him for them. Because of who he was deep in his soul, rather than what he thought should be. He was free. Finally free. As if in being told he wasn't a king, he found the reason to *be* a king.

His blood burned hot. The veins of his neck throbbed, a roar licking at his throat. He raised his eyes to the Lady.

"I'm ready."

Agatha's hand wrapped around his, the princess at his side. Young Merlin flanked the prince, his hand on his back.

The Lady smiled at Tedros, an inscrutable smile like the Lady of old . . .

Suddenly the glow on her face darkened, like a candle blown out.

She spun to the night sky—

Lionsmane's message.

It was gone.

For a moment, no one seemed to understand.

But the prince did.

His blue eyes knifed the dark.

"He's found it."

~ 28 ~

Beasts and Beauty

Arthur certainly hadn't been subtle about it.

Marking the house with a sword through the roof, like Zeus hurling a thunderbolt.

The house of the true heir to Camelot.

Sophie remembered the first time she ever saw Chaddick of Foxwood, strutting into the Welcoming with the rest of the Everboys, flaunting his swordplay and puffed chest and flirty gray eyes. And yet, all her attentions had gone

to Tedros, even though Chaddick was handsome, charming, capable . . . But Tedros was the prince. Camelot's future king. That's why all the girls wanted Tedros. That's why all the boys wanted to *be* Tedros. What would have happened if they'd known the truth? Where would Chaddick and Tedros be now? Where would *Sophie* be—

The carriage hit a snag and her head thumped the roof. Sophie looked down at her rope-tied hands and the metal cuff around her neck attached to a chain, held by three women sitting opposite, with long gray hair, hawkish eyes, and bare feet snaking out from lavender robes. A single scim hovered in front of Sophie's heart with a fatally sharp tip. Through the window, she could see at least fifty Camelot guards protecting the prisoner's transport, the guards sealed in armor and carrying crossbows, marching with the carriage through the twilit Woods, dappled with copies of Excalibur.

"Is all this really necessary?" Sophie growled.

"You escaped once under our watch," Alpa pointed out. She twisted her fingers and the eel at Sophie's chest pinned closer. "We'll return you to Camelot and seal you in the dungeons until it's time for you to wed the One True King."

"I always wondered how you could control his eels," said Sophie coolly. "Until I realized: you have his blood, too. Rafal's sisters. Japeth's aunts. You have access to his magic. Too bad magic can't save you. Not from what's coming."

She summoned the wickedest grin she could, but the Mistrals saw through it.

"Sent word to the king that you'd been found in Foxwood prowling around a house hit by a sword," Bethna said. "Didn't take long for him to figure out which house it was."

Outside, Sophie could see Lionsmane's message vanished from the sky.

"He's on his way to the Gremlaine place now," said Omeida. "Fitting, isn't it? Tedros once thought Excalibur was his by right. Now it'll lop off his head. But what to do with that head?"

"Auction it to the highest bidder," Bethna proposed.

"Mount it in the king's chamber," Alpa offered.

"Send it to Agatha in a box," said Omeida.

Sophie swallowed her nausea.

"Once Tedros is dead and the last ring in the king's hands, then the wedding will resume," said Alpa. "King Rhian and Queen Sophie, finally united. Queen for a night at least, then a return to the dungeons, where you'll never again see the light of day."

"There'll be no wedding, you hobbit-footed trolls," Sophie snarled. "And with no wedding, there's no One True King. That's the Snake's only path to the Storian's powers. My blood with his. *Me* as his queen. Like his father Rafal needed me. And just like Rafal, he'll never *get* me."

"Don't think you'll have a say in the matter," Alpa replied.

The scim floated up from Sophie's chest to her head, cleaving into two eels, then three, then four, poised to spear into her ears, her mouth, her nose . . .

"This time, we'll use more than two," said Bethna.

The scims rejoined, aiming back at Sophie's heart.

She pursed her lips and returned her focus outside the window, projecting an unruffled calm. But inside, her bones had gone cold. Japeth was on his way to Chaddick's house to win the third test. Tedros was in Avalon with Agatha, likely without a clue where the sword was. Sophie was their only hope—and yet here she was, back in the hands of her old captors. *Think, Sophie.* She was trapped in a carriage at scim-point, walled in by soldiers, outnumbered a hundred to one. But every fairy tale had a moment like this, with Good beaten by Evil . . . until Good found a way to escape by the grace of true love. But Sophie wasn't Good. And no one was coming to save her, because she didn't *have* a true love. She peeked at her dress, praying that it might help, the way it had so many times, but it shrank from the scim, as if Evelyn's spirit was on her son's side.

So why had it helped Sophie before?

She thought about the moments the dress had come to her rescue: breaking her out of Camelot, hiding her in the Woods, thwarting the Empress's geese . . . all times when the Snake was far away. Then she thought about the instances the dress failed her: when the Snake killed the Sheriff or when the Snake attacked her in the wizard tree or now, when a scim held her hostage . . . all times when the Snake or his eels were near.

In a flash, Sophie understood.

Evelyn's dress only helped her when it wouldn't get caught.

Because Evelyn's spirit was afraid of her son.

This son.

Back when Rhian was king, Evelyn's dress was a loyal henchman, binding Sophie like a puppet. Because Evelyn loved Rhian. She wanted Rhian to become the One True King, even if it meant him marrying Sophie—the bride of Evelyn's once true love, the girl responsible for Evelyn's death. Because with Rhian as king, Evelyn knew she would get a second chance at life. She trusted her son to bring her back.

Rhian.

Not Japeth.

Which is why the moment Japeth *killed* Rhian . . . the dress's allegiance changed. Evelyn knew what Japeth was. She knew what he'd done to his brother. He had to be punished. But Japeth couldn't get a sniff of what she was up to. So his mother's ghost took her time. Slowly, carefully, the dress began helping his bride, each time out of the Snake's sight, until the time came at last when Sophie could see that Japeth's mother wasn't loyal to Japeth. She was loyal to the girl trying to kill him.

The dress's white folds softened, caressing her like rose petals . . . before the eel sensed something afoot and pierced into the silk, grazing Sophie's skin. Instantly, the dress stiffened like a straitjacket, afraid for its own preservation.

Loyalty could only go so far, it seemed.

For now, Sophie was on her own.

They rolled deeper into the Woods, past the evergreen

edges of the Stymph Forest, into the autumn hues of Camelot's wood, the king's castle only a few miles away. Dusk thickened, embers of sun widening to dark shadows around the hilts of buried blades. Trees began to tremble, the scufflings of metal echoing to the east. Through the window, Sophie glimpsed a thousand men riding past on horseback, outfitted with red-and-black helmets, armed with Camelot swords and shields . . . followed by another battalion, seven-foot nymphs with colorful hair, floating over the ground in neat lines, also with Camelot weapons.

"Fleets from Akgul and Rainbow Gale," said Alpa. "On their way to Foxwood."

"Camelot offered free arms to kingdoms that help the Lion win the third test," said Bethna. "They'll keep guard over the king while he's in Foxwood—"

"—in case Tedros tries to get anywhere *near* the sword," said Omeida.

More armies followed, silhouettes gliding across the trees: the red-horned goblins of Ravenbow . . . the giantesses of Gillikin with clouds of fairies in their hair . . . the blue-jacketed soldiers of Pifflepaff, wearing blue masks . . .

The air went out of Sophie's chest.

Even if she could get out of this carriage, she'd never find her way to Avalon, track down Tedros, and somehow sneak him a hundred miles into Foxwood, let alone into Chaddick's house before Japeth got there. Not with this many men out to kill him. There would be no rescue for the prince. Or for her.

Then she noticed one of the Pifflepaff soldiers.

He was glaring at her through his blue mask, his eyes sparkling in the dark. A tiny blue glow lit up his finger. Then he breathed out a trail of smoke towards Sophie's carriage.

Sophie spun back to the soldier but the carriage had already veered to the west, into the heart of Camelot's forest.

Sophie held still as treetops blacked out the sky, the Mistrals watching her in the window reflection. Outside, Camelot guards faded to inky outlines. She'd sung a thousand songs in her life, songs of love, but those had come to nothing and she couldn't remember a one . . . No time to think. Sing! Sing something—

"I'm Whisky Woo, the pirate queen!"

Not that.

A new tuft of smoke appeared out the window.

LOUDER

"I'm Whiskey Woo, the pirate queen!" she belted again.

"Stop it," Alpha snapped.

"Whiskey Woo! Whiskey Woo!" Sophie crooned at a hellish pitch. *"I'm Whiskey Woo, the pirate queen! Not yet eighteen, but still damn mean!"*

"Enough!" Bethna barked.

"I'm Whiskey Woo, the pirate queen! Formerly known as Evil's Dean!"

She yowled so loudly the carriage seemed to shake, her voice drowning out a strange rustling outside. *"I'm Whiskey Woo, the pirate queen! No autographs please, don't make a scene!"*

"We said *stop*!" Omeida twisted her hand, the scim puncturing Sophie's skin.

But she kept warbling, the carriage jostling to more muffled sounds in the forest while the scim cut Sophie deeper, her song exploding to a wail of pain: *"Whiskey Woo! Whiskey Woo—"*

The carriage stalled violently, launching Sophie and the Mistrals at each other, the eel crushed between Alpa's and Bethna's colliding skulls, leaving sisters and prisoner in a heap on the floor.

Outside, the forest was silent, the carriage unmoving.

The Mistrals gaped in confusion. Then they threw open the door, stumbling out, dragging Sophie with them.

A slew of guards were on the ground, faces slashed, helmets crushed, knocked out cold. She'd seen this kind of carnage before, Sophie thought . . . Then she spotted the rest of the guards huddled around the carriage, eyes haunted through their helmets, swords and crossbows pointed wildly in the dark at whatever had just attacked them. The Mistrals, too, scanned the night, gripping their prisoner by her chain, Sophie's singing having distracted them from the force that just eviscerated half their guards.

One thing was for sure.

Whoever did this was angry.

Very angry.

Sophie smiled to herself.

She had that effect on men.

From the trees came a snarling mass of teeth and fur, crashing down onto the carriage and shattering it to splinters, before sweeping Sophie into its claws, grabbing hold of the nearest branch, and swinging limb by limb into the black mass of trees.

She relaxed into the beast's chest as he flew through the forest, his paw manhandling the cuff around her neck and busting it free.

"My prince," she sighed. "Only hairier."

"You like me like this, don't you."

"If only you didn't smell like wet dog."

"If only you didn't keep putting yourself into trouble, making me sweat *after* you like a dog."

"Me without trouble is like you without . . ."

"You?"

"I am a *lone* wolf, thank you."

"A lone wolf who has to keep getting rescued."

"Are you saying I can't take care of myself?"

"I'm saying that letting me take care of you *is* taking care of yourself."

"Oh, darling. When you shrink back into a wee little weasel without your clothes on, we're going to pretend we never had this conversation."

His snout brushed her ear: "Beauty and the Beast. That had a happy ending, didn't it?"

"Depends on if you think a girl kissing a beast is a happy ending. I don't."

"I'm half-tempted to drop you right no—"

An arrow impaled his thigh.

He yelled with pain, as Sophie swiveled to see Camelot guards rush in, crossbows raised, along with blue-masked Pifflepaff soldiers firing arrows of their own. An arrow struck the man-wolf's ribs, then his shoulder, his eyes numb with terror. More arrows speared for their tree—

Sophie thrust her lit finger and turned them to flowers—razor-toothed, man-eating flowers—raining them like piranhas over the screaming soldiers. She whirled back, but the wolf was drenched in blood, his paw weakening on the tree.

"We need to get down," Sophie ordered, her cheek against his. "Put your arm around me. We'll go together."

He shook his head, saying nothing.

"Please," Sophie begged. "We need to find help."

He looked at her, a scared boy in a man-wolf's body. "I love you, Sophie," he breathed. "I love everything about you. Even the terrible parts of you. They're as beautiful as the good parts. I knew from the moment I met you that I couldn't love anyone else. Not like I love you. I tried, Sophie. I tried to let you go. But love doesn't give you that choice. Not real love. At least you'll know now. That your story had a happy ending all along. That you had true love. Always."

Tears flooded Sophie's face, stained with his blood. "Don't talk like that. You're my Beast. And that story has a happy ending, just like you said. We'll find a way. Stay here. With me. Don't let me go, okay? Don't give up on me."

But life was already fading from his eyes. In their reflection, she saw more guards swarming, hundreds of them, arrows and swords raised—

A sea of white clobbered them, like snow sweeping a field, dragging the shrieking armies under. *I'm seeing things*, Sophie thought. Phantom swans come to save her and her beast. But as the white wave swept closer, surrounding her tree, she saw they weren't swans at all.

Goats.

Scores of them, led by an old, gray-whiskered librarian from the School for Good and Evil. Sophie smiled down at this flock of heaven-sent angels . . . then looked back at her wolf to see his eyes closed, his body collapsing against a branch, his claw losing grip—

"No!" Sophie cried.

He let her go, Sophie reaching for him as she fell, gasping his name like a love song, *Hort, Hort, Hort*, until she felt the hug of soft white fur, nothing like the beast's she left behind.

SOMETHING WARM AND cuddly nuzzled her cheek.

"Hort?" she whispered, stirring from sleep.

Her eyes quivered open to a bath of sunlight and a big pink udder pressed against her face. She was stuck to the underside of a goat, her chest against the animal's fat belly, her face jammed near its backside. Sophie was about to unleash a scream . . .

. . . until she saw two more goats jogging behind hers in the middle of a crowded market, Willam and Bogden clinging to their stomachs.

Both boys put fingers to lips, telling her to stay quiet.

For a moment, Sophie didn't understand how she was beneath the goat, until she realized it was her dress's doing, magically adhering to the animal's paunch. Craning her neck, Sophie spotted more goats ahead, a green-hooded shepherd leading the flock through hectic stalls, fragrant with pome-granates and peaches, sandalwood and rose oil, cinnamon and cardamom spice. Villagers in expensive coats bustled between copies of Excalibur, too concerned with their shopping to pay much notice, while the alleys of the market were crammed with grimy peasants who used Arthur's swords as tentpoles for their shanty houses.

Sophie knew this route.

They were in Maker's Market, the main thoroughfare of Camelot City. Sophie's dress hugged her tighter against the goat, camouflaging her to the animal's peach-cream skin. Soon they were out of the market, crowds receding, as the shepherd led the goats up the path towards the king's castle.

Sophie swiveled to the boys: "Where's Hort? What's

happening! We need to go to Foxwood—"

Bogden was holding his nose as his goat pooped. "Tell her, Will."

His redheaded friend prattled quickly: "While you were in Shazabah, Bogs and I came to Camelot. That's what Tedros told us to do: come see my old priest, who I used to altar boy for, in case he could help us. Then Hort comes from Shazabah with two old goats he found along the way—librarians, actually; one from school, one from the Living Library—who know Pospisil and wanted to help find Excalibur. But then we hear you *found* the sword in Foxwood and were being taken prisoner to Camelot's dungeons. Hort freaks out and insists we rescue you. Luckily, the goats had friends. So Hort tracks you down and tells us to wait in Camelot forest with the goats until we hear the signal."

"What was the signal?" Sophie asked.

"Really bad singing," said Bogden.

Sophie reddened. "But where is he, then—"

"Hort told us no matter what happened, Bogs and I had to get you out the moment we found you. That *you* were the mission. He'd find us at the meeting spot later," said Willam.

Bogden saw the panic in Sophie's face. "He's *Hort*. Nothing bad can happen to Hort."

"He'll be at the meeting spot," Willam assured. "Then we'll all go help Tedros together."

Sophie swallowed a sick feeling. These boys were young and in love. They believed in Ever Afters. They believed in the rules. But the world had changed. Rules didn't mean anything now or else Lesso, Dovey, and Robin Hood would still be alive. In this story, bad things happened to good people. And something bad had happened to Hort. But Sophie couldn't stop believing. Not yet. Hort always kept his promises. And if he told them he'd be at the meeting point, then he'd find a way.

"You said we're going to the meeting place." Sophie looked at the boys. "Why would the meeting place be the Snake's *castle*—"

Except now the goat herd was veering east, away from the castle and down a road that Sophie knew well.

The church.

But that couldn't be the meeting place either. Because ahead, she glimpsed the spire of Camelot's chapel, two armed guards blocking the entrance, the door barricaded.

"Japeth is keeping the priest locked up. My old chaplain, Pospisil," Willam whispered to Sophie. "Snake didn't trust him after that speech he gave at your Blessing."

Sophie remembered it well. The priest had known her marriage to the king was a sham. Pospisil had used his speech to warn that in the war between Man and Pen, the Pen would always win: "*In time, the truth will be written, no matter how many lies someone might tell to obscure it. And the truth comes with an army.*"

But the truth also came with consequences: the priest was now a prisoner in his own church. Another friend to Tedros dealt with.

The men in front of the chapel pried open their helmets, revealing greasy faces, as the shepherd led his goats past, the guards' eyes flicking over them with disinterest.

"Most action we've got," the first guard grouched.

"Cheer up. On dungeon duty next, ain't we?" said the second. "Ya know, once Sophie's innit."

The first guard flashed a sordid grin. "Shame we gotta keep 'er alive 'til the weddin'."

"Accidents happen," the second quipped.

Sophie memorized their faces.

One day she'd come back for them.

Onwards the goats trotted, winding past the church, past farm fields, towards the Camelot stables. A few muddy hogs poked heads through a pen, watching. Ahead, the doors to the chicken coop were open, a gaggle of confused hens fleeing into the sun. There were some dead ones too, heads removed, as if one of the hogs had escaped. (*And they say pigs are vegetarians!* Sophie thought.) The shepherd led his goats into the coop, Sophie and the two boys sliding in last, before the shepherd shut the doors and barred them with a stick. Darkness settled, rich with the scent of overworked goats and a few last chickens, squawking shrilly, then going quiet.

"What now?" Sophie whispered.

Somewhere a flame ignited, spraying the coop with light.

Willam and Bogden dropped from their goats' bellies, the boys shaking off cramped hands and legs, while Sophie's dress released her to the pebbly floor. She stood up and saw the shepherd, hood pulled low, holding a torch.

"There is a reason goats take a shine to me," spoke a dry, wheezy voice.

The shepherd pulled back the hood.

"Because I am an old goat myself," Pospisil chuckled.

Sophie's eyes widened at Camelot's perilously ancient, red-nosed priest. "But those guards . . . how did you—"

Pospisil waved his arms over the goats. "Well done, my little kiddies! Shall we do a roll call? Bossman! Ajax! Valhalla! The rest of you! Call out your names and be accounted for!"

Sophie held in a groan. Just her luck. The one adult to help and he was a senile crackpot—

Thumps echoed around the room.

Bodies dropping to the floor.

That's when Sophie realized.

It wasn't just a few goats hiding passengers.

It was all of them.

⌁⌁⌁

"FIRST OF ALL, it's Bossam, not Bossman," said a hairy, three-eyed Neverboy.

"I'm *Valentina*, not Valhalla. And this is *Aja*," said a thin-browed Nevergirl.

"Ajax sounds like a gorilla name," sniffed a waifish Never-boy with flame-red hair.

Sophie glimpsed two old goats giggling in the corner—one the librarian from school, the other name-tagged GOLEM—as if they found their priest friend's ineptitude with names an inside joke. Sophie did the mental roll call herself: Valentina, Aja, Priyanka, Bossam, Laithan, Bodhi, Devan, Laralisa,

Ravan, Vex, Brone, Mona, Willam, Bogden—

"Hort?" Pospisil called. "Where's Hort?"

Sophie looked around the crowded coop, packed with friends and first years, many that she used to teach.

But no Hort.

"He was our leader," Laithan worried. "What do we do now? How do we help Tedros?"

All eyes shifted to Sophie.

But she was still watching the door, hoping Hort would walk through.

Her mind went to him in the tree, shot through with arrows—

She steeled her heart. She couldn't let herself go there. He was alive. Hort was still alive.

"Where did you come from?" Sophie asked her charges. She turned to the priest. "How did you escape the church?"

"Any priest knows not to rely on the good graces of a king," Pospisil replied. "The church has had secret escape routes since its beginnings. Luckily, Willam paid attention in his altar boy lessons and knew where to find me. Together, with Hort and my old goat friends, we made a plan."

"As for us, Princess Uma came to school after she escaped Shazabah," Ravan answered. "She heard from her animal friends that you'd been captured. Teachers can't interfere in a story, so Manley and Anemone sent us to rescue you—"

"—and we ran into Hort in the Woods," finished pointy-eared Vex.

"What about the Knights of Eleven?" Sophie pushed.

Valentina waved her off. "Listen, Señora Sophie, the *serpiente* is on his way to Foxwood to win the third test. Princesa Uma's animal friends will try to slow him down, but it's only a matter of time before he gets to Excalibur and then *pew, pew, pew!*, we're all dead and buried under the guanabana tree. So you need to lead us, like Hort once did. We are your army, like we were his. Ever and Never. Smart and talented and *elegante*. Most of us, at least." She gave Aja a darting frown. "We'll do anything you ask, Señora Sophie. What can we do to help Tedros win?"

This is where Sophie shined. Taking command. Hatching schemes. And yet, all she could think about was Hort. His eyes closing. His paw letting go.

She shook her head. "Japeth has thousands of men, armies from Good and Evil, plus the King of Foxwood on his side. And the boys who live in the house where the sword is, Cedric and Caleb, both support the Lion . . . Japeth will walk right in . . ." She looked to Pospisil, the embers of his torch popping loudly, lighting him up and his goat friends, but they all seemed at a loss, as if they'd gotten Sophie as far as they could. Sophie appealed to her dress, but it, too, had no answers. "There's no move for us to make. Not with the whole Woods on his side."

"This is ridiculous. You're *Sophie*, grand high witch *queen*," Aja puffed, hands on hips. "You led a school of Nevers in a glam revolution. You won the Circus of Talents and invented the No Ball. You killed Rafal, kissed Tedros as a boy *and* girl, turned the School Master's tower into your own personal hotel, and you looked like a boss witch doing all of it. You don't make excuses. You don't give up. You always find a way. That's what *makes* you Sophie."

Sophie gazed at Aja, at Valentina, at all the students looking up to her, like she was still their Dean, Evil's mistress of mischief and manipulation. But she wasn't any of that now. She was just a girl. A girl who'd finally opened herself to love, real love, right when it was too late. "Tedros is the one who has to pull the sword. And he's far away," she said, trying to swallow the lump in her throat. "He and Aggie don't even know where the sword is . . ."

The embers off the priest's torch were popping louder, snapping at Sophie's words. Suddenly, more and more spewed off the flame, as if the entire fire was breaking apart. For a split second, Sophie thought the whole coop might go up in smoke, but then she noticed the embers hanging strangely in the air, as if they had a life of their own, little pearls of amber buzzing and glittering about like . . .

Fireflies.

Instantly, the glowing bugs swarmed into a glowing orange matrix like they once had in Gnomeland. On this magic screen, Sophie glimpsed grainy footage of Tedros and Agatha in a snowfield, riding some kind of humped creature, away from Avalon's castle. Then Sophie saw Agatha staring at her, eyes flaring, as if she could see her friend in her own fireflies.

"Sophie? Is that you?"

"Aggie!" Sophie gasped. "I found the sword—"

"Chaddick's house," Tedros cut in.

"Y-y-yes!" Sophie said, startled. "How did you—"

Tedros thrust his face into close-up. "Meet us at Snow White's cottage. In Foxwood. Hurry!"

"No! Foxwood's a death trap!" Sophie said as the screen flickered, the connection severing. "There's armies! Thousands of men! You can't go!" But the fireflies had dimmed, her friends gone. "No! I can't lose you too!" she cried. All the fear and dread she'd been holding back broke through. Grief poured out of her, her face in her hands, her chest heaving. "He's dead. I know he's dead . . . I tried to save him . . . I did everything I could . . . But he let me go . . . I told him not to let go . . ." She sobbed so hard, her whole body shook. "They can't go to Foxwood . . . Please . . . I can't lose anyone else . . . Not after him . . ." Then slowly her sobs softened. "Only I will lose them, won't I?" Sophie lifted her head, her cheeks wet. "Letting the Snake win means we all lose. It means everything Hort did to save me was for nothing. That's what Hort would tell me. To be brave for him. To finish his work." She sat taller, wiping her eyes. "But how? Aggie and Teddy will be dead the second they come near Foxwood. Unless there's a way into the kingdom . . . a way to *get* them in . . ."

"Same way I got into all these chickens, of course," a droll voice replied.

Sophie turned to the corner.

The two librarian goats parted, revealing a bald, wrinkled cat, pawing at a pile of bird heads.

"I acted like their *friend*," he said.

Fireflies settled into a crown over his ears.

"Witch of Woods Beyond," the cat greeted, yellow eyes twinkling.

"King Teapea," Sophie breathed.

She held the thought of Hort close to her heart.

This time, there were no tears.

Instead, her eyes twinkled right back.

29

Chateau Sugar East

She'd never seen that kind of pain in Sophie's eyes. Not in Gavaldon, not at school, not in the years that followed.

Something had happened to Sophie in their time apart. Something that changed her.

And yet, Sophie was still alive.

Not just alive, but with an army.

She'd found Excalibur too.

Just like Agatha and her prince had.

Of course she did, Agatha thought.

She expected nothing less of her best friend.

As if *The Tale of Sophie and Agatha* had never really ended, the Pen still writing their fates with inextricable symphony, even when they were apart, harmony and melody to the same score—

A gob of snow slapped her in the face.

The giant black rat bounded across the Frostplains, weaving between swords, kicking up icy snow, forcing Agatha to hold tighter to Tedros' waist and duck behind his back like a shield. Her prince gripped the leash around the rat's neck, absorbing a stinging spray of cold as he kicked the rat's flank, driving it faster. On a second rat behind them, Anadil and Hester rode with Merlin, the boy wizard puking over the side as Anadil's rat pulled next to Tedros.

"It's because you ate all that junk from your hat," the prince chided.

"You're . . . not . . . my . . . dad," Merlin wheezed, before retching again.

"This is why I don't like boys," Hester growled. "Can't go through puberty without making a mess of it."

"To be fair, you don't like boys for a lot of other reasons," said Anadil.

"How'd you find us?" Agatha asked the witches.

Hester nodded up at her demon, high in the blue night sky, scouting the landscape for danger. "After Shazabah, I told him to fly over the Woods and look for you two."

"Told her not to do it. If her demon dies, *she* dies," Anadil said sourly.

"Found them, didn't he? And when he did, I felt it, just like you felt your rats nearby before we found them in the Woods. A little worse for wear, maybe," said Hester, stroking the bald patches on the rat's fur where it had been hit by camel fire, "but aren't we all." She turned to Agatha. "And you're sure the sword's at Chaddick's house?"

"Has to be," said Tedros, almost to himself, still thinking about what happened in the Lady's cave. "Only place that makes sense."

"And Sophie confirmed it," Agatha said to the witches, who seemed unsettled by everything she and Tedros had told them after they retrieved their friends from Avalon.

"Chaddick, the King," said Anadil softly. "Doesn't seem right, does it?"

"Which is why Chaddick never *became* king," Hester surmised. "Storian finds a way of making things right, even if its way of doing it feels all wrong."

Witches and Agatha looked to Tedros, gauging his emotions, but the prince kept his eyes on the icy path.

"Are we . . . there . . . yet?" Merlin rasped—

He puked again, waking a cluster of fireflies in the rat's fur. They flickered slightly, then went back to sleep, exhausted from the journey and helping Agatha see Sophie.

"Gnomeland fireflies . . . There must be some with Sophie too . . . That's how she saw us . . . ," Tedros said, glancing at Agatha. "Which means the gnomes know where she is . . ."

She caught on to his thinking.

Reaper.

Her cat was *king* of the gnomes.

The wind picked up, the rats grunting loudly, laboring against it. "Sophie found the sword. Which means she knows where Chaddick's house is, while I don't have a clue," Tedros called to Hester. "Told her to meet us at Snow White's cottage in Foxwood. First place I thought of. Been deserted since Rafal's zombies killed the dwarves. If Sophie knows where Chaddick lived, she can take us there."

Agatha saw Hester and Anadil eyeing each other. "What is it?"

"Japeth must know the sword's in Foxwood," said Anadil. "That's why Lionsmane's message disappeared."

"These rats are as fast as his horses," Tedros started—

"Japeth's only one of your problems," Hester cut off. "The entire Woods is sending armies to protect him until he wins the third test. We saw them on the move. Right after Lionsmane's message vanished. Which means if the sword's at Chaddick's house, then there's thousands of soldiers heading there too."

"Which means getting you anywhere *near* Foxwood will be . . . a challenge," said Anadil.

Agatha thought of Sophie last's words over the firefly broadcast: *"No! Foxwood's a death trap!"*

She could feel Tedros' muscles steel under her arms. "Whatever is waiting for us, I'll handle it," he said soundly.

Agatha didn't argue.

Which was . . . strange.

She was so used to being afraid for her prince, a fear that made her meddle with his quests and strain to protect him.

But something had changed in Tedros ever since he'd heard the Lady's story. His old doubts had vanished, replaced with a sureness of mission. Agatha trusted him now. Because he trusted himself. Over his shoulder, she could see the heat in his stubbled cheek, the crystal blue of his eye. His chest was proud and full, his golden curls wild in the wind. Agatha stayed silent, letting him be, the same way she'd stayed back as he'd said goodbye to the Lady at the shore of her lake. Agatha had watched their silhouettes, Tedros' strong and straight, the Lady's shrunken and cowed, the prince whispering to her, before the Lady's expression suddenly changed. Something Tedros said had broken through, the darkness and pain in her beginning to lift. Behind them, her frozen lake thawed. From its silver waters the Lady drew an apple, greenest of greens, and bestowed it on the prince as a gift. It would have no magic, Agatha thought, for the sorceress's powers were lost. But Tedros didn't seem to care. He kissed her on the cheek, his own gift of forgiveness for the Lady's mistakes. Gone was the anger, the secrets, all washed away. This would be the last time they'd see each other. That Agatha knew for sure. The Lady was at peace now. Her days soon over, by her own wish. But Tedros still had more days to fight for. A fight that had an uncertain end. Agatha held him tighter, hand on his chest, the apple there in the lining of his coat, firm against her prince's heart.

"Let's share it," she said. "The apple, I mean. We haven't had anything to eat since Shazabah."

Tedros pulled her hand away and kissed it.

"Where's Dot?" he asked the witches.

"Her mother took her to a witch doctor in Sherwood Forest to try and de-age her," said Hester.

"Dot's mother knows Sherwood Forest well," Anadil quipped.

Agatha gave them a surprised look and Hester winked back. They'd figured it out too.

"Her *mother*?" Tedros said, eyes still ahead. "Who's Dot's mother?"

"Don't worry. Not yours," Merlin croaked, finally righting himself.

Tedros' head swung to the wizard boy. For a second, Agatha thought the prince might beat him up. Then Tedros burst out laughing. "Same old Merlin . . ."

Night deepened, the sky bruising black. Still, the rats carried on, their eyes glowing in the dark, Merlin clearing swords in front of them with strikes of pink lightning, growing bigger and stronger as the young wizard gained control. Soon light cut over the iceplains with angry whipcracks, lashing out in every direction, a teenager's chaos given full outlet to bloom, sending the ashes of Arthur's game up in pink smoke. Then, all at once, trees encroached around them, closer, closer, trapping them in the darkness of a forest. Movement rustled in the branches, the glint of white bones and hollow eye sockets, leering down at the trespassers, before the birds reared back, letting them pass. Here in the Stymph Forest, there would be no enemy forces, since it was school territory and no one trespassed near the School for Good and Evil without consequences. (Rafal's zombies and Rhian's pirates learned that lesson harshly.) Even now, it was the only part of the Woods untouched by phantom swords, as if Arthur too had known the school was beyond his power, equal and separate to Camelot. Hester's demon returned to her neck, its job done, as the rats hurtled faster down swordless paths. Tedros' rat pulled ahead, leaving the witches and Merlin behind. His pace was so smooth, Tedros' back so warm and taut against Agatha's breast, that her eyelids grew heavy. When her prince spoke at last, she wasn't sure if she was dreaming.

"Agatha, when we get to Foxwood, I need you to make me a promise."

"Mmm?"

"If anything happens to me, don't mourn for me."

Now she was awake. "Tedros—"

"Listen to me. You're to go on. You're to keep fighting. You're to do what needs to be done. Don't let what happens to me stop us from getting to The End. I'm with you in life and death."

"I won't let anything happen to you."

"Promise me you'll keep going. Promise me you'll fight on."

"Tedros, you and I . . . we're one. Whatever happens to you happens to me—"

"*Promise* me, Agatha." He gripped her thigh. "Please."

There was such clarity in his voice, as if they couldn't go further without her vow. How could she tell him she would never agree to such a thing? That his death would be her own? But he'd left no room for her feelings. This was the king commanding something of his princess. For the sake of his kingdom. For the greater Good. And Goodness was sacred to

Agatha, even more than love.

"I promise," said Agatha.

Tedros exhaled, his shoulders easing, as if her words had unchained him.

"Will you make the same promise?" Agatha asked. "If something happens to me?"

But now the second rat was catching up, Merlin and the witches snapping at each other.

"You couldn't have found a useful aging potion? Something that doesn't work at a *glacial* pace?" the wizard boy was saying. "You could have gone to any witch—"

"This was my mother's recipe and she *was* a witch," Hester retorted. "Teachers at school didn't have anything better."

"Then use a *library*," Merlin bit back. "There's a thousand aging potions more effective than this one. The old me could recite them in my sleep!"

"Then make one yourself!" Anadil scolded.

"Your potion is so worthless I can't remember my spells!"

"And here I thought you'd be grateful to us for everything we've done for you," Hester griped, like an aggrieved parent.

"If it wasn't for us, you'd still be a baby in a cave instead of here picking fights and harassing us with your mood swings," Anadil piled on.

The wizard boy groaned. "This is insufferable, being ganged up on by two girls who have no interest beside each other's loyalty."

"That's what a good girlfriend does," Hester trumped.

"Oh, I'm your girlfriend now?" Anadil said, peeking back

at her. "Shouldn't that warrant some conversation?"

"Girl friend. Two words," said Hester.

"That's not what it sounded like," said Anadil.

"God, please let me not be a teenager much longer," Merlin begged.

"You want me to say 'I love you' like all the Everboys?" Hester baited Anadil.

"Say it like that and I'll cut your throat," Anadil spat.

Agatha could hear Tedros chuckling, the seriousness of the promise between them passed, her own question to him forgotten. She knew not to press the point. The witches' voices faded as the rats diverged onto separate paths around a patch of trees, leaving Agatha and her prince alone.

"I can hear you thinking back there," Tedros teased.

"Oh, just about all the different kinds of love," said Agatha.

"You mean, like what happens if Hester and Anadil get married? Does it end in a massacre instead of a dance?"

"Only of closed-minded princes."

"I've kissed boys, turned into a girl, and am marrying *you*. No one can say I'm closed-minded."

"Funny, isn't it? So many ways to love," Agatha said wistfully. "You and me, me and Sophie, you and . . . Filip."

"I am ashamed of nothing. Other than who Filip turned out to *be*."

"Sophie did make a beautiful boy."

"No argument. But what good is beauty when it's based on a lie?"

"Sometimes your whole *world* seems like a lie."

"What do you mean?"

"Just that nothing is as it seems here. I always have the story wrong, right when I think I've figured it out."

"It wasn't the same in the Reader realm?"

"Here, anything is possible. In real life, people are afraid of what they can't understand." Agatha thought of her mother, Callis, hunted by those who thought her a witch. "That's why only children read fairy tales where I come from. At some point, people become afraid of life's mysteries. With age, their lives get smaller and smaller. They judge with their fears instead of their hearts. In your world, not everyone can have a happy ending. The Pen won't allow it. But in my world, every Man thinks they deserve one. They turn on each other when things go wrong. They try to beat back the hand of fate. And when they can't . . . that's when Evil is born. Real Evil. The kind that killed my mother."

"Sounds like Japeth would fit right in there," said Tedros.

Agatha held the thought in her head. "Tedros?" She looked up at her prince. "What if Japeth cheats? What if he has Chaddick's blood hidden on him like Rhian did? What if Excalibur thinks *he's* the heir?"

Tedros smiled back at her. "I'm counting on it."

Agatha had no idea what he meant, but the pureness of his gaze preempted any questions, as if for once, her prince was well ahead of her. The forest opened up into a field of willow trees with silver, shimmering leaves, like Christmas tinsel, the glow of dawn pressing against the dark. Agatha looked back to see the second rat lag out of the Stymph Forest, well behind theirs. Hunger stirred in Agatha's stomach, with no time to stop and Merlin's hat out of reach.

"Do you think Chaddick would have made a good king?" Tedros asked.

"No, not really," said Agatha. "He would always look to you."

"You're just being nice."

"Too hungry for that. Chaddick was a born knight."

"A *loyal* knight," said Tedros.

He paused, thinking about his friend and liege.

"But not meant to lead," he admitted.

The prince and his princess fell quiet.

Agatha kissed the back of his neck. "Can I eat your apple?"

Tedros sighed. "Think I'm going to hang on to it a little while longer."

He sounded far away, Agatha's head suddenly heavy and slow. Sleep assailed her, stronger than before, a strange powerless feeling she knew. She looked up at the willow trees, shedding silvery leaves over her like stars . . . *Sleeping Willows* . . . She grabbed at Tedros' chest to warn him, her eyes closing, but he showed no signs of flagging, muscles hard and eyes flared, his will and desire fending off the spell. Agatha strained to stay awake, fists clenched, determined to protect him . . .

The next time she blinked, it was morning, the sun bright over Foxwood.

Her prince was gone.
So was the rat.

AGATHA WAS CURLED up deep under a magnolia bush, a sweet honey smell breaking through her dull senses, along with the buzz of a crowd and the crisp clanging of metal. She pried apart a bough of flowers and spotted the thin towers of Foxwood's royal castle fanned against the horizon. But in front of that castle was a wall of soldiers, thousands of men deep, dressed in varied armor and shields, gathered under flags of different kingdoms: Kyrgios in pea green, Netherwood in glossy purple, Hamelin in checkered yellow and orange, Akgul in red and black . . . Then, from behind, Agatha heard voices: two Akgul guards in helmets and armor, hacking through bushes with their swords, coming straight towards her.

"Saw him myself. Prince Tedros it was," grunted one. "Ridin' somethin' like a big rat."

"Must be with his witch friends," guessed the second guard.

They slashed through more bushes, getting closer and closer to Agatha. She pulled out of the bush to flee—

—only to be yanked back.

She spun to see Hester and Anadil, fingers to lips. Agatha started to ask something, but Anadil's rats hissed "Shhh!" from her pocket. Hester pointed across, to Tedros and Merlin, camouflaged in a bush. Tedros mouthed to Agatha: "Don't move."

The two guards eviscerated the bushes, only a few feet

from Agatha's. With fingers, Tedros counted at Hester: *3 . . . 2 . . . 1 . . .*

Merlin and Hester sprung out of the bushes, each shooting a spell at a guard. Hester's knocked her guard out; Merlin's didn't, instead swelling his guard's helmet ten sizes, so the guard bumbled inside it like a barrel, slashing his sword blindly. The boy wizard shot another spell. This one turned the guard's sword into a ferret. Merlin tried one more, only to vanish the guard's pants.

"For God's sake, Merlin," Tedros growled.

He punched the guard out.

"It's that age potion. I'm telling you," Merlin complained.

"Don't even start," said Hester, freeing the ferret into the bushes.

A few minutes later, two soldiers in red-and-black armor crammed into the mob of armies, who were all on the lookout for Tedros of Camelot.

"Snow White's cottage is to the east," Tedros whispered through his helmet.

"It'll be guarded too. The whole kingdom is," Agatha whispered back. "Let's go straight to Chaddick's house—"

"We don't know where it is! That's why we need Sophie!" said Tedros.

Through her eyehole, Agatha spotted Merlin, Hester, and Anadil scuttling to the citizens' checkpoint, where guards hunting for Tedros assessed them with Matchers and allowed them to pass (Merlin's name popping up made them give the well-suited teenager a second glance, before they shrugged and let him go). Tedros knew that he and Agatha would never survive the Matchers, which is why he'd suggested sneaking through the armies and meeting the witches and Merlin at Snow White's. But now the plan seemed foolish.

"I can't move," Tedros gritted, stuck between trolls.

"Neither can I," said Agatha, a throng of Rainbow Gale nymphs blocking her.

Drumbeats thundered in the distance.

"Quit your pushin'," a troll snarled at Tedros. "King Rhian's comin'. We'll all get a good look."

Tedros and Agatha ducked their heads, hoping the troll hadn't inspected them too closely.

Drums boomed louder, followed by a flourish of horns.

"That must be Japeth!" Agatha whispered to her prince. "We need to hurry—"

Fanfare exploded behind them, the trumpets of a royal procession, as the trees and bushes around Foxwood's border began to shake. The foliage burst open, a parade of toy horses rolling through, every horse the size of an elephant, each completely covered in mosaics of . . . *candy*. There was a gumdrop horse, a lollipop horse, a marzipan horse, a caramel brittle horse, a cake truffle horse, a macaron horse, even a horse wrapped in tiny butterscotch balls. But the greatest horse of all, twice as tall as the rest, was latticed in bright red licorice, and atop this horse rose a figure in a red head-to-toe veil, her eyes gleaming through diaphanous silk, an enormous crown of white spun sugar extending off her head like antlers. The fanfare seemed to be coming from inside her horse, the veiled stranger striking poses to each new beat—tree pose, wheel pose, even a head-stand in her saddle—like some sort of equestrian yoga, before the toy animals all rolled to a stop and the drums fell to silence. Hands on hips, the red woman stood with a high-heeled boot on her horse's head and glared down at the hundred armies of the Woods.

"Who claims to have authority here?" she announced in a mystifying accent at once low-class and posh.

A sea of men gaped back at her.

"I said, who claims *authority* here?" she drawled.

"Me! Me!" yelped a voice far away, before a short, bald-ing man in a lopsided crown popped up amidst the armies, wrestling his way through. He was red-faced and sweaty, with an egg-colored tunic and hideous brown scarf that made him look a bit like Humpty Dumpty. "I'm King Dutra of Fox-wood! This is my kingdom!"

"Incorrect, wee little man," said the red stranger. "This is *my* kingdom. This entire *Woods* is my kingdom. I am the Sugar Queen, diva supreme and mistress of realms across the Savage Sea, come to claim the throne of Camelot, as is my right."

The king looked as gobsmacked as the soldiers around him. "B-b-but this is King *Rhian*'s land—King Rhian of Camelot—"

"As far as I know, there *is* no king of Camelot at present," the Sugar Queen snipped. "Arthur's will specified *two* con-tenders for his throne. I don't care who the second contestant is, but one of them is *me*. The Tournament of Kings is ongoing, is it not? A sword trapped in a stone that will *decide* the next king? Well, when Excalibur feels my touch, I assure you . . . *I will be king.*"

Tedros squeezed Agatha's arm. "What in the—" But Agatha was studying the Sugar Queen, who seemed to be staring right at her.

Meanwhile, the Foxwood king puffed his belly and stood taller. "I am loyal to the Lion. Every man here is. You have no jurisdiction on this side of the sea. Return to your sugar swamp and be gone!"

The Sugar Queen's eyes fell on him through her veil. "You are short and incompetent. An unforgivable combination in a man. One more word and I shall open my horses, unleashing a poisoned sugar mist that will slay you and all your armies with a single breath. Then I can conquer your lands as I have all others: in silence and peace." The king looked appalled, but the Sugar Queen went on: "That said, I am known for my fairness and generosity. If King Rhian believes he has a claim to the sword, then let him come to me and explain why, before we each take our turn in full view of the people."

The Foxwood king was sweating so profusely it was dripping into his mouth. "King Rhian has not yet arrived . . . delayed by an attack of traitorous mongooses in the forest . . ."

"Then I'll proceed to my accommodations at Snow White's cottage. Snow and I met years ago before her unfortunate death. She would sail across the Savage Sea and come stay with me at Chateau Sugar. Became dear friends, she and I. Left me her cottage in her will. Now to be my royal palace on *this* side of the sea," the Sugar Queen declared, her horse procession gliding in Agatha's direction as stunned soldiers made way. "Bring King Rhian to my palace the instant he arrives. Failure to do so will result in all of your deaths, including his. And given I trust not a one of you, I shall take two hostages, who will be killed if you disobey."

From the butterscotch horse, tiny hands suddenly reached out from its mouth and yanked Agatha and Tedros inside.

Agatha heard Tedros yowl in surprise, her hand holding his in the dark, before they were pulled apart, Agatha caught by warm bodies she couldn't see. The smell of sweet, cloying candy overwhelmed her. She threw off her helmet: between cracks in the licorice shell, she glimpsed the King of Foxwood chasing their horse. "You've kidnapped Akgul soldiers! This is illegal! You have no right!"

"Bring King Rhian to me or their blood will be on your hands!" the Sugar Queen bellowed, her procession picking up pace, breaking through the last of the soldiers. The king toddled after them with his coterie of bodyguards, shouting things Agatha could no longer hear, her body tossed and jostled by whoever it was that was holding her up.

A boy gasped behind her—

Agatha whirled to see Tedros, helmet off, holding his lit finger like a spotlight. "*Gnomes!*" he said.

Agatha followed his glow to an entire fleet of the ruddy, cone-capped dwarves packed into the horse, jogging their tiny feet on the ground and pushing the candied procession along. They shielded their eyes from Tedros' glow, before a toothless granny gnome cupped her fist over the prince's finger, plunging them back into darkness. Outside, they were approaching Snow White's cottage, nestled into a clearing. Colorful shrubs had grown around the ramshackle two-floor house made of lumpy wood with a domed roof shaped like a princess's hat. "Oh, no, no, this won't do at all," Agatha heard the Sugar Queen sigh, an array of hot pink spells firing at the cottage, refitting it into a chic candy chalet, with gingerbread eaves, gumball stucco, and powdered sugar windows, along with a lethally sharp rock-candy fence around the house and a blinking sign:

Chateau Sugar East
No Visitors Allowed
(Except King Rhian)

Horses plowed forward and the door to Chateau Sugar East magically swung open, sugarcoated ponies all jamming into the dusty foyer one by one, before the licorice horse piled in last and the door slammed and bolted shut, the Foxwood king's belligerent shouts still echoing outside.

Instantly, Agatha felt her horse bust open, the licorice shattering, as all the gnomes dispersed, wagging their bottoms and eating up the sweet debris. All the other horses erupted in a carnage of candy, not just gnomes flooding out (including a full marching band), but friends and first years too: Willam, Bogden, Valentina, Aja, Laithan, Ravan, Vex, Brone . . . But Agatha couldn't count them all, for there was a ghostly heap of red silk sweeping towards her, snatching her and Tedros and pinning them against a wall, before the Sugar Queen flung off her veil and leveled them both with an emerald glare.

"I'm going to kill that dirty, rotten Snake and here's *how*," said Sophie.

HER PLAN WAS brutally simple.

Step 1: Bait Japeth here, already in progress. The moment he arrived in Foxwood, he'd hear of his new rival and come straight to Chateau Sugar East.

Step 2: Act like his friend. A fellow ruler simply here to iron out a misunderstanding.

Step 3: Lure him into the house alone.

Step 4: Ambush him with a hundred gnomes and students from the school and rid the Woods of the Snake once and for all.

"All done in a matter of minutes," Sophie said, her red veil magically refitting into Evelyn's familiar white dress. "Then while Japeth is nowhere to be found . . . Tedros appears, pulls the sword out of the stone, and *voilà!*—the true Lion reveals himself. An unassailable plan. The End of Ends. Absolutely foolproof."

"You know I'm not one for Sophie's schemes, especially one that traps me in a knockoff of my mother's house," said Hester, tramping in from another room with Anadil, the two having arrived before. "That said, the plan isn't shabby."

"Could have done without the circus, though," Anadil grouched, gnomes around her gorging on candy.

"We have lookouts to alert us when he's coming," Sophie added, peeking through shutters at Bodhi and Laithan, posted at the rock-candy gates and wearing Tedros' and Agatha's stolen Akgul helmets. Sophie sealed the shutters once more, so no one could see into the house. She turned to her best friend. "What do you think, Aggie?"

There were things about the plan Agatha hated.

Inviting the Snake here.

Sophie taking on the burden of danger.

But there were also things that Agatha liked: Tedros would have a clear route to winning the third test. And no matter how unfairly Japeth fought, this was too big an ambush for him to survive. His death would truly be a taste of his own medicine.

Only Tedros didn't seem to see it that way.

He had a pensive frown on his face, his back against the wall, his eyes on the closed-up windows.

"It's a good plan, Teddy," said Sophie. "But I can't take all the credit. I had a little inspiration from a friend."

She looked over Agatha's shoulder. Agatha turned—

"Reaper!" she said.

Her cat glided towards her on a blue-velvet pillow, hoisted by two gnomes. Reaper bowed his head to Agatha, his crown slipping over his bald, shriveled ears. "The gnomes care little about the human world. But they do care about their king," he said. "So when I found out you and your friends were in danger . . . they were willing to leave the comforts of Gnome-land to follow that king into battle."

Agatha plucked him off the pillow and hugged him tight. Reaper scowled: "When in the presence of my subjects, I'd prefer a more distant approach."

"When in the presence of *my* cat, I know nothing but love," said Agatha, squeezing him harder. "I thought you could only talk to humans if you were under a spell."

"Turns out learning man's language isn't difficult," said Reaper, "given its dim-witted constructions and lack of finesse."

Brone poked his doughy head in from the back room: "If anyone wants *real* food, Merlin's hat is cooking!"

All at once, students ganged towards him, the gnomes content with their candy, while Reaper took advantage of the hubbub to hop from Agatha's arms and scamper away.

"Might as well be well-fed when the Snake comes," Sophie said, dragging Agatha ahead.

Agatha pinched her arm playfully. "I really do like this new Sophie who eats honeycake, is the queen of candy, and makes feasting a priority while in the throes of danger."

"You know how one day you woke up and discovered boys aren't the toxic poison you thought they were? Well, boys and cake have a lot in common, it turns out," Sophie said with a wink.

Agatha let go of her hand. "Sophie . . . is everything okay? When I saw you in the fireflies, you looked . . ."

Her best friend's smile evaporated. She avoided Agatha's eyes and whistled at Tedros: "Teddy, sweetie, what are you waiting for? When have you ever turned down a meal?"

But the prince stayed in place, fluttering his hand back as if to say he'd be along soon, before he was cornered by first-year girls, Valentina and Laralisa and Priyanka, asking obsequious questions about his time at school ("Which bed was yours in Honor 52?" "What was your favorite thing to do in the Groom Room?").

Agatha gave Sophie a look. "We should wait for him."

"There will always be someone chasing after him, darling. He's Tedros, for goodness' sakes. But he'll always love *you*," Sophie said, pulling her into the living room. "Speaking of chasing, who's *that*?" She ogled a tall, stylish boy laying out a banquet of plates on a wooden table.

"That's Merlin," said Agatha.

"I've lost my appetite," Sophie sighed.

The living room was a hive of activity, bodies packed around snuggly calico chairs and shuffling along the fluffy red-brown rug towards a colorful spread—kale pakoras, spice-baked root vegetables, crispy-fried mushrooms with garlic chutney, pasta Provençale, beet-glazed radishes, squash and okra curry, fava beans with sungold tomatoes, cinnamon-coconut rice, and chocolate-dipped churros—as if Merlin's hat was determined to make its young ward and all his fellow teenagers eat their vegetables.

Meanwhile, between bites of churros, Ravan and Vex were comparing iron pokers from the sooty fireplace, looking for the best weapon to ambush the Snake. So, too, were Bossam and Devan and other first-year boys searching the kitchen for knives that might work as daggers. Near the boys, Agatha spotted Beatrix, Kiko, and Reena in Knights of Eleven armor, boiling up a big pot of oil—

"You're *here*!" Agatha said, racing in.

"After Shazabah, Maid Marian took some of us to Sherwood Forest," said Beatrix, accelerating the boil with her fingerglow. "Met this witch doctor, who had a crystal ball."

"Showed us you were headed this way, so we came as fast as we could," said Reena.

"Got here last night," Kiko added, giving Agatha a sleepless frown. "The beds are made for *dwarves*."

Agatha stood straighter. "Wait, if you went with Maid Marian, then that means you were with—"

"Hello, dears," a voice chimed.

Everyone turned to see Dot swanning down a small staircase, a round-faced, young teenager once more, munching on a plate full of vegetables turned to chocolate.

"Think I'm going to be a witch doctor when I grow up," Dot beamed.

Near Agatha, Hester growled: "Just when I was getting used to hausfrau Dot."

"At least that one moped instead of talked," Anadil agreed.

But Dot was already hugging and kissing them both, her two witch friends squirming and gagging, but doing nothing to free themselves.

"Marian's still with you?" Hester asked.

"She and Nicola went to help Queen Jacinda in Jaunt Jolie," said Dot. "The old knights turned against Jacinda after we replaced them. Staged a coup and tried to take over the castle. So much for being loyal to their queen! Never seen Marian so determined to put men in their place. Perhaps she wants history to remember her as more than the damsel of thieves and sheriffs." Dot winked. "Her daughter too."

Hester and Agatha gaped at each other.

"Oh, don't give her *too* much credit for figuring it out," Anadil moaned. "Wasn't like she solved the riddle of the sphinx."

"Means I'm half-Ever, though," Dot said, looking tense. "Not exactly a witch." She eyed Hester and Anadil nervously, as if she might be expelled from the coven.

"Well . . . ," said Hester. "Nobody's perfect."

Willam came up behind the witches: "Want to stake out upstairs with us? We can dive-bomb the Snake once he comes in."

"My idea that Will's taking credit for," Bogden chirped.

Agatha smiled, watching the witches and boys go upstairs, so much love amongst them that Agatha nearly forgot her own true love's head was at risk and his enemy on the way here. She turned to look for Tedros—

Sophie intercepted her, nibbling on churros. "You know how Merlin always smelled a little like an old sweater left in a trunk too long? The younger Merlin doesn't smell like that at all. Not that he seemed thrilled to see me. But you know I love a challenge. *Grrr.* Agatha, are you really not eating? Do I have to make a plate for you?"

There was something in her tone, manic and forced, that bothered Agatha. It reminded her of the old Sophie.

The performer. The actress. That's when it dawned on her. "Sophie?" said Agatha, looking at her friend. "Where's Hort?"

The facade cracked. Pain spilled through, tears rushing to Sophie's eyes. Agatha lost her breath, her hand flying to her mouth—

Two horns clashed outside, urgent and badly played.

"That's the signal!" Sophie gasped, forcing composure. She spun on her heel. "Places, everyone! He's coming! Snake's coming!"

Everyone sprung into motion like guests at a demented surprise party, toting makeshift weapons: chairs and cutlery and porcelain dinner plates. Quickly, Agatha peeked through the window shutters. In front of the rock-candy gates, she glimpsed Bodhi and Laithan tooting gnome-sized trumpets as a crowd of thousands swarmed towards Chateau Sugar East: soldiers from other kingdoms, citizens from Foxwood chanting "*Lion! Lion!*," along with a phalanx of gold-shielded Camelot soldiers, and at the fore of them all, a boy in blue and gold, atop a white horse. Agatha snapped the shutters and whirled around, scanning for Tedros. But Sophie shoved her down behind a couch, the Sugar Queen morphing back into her red veil, directing her own army through the house.

"Everyone hide! Out of sight! And complete silence from here on out!" she commanded. "Once he knocks, I'll let the bastard in. Then *attack*!"

The house plunged to an anxious hush, every last body stuffed behind a wall or chair or chaise or stashed in the kitchen or upstairs, leaving only Sophie standing in the middle of the living room. Agatha scrambled back up, grabbing Sophie's arm—

"Hide, you goose!" Sophie hissed, burying her friend in a gaggle of gnomes, who were armed with jagged pieces of candy. But Agatha clung to Sophie's wrist.

"Where's Tedros?" she pressed.

"Hiding quietly, like you should be!" Sophie said. She wrenched free of Agatha, sweeping towards the foyer in blood-colored silk—

Sophie stopped cold.

"Teddy?" she breathed.

Agatha leapt up.

He was at the door.

His hand on the knob.

Tedros gazed at Agatha.

"Remember your promise," he said.

Sophie's eyes shot to her friend: "What promise?"

Tedros had already opened the door.

Sophie and Agatha both dashed for him, stumbling through the mess of candy, Sophie throwing off her veil, Agatha hurtling into the sun first. "Tedros, no!" she cried—

Her prince stood unarmed at the gates, a thousand swords and arrows and spears pointed at him.

The white horse cantered to within a few feet of him, the forest falling quiet as Japeth dismounted, still disguised as his dead brother.

The Snake stared at Sophie and Agatha, frozen at the door to the house.

His focus lowered to the prince.

"One turn at the sword each," Tedros declared. "Excalibur decides the king."

The prince reached his hand through the gate.

For a moment, his enemy said nothing.

They just looked at each other, two rivals for a throne.

Truth against Lies. Present against Past. Pen against Man.

All the Woods held its breath.

The Snake's eyes glittered.

"Excalibur decides the king," he said.

He took Tedros' hand.

The deal done.

Arthur's son and Rafal's.

Agatha's legs buckled, Sophie there to catch her, asking again and again in scared whispers what Agatha had promised him, what vow she'd given, but all Agatha could remember was the last time she touched her prince, somewhere in the dark, lost in the smell of bad candy.

~ 30 ~

AGATHA

The Sword and the Lion

When making a deal, one must be specific.

That's all Agatha could think as she lurched through the streets of Foxwood, yoked to a chain, her mouth gagged with rope. As soon as the terms between Tedros and the Snake were settled—Excalibur to decide the king— Chateau Sugar East was raided by

a hundred armies, all of Tedros' friends captured and bound. The prince said nothing, watching this happen, even as his friends were cuffed into a prisoners' parade, even as Reaper and his gnomes were kept behind and jailed inside the cottage, even as Tedros' princess was kicked into the back of the line with Sophie. At their wings were thousands of soldiers marshaling them along, Good and Evil, prodding Tedros' friends with swords and spears, while Foxwood citizens pelted the rebels with rubbish, chanting *"Rhian is King! Rhian is King!"* In front of Agatha, a soiled rag smacked Dot in the face, while a rotted peach slapped Agatha's ear, spurting her cheek with juice.

She remembered one of the first times she'd left the castle at Camelot when she was its new princess, citizens in the village attacking her with mashed hunks of food, rejecting Tedros as king. Back then, Agatha too had her doubts about Tedros. So much had happened since. A Snake unmasked. A Lion brought to light. And yet the people of the Woods were still deep in the dark.

Agatha could hear Sophie's choked breaths behind her, her friend the last in the chain, her mouth stuffed with King Dutra's brown scarf, the runty Foxwood king waddling alongside and giving Sophie a boot whenever she slowed, sniping, "Sugar Queen! Ha!" Farther ahead, the witches were chained too, Hester's demon hemmed by an iron collar around its master's neck and Anadil's two rats tied with rope around Anadil's belly. A grim déjà vu came over Agatha, remembering the last time she, Sophie, and the witches were in a chain gang, captive to pirates who took them to their leader.

That was the first time they'd met the Snake.

Now here they were again in his grip. They had magic at their disposal and the will to fight back, but resistance was futile; they were both outnumbered and irrelevant, the outcome of the tournament confined to a contest between Tedros and the Snake, just as King Arthur had intended. Even Merlin slogged along the chain dutifully, peeking back at Agatha with a glum expression, as if whatever incited the prince to challenge Japeth had been done without consulting him.

Tedros was the only one free, walking at the front of the chain gang, his black coat buttoned up tight, Japeth riding next to him on a white horse. Twelve Camelot soldiers guarded Tedros from the front, crossbows cocked at him, the soldiers shuffling backwards along the last bumpy cobblestones of the square, Agatha terrified that any misstep might trigger one of the bows. Still, Tedros looked impossibly calm, as if he himself had seen the future and picked this path, knowing where it would lead. And yet, Japeth had the same serene expression, towering high over the prince, having seized Tedros' friends preemptively, as if there could only be one outcome to whom Excalibur would choose.

They couldn't both be right.

Agatha wanted desperately to trust Tedros' instincts. No doubt he'd assumed that under fair conditions, in full view of the people, his father's sword would anoint him king. But the Snake was always one step ahead, just like his own father, and to play by the rules against him was the surest way to lose.

Hoping to calm herself, Agatha looked back at Sophie, but her friend was quailed silently in her white dress, her eyes pinned downwards. She sensed Agatha watching her, about to look up, but Agatha turned, letting her be. It was the same consuming grief she'd seen in Sophie at Snow White's. She could almost read her friend's mind: that Hort wouldn't have stood for this or gone along quietly. He would have erupted into a raging man-wolf and smashed soldiers with his fists and raised holy, apocalyptic hell, no matter what deal Tedros had made. And even though it would have served no use and certainly made things worse, Sophie would have loved him all the more for it.

That Sophie had fallen in love with Hort was as natural as it was surprising. On the one hand, Agatha couldn't believe it had happened and on the other, she couldn't fathom it *not* happening, even after Sophie had rejected the possibility time and time again. Around Hort, Sophie was the Sophiest of all and the Hort the Hortiest, each the deepest version of themselves, bared to each other without shame or fear or regret, and isn't that what love is? That magical force that makes you *more* you. The way Agatha made Tedros more Tedros and Tedros made Agatha more Agatha. Sophie had tried to find another equation for love. All the boys she'd loved before were gorgeous or edgy or mystical, but they'd held her back or pushed her towards something she didn't want or couldn't be. Hort loved Sophie as herself. And any boy who could love the *real* Sophie in all her incarnations was the only prince deserving of her love. It just took Hort dying for Sophie to see it.

Tears stung Agatha's eyes. Is this how the story would end? Sophie stripped of her Ever After and Agatha robbed of her own? Two friends alone again, love found and lost? For a moment, Agatha felt like they'd returned to Gavaldon, she and Sophie pulled through streets of ordinary, tulip-lined cottages . . .

Then she saw the house with the hole in the roof.

Atop the two-level, pale yellow home, the blue tiles had been blown open, guards stationed around this crater, armed with crossbows, pointed at Tedros as he approached. Down on the ground, a thick ring of guards walled off the house, the strongest soldiers Good and Evil, an elite force protecting the third test. Agatha could hardly see Tedros anymore, the guards closing in on him from all sides before the prince stopped in front of the house.

Japeth halted his horse.

Tedros waited for him, as if they were friends.

Watching them were two boys in school uniforms, standing on the porch in front of an open door. Both wore Lion pins, one older, about eighteen, who looked a bit like Chaddick, the other boy ash blond, no more than eight or nine years of age. In the doorway waited a woman in rose-pink robes, who had Grisella Gremlaine's tan skin and sharp-drawn face. It was here that Lady Gremlaine must have left her son to be raised by his aunt, where Arthur would never learn of his existence. Why Grisella hid Arthur's true heir from him they'd never know for sure. But Agatha suspected it was so the story of Arthur and Grisella would end on that fateful night they'd spent together in Sherwood Forest. For Grisella, that was their Ever After. Their secret to keep forever. Anything born of that secret had to be hidden, not just to protect Arthur and Camelot, but to give the child a fresh start, a *new* life, away from the tangled web of its parents.

Japeth dismounted. He left his sword behind and joined Tedros on the patch of grass in front of the house.

The prince nodded, ceding way to his rival.

Silently, the hierarchy played out.

Japeth made his way to the porch, the two Gremlaine boys bowing to him. At the door, Japeth didn't enter, but instead signaled to the crowd, drawing forth the leaders of the Kingdom Council—King Dutra of Foxwood, Empress Vaisilla of Putsi, the Maharani of Mahadeva, the Wolf King of Bloodbrook, and dozens more—who would all bear witness to the test, each gliding into the house one by one until the parade of royals was done.

Japeth waited by the door and nodded at Tedros.

Tedros moved to join him, the Gremlaine boys giving him cold glowers, which the prince solemnly endured. From the porch, Tedros glanced back at the chain of prisoners, signaling to the guards at their flanks that he wanted them as his witnesses. The soldiers all looked to Japeth, who made no objection. Guards sheathed their weapons and stood down.

At the front of the line, Vex and Ravan pulled the chain forward, drawing Tedros' friends into the house, past the prince and Japeth, who watched them enter: fourth years, first years, followed by Merlin, then the witches towing Agatha and Sophie last. As Agatha jerked onto the porch, she stared urgently at Tedros, but he wasn't looking at her, his eyes on his own cloak-covered chest, where Agatha had wrapped her hands only a short while ago. Was this the last time they'd be close to each other? Why couldn't he look at her? Was he afraid? Was he regretting his deal? Overwhelmed with feelings, Agatha spun to the Snake, cutting him with a glare of fire and pain, but it was too late, the chain already dragging her inside—

That's when Agatha saw Japeth's collar.

Fluttering in the breeze, just long enough for her to catch what was pinned underneath . . .

A tiny piece of gray fabric that matched the color of Chaddick's eyes.

A golden *C* stitched into the gray.

All of it, dried through with blood.

HE'S CHEATING! AGATHA wanted to scream.

He has Chaddick's blood!

She needed to warn Tedros, but she couldn't see him any longer, her body hauled into the crowded house. She couldn't cry out to him either, the rope pulled too tight in her mouth. Down the chain, Merlin was peering strangely at her, but now the chain dragged them forward, her feet staggering over broken blue tiles, Agatha wrenched between gathered leaders, the Ice Giant of Frostplains, the Fairy Queen of

Gillikin, the Dwarf Queen of Ooty, who all recoiled at her touch, until she was tugged up a staircase to the second floor, giving her a view over the banister of the Gremlaine home.

Japeth's allies occupied the first floor, packed around Excalibur, its blade stabbed into a pile of shattered stone that had crashed in from above. Noontime sun spotlit Arthur's sword through the hole in the roof, casting gold sparkles in the sapphire-colored stone, matching the hues of Japeth's suit. The two rivals came through the door, Japeth and Tedros hewed close as they took their places in front of the sword. Trapped against the upstairs banister, Agatha saw Sophie flash her a look, no doubt recognizing the irony of crowding her candy chateau with friends to keep Tedros away from the Snake, only to end up in a house of enemies, the two boys hip to hip. With Tedros directly below her, Agatha couldn't see more than the top of his curls, eye contact between them impossible. How could she tell him what she'd spotted on Japeth's collar? That Japeth was tricking Excalibur the same way Rhian had, which is why the sword rejected Tedros the first time? How could she tell Tedros that Excalibur was about to spurn him again? And this time, it would *kill* him?

She tried to choke out sounds, but there was no way to hear her from up here, the house too jammed with shifting bodies, her prince's eyes fixed on his father's blade. Slowly, a wave of quiet rolled across the house, the stakes growing clear. That this was the final test of the Tournament of Kings. That in a matter of moments, the sword would surely be pulled by one of these two boys and the other would die. Agatha could see her friends chained down the staircase, all of them with the same pale, petrified faces, especially the first years who still believed in a world where Good always wins, where the true heir to Camelot must be king. The silence grew and Agatha seized her chance, drawing a breath and forcing a cry through her rope, a cry Tedros had to know was hers—

He didn't look at her.

Tedros cleared his throat. "We have our witnesses, Rhian. We have our test. We have only our last words that the people will remember us by, whether we rise to the throne or go to our grave."

"Then speak first, young prince," Japeth simpered. "The last time you gave a king's speech, it was something to behold."

Agatha saw Tedros flinch. She remembered the moment well. The speech King Tedros had to give to rally his armies against the Snake and faltered so badly, his words so uncertain and timorous that another boy stepped in to do the job. In that instant, Tedros had opened the door for his throne to be stolen. And here he was, against a boy who wore the same face as the one who'd humiliated him. *Past is Present and Present is Past. The story goes round and round again . . .*

Unless you learn from that past, thought Agatha, watching her prince turn towards the crowd. Because the story might be the same, but this Tedros was different. His eyes were clear, his stance proud. When he spoke, his voice was dark and commanding, his breath low and deep, as if he was holding back a roar.

"Kings are born, not made. That is the law of our land.

That is what we are taught," he said. "Even the mightiest and worthiest cannot ascend to the throne without the blood of his predecessor. Blood is the magic of how kings are made. Only blood. It is why my rival and I stand before this sword. Each of us claims the blood of my father. My father, who created this tournament to find his heir." Tedros paused. "And yet, why make three tests? Why not return the sword to the stone and ask one of us to pull it out, just as he did to prove himself a king? Why declare a tournament to make us quest for answers and risk life and limb across the sea and back, only to then end here, with the same task my father passed, by the magic of his blood? Maybe because he learned that blood *wasn't* enough to make him a king. What made him a king were the tests of leadership he faced over and over. Tests that made him a king in more than blood. Tests of humility. Forgiveness. Sacrifice. Love. The *real* tests. Ones I failed my first time as king. Because I, too, believed in the magic of blood. That it made me king, even if I didn't *feel* like a king or know how to act like one. I ruled with fear in my heart. Fear that I wasn't worthy of my blood. Fear that I wasn't good enough. I shrank from challenges, worried for myself instead of my people, desperate to protect a throne I didn't think I deserved. Guilt. Shame. Doubt. These were my guides. It is no wonder a usurper came to rob that throne. I conjured a Snake into existence. Yet it was this Snake who gave me a second chance to pass the tests I'd failed. That's why my father left three tests. To let me prove the humility, love, and courage I once lacked. But there is more at stake here than a crown. One of us fights to protect the Storian. The other seeks to destroy it and replace it with himself. Man versus Pen. Yet, without the Pen, we are lost. For it is the Storian who truly knows our fate and gives each of us the chance to fulfill it. It is why Man cannot rule these Woods alone. It is why the One True King must never replace the Storian. Because Man doesn't have the courage to face his own worst fears, to rise to his greatest self, not without the help of fate. Fate and free will must work together. Man and Pen in perfect balance. We are all objects of our fate, but our *will* decides whether we overcome the challenges fate brings us. The Storian only begins our tale. *We* must end it. And my end is to grow beyond my failings and become more than my blood. It is why I stand here today, made stronger by my mistakes. Because the Pen always gives the best of men second chances. And the best of kings."

He stood taller, speaking at full thunder. "Maybe Excalibur will choose me now. Maybe it will not. But I will not step back from the challenge. Not this time. I will risk losing my head to claim the truth of who I am. A leader who will bring all of us, Good *and* Evil, into a new realm. Where Truth wins over Lies, where the Past doesn't dictate the Present, where Man and Pen share power. A future where a king doesn't look down on the people but is one of the people. I will be your Lion. I will be your protector. I will be your *king*. Not for my glory, but for all of us. *All* of us, even the snakes. Which is why my father made this the third test. It is not a test of blood or birth. Both of those can be faked." Tedros set his eyes on Japeth. "But the truth can't be faked. And this is a test of truth. Only one will face it with courage instead of cowardice."

The Foxwood house was still, leaders and students captive to the prince's words. Through an upstairs window, Agatha could see the mob of citizens outside, mesmerized to silence, having listened to Tedros' voice boom from the blown-open house. She gazed down at her prince, his face flushed with belief, and though Agatha was chained up and robbed of speech and Tedros still wouldn't look at her, she'd never felt so hopeful in her life. For her true love no longer belonged to her, but to all the Woods. The Lion. The King.

Japeth broke the silence with a chuckle.

Agatha's stomach sank as the Snake raised slitted eyes to his rival.

"Are you calling me a coward?" Japeth asked.

Tedros stared back. "I'm calling you a liar *and* a coward."

"You would know, wouldn't you?" Japeth leered. "Tell me what I've done, other than obey Arthur's will. Tell me what I've done, other than honor the one I *love*." He burned with fury, as if in Tedros he still saw the fraud of Aric. "You have your truth and I have mine. The people believe me. They've burned their rings for me. *Me*, the One True King." He hissed in Tedros' face. "*That* is the truth."

Tedros gazed purely at the Snake. "The truth cannot be spoken. It must be seen. And your crimes will be seen."

Tension froze the house. Japeth pulled back from Tedros, a wry smile on his face.

"And if they are not, soothsayer?" he baited. "If *I* have the blood of the heir and the blood of the king?"

Tedros hesitated, the veins tight in his neck. He looked at the Snake. "Then I wish Excalibur take my head for as long as it is true."

Japeth smiled. "So it is written." He straightened his collar, touching it just long enough to make sure Tedros caught sight of Chaddick's blood underneath. Agatha watched Tedros' body go stiff, his throat constrict.

The Snake turned back to the sword. "I see no reason for more empty words. The test to decide the king is clear. Let us draw as to who pulls Excalibur first."

"A coin toss!" pipped the King of Foxwood, rushing forward, a gold piece in his hands. "Heads for King Rhian and tails for . . . the other one." His fingers were shaking as he pinched the coin and tossed it clumsily in the air, nearly hitting the Empress of Putsi. "Heads, it is. King Rhian?"

"I'll go second," said Japeth.

Agatha broke into a clammy chill, her cuffed hands dripping sweat. Sophie squeezed against her, their arms touching, both holding their breath.

Tedros stepped into the arena of sun beneath the broken roof, just him and his father's sword. He wedged his worn boot into the mass of stone and put one hand on the Lion-carved hilt, then the other. Every sound drained out of the house, the prince's chest rising and falling, his breaths heavy like an ocean wave. He grasped the sword hard. Then he pulled it with all of his force.

Excalibur didn't move.

Tedros clamped his knuckles and yanked a second time,

his forearms pumped, his cheeks hot red.

The sword stayed in place.

Air went out of Agatha's lungs, Sophie's chained arms hugging her close. Agatha could hear her friend gasping through her gag to comfort her, drowned out by the murmuring leaders, who'd been so thoughtful after Tedros' speech as if reconsidering who they'd chosen as king, now relieved that Excalibur had silenced their doubts.

Tedros stepped back, his eyes on Arthur's sword.

He said nothing.

"My turn," said Japeth.

He came around the side of the blade and faced Tedros head-on, his tan hands clasping the carved Lion, rays of sun lighting up his collar. With a quick, shallow breath, he seized the hilt and pulled the sword.

It glided out of the stone, into the Snake's raised fists.

"No!" Agatha yelled into her gag—

But leaders were already on bended knees, bowing to their king, and so were the students, pushed down by guards, Agatha and Sophie with them. Agatha thrust her head through the railing, just in time to see Japeth grinning at Tedros, Excalibur gripped in his thin fingers, its blade magically glowing gold. Slowly, the sword floated out of Japeth's hands into the sun, suspended in midair by its own force.

Arthur's spirit resounded from within:

"My blood lives on.
The third test is complete,

The tournament done.
A king is found."

Camelot's crown appeared like a phantom over Japeth's head and fitted down onto his copper hair.

Excalibur turned to Tedros.

Arthur's voice spoke once more, sharper this time.

"And so is the loser."

The sword glowed red with punishment.

Agatha lunged in vain for the stairs, trapped by her chain. That's when Tedros locked eyes with her, finally looking at her, finally seeing her, strong and true, the way he did when he asked her to make a promise. To go on without him. To keep the fight.

Tedros looked back at his father's sword.

Agatha screamed—

The blade swung for her prince's neck.

Light caught its edge.

Then Tedros fell, cut into two pieces.

31

Return to Ender's Forest

Nearly ten years before, Tedros and I had a lesson in Ender's Forest.

I hadn't intended it to be a lesson.

It was supposed to be a goodbye.

Arthur had killed Kay and I'd resolved to leave Camelot altogether, but not without seeing the young prince one last time.

As I'd waited beneath a purple oak, my eyes clouded with tears behind my spectacles and my hand grasped anxiously at my beardless chin. How could I leave the boy? Just when we were getting started? I'd intended to stay with his father and then with the son until a day far into the future when the work was done. But things had changed. Arthur had become secretive and volatile; instead of his mentor, I'd become a nuisance to rebel against. Somewhere inside him, he'd either lost faith in me or more likely, himself. The only cure was to leave and make him face his fate on his own. As for Tedros, I'd keep an eye on him from afar, like a hawk on high, until a day came where he needed me most. I couldn't tell him this, of course, or he'd spend his life searching and waiting for my return, instead of learning to stand on his own two feet. No, the farewell had to be a clean blow, no matter how many tears were shed between us—

"Merlin!" a voice chirruped.

I'd turned to see him scooting between lavender bushes, his gold curls strewn with leaves, his princely vest torn. He was so small then, perpetually flushed and in motion, like a rambunctious fox.

"Merlin, it only took me five tries to get in! I did everything you taught me! I closed my eyes and thought about finding the portal and then I focused on relaxing my brain and let my feet take me and then I opened my eyes and there it was! But I tried to jump in too fast, so I took deep breaths and that didn't work but then I calmed down and—*poof!*—the forest opened and that's the first time I did it on my own without you feeling sorry for me and letting me in. Only five times! Aren't you proud of me? Merlin?" He suddenly screwed his eyes on me and cocked his head. "You look very strange without a beard. Can you put it back?"

In that moment, any plans to tell him this was our last lesson evaporated.

He'd just turned nine and having been nine years old myself a week ago, I know firsthand how sensitive one is at that age, how live-wired with energy and ambition, especially Tedros, who used to stand so upright, almost on his tiptoes, as if he couldn't wait to grow taller. He'd lost his mother only weeks before and now I'd lost the strength to admit that I, too, was about to desert him. Instead, I vowed to make our last lesson one he would remember.

"Tell me, future king," I'd said, picking leaves out of his hair. "What would you like me to teach you more than anything else in the world? This is your chance. No limits. Anything you desire."

"How to die and come back to life," the prince said instantly, as if he'd already given it a good thought.

I kneeled in front of him. "Well, that's impossible, unless you're a wizard with a Wizard Wish—"

"No, it isn't," Tedros contended. "That Green Knight who came got his head cut off by Dad and then he put his head right back on his neck. Everyone at the castle is saying it. He did it

right there, in front of Dad! *Slash! Plunk! Peekaboo!* I want to
be able to do that! I want to be strong and never die! I want to
be a Green Knight!"

"The Green Knight *is* dead," I pointed out.

"Fine, then give me your Wizard Wish, because you just
said it'll let me die *and* come back to life."

"I don't have it."

Tedros balled up his fists, his cheeks hot. "You asked what
I wanted you to teach me, no rules, and now you're going back
on it." He looked like he was about to cry.

Then and in the years to come, Tedros clung to a profound
sense of justice. I looked into his quivering blue eyes and saw
there'd be no reasoning with him. Of course, there wasn't any
way to teach him to die and come back to life—Kay's immortality had been a unique curse—but perhaps if I could give the
boy the *feeling* of death, so he'd no longer see it as an enemy, he
might let go of his wish altogether.

"Come," I said, striding into my forest, the lilac spruces, purple pines, and plum-colored dragon trees bowing their limbs to
me, sensing my tendency to reimagine the foliage of Ender's
Forest at any moment and hoping to stay in my good graces. I
could hear Tedros bopping along behind, singing coded songs
about his mother and Lancelot (*"When I'm a headless knight,
I'll go hunting other knights! Knights that I don't like!"*), eagerly
scrambling over rocks and logs I conjured into his path ("Merlin, make them harder!"), and spooking every bird and squirrel
he could: "Peekaboo! Peekaboo!"

In time, the forest opened up and we arrived at a mirrored

pool, surrounded by neat purple grass, an oasis in a field. Overhead the sky was clear, nothing beyond the pool except more amethyst lawns, none of Tedros' favorite squirrels or flowers or insects, the scene conjured to induce zero distractions in the boy, so he would focus keenly on what we were about to do.

"Never been to this part of the forest!" he pipped, dropping to his knees at the pool's edge and plunging his fist into the water.

"What did I tell you about *looking* before doing, Tedros. For all you know, this pool is filled with piranhas."

"Is it?" Tedros said, wide-eyed. Now he put both hands in and his whole face to it, hunting its depths. "I heard they have sharp teeth and eat people!"

I shook my head. He was stubborn, rash, prideful, overemotional, and had poor instincts . . . and oh, how I'd miss the boy. "Let's get on with it," I said.

Sparkling nuggets rushed to the surface, spitting him with water.

"Wish Fish!" the prince chimed, ogling the silvery creatures swirling through the pool. "Dad says the School for Good has a lake full of them! That's where I'll go when I'm thirteen, as long as I keep eating vegetables and cleaning up after myself. That's what Dad told me. But don't know how much I believe him these days . . ." He looked up at me. "These are *real* Wish Fish?"

"Put your finger in and see," I said. "If dying and coming back to life is your greatest wish, that's what the fish will show you."

Tedros stuffed his tiny finger in the water.

The fish darted away from each other, like a firework dispersing, before shuttling back together, painting a picture of . . . Guinevere. Instantly, the prince withdrew his finger, his face pale. "Stupid fish!"

He closed his eyes, as if wishing the vision of his mother away, and shoved his finger in again.

This time, the fish painted Lancelot, cuddling him with love.

Tedros sprung to his feet, kicking the water, sending the fish diving deep for cover. "I hate this game," he said, sprawling onto his stomach in the grass. Not realizing, of course, that he'd just seen the wishes he *truly* wanted most.

So I sat down beside him. "Tell me. Why do you want to die and come back to life?"

He didn't look at me. "It just seems amazing."

"But *why*, Tedros?"

He thought about this awhile, before craning his head up. "Because if I can die and come back to life, then no one can hurt me."

"Oh, my boy," I said. "I'm afraid being able to come back from death can't stop you from getting hurt. If anything, living longer means you'll get hurt *more*. Because life is also about opening yourself to all emotions, even the bad ones."

Tedros turned away. "I don't like being hurt."

"Who is hurting you?"

"No one." He swallowed. "I'm okay."

"You're lucky, then, because I feel quite hurt myself."

He looked back at me. "You do? Where are you hurt?"

"Here," I said, my hand on my heart.

"Oh." He nodded. "Who hurt you?"

"Someone I loved very much," I said.

Tedros nodded. "Me too." He sniffled and curled into a bean shape, his back against my knee. "When does the hurt go away?"

"Once you make friends with it. Once you come to see the hurt not as something to fear or run away from, but as an important part of you. As important as love and hope and happiness. All of them are pieces of your heart, each as important as the other. But ignoring the hurt or pretending it's not there doesn't make it go away. It just means you're not using all of your heart. Soon that piece might even dry up and break away. We don't want that. A strong king needs *all* of his heart. And the funny thing is, once you're bold enough to welcome the hurt, to give it a hug and face it unafraid . . . then suddenly, it's gone."

Tedros was quiet, his big blue eyes fixed on his chest, where his heart would be. He rolled over to me. "What happened to your Wizard Wish?"

I hunched forward and sighed.

"Come on, give it to me," he pleaded.

"I don't have it, Tedros."

"If you did, would you let me take it?"

"No."

"I'm going to find it and steal it. Or another wizard's. And I won't tell you when I do," he snapped. "At least tell me what you were going to wish *for.* To die and come back to life? Like me?"

"Oh no. When it's my time to die, I won't need to come back," I replied.

Tedros sat up. "Why not? Why not live forever?"

I ruffled his hair. "Because the work will be done, dear boy."

"You never make any sense," the prince growled, before lunging forward and dipping his finger back in the water.

"Concentrate now . . . ," I urged. "Think hard about your wish . . ."

The fish swerved into formation, colors dancing across their shiny scales, steel blue and treasure gold and dusty peach, a rich vision reflecting back at the young prince . . . of his own small head, the eyes closed, severed from his body and carried under his arm . . .

"Merlin, I did it! I'm dead! Like the Green Knight!" he yipped, gaping at the water. "I made it come true! Look! See, Merlin! See!"

"I'm seeing, Tedros."

He whistled proudly, hopping and pointing at his decapitated twin . . . then quieted suddenly, as if absorbing the scene of his death, the reality behind his wish. His smile disappeared, anxiousness surging to his face. But he was looking at the painting closer now, at the calmness in his imagined self, the peace in his shut eyes, for this was the wish he'd wanted, the death he *chose* to prove something to himself, so that he could come back stronger. The fear went out of him, a new sense of power alighting—

His eyes shot open in the painting, the head roaring to life: *"Peekaboo!"*

Tedros screamed and took off into the fields.

"Well, you did say you wanted to come back to life, didn't you?" I said when I found him.

But he just hugged me tightly, gripping at my robes, long after the fright was gone, as if somewhere deep inside, he knew that he and I were about to have our own death, our days together at an end.

I left Camelot with a heavy heart, plagued with doubts as to what would happen to Arthur and his son in the years to follow. But I knew two things for sure about Prince Tedros after that last lesson in the forest.

He wouldn't be scared of death when the time came.

And he'd steal another's Wizard Wish the first chance he got.

THE APPLE.

The one the Lady of the Lake had given him.

Kept in Tedros' coat, near his heart.

I'd thought it a strange parting gift, since it couldn't have any real magic, her powers mostly gone. But from what I'd seen, Tedros had laid it on thick, whispering in the Lady's ear, eliciting a smile of love and gratitude, until she'd drawn the apple out of her waters, a token of affection for him. I'd assumed the prince had told Nimue that her sins were forgiven, that he still loved and admired her, so she would have the peace she needed . . . but now, looking back, it was more than that . . .

He wanted something from her.

He wanted her *Wizard Wish*.

And whatever he'd said to her at the lake had made her give it to him.

These are the thoughts that run through me watching Tedros' head severed from his body, like I'd seen in the boy's Wish Fish painting so long ago. Trapped on the staircase, I calculate quickly, my fists cuffed to the prisoner's chain, my mind firing with teenage adrenaline.

If Tedros has the Lady's wish, then he had to have *said* his wish. He had to have spoken it out loud.

Of course!

He *did* speak it out loud.

After the Snake had taunted him about having the blood of the heir, the blood of the king.

Tedros had looked right at him: "Then I *wish* Excalibur take my head for as long as it is true."

As long as it is true.

As long as *what* is true?

Japeth having the heir's blood.

Japeth having the blood of the king.

But Chaddick was the heir.

Which means Japeth has Chaddick's blood on him.

And Agatha *knows* it.

That's why she looked stricken when she passed Japeth at the door.

That's why she screamed through her gag to warn Tedros.

That's why Tedros looked right at her before Excalibur cut off his head.

Because he *knows* she knows it.

He's counting on her to know it.

Only she hasn't made the connection yet . . . My head swivels to Agatha and I see why. She's too shocked, her face dead white, her whole body tremoring, lost to the horror of seeing her prince cut in two. Meanwhile, Japeth stands triumphant in the chaos of fawning leaders, Excalibur back in his fists. I need Agatha to look at me, but Sophie and the witches are huddled around her, all of them a mess of tears. Guards will come any moment to take us to the dungeons. *Look at me, Agatha*, I think. *Look at me. Look at—*

My hat pokes out of my pocket, hearing my thoughts.

Not you. Agatha.

My hat launches up the stairs and smacks Agatha in the head.

Good boy.

Agatha glances at me.

For the slightest second.

The magic is already forming between my bound hands, my fingers prying apart just enough to release it into the air . . . floating out of my palms . . . a pink orb of light . . . in the shape of . . .

. . . an *apple*.

Agatha stares at it through tears, then at me, confounded.

I glare at her hard, willing her to think like *me*.

She looks at the apple again.

The apple Tedros wouldn't let her eat on our journey, even when she'd asked.

Her gaze sharpens like a knife.

The apple.

The Lady.

The magic.

She understands.

Tears dry up.

Her jaw sets.

Sophie sees the shift in her, follows her eyes to me—

But Agatha is already jumping on top of the banister, diving with her cuffed arms out, swooping like a phoenix towards the Snake.

Only one problem: all of us are chained to her—

Sophie goes jerking up after Agatha, tumbling with a scream towards the first level, before the witches and I and the others yank the chain back, suspending the two girls in air, upside down, their heads swinging for the floor. Japeth whirls around in surprise, but Agatha is right there in his face. She bludgeons him with shackled hands, knocking him off-kilter, then snatches at his collar, grabbing something from beneath it. Dot manages to fire a spell from her lit finger, turning the chain over Agatha to chocolate. Agatha and Sophie snap free, crashing down onto King Dutra and Empress Vaisilla, who shriek and swat at them, pinned beneath the girls and yelling for their guards. Meanwhile, Sophie angles her bound fists to burn her glow through Agatha's cuffs, Agatha doing the same to Sophie's. Chains break at the same time, before Sophie swipes a brooch from Vaisilla and spears through her and Agatha's gags. But now soldiers are running for both girls, Japeth leading them, swords out to slash them through—

The soldiers pull back, startled.

Because Japeth's crown is . . . moving.

Rising off his head without a sound.

It drifts across the room, five spires of gold, shining in sunlight through the roof, passing over stunned leaders, before Camelot's crown fits down onto another's head.

Agatha's head.

Japeth surges for her, but Sophie blocks him, her fingertip glowing hot pink.

"Bow down, *worm*," Sophie hisses.

Then she peeks back at King Agatha, mouthing: "*What's happening?*"

Agatha's eyes stay locked on Japeth.

Baffled guards pivot their weapons between them.

When Agatha speaks, it is with pure fire.

"Here is your liar. Here is your *Snake*. He stole the blood of the heir and faked being king this whole time." She holds up a piece of fabric, stained with blood. "Excalibur never chose him. Not the first time. Not now. It chose this. Without it, he's not king. He's no one. He's *nothing*."

"More rebel tricks—" Japeth mocks, appealing to the leaders.

"Oh?" says Agatha.

She thrusts the scrap of fabric at Sophie, who's caught on to the game. Sophie takes Chaddick's blood into her hand, smiling imperiously as the crown flies from Agatha's head to her own. Her white dress magically morphs into a coronation gown.

"I could get used to this," King Sophie says.

King Dutra of Foxwood stumbles to his feet. "Explain this, Rhian!"

"I don't understand!" Empress Vaisilla cries. "Why would the crown go to them, Rhian—"

"*Rhian?*" Sophie puffs. "Oh, no, no, no. Rhian is *dead*." Her emerald eyes cut through the Snake. "This is *Japeth*. He killed his twin and has been pretending to be Rhian ever since, like a grand old stooge. All of you are his fools."

At first, they think she's joking. Then they see the steel in Sophie's glare, coupled with the crown on her head . . . The room erupts into commotion, demanding King Rhian respond to the charges and punish the girls' lies.

I can see Japeth's cool shell cracking. He wants to turn into the Snake right here, to crucify these girls with a thousand scims. But he can't give himself away. He's playing his brother now. His Good, kingly brother.

Japeth turns to his soldiers. "*Kill* them!"

But they don't move, even his Camelot pirates stupefied by the crown on Sophie's head.

Japeth's facade breaks. He roars with murder, his face monstrous and gnarled. Excalibur out, he rushes at Sophie, for the blood clasped in her hand. Sophie rears in surprise, the scrap of blood fumbled from her palm, into the air, about to catch on Japeth's sword—

Agatha's glow scorches the blood, setting it aflame, incinerating it to nothing.

Ashes dangle in the sunlight like dust . . .

Then they're gone.

So, too, is Camelot's crown.

Excalibur rips from Japeth's hands and plunges back into the pile of stone.

No one moves, the house silent as a grave.

Japeth faces Agatha, her gold fingertip still smoking.

"There is only one true heir now. Only one true king," Agatha says, her voice big as thunder. "A king who warned you. The truth cannot be spoken. It can only be *seen*."

A truth Japeth doesn't see at first.

Then he hears the gasps.

Slowly the Snake turns.

Tedros rises, the Lion, the King, the crown of Camelot glittering in his hair.

Leaders drop to their knees, awed and overcome, a wave of humility and allegiance.

"Long live the King!" Agatha proclaims.

"*Long live the King!*" the leaders resound.

Tedros steps into the sunlight and pulls Excalibur free, the stone shattering from his force.

His gaze never leaves Japeth.

Arthur's sword soars out of Tedros' hands.

It lifts over the Snake, glowing hot red.

Japeth's eyes widen, reptilian blue—

"Like father, like son," says the King.

The sword falls.

This time, no mistakes.

32

THE STORIAN

Samsara

When it comes to wedding preparations, a witch can only take so much.

Which is why Sophie was in a dank sewer, her black-spike heels clacking along the path that bordered a river of sludge. When she was Dean, Sophie had tried to make the School for Evil more enticing, fumigating these sewers with sandalwood incense, changing the color of the sludge to a resplendent blue, even turning the dungeons into a nightclub party on Saturday nights for the highest-ranking Nevers. But in her absence at Camelot, Professor Manley had seized control of the school and restored everything to its old, decrepit gloom.

Evelyn Sader's dress hugged her tightly, refitted into a black leather sheath. Once, she'd have done anything to get the dress off; now, it was her loyal companion, shape-shifting to her moods and desires, like her own version of Hester's tattoo. If it was up to her, she'd mold the dress into a black vampire gown for the wedding, complete with thigh-high boots, a shimmering red cape, and heavy necklaces laden with blood rubies and signs of the cross.

But that wouldn't go over well with the groom.

Boys, Sophie sighed, running her fingers over walls, struggling to see down the tunnel. Soon the solid stone turned to rusty grating and Sophie found the keyhole, using her old Dean's key to pry the door open. She'd wanted to escape the wedding planning for just a moment, to catch her breath and be with her thoughts, but something had compelled her towards the Doom Room, even though she hadn't the faintest clue why. She only had terrible memories of this torture chamber for wayward Nevers and the big, hairy man-wolf that probed for weaknesses and made nightmares out of them. She still remembered the way he sniffed her hair, his paws stroking her. He'd paid the price in the end. Pushed into the sludge and left to

drown. For daring to touch her. For awakening her Evil. The
Doom Room had stayed beastless ever since, the punishment of
students left to the teachers.

But now she'd felt called back, all these years later. Sophie
stood alone in the dark, taking in the bare walls, as if there
was still something here for her, something she couldn't yet
see. She closed her eyes, listening to the silence, the creak
of the grate, the flit of a moth. Her heartbeat picked up, a
tight pitter-patter, as if struggling to keep control. She tried
to focus on the river sounds, a thick, soothing rush. But now
the sludge had a life of its own, churning faster, harder, its
roar thundering in her chest, swallowing her up. Something
brushed her ear, the kiss of fur. Heat clawed her body, the
threat of an animal's touch. She tasted tears. "I'm sorry," she
gasped. This is why she'd come: to find her beasts, to make
peace with them. The one she'd killed. And the one she
couldn't save. Both had to forgive her if she was to be free.
She could feel them now, the two beasts inside her, entwined
around her heart, pulling her towards an ending, life or
death, she couldn't know—

A chill hit her.

She startled awake.

Something was there.

In the darkness.

Two coal-black eyes.

"Sophie? Is that you?" a voice echoed.

She turned, a thin shadow coming down the tunnel for
her—

Sophie spun back to the dark, her fingerglow lit.

But there was nothing, except the memory of ghosts.

A SHORT TIME before, the bride had been in her last fitting, poised on a pedestal in Good Hall as tall, floating nymphs poked her with pins and clips and measuring sticks. The groom lay on his back on the blue marble, sweaty and shirtless from a workout, eating chips out of Merlin's hat and reading the *Royal Rot*.

"You shouldn't be here, you know," Agatha warned him, as the neon-haired nymphs hovered over her. "Bad luck for you to see the dress before the wedding."

"Bad luck for me to get my head cut off too, but here I am," said Tedros, his nose in the paper. "Besides, I can't see anything with all those overgrown pixies around you. Listen to this hogwash: *Tonight, King Tedros and Princess Agatha will be married at the School for Good and Evil by their own choosing, even though every king of Camelot has married at Camelot Castle since the founding of the realm thousands of years ago. In an exclusive interview, King Tedros insisted this is because he wants to 'show unity between the School and Camelot,' after Rhian and his brother sought to overthrow the school and the Storian kept within. But privately, sources tell us King Tedros moved the wedding because the castle is under repair, due to a 'de-Snake-ification,' which the king ordered to rid Camelot of every last vestige of Rhian and Japeth's reign.*"

"Um, that's all true," said Agatha, but Tedros barreled on—

"*We at the* Royal Rot *will keep a keen eye on the king's expen-
ditures, now that the Camelot Beautiful funds have been unfrozen.
Word is he's also spending a pretty penny to revive the* Camelot
Courier *with a new staff, so the* Rot *isn't left 'unchallenged,'*"
Tedros scoffed.

"That's true too," said Agatha.

"Don't encourage them," Tedros growled. He grabbed more
chips from the hat and kept reading.

His bride sighed. "There will always be people looking over
our shoulder. But that's why I wanted the wedding here," she
said, the nymphs finishing their work. "This world is powered
by its stories. Stories that are real to those who live them, but
stories that also inspire and teach and belong to every last soul
in these Woods. And this wedding is about *our* story: a prince
from this world and a girl from beyond it, brought together by
an unlikely education." Agatha looked out the window into the
golden afternoon, my steel edges glinting high in the School
Master's tower, writing the words she was speaking at this very
moment. "Camelot might be our Ever After," said Agatha.
"But this is where our fairy tale began."

"See? Why didn't they write *that*?" Tedros asked, mouth
full, finally looking at her—

He dropped Merlin's hat, his eyes wide.

Agatha smiled down, the nymphs parted. "Because they
only talked to you."

The dress was as white as a summer cloud, a three-quarter-
sleeve gown with a plunging neck and a cascade of shimmering
tulle from the waist sweeping out across the floor, catching the

light of the hall's torches and casting sparkles on Agatha's face.
Her hair had been pulled into a delicate twist and wrapped in a
wide white-silk band, her makeup fresh and light with a peach
sheen on her lips. Diamond studs shined in her ears, a matching
bracelet on her wrist. As for the shoes . . .

"The nymphs had their ideas," said Agatha, lifting her
dress to reveal two silver clumps, covered in crystals. "And I had
mine."

Tedros had no words, his skin so pink in his neck and chest
that Agatha thought he might burst into flames.

Luckily the nymphs needed the dress for final adjustments
and stripped Agatha of it, along with the hairband and jewels and shoes, leaving her in the unfussy blue frock she had
on underneath. She wiped away her lipstick, hopping off the
pedestal—

"Can you please wear your wedding dress every day?"
Tedros asked.

"Can you please wear clothes in public?" Agatha replied,
sprawling onto his chest.

They were alone in the vast hall, the half-dressed king and
his barefoot princess, like two first years who'd snuck out after
curfew. Neither spoke for a long while, Tedros running his fingers through her hair, their breaths falling in synch.

"Only a few hours now," said Agatha. "They'll start letting
guests in soon."

Tedros didn't say anything.

Agatha rolled over, her chin on his chest. "Something's
bothering you."

"No, no. I mean . . . it's just strange, isn't it? Not having anyone to give us away?" said Tedros. "No mom. No dad. For either of us. Dad's at peace now, his ghost finally at rest. But still . . . No Dovey or Lesso. No Robin or Sheriff or even Lance. Not even Tink. None of them lived to see the end. But we did. We made it somehow. Through the tests. Through the darkness. I just wish the others had made it with us."

Agatha saw the emotion in his eyes, the elation and sadness of everything that had happened, and she, too, felt it in her throat. "I wish the same thing, Tedros," she said, lying back and holding him. "We do have Merlin, though."

Tedros smiled. "Nineteen-year-old Merlin who we'll get to watch grow old, day by day."

"Where is he? Haven't seen him since we got to school."

"In the Gallery of Good," said Tedros, fidgeting with his ring. "They have an exhibit there with some of his old spellbooks and things. Probably wants to break the glass and get them all back."

Agatha laughed. "Doesn't seem happy to be young again, does he?"

"Merlin's happy as long as he has a pupil to badger and nitpick," said Tedros. "Thankfully, he'll be badgering me for a very long time."

He fell quiet, turning the ring round on his finger, studying its carvings. "On our carriage ride here, he asked me what I was going to do with it. The last of the Storian's rings. He said all the leaders look to me as the Lion now. If I burn Camelot's ring, I'll be the One True King, with the power to write others' fates.

The power to claim the Storian's magic and remake our world as Good as I want."

Agatha sat up. "And what did you tell him?"

"That I will never be the One True King," Tedros answered calmly. "Because a true king knows there is *more* than one king. I will be followed by another and another, each protecting this ring, each leading the Woods for as long as we are alive. And with my time on the throne, I'll be the best leader I can, while knowing that the Storian is the true master of our fate. I can't stop new tests from arising, but I can will myself to conquer them. Man and Pen in balance. Me and the Pen. The Storian has a larger plan for all of us. I am only one part of it."

Agatha held her breath, looking at him, the boy she once knew, become a man.

High in a tower, I paint this in their storybook: Agatha and the King. The last swan in my steel goes calm, my days of writing out of turn at an end, a Pen returned to its familiar rhythms . . .

Tedros shrugged. "But then Merlin's hat bit him, insisting it was time for Merlin's nap, and M said he's not a child anymore and they had a holy row. That's how I ended up with his hat. M said he wanted to be left alone for once—"

He saw Agatha still staring at him. "What?"

She traced the faint pink scar on his neck, Excalibur's mark. "Of all the tales in all the kingdoms in all the Woods, you had to walk into mine . . ."

"Now she's stealing my lines," said the boy, wrestling her playfully. "Did you really think I was dead for good?"

"I still haven't forgiven you for it," Agatha said, trying in vain to pin him. "What if *I* had died from the sheer shock and then you came back to life?"

"Dunno. Marry Sophie instead?"

Agatha smacked him. Tedros pinned her. They kissed passionately on the cold marble floor.

"Oh, kill me *now*," a voice grouched—

Agatha and Tedros turned to see Beatrix tramp in with Reena and Kiko.

"Romping like rabbits while we manage the wedding," said Beatrix.

"You?" Agatha asked. "I thought Sophie was in charge!"

"Sophie went running off right when we were doing decorations," said Reena. "Professor Anemone helped us instead."

"And the witches," Kiko chimed.

"Witches," said Tedros, his face clouding. "Helping with *wedding* decorations . . ."

"But why would Sophie run off?" Agatha pressed. "Did anyone see where she went?"

"Towards the Doom Room, last I saw," said Reena.

Agatha sat up. "The *Doom Room*?"

"You okay?" Agatha panted, pulling Sophie out of the dungeon cell. "Why are you in here?"

Sophie stammered, her skin damp: "S-s-sorry, I didn't mean for you to . . ."

But Agatha wasn't looking at her anymore, her gaze over Sophie's shoulder into the Doom Room. Agatha's eyes narrowed before she closed the grating, hugging her chest to it, making sure it was shut.

"What is it?" Sophie asked.

"Come on," Agatha said, dragging her down the tunnels. "This place gives me the spooks."

Sophie expected her friend to hound her as to why she'd gone to the dungeons or at the very least berate her for abandoning the wedding planning that Sophie herself had volunteered for. But Agatha was quiet, as if in rescuing Sophie from her ghosts, her friend had seen a ghost herself.

Finally Agatha turned to her. "What time is it?"

"Nearly four, I think," said Sophie.

"At five, I need to get ready," said Agatha. "I used the castle tunnels to come here, so I haven't seen the decorations yet. Maybe we should check on them. Heard the witches are involved . . ."

Sophie's eyes flashed. "Prepare for war."

They surfaced from the sewers and hustled up the banks of the bay towards the sun-gilded grass in front of Good's castle—

Both girls stopped.

The Great Lawn had turned into a feast of color. Everywhere they looked, bubbles of red and blue and gold light floated through the air like lanterns, a few filled with tuxedoed frogs playing a bright waltz on tiny violins. Professor Emma Anemone cast more glowing orbs, the Beautification teacher draped in a yellow gown with a pattern of tiny diamond mirrors.

She was helped by a coterie of Evers, Bodhi, Laithan, Priyanka included, dressed in their finest clothes for the wedding, while Professor Anemone led them in blossoming more brilliant bubbles from lit fingers: "Fill your hearts with love and well-wishes for our new king and queen and the beauty will show in your work! Bert, Beckett! Those better not be dungbombs!"

Meanwhile, a stained-glass altar gleamed atop the hill, which Aja and Valentina carved with rich fairy-tale scenes: Agatha and Tedros battling witch Sophie at the No Ball . . . Sophie beheading Rafal . . . Sophie as the Sugar Queen—

"What is this foolishness!" Professor Sheeba Sheeks yelped. "This is the wedding of Tedros and Agatha! Not a valediction to Sophie!"

"But Sophie is the best," said Aja.

Down the hill were columns of red, blue, and gold seats, which Willam and Bogden wove through, both boys in ruffled blue suits, placing name cards on cushions. They saved the best seats for C. R. R. Teapea of Gnomeland, Queen Jacinda of Jaunt Jolie, Maid Marian of Nottingham, Golem of Pifflepaff Hills, followed by rows for the faculty of the School for Good and Evil. Behind the teachers was a section for Teapea's gnomes, a testament to their help in fighting the Snake, followed by rows for all students of the school, Ever and Never. Then the seats for journalists and artists, who would document the wedding, along with room for families of students as well as Camelot maids and staff. And way, way, way in the back, sunken and teetering at the lake's edge, were chairs for the leaders of the Kingdom Council.

"EXCUSE ME!" Castor boomed, assessing their seating plan from atop Honor Tower. "YOU'RE PUTTIN' THE KINGS AND QUEENS OF THE WOODS, THE 99 LEADERS OF THE FOUNDING REALMS, BEHIND FIRST YEARS AND PEONS AND A BUNCHA GNOMES, WITH SEATS HALF IN THE LAKE, SO THEY CAN'T CATCH ANYTHIN' OF THE WEDDING BUT SOGGY KNICKERS?"

Willam and Bogden looked up. "Yes," they chorused.

Castor grinned. "Good lads."

Between the columns of seats was an aisle of white silk, aglow in more floating bubbles of color, filled with lovebirds singing along to the frog's symphony. Hester popped a bubble, the bird inside shrieking and fleeing past the black-clad witch.

"Couldn't help it," Hester said as her demon whittled an ice sculpture of Agatha in a fierce warrior pose.

"How's this?" Anadil asked, in matching black across the aisle, her rats chiseling an ice statue of a short boy with clownish curls and a wide, grotesque smile.

"Looks like an overeager dwarf," said Hester.

"But this is what Tedros looks like," Anadil maintained.

A blast of glow hit the sculpture, coating it smooth and milky white, obscuring its worst details.

"Chocolate solves everything," Dot trumped, arriving in a voluminous, bright pink gown with an explosion of bows. She zapped Hester's statue with a white chocolate sheen too. "And it goes better with the theme. Unlike your outfits. Who wears *black* to a wedding?"

"Witches with dignity," said Hester.

"Witches who don't want to look like they fell out of a fla-mingo," Anadil echoed.

"Well, now that I'm young again, I want to *enjoy* it," Dot vowed. "Get enough darkness and pointless cynicism hang-ing around you two. Oh, look. Aggie! Sophie! Why are you hiding!"

Dot spied the girls beneath the hill and hustled towards them.

How quickly things turn from dark to light, Agatha thought, the sun sending glittering shivers up Good's glass spires. She soaked in the sumptuous scene, a wedding in full bloom. No more dark edges lurking. No more tests to pass. Just color and chaos and love.

Sophie clasped her best friend's hand.

"You're getting married, Aggie," Sophie said softly.

Agatha saw nothing but happiness and joy in her friend's eyes, as if this was Ever After enough for them both. Which was a testament to how much Sophie loved her, Agatha thought. Because Sophie had lost her happy ending, just as Agatha had won hers.

"Oh, not you *too* in black," Dot chided Sophie, sweeping in.

"Everyone can wear what they wish," Agatha corrected, for Sophie had been wearing funeral colors for several days now. "All that matters is we're here together."

"For now," said Hester, appearing with Anadil. "Ani, Dot, and I were thinking about what comes after the wedding."

"Agatha and Tedros will live at Camelot, obviously," Anadil

pointed out, "and first years and teachers will stay here at school, Nicola, Bogden, and Willam included. Willam was officially invited to be an Ever by Professor Anemone."

"A lot of our classmates want to go back to their quests, like Ravan, Vex, and Brone," Dot added. "And Beatrix, Reena, and Kiko are planning to sail the *Igraine* across the Savage Sea to chart the unmapped realms . . ."

"Which leaves us," said Hester, glancing at her coven mates.

"You'd be perfect as Deans of Evil," Sophie proposed sincerely. "Patrolling halls. Managing curriculum. Disciplining students. I mean, you almost took as much delight in dumping those Mistral Sisters back in the Camelot dungeons as I did. *Almost*."

The witches stared at her. So did Agatha.

"But if they're the Deans . . . what about *you*?" Agatha asked.

Sophie smiled at her friend. "Thought I could come live at the castle with you and Teddy."

Agatha hesitated, looking tense, and Sophie instantly flushed, with Hester jumping in to stop the awkwardness—

"Appreciate you thinking of us as Deans, but we're not meant for office jobs," Hester touted. "Besides, now that Manley has the title, it'll have to be pried out of his cold, warted fingers."

"He and Professor Anemone already brought in sorcerers to dismantle Sophie's suite in the School Master's tower," said Anadil. "Looks like they have both schools well in hand."

"So what will you do, then?" Agatha asked, fixing on Dot. "Still thinking about being a witch doctor?"

"Our coven had something else in mind, actually," Dot volunteered. She peeked at Hester and Anadil, who nodded at her, urging her to go on. "Well, with Daddy gone, there's no Sheriff in the Woods anymore," said Dot. "No one protecting law and order. As king, Tedros will have his knights, but if we've learned anything, Good has a blind spot to the worst kind of Evil. More Snakes could pop up. The Woods needs a real Sheriff. Like my dad was. So we thought maybe . . . *we'd* do it. Be the new Sheriff. Be the new law and order."

"Go searching for villains that don't play by the rules," Hester explained, her demon twitching on her neck. "And bring them to justice, *our* way."

"Hell hath no fury like three witches who think you're giving Evil a bad name," said Anadil, rats poking from her pocket with a hiss.

Agatha smiled, looking at Sophie, but there was still tension between them, Agatha quickly turning to assure the witches: "That's a magnificent idea. Tedros will give you any resources you need—"

"No, no, no. Covens don't work on behalf of kings," Hester retorted. "We are independent witches, with no master or patron or affiliations, working in the shadows on our *own* missions. You will reap the benefits of our work, but you won't hear about it and we intend to keep it that way."

Dot whispered to Agatha: "I'll send postcards."

"Did you hear?" Kiko gushed, cramming in. "Reena's boyfriend is coming from Shazabah!"

"Jeevan is *not* my boyfriend," Reena objected behind her.

"If a boy's flying in on a magic carpet for you, he's your boy-friend," said Beatrix. "Speaking of, who is *that*?"

From the South Gates came a sultry boy in a gray suit, with a pompadour of blue hair, a gold earring in one ear, and thin, intense eyes.

"That is Yoshi," Kiko ogled. "She found him in Jaunt Jolie."

"*She?*" said Beatrix.

But now they saw the girl on his arm, coming through the gate: Nicola, nuzzled against him, in a matching gray dress.

"Rebound boys are the *best*," Dot marveled.

"How do *I* get one?" Kiko complained. "I figured out Willam doesn't like girls like me." She paused. "He only likes tall girls."

Everyone else groaned.

All this talk of boys made Agatha remember the days when she didn't believe in princes or castles or fairy tales.

She, the new Queen of Camelot.

She, who dreamed of an ordinary life, only to have the most extraordinary one of all.

Then she noticed Sophie, as the other girls dispersed into their groups, her best friend shifting in her boots, as if she didn't have a place to go. Agatha knew the pain Sophie was feeling: deep in her heart, Agatha would always be the old Graveyard Girl.

The castle clock sounded five, strong and bold.

Agatha breathed a sigh of relief, touching Sophie's wrist.

"Come and help me get ready, will you?" Agatha asked.

HOW THE TABLES TURN, Sophie thought, following Princess Agatha through Valor Tower.

Once upon a time, it was Sophie with a prince, eager to get rid of Agatha as a third wheel. Now Agatha had the prince to herself and was leaving Sophie out in the cold. For Sophie, there would be no royal triumvirate, no busying herself at the castle with her best friend, no escaping her deepening loneliness. She had never wanted to end at Camelot, of course. But she had nowhere else to go to feel loved. And she thought Aggie of all people might understand that. Until she saw the way Agatha hesitated when she'd proposed it . . .

Not that Sophie blamed her. Of course Queen Agatha wouldn't want Sophie swanning around the castle, stealing focus away from her and King Tedros. Sophie would have been a good girl and done everything possible to cede the stage . . . but Agatha knew her friend too well. The spotlight always found Sophie, especially when Sophie felt lost and scared like she did now.

Where to go? What to do?

She was so caught up in her thoughts she hardly noticed Agatha lead her up a staircase and through an office door, already cracked open. Agatha closed the door, while Sophie glanced at the cramped room with a single window and broom closet and a mess of soggy books, scraggly-written scrolls, and moldy food crumbs.

"Professor Sader's old office?" Sophie asked. "You want to get ready for your wedding in *here*?"

"Don't want Tedros seeing my dress. Bad luck," Agatha

said, peering around. "No mirror, though."

Sophie frowned. "Where are the nymphs? Who's helping you get ready?"

Agatha pulled a small mirror from her dress. "Brought one with me in case," she said, handing it to Sophie. "Show me what I look like, will you?"

Sophie stared at her.

Agatha who used to hide from mirrors.

Now carrying one with her.

Sophie shook her head. *You really have changed*, she thought, reflecting her friend in the glass—

Only then did Sophie look at the mirror closely.

A mirror she'd seen before, in a land far away.

Agatha's eyes reflected yellow.

Then Sophie was falling through them.

AGATHA'S SECRETS.

She was inside Agatha's secrets.

That's all Sophie had heard about the mirror. It revealed the things a person wanted to hide.

But now Sophie was in a familiar place, dank tunnels melting into view around her, a river of sludge rushing past . . .

The sewers.

"Sophie, is that you?" a voice called.

Sophie spun to see Agatha hustling towards her, barefoot in her blue dress—

Sophie grabbed at her: "Aggie! Why are we here!"

But her hand went through her friend like a ghost, Agatha continuing to move along the sludge, heading towards a blond girl in a black leather dress, farther down the tunnel . . .

Me, Sophie realized.

This isn't now.

This is *before*.

When Agatha found her in the dungeon.

Quickly Sophie chased after Agatha, catching up to her just as her friend pulled the old Sophie out of the cell.

"You okay?" Agatha was panting. "Why are you in here?"

Sophie's past self stammered, her skin damp: "S-s-sorry, I didn't mean for you to . . ."

But Agatha wasn't looking at the old Sophie anymore. She was looking over her shoulder into the dungeon. Agatha's eyes narrowed before she closed the grating, hugging her chest to it, making sure it was shut—

Except now the scene magically pivoted, like a projection rotating on itself, allowing Sophie to see what was happening on the other side of the grating, *inside* the cell . . .

A shadow, crouched on the floor, seizing onto Agatha's wrist and handing her a mirror through the grate.

And on this mirror, a message etched in dust:

**MY OFFICE
5PM**

Agatha hid the mirror in her dress before spinning on her heel and ushering Sophie out of the sewers, that strange, spooked look on Agatha's face that Sophie remembered—

But now the scene was vanishing, the secret exposed, as Sophie felt herself pulled back into Professor Sader's office, her head faint and blood throttling, her eyes flying to the desk . . . the food crumbs and soggy books and bad penmanship that hadn't belonged to Professor Sader at all . . . but to the boy who had taken over as History Professor once the old seer was gone . . .

My Office.

My.

Slowly Sophie turned to Agatha, her heart on fire, her body shaking so hard she couldn't see straight.

Agatha nodded towards the broom closet.

Sweat dripped off Sophie's palms. Every step she took seemed as if she was taking eight steps back, like she was clinging to the fringes of a dream just when she was waking up. She couldn't breathe, her hand grasping for the closet door, stuttering onto the knob, turning it the wrong way, then the right way, the jamb stuck before she shot it with a spell, blasting the door off its hinges, the darkness inside overwhelmed with light—

Sophie dropped the mirror, shattering the glass.

Every shard reflected him.

He was skinnier than before, weakly pale in a thin black shirt and black breeches, his hair dark and jagged, his arms and legs cut up and heavy white bandages peeking out from his shoulders and chest. But his eyes were strong, hot with life and locked on Sophie, as if he was afraid to blink.

"It's a trick . . . ," Sophie croaked. "It's impossible . . ."

The boy stepped out of the closet.

"Every good story needs a little impossible," said Hort. "Otherwise no one would believe it."

Sophie's legs jellied, the distance between them feeling as wide as an ocean.

"I'll leave you two," said Agatha at the door—

"Aggie?" Sophie gasped.

Agatha looked back at her, her eyes shining with happy tears, brimming with love. And suddenly, Sophie realized that she had it all wrong. Agatha would do anything for her. She always had. She always would. And on this, her wedding day, it wasn't her own happy ending that Agatha had been determined to make happen. It was her best friend's.

Agatha gave her a wink, then closed the door behind her.

Sophie swallowed, struggling to focus on Hort, as if gazing into the sun. "How?"

"Kept myself alive just long enough to be rescued," he said. "An old friend found me, who happened to be an expert in forest survival. Nursed me back to health."

"An old friend? Who?" Sophie asked.

"I mean . . . really, *really* old," said Hort, nodding out the window.

Sophie peeked through and glimpsed a wrinkled, bearded gnome on the lawn, swatting at Neverboys with his staff: "Eating the wedding cake! Hooligans! Yuba is back! Shipshape! Shipshape!"

"This whole time, Yuba was searching for missing files on

Rhian and Japeth from the Living Library," Hort said behind her. "Never found them, but he found Aladdin's mirror in a Pasha Dunes pawnshop. Tedros must have lost the mirror in the desert before one of the Sultan's soldiers sold it off, not realizing what it was. I had a plan to use the mirror, to bring you into my secrets, but then Agatha showed up and ruined everything as usual . . . so I had to improvise . . ."

This is real, Sophie thought.

This is happening.

She turned back, taking Hort in, finally letting herself believe it. "I thought I'd lost you . . . I thought you were dead . . . ," she rasped, moving towards him. She reached for him—

"Wait," he said, drawing back. He turned away, his face quivering. "There's something I need to tell you."

Sophie's stomach wrenched.

She'd been waiting for it.

Her happy endings always came with a catch.

Tears slid onto Hort's cheeks. "The wolf part of me," he said quietly. "The wolf that was shot in the tree . . ." He couldn't look at her. "It's . . . dead."

Sophie went still.

"The part of me you liked. The strong part. The beast. My wounds were too great for it to survive," Hort confessed, his voice broken. "It's just me now. Weaselly old me. And I know that isn't enough for you."

Sophie didn't say anything for a moment. She stood taller on her heels. "No, it isn't enough for me."

Hort hung his head.

Tears frosted Sophie's eyes, watching him. "It's *more* than enough."

He froze, slowly raising his chin.

"You've always been enough, Hort of Bloodbrook," said Sophie. "You, who are strong enough to die for the girl you love and still find your way back to her. You. Bold, big-hearted, beautiful you. It's me who wasn't enough. Me who kept searching for fantasy love instead of real love. It's me who didn't deserve you." She touched his cheek. "Until I opened my heart big enough and found you there, waiting patiently, a piece of me all along."

She kissed him, holding on to him tight, his lips so soft and perfect they felt like home. Where they would go from here, who they would become, she didn't know, the two of them bound by nothing except their feelings for each other and thankfulness for this moment. For the first time, Sophie didn't need to know the future to be happy. She didn't need promises or princes or a storybook life. All she wanted was the most ordinary of ends: to love with all of her heart and to be loved the same way in return.

Their mouths parted, Sophie taking in air. "Should we go and tell the others?" she asked, moving for the door.

"Not yet," said Hort, locking it sharply. "They can wait."

Sophie grinned as he came for her. "Who says the beast is dead?"

TEDROS WAS TEMPTED to peek into Sader's office and see Hort in the flesh, but from the scene Agatha had described to him and the rapture between Sophie and her weasel . . . better he didn't.

Leave it to Agatha to execute the perfect love plot on the day of her own wedding, Tedros thought, heading through a glass breezeway, dressed in a white-and-gold suit and matching white boots, his golden hair perfectly arranged, his heart pumping with happiness. Happiness that he'd kissed his bride before he'd left her with the nymphs to get ready. Happiness that Hort was alive and on the way to recovery. Happiness that Agatha could get married, knowing her best friend had found love. And happiness for Sophie, who he no longer thought of as a thorn in his side, but as a true, irreplaceable friend. His castle would be open to her always, his once-nemesis now part of his family, and no doubt fresh challenges would arise in the course of his reign where the King of Camelot would call upon the Witch of Woods Beyond for her help.

Through the glass breezeway, he could see guests arriving: Maid Marian, with some of Robin Hood's old Merry Men . . . Queen Jacinda, looking resplendent, with eleven new female knights flanking her like bodyguards, the coup in her castle put down . . . Boobeshwar and his troop of mongooses, each kissed on their furry heads by Princess Uma for their work slowing Japeth's armies . . . Caleb and Cedric and Headmistress Gremlaine, who Tedros personally visited a few days earlier to tell them the truth about Chaddick of Foxwood, his liege, friend, and brother . . . Hansel and Gretel and Briar Rose and giant-slaying Jack, old members of the League of Thirteen . . .

All made their way to the lawn, savoring cups of masala tea and plates of saffron pudding and pistachio cookies from Reena's mother, who insisted that she and Yousuf handle the food and drink for the wedding, including the elaborate feast to follow and the twelve-layer cardamom and rosewater cake.

Then Tedros noticed Pollux slinking up the hill, his oily head atop a poodle's body, the dog trying to keep away from Castor, who'd already spotted his brother and was giving him a rabid glare. Pollux hadn't been invited, of course, but he always came sucking up to power when he saw the chance. More guests flooded in: the Fairy Queen of Gillikin, the Ice Giant of Frostplains, the Dwarf Queen of Ooty, mixed amongst the students and teachers of the school. Pospisil, too, had come, the old priest dressed in gold and brought to the altar, where he would conduct the wedding. Everyone was here, Tedros thought, past divisions and sins forgiven, the Woods united under the Lion, all friends accounted for . . .

Except one.

Tedros hastened towards the Gallery of Good. He would have forgotten entirely about Merlin, except Merlin's hat was making such a fuss about being away from the wizard that Tedros had stuffed it under pillows where the nymphs were dressing his bride.

At first, Tedros had assumed Merlin was down on the lawn, but Tedros hadn't seen him and at nineteen years old, the wizard couldn't be expected to be a model of timeliness and responsibility. Most likely he got sidetracked in the Gallery of Good, practicing his old spells, determined to return to the master wizard he once was. Tedros hopped off the staircase, jogging past corridors to the double doors at their end, shoving through and ready to give the boy a stern talking-to—

But he wasn't there.

Tedros glanced around the deserted gallery and its exhibits and displays, celebrating the best of its alumni. Merlin had his own corner in the museum, a tribute to the wizard's humble beginnings as a student at the school a long time ago. But nothing in Merlin's display had been disturbed, not the glass cases with his old spellbooks or his first-year assignments or his medal for winning the Trial by Tale, as if the wizard boy had never come here like he'd said.

Must be with the guests after all, Tedros sighed, heading back—

Then something caught his eye.

One of the spellbooks.

It was open to a young painting of a radiant beach at sunset with pink sand and purple waters, the sea leading out in calm, brilliant waves . . . where it abruptly stopped. The waters, the waves: it all went blank, as if the painting was unfinished.

But it was the title that Tedros noticed.

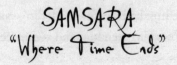

Samsara.

Tedros had heard it before.

Merlin had used the word in Avalon, when the teenage wizard was annoyed with him and Agatha.

"Think I would be here, decades younger than I'm supposed to be . . . instead of basking on the beaches of Samsara?" he'd groused. *"That's where I'd like to spend my future."*

Tedros looked at the painting again, the vibrant purple waters cut short.

Where Time Ends.

Something in Tedros went cold.

"Tedros?"

He turned.

Agatha.

She was in her wedding dress, Sophie and Hort at her side. Their faces were pale, watching something in Agatha's hands.

Merlin's hat.

The blue velvet fading, the threads coming apart, magically aging in front of their eyes.

It hacked out a cloud of dust: *"Honor Commons."*

Tedros was already running.

BY THE TIME they arrived, his hair had gone gray, wrinkles creasing into his smooth face.

He was reclined on the couch, his old, velvet robes fanned around him like a purple sea, while a fire burned in the fireplace, casting light on murals of mermaids and kings.

They gathered around him, Tedros on his knees.

"My boy," Merlin said.

"M, what's happening . . . you have to make it stop . . . ," the prince begged, watching him grow older, forty, forty-five, fifty at Tedros' best guess, his cheeks weathering, his skin loosening on his bones. "Please, Merlin."

"No one gets to be young again for free, Tedros," the wizard spoke. "Once upon a time, the King and Queen of Borna Coric learned that lesson when they tried to stay young forever, only to learn they were on borrowed time. I, too, was on borrowed time. Nineteen years of added life, lived in nineteen days. More years than I had left to live. And now Father Time has come to collect."

"But surely you can fight it," Agatha pressed. "Surely you can do something—"

"What I want to do is be right here, with you," said the wizard, his hair gone white. He looked at Tedros in his suit and Agatha in her wedding dress, Sophie's lips smeared and Hort's hair in disarray. "The great things you will do. So much love between you."

His shoulders hunched, liver spots dotting his arms.

Sixty. Seventy. Seventy-five.

Tears wet Tedros' face. "Stay with me, Merlin . . . We can be together . . . We can see the world . . ."

Merlin's eyes fogged behind his spectacles. "I've seen the world in you, my boy. Now it is time to go where time ends. To cross the line between seeing and silence . . ." His words slowed.

"Tell me . . . what did you say to the Lady of the Lake . . . What did you say that made her give you her Wizard Wish?"

Tedros watched him turn bony and limp. "Merlin—"

Merlin clutched his hand. "Tell me, my boy."

Tedros held down tears. "I told her how I proposed to Agatha."

Merlin's chest rose and fell.

Agatha looked at Tedros, nodding at him to go on.

"I woke Agatha in the middle of the night," said Tedros, gripping the old man tight. "We were at Camelot. Not too long after we came from school. She was asleep in her chamber. I said that I needed her help. Naturally, she came at once. We snuck past the guards, through the gardens, and down the shore to the Savage Sea. I explained that I'd found a seer, who told me my reign could be protected from Evil by a magical talisman. A secret jewel that appeared once a year where the moon met the sea. Tonight was that night, I told Agatha, pointing to a moonlit rock far out into the waves. The waters were frigid, the currents rough. But I promised her: if we could get the jewel, we'd be shielded against Evil forever. No surprise, she dove in before I could. We swam together, through the ripping undertow, she dragging me out when I got pulled down, me chewing through seaweed that had snared her, both of us chilled to the bone and losing steam as we pushed length after length into icy water. And just when we thought we could swim no more, our lungs failing, our eyes too salt-stung to see, we were there, at the end, the surface of the rock polished by the light, the talisman in plain sight. That's when Agatha found it: the diamond ring I'd left there. Now, she understood. The talisman was a question. Our journey to get to it the proof of our love. I was asking to be her husband and she my wife. That we would risk our lives for each other in a winter sea was answer enough. Death would be no obstacle to our love, only another challenge to overcome. Which is why I need your Wizard Wish, I told the Lady. To hold on to the love I fought so hard to find. Love that the Lady could still find herself, even without her powers. She had to give her story a chance. She had to trust the will of fate. Fate that had brought she and I together. It is not your time for death, I told her. And it is not the time for mine. We're part of each other's story now, the way you and I were part of my father's, bound by love and pain and forgiveness, but most of all hope. Hope that we can all be as valiant as the Lady, to face our mistakes, to accept our weakness and keep going, wherever it takes us, not for Good or Evil, not for glory, but to find the truth of who we are meant to be."

Merlin gazed into Tedros' eyes.

"My king," he whispered.

The room was quiet, the four youths kneeled over the wizard.

Merlin looked at them all. "The End of Ends . . . the stories told . . . What wondrous souls you are."

He let go of Tedros, fading deeper into purple velvet.

"Please, M," said the king. "Stay a little longer."

Merlin breathed out a smile. "Don't you see . . ." He closed his eyes, on to new shores. "The work is done."